GOLD SIN

AVELINE KNIGHT

First paperback edition September 2024.

Edited and proofread by Bryony Leah

Development edit by Thebluecouchedits

Cover design © SeventhstarArtServices

TRIGGER WARNINGS

Please be aware: this book contains subject matter that might be difficult for some readers.

Some of the things you can find inside the book are graphic sexual scenes, graphic violence, domestic violence (not between the main characters), murder, knife play, Breath play, Primal kink, Drugs, Slut shaming (not between the main characters) , Torture, Mention of SA and attempted SA.

Despair burns like fire on a match. And when the flame is wild . . .
You become rage.

To my flames.

To the women that the world turned into rage. This book is for you.
Let them all burn to hell, and while you're at it, have some goddamn fun.

You deserve it.

Set the world on fire.

CHAPTER ONE
AURELIA

Wolfsbane.

Such a delicate flower for something so lethal.

It took me weeks to learn every aspect of the plant—how much to use, how long it would take for the poison to start to work, and how *untraceable* it is.

Then it took me even longer to persuade Valentine, my adoptive father and the only person who knows of my revenge plan, to order me some through his network.

And not because he didn't want me to kill DeMarco, but because he wasn't too excited by the idea of using poison. He preferred brutality and wanted to see me stab him to death.

Valentine was just projecting his boredom onto my plan. Once I showed him all the information I'd gathered about the plant online, he decided using wolfsbane would make the cleanup easier, help him erase any trace of my presence at the scene.

At the end of the day, attention to detail is everything when it comes to murder.

I can't tear my eyes away from the slosh of liquid as I sway the vial between my fingers. How can something so innocent-looking be the vile solution to my problems?

I mix a few drops into his drink while he's busy, probably stroking his ego, in the bathroom. His reflection in the mirror is the only person he'll ever truly love in this life.

"Cheers." My lips curve to the side as I lift my glass and slip the vial back into my purse just as he comes out.

"Are we going to toast or what?" His raucous voice attacks my senses, hairy fingers eager as they clasp the flute.

"Of course," I say with faux sweetness. "To new beginnings."

Standing in front of me is the powerful Vincent DeMarco. Not so powerful, with the way I've been playing him the whole afternoon. It didn't take me long to seduce him into bringing me to his hotel room just a few floors above the Harrows' fundraiser, which we'll be attending soon. Well, I will. He'll be dead by then.

He was drinking by himself at the hotel bar, deep in his third glass of scotch, when I appeared at his side pretending to order my drink. He didn't wait long to strike up conversation, and after a few sways of my hips and whispers of sweet nothings in his ear, he invited me up to his room.

Eleanora, my best friend, was right: give men a shallow version of yourself, and they'll become enslaved to it.

A smug grin stretches his lips as he peeks at me over the rim of his glass.

He thinks I'm just another dumb bitch he'll get to take to bed—one who approached him for his money. He thinks I'll be easy to manipulate and use on his own terms, because I laugh at his dry jokes and touch his arm here and there.

He thinks he's one step ahead of me.

If only he knew.

I take a small sip from my glass, the sweet taste of champagne dancing on my tongue. While the bitter taste of wolfsbane pierces his.

He would have tasted it if he hadn't swallowed most of the drink so fast.

The clear liquid I mixed with his champagne is enough to kill him twice.

"Ah, that's the stuff," he grunts, wiping his mouth with the back of his hand like the true head of South Seattle's drug distribution he is.

They don't really teach you manners when you're part of the Inferno Consortium. Well, they don't teach you manners if you're a *man* in the Inferno Consortium, the secret society of powerful families who launder money from their legitimate businesses.

Only, that's not all they do.

His broad shoulders stoop and he threads his fingers through his slicked-back dark hair as his eyes roam over my body. As if he owns it. Owns me for the night.

I feign a smile as I try to hide my disgust.

Just a few more minutes and no one will ever have to

experience his eyes burning down their skin, the sickening feeling it leaves you with, again.

There's no going back now. My plan is set in motion. The poison is coursing through his body right now, so close to reaching the first vital organ.

This is all for you, Mother.

One less monster in the world. Many more to go.

Vincent's grip on the glass weakens as he tries to keep up the façade. His hand shakes a little, and he clears his throat, brushing off whatever is happening to him.

The loathing I feel for him slips between the cracks in my mask as I watch him struggle.

His role in the Inferno Consortium wasn't what made me want to draw his fate for him. He's done something far more personal.

Vincent took his role in the Inferno Consortium, and the power that came with it, and used it against my mother. He humiliated her, alongside other members, at Lucian Harrow's exclusive parties.

Lucian is the leader of the Inferno Consortium, and his gatherings allow powerful men to indulge in their darkest fantasies while talking business, with no regard for the women they use and abuse.

My mother was one of those women.

"Tell me, Aurelia." His words are barely coherent as he slurs, his eyes fluttering closed as he struggles to maintain eye contact. "Is this the first time you've attended the Harrows' fundraiser? Have you ever been to one of Lucian's parties? They're quite the experience." He chuckles.

I clench my fist behind my back to keep my boiling

anger under control. "Oh, I've heard stories," I reply. The images of those events that ultimately led my mother to her death blind me for a second. "What exactly goes on at these ... parties?"

Vincent smirks, unaware of his life slipping away by the second. "Let's just say, the men in attendance have ... particular tastes." He glances down at my cleavage, and I swear, if the poison takes any longer to kill him, I'll do it with my bare hands. "Beautiful women like yourself are put on display for our amusement. We drink, get high, and enjoy the pleasures of the flesh without consequence."

Beautiful women like yourself. He means like my mother.

Something flickers in his eyes. It lasts seconds, but I see the way they round slightly as he looks me over.

I remind him of her.

Of course I do.

I don't remember my mother, but Valentine, the one who adopted me after her death, does. And he always says I'm a carbon copy of her. Same red hair, and green eyes with the right number of brown flecks.

My identical twin.

If you don't count her lack of a sense of justice, and her lack of hunger to live.

"Sounds like quite the spectacle." My throat constricts with the force I use to fake my admiration. Images of my mother surrounded by men like Vincent clog my vision. "I can see why they're so popular with men like you."

He scoffs. "Men like me?" Shaking his head, he adds,

"You mean powerful men who know how to enjoy themselves? Damn right, sweetheart."

Nausea crawls up my throat.

"Powerful men who exploit others for their own gain," I correct him, letting the cracks in my mask slowly show as what I really think of him seeps into my words. "But I suppose that's just the way the world works, isn't it?"

"Exactly." He coughs so abruptly some of his drink spills onto the floor. His hand trembles slightly as he tries to hide what he doesn't know are the effects of the poison. "And if you play your cards right, you might find yourself enjoying the finer things in life too."

God, how oblivious is he?

"Or perhaps," I muse as I catch the first signs of his body convulsing, "the tables will turn, and those who thought they held all the power will find themselves at the mercy of someone else."

He coughs again, this time harshly, as he bends down. "Wh-what is happening?"

"Karma, Vincent." I lean closer to him as his breathing becomes labored. "It always finds a way of catching up with us in the end."

His face contorts, freezing like the elegant statue on the table in the center of the room. I wonder if his body will make the perfect complement to the creamy furniture. The drawn curtains and the soft ceiling are soothing to watch while Vincent's gurgling noises fill the air.

His hand clutches at his chest, wrinkling his white shirt. "Wh-what did you do to me?" he gasps.

"Nothing you don't deserve."

He falls to his knees in front of me. His glass slips from his hand and shatters on the floor.

It was too easy to get him here, pleading at my feet.

"Please," he chokes out. "Help me."

I look down at him in disgust. How many times did my mom repeat those two words to him? How many times did he laugh in her face before making her scream?

"But Vincent, I thought powerful men like you didn't need help from anyone."

He coughs, his body convulsing violently. Terror widens his eyes.

"Was this how you imagined it, Vincent?" I step around him, sneering. "Begging for your pathetic life on the floor of a hotel room."

How many times did my mom beg? How many people heard her before someone stepped forward?

Did anyone even step forward, or did they all just watch in amusement?

His eyes plead with me, beg me for mercy, as I revel in it.

The once powerful Vincent DeMarco, who stood tall within the Inferno Consortium, is now nothing more than a groveling, dying mess at my feet.

He doesn't deserve my pity. He deserves far worse than death for taking part in my mother's suicide.

"Y-you could've killed me . . . any other way," he chokes out between gasps for air. "And you chose the weakest way?"

"I didn't choose the weakest way, Vincent. No—I

wanted you to feel the slow burn of betrayal, just as my mother did when you took part in using her."

The intensity of my desire for revenge blazes through me.

He violated my mother. He pushed her to kill herself.

"Look at you now," I spit. "A lifetime of power and wealth, and it all comes down to this. You're not even worth a bullet or a blade, Vincent. Your death should be as insignificant as your soul."

He extends his hand toward me, fingers clawing at the air between us. Stepping back, I let his hand fall in a thud, not wanting his filth on me.

"Please . . ." His voice is barely above a whisper.

I look down at him, his attempts to survive weakening with each fleeting second. "Save your breath," I reply coldly as I lean closer. "You're not worth the air you're choking on."

Blood splatters out of his mouth, and he chokes on it before his body convulses one final time.

He lies there dead, and I stand over him, ticking his name off my list.

I brush my hands over my silver gown, quickly checking he hasn't ruined what I'm supposed to wear for tonight's fundraiser.

With one final glance at the lifeless body on the floor, I turn and leave.

The sound of my high heels on the marble vanishes beneath the intensifying chatter coming from behind the double doors. The corridor is covered in shadows, the lack of light a jarring contrast to the fundraiser, which is bright with candles and chandeliers.

The whole room is cast in a warm glow as tailored suits and couture dresses mingle around. Laughter and the soft notes of music fill the ballroom.

A hint of expensive perfume overpowers the delicious scent of finger food being served by waiters. Slender flutes of sparkling champagne accompany the shrimp in phyllo pastry cups.

Countless eyes follow my every move as I make my way across the hall, judging my hairstyle or praising the way the silver complements my skin tone.

I already feel like I'm drowning in a pool full of people hungry for the one thing they don't own: a soul.

"Ah, there you are!" Lady Harrow, the wife of Lucian, the leader of the Inferno Consortium, approaches me with a drink in her hand. Her lips attempt to form a smile, but it's impossible after the countless injections she's had. "You look stunning, dear."

You look average, is what she's really saying.

I dated her son for ten years, and the only time she ever complimented me was when I picked up the correct fork for the first course of our meal. As if I'd never attended a banquet before.

"Thank you." I give her the warmest smile I can fake. I can't afford to raise any suspicions now—not with a dead body upstairs. "It's a beautiful event, Lady Harrow. You've outdone yourself."

"Of course, dear. Only the best for our esteemed friends."

She says the last words with a drop in her voice, but I can't seem to focus on her underlying message. Not with the way Adrian Harrow, the Harrows' eldest son—*and my ex-boyfriend*—is watching us from across the ballroom.

Watching *me*.

His dark blue eyes narrow, and I swear, if they could, they'd swallow me whole. He just stands there observing. Unreadable.

I shouldn't be surprised. Adrian's always been stoic. As the eldest Harrow brother, he was taught to be like this, in stark contrast to his younger brother Julian's nonchalant ways.

But tonight . . . something feels different.

"Excuse me. I should probably go and greet some of the other guests." Without waiting to hear Lady Harrow's response, I extricate myself from her presence. But even after I've walked the perimeter of the ballroom, Adrian's eyes are still glued to me, leaving a trail of unease down my spine.

Brushing off the heaviness of his gaze, I move through the crowd, engaging in trivial conversation while collecting whispered secrets. Each spoken word is a weapon, a tool I'll get to use against those I promised to destroy.

"Golden one!" The nickname the Inferno Consortium gave me scratches down my skin as the woman's eyes do the same, appraising the way I look. "Your dress is simply divine."

They've called me that since I can remember. No one calls me by my given name except Valentine, Adrian, and Julian. Although Julian hasn't really called me anything for a while.

Whenever I hear those two words, they make me feel

dirty, like a pet for them to toss around. No one else has a nickname in the Inferno Consortium but me.

I match the woman's saccharine tone. "Thank you, Mrs. Caldwell."

Another guest appears next to her. "Isn't this a fabulous party?" His cheeks are a shade of red from the countless flutes of champagne he's probably had. "The Harrows always know how to throw the most exquisite fundraisers." His fingers are covered in cream cheese as he stuffs his mouth with cucumber sandwiches.

I force a polite smile as I nod in agreement.

As exhausting and boring as it may be, engaging in small talk is the only way I can gain valuable information on the members of the Inferno Consortium. Unless I resort to stalking, but I'm not about to waste my time studying these pigs.

"Is it true what they say about Julian Harrow?" he asks before sipping on his flute of Krug Clos d'Ambonnay. His fingers are *still* covered in cream cheese as he dirties the glass. "That he's involved in some rather . . . unsavory business dealings?"

His name chills my heart as I try to suppress a sigh of frustration.

As if it wasn't bad enough that they had to bring him into our conversation, they clearly have nothing to do with the Inferno Consortium. They're just wealthy associates of the Harrow Enterprise, relying on their money for influence.

This is a waste of time. I need to find members, not outsiders.

"Who can say for certain?"

This man is playing my game. He's the one digging for information from me. But in this world, gossip is a currency, and I'm not about to give it away.

I'd trade it, but he clearly knows nothing apart from the taste of those cucumber sandwiches.

At my silence the man continues. "Either way, it would seem there's more to the Harrow family than meets the eye."

No shit. The words beg to leave my lips.

Instead I ask, "Isn't that always the case with powerful families?"

My gaze drifts across the room to where Julian stands. His torturous blue eyes are already fixed on me. I can't decide if it's how unreachable he looks between the laughter and chatter of others, or if it's the way only his attention can scorch my insides, that truly feels torturous.

One look from him and I feel things I'm not supposed to. Not ever.

It's just a look . . .

But it's one I haven't felt in years.

"Wise words," the man murmurs in agreement, licking his fingers. "Very wise indeed."

———————————

The night drags on, and I start to itch with the pestering thought that DeMarco's body is still upstairs and at any minute someone could find it.

What if I messed something up? What if they can trace his death back to me?

I try to distract myself with every loose-lipped guest, but no one seems to hold anything of value. They clearly believe I do, charming me into spilling every Harrow secret.

Gathering information is more boring than I thought.

"Ah, there she is." A smooth voice interrupts my train of thought as I approach the bar.

I know that voice. The sweet tone is a pretense as it slithers down my body, stiffening it, stealing the serenity away from me and leaving me on my toes for what's to come.

Not bothering to turn to my right, I pretend to ignore Adrian as he leans against the polished walnut counter. But we're standing so close to one another it's hard to ignore him completely.

He doesn't waste time. If he's talking to me, there must be a reason, and since getting me into bed isn't one, there must be something else he wants. And I don't like how uneasy it makes me feel.

Adrian studies me carefully, the ice cubes gently knocking on his glass as he twirls it in his hand. "Enjoying the festivities?" His lips curve into a lopsided smile.

Not good. That smile is never a good sign.

"I can't complain." I finally turn to face him. "Your family certainly knows how to throw a party." I match his tone with practiced ease.

"I have to admit, I find these events somewhat boring. The same faces, the same conversations—it all becomes dull after a while. Don't you agree?"

"Dull" seems like the correct word coming from Adrian. Our relationship was dull. His love for me was dull. And the sex . . .

Actually, "dull" seems too exciting a word.

"Depends on the company." I try to hide my smirk. Instead I pick up a champagne flute from the ones left on the bar for guests to take.

He follows my every move, and I see the gears turning in his head before he glances past me.

"Speaking of which." He tilts his chin at something behind me. "It seems my father has taken an interest in tonight's proceedings."

Following his gaze, I suppress the urge to stiffen as I spot Julian and Lucian Harrow locked in what appears to be an intense conversation.

Is this another one of their family feuds, or is this about DeMarco?

Lucian's jaw is clenched. His ice-blue eyes narrow slightly. He's visibly irritated, yet he maintains a polite façade.

"Family business?" I ask, turning back to Adrian.

"Something like that. My father has a habit of involving himself in matters that don't concern him. It's a trait Julian and I both find . . . tiresome. But you already know that."

Why is he telling me this? Why does it feel like we're talking about something else?

How can I exploit it to my advantage?

"Tell me," Adrian continues, "what do you make of all this? The wealth, the power, the constant maneuvering for position."

What does he know that I don't?

"Life is a game, Adrian." I maintain an unwavering gaze. "And we're simply playing our part."

His eyes flick back and forth between mine before he raises his glass in a silent toast. "May the best player win."

"May the best player win."

CHAPTER TWO

JULIAN

I spot her fiery red hair first.

She's straightened it, pinning it in such a way that it falls seamlessly down her open back. I've never liked it when she does that, because the locks of curls that fall over her forehead when she gets frustrated have a different kind of appeal. They make me mad with the need to thread my fingers through them and pull her to me.

It suits her better, being wild and untamed.

There's a sudden shift in the room as she weaves her way through the crowd. The chatter buzzing around me vanishes as I watch those defiant green eyes scan the room before landing on me.

She gives me a once-over, indifference evident in her posture. Yet I see the flutter of her lashes the moment she notices I'm staring back. The rise and fall of her chest is impossible to miss.

Yet she doesn't come to me. Instead she turns around and heads in the opposite direction, far from me.

Snatching another full glass from the passing waiter, I drown myself in alcohol.

Ten years of ignoring her and it's taken only one second of her ignoring me for me to lose it.

"Mr. Harrow, I must say, your family throws the most exquisite parties!" a woman gushes next to me, her neon-pink lips stretching into a smile, and I fight the urge to roll my eyes at her.

Instead I lean against the wall, already exasperated by the charade. It's not been long since I arrived at this hellhole, and I can barely feign interest.

I grunt in response.

She mentioned her name not too long ago. But I already forgot it.

I don't give two shits about the family business; even less about these time-consuming events that serve no purpose. I'd rather be out there bashing some fucker's face in at the Den, my underground fight club. Or watching a fucker's face get bashed in by someone else. I'm not picky really.

"Your tattoos are quite fascinating." The woman brushes her finger over the ink peeking out from beneath the sleeve of my tailored suit. "I've always loved a man with art on his body."

If it weren't for Aurelia commanding my full attention, I'd be sick to my stomach at how this woman is touching me. Flirting with me when I'm young enough to be her son.

Unable to tear my eyes away, I follow Aurelia's every move.

She stands tall and confident in the room,

commanding attention, her chin jutted out defiantly as she sways through the crowd. The silver material of her dress hugs her curves perfectly.

She's in the middle of the ballroom when my mother approaches her. A warm light cascades over them from the nearby candles. Flecks of burned honey make Aurelia's eyes appear almost angelic.

Almost.

In an instant, images of that night consume my mind. I grind my teeth at the memory of her touch. Her taste—

Fuck.

"Julian, are you even listening to me?"

I inhale a deep breath at the interruption. The woman stares at me expectantly.

"Whatever you say won't convince me to fuck your dry cunt tonight," I grunt, my gaze glued to Aurelia despite the gasps and scoffs coming from Stevie.

Or maybe her name was Stacie.

I don't even notice Lacey leave, nor that my glass is empty now.

All I see is *her*.

Until my gaze flickers across the room, over to my brother, and I notice the way he's staring at her, his dark eyes narrowing as if he's seeing something I'm not.

Without a second thought I march toward him.

"Enjoying the view?" As I sidle up to him his lips curl into a thin smile, betraying nothing. Yet his eyes remain glued on her, assessing.

"Can't say I am." He takes a sip from his glass. "But it

seems you are, little brother. Don't bother. She's nothing more than a tight ass."

"She wasn't even that to you," I bite out.

If the dickhead talks about her ass so carelessly one more time, I'll make sure he's sitting front-row while I make every inch of her mine.

"Come on, Julian. You think she'd ever want to fuck someone like you?" He peeks at me before adding, "She's out of your league, and you know it."

"Is that a challenge?"

I kept my distance all those years. Never looked at her or even acknowledged her existence.

You fool. What about that night at Emeric's party? the voice in my head taunts.

But they aren't dating anymore. He got his ass dumped.

And I can finally look at her.

"Take it however you want." He returns his gaze to her. "Just remember who she belongs to."

"*Belonged* to, brother. Now she's mine to take."

"Boys." Lucian appears at our side, his greeting dripping with distaste. "I see you're enjoying yourselves." His eyes flick to Adrian then me, and when they do, something flashes behind his eyes as he measures my worth.

And I know he sees none.

Adrian's quick to respond. "Of course, Father." His voice is devoid of the emotion I roused in him.

Lucian nods, content, before turning his focus to me. "Julian, I hope you're not bothering your brother. He has important matters to attend to."

The meaning behind his words is clear: I'm not worth his time.

"Everything's fine."

On instinct I glance over at my mother, who's now laughing at whatever the guest is saying. She looks beautiful. Elegant and carefree despite the bruises she hides beneath her long-sleeve gown and her makeup. Courtesy of our dear father.

"Good. You two should focus on your roles within the family, not on petty squabbles," he orders harshly.

"Understood," Adrian replies.

Emotionless.

The perfect son.

"Right," I say instead.

A wave of anger boils my blood just below the surface. I know better than to provoke Lucian, but that doesn't mean I have to fake how much I enjoy his company.

Adrian's next words are barely above a whisper, loud enough for only me to hear. "Remember, Julian. She's off-limits."

But they only stoke my determination to prove him wrong.

"Excuse me." Adrian nods curtly and then walks away, leaving me alone with Lucian.

Lucian turns his nose up and curls his lip in contempt as he looks me up and down. His gaze falls to my knuckles, still red from the punches I threw last night. "What a waste of time," he mutters. "You should focus on more important things, Julian. Like the family business."

"What I do in my free time doesn't affect the family."

"Everything you do affects the family," he snaps, causing some of the nearby partygoers to glance our way. "You should be grateful for everything I've provided for you. Instead you squander your time in those filthy clubs."

Filthy clubs? I'm tempted to laugh in his face.

"Filthy" are the brothels he runs.

"Filthy" are the parties he hosts as cheap excuses for business meetings.

The true "filth" exists in what he does to my mother every single day.

My clubs aren't filthy. *He* is.

I take a deep breath and look away.

"Enough about that." He clears his throat, eyes sharp with a sinister intent I know all too well. "There's something you need to take care of tonight."

Chills skitter down my spine at his words.

"But before that, have you seen DeMarco?" He gives the room an impatient scan. "He has a room in this goddamn hotel and dares to make a late appearance?"

I press the bridge of my nose with my fingers, already over the conversation. "Can't say I have."

"Find him," Lucian orders. "And make sure you get the job done. You'll soon know what it is. And remember, you're a Harrow. It's time you started acting like one."

I grit my teeth and nod.

The last thing I want is to follow his order. But my gaze returns to my mother. Her delicate features are in stark contrast to the darkness we're forced to live in.

She's my anchor, and I will do whatever it takes to protect her.

Starting with whatever Lucian tells me to do.

"Fine," I say reluctantly. "I'll find DeMarco and handle the job."

"Good."

As he walks away his presence persists, bearing down on me. He expects me to be a reflection of him, but there is nothing I'd hate more than to become like him. Nothing. I'd take death in a heartbeat before becoming the monster he is.

Sure, I enjoy the perks of being a Harrow, but the price is steep. Too steep.

And once you keep taking, life will soon expect something back.

Dejected, I force myself to get the task done as quickly as possible. Scanning the room, I search for any sign of DeMarco, but I can't seem to focus. I can't keep my mind away from Aurelia.

The way she holds herself in the middle of these predators, the way her eyes seem to see right through their masks—it's admirable.

Intoxicating almost.

I need to keep my head on the task.

The last thing I need is to give Lucian an excuse to go after my mother even more than he already does. He'd love that.

And I would love nothing more than to lose myself in the adrenaline the Den offers. There, the only rules are the rules I make.

There, I'm in control. Here, I'm just another pawn in his twisted game.

But things are different here. My actions don't only affect me.

For my mother's sake, I have to do whatever it takes to keep her safe. Even if that means diving headfirst into the darkness that is Lucian's world.

I weave through the crowd. There's a tension in the air that seems to grow thicker with each passing second, but I can't pinpoint the source or the reason.

Feeling eyes on me, I catch sight of a woman with long, slender legs sauntering toward me from across the room.

I've seen her somewhere before . . . but where?

Her dress is a burgundy silk, cut low to reveal flawless skin.

And as she nears, I know exactly who she is. She's part of the job Lucian mentioned.

"Julian Harrow," she purrs, running a long, perfectly manicured finger down the lapel of my suit. "It's such a pleasure to finally meet you. My name is Victoria."

"Is it now?"

"Absolutely." Her black eyes roam the length of me. "I must say . . ." She lingers on the tattoos peeking out from under the open buttons of my shirt. "I've heard quite a lot about you."

"Good things, I hope."

She leans in closer, her rose perfume burning my nose as I feel her whispered words on my ear. "How about I show you just how good things can be?"

She's attractive, sure. A pretty face. Any man's dream.

But when everything's this perfect, it becomes boring. Nightmares have depth to them. Nightmares keep you on your toes—a fire that never stops sizzling.

She's none of these things. She's just Lucian's task.

My gaze drifts past her.

This intense feeling brewing inside of me consumes me whole when I see my brother talking to Aurelia. He steps closer to her, eating up the space between them and setting my teeth on edge.

They clink their champagne flutes together in a toast.

What the fuck?

"Julian?"

I barely register Victoria's voice.

"Excuse me," I murmur, not bothering to look at her as I step away.

My focus is solely on Aurelia.

Her green eyes sparkle with a challenge as she looks at Adrian, and I catch the faintest hint of a blush staining her neck. Spreading to her breasts.

I guess it's time for me to play my part.

Game on, brother.

Aurelia excuses herself, walking out of the ballroom. She turns a corner and disappears into the corridor.

And like her shadow, I quicken my pace to catch up.

The clicking sound of her heels beckons me closer. I could close my eyes and I'd still be able to find her.

There's nowhere for you to run.

She continues to walk until she abruptly stops, leaning against the wall. Her chest heaves as she takes in deep breaths.

I hesitate for a moment, not sure if I want to interrupt this view in front of me.

She looks just like she did the night she straddled my hips.

But I didn't keep her from leaving then. I was too immature to know I had to trap my prey before sinking my teeth into it.

But now . . .

All bets are off.

You're mine now, golden one.

CHAPTER THREE

AURELIA

H*e doesn't know.*
He can't know.
No one knows.
If Adrian knew, why didn't he throw it in my face? Why act so damn vague?

If all those years of dating served as anything, I know he would have at least used this as leverage to get us back together. Anything. He would have done anything.

But he didn't.

I slip into the dimly lit corridor and walk as quickly as I can with these heels on. I need someplace quiet, where I can clear my mind and uncoil my nerves.

Yet the more distance I put between myself and the ballroom, the louder Adrian's words echo between the walls.

I can almost see his piercing eyes when I close mine. How he dug past my carefully constructed façade, reading every tiny secret I was hiding.

As much as I want to believe he was trying to rattle

me, I can't lie to myself. He's never been the type to waste his time—not in all the years I've dated him.

If Adrian does something, there's a good chance he has a valid reason for it.

The realization twists my gut. *I'm fucked.*

Maybe I'm losing control of my plan. I've only killed one person and I already feel like I can't manage.

Valentine taught me how to kill. I know how to use a gun without getting a black eye or falling over from its force. I know how to stab someone, to thrust through bone, without panting afterward. I know where the arteries are, so I know not to stab those, making it painfully slow for the victim to die.

But all the strategy that comes with it? There's only so much the internet can teach.

I can take a life, but can I stop it from taking mine?

Adrian's a cunning little shit and Lucian's favorite son, but he still knows how to act dirty when it doesn't involve pleasing his old man.

So if he hasn't shown his cards yet, it's because he has none.

I snort at the irony of the situation.

I can't believe there was ever a time where I thought—no, I was *certain*—we could be happy together. That illusion was shattered when I realized how deeply rooted his family's illegal activities really were.

I've always known the Harrows have secrets—any powerful, wealthy family has them—but I never knew they were this twisted and disturbing. My mother's diary didn't just contain her pain and suffering; it gave me an inside look at what being part of the Inferno Consortium really means.

I learned the truth a few months before breaking up with Adrian. Somehow, I'd convinced myself staying with him would keep me safe, never make me a suspect, as I used him to get the information I needed to form my plan. But in the end, all it did was suffocate me.

Our relationship was more about power and control than real love.

Adrian never seemed like a controlling type. At least, he didn't give me that impression before we started dating.

He decided what I should wear, gifting me most of what makes up my wardrobe today. He also liked to tell me how to act before any event we attended together.

Dinner parties and business events were for me to act innocent and indifferent. I could never let my eyes roam around the place, instructed to only ever look at the person talking to me in the moment. I had to keep quiet and . . . act like I wasn't there.

Friends' parties were the only places I could be myself—on the understanding I couldn't be the center of attention.

And I was never allowed to attend Adrian's house parties. Which I didn't really mind, since I didn't want to run into Julian.

In the beginning of our relationship I wasn't too bothered by any of this. I loved the attention Adrian was giving me—even if it was toxic. Because I'd gone from spending most of my time with Julian to becoming invisible, I craved Adrian's attention. It made me feel important.

Until it didn't anymore, so I broke things off with him weeks ago.

Yet Adrian still haunts my thoughts. Still suffocates me.

Pressing my back further into the wall, I close my eyes, seeking the cold to steady my racing mind.

My breaths come in short gasps as I try to regain control of my emotions.

Breathe in and out. In and—

The scent of Julian's cologne, a mixture of cedarwood and something indescribable, drifts past me, tickling my nostrils. Clouding my judgment.

I miss the way he smells.

The sound of his footsteps comes next, and I snap my eyes to the side. His menacing gaze pierces me in place as he prowls toward me.

When was the last time Julian Harrow looked my way? No. When was the last time Julian Harrow was *heading my way*?

Panic thrums in my chest, each beat heavy on my heart, before freezing it in agony. His presence has always invoked such an effect.

Call it instinct, but his good looks won't take me for a fool.

Again.

"Looking a bit flustered there. That's unlike you," he drawls.

Taming the shadows like it's child's play, Julian stands out in the darkness. As if he holds power at his fingertips, the lack of light doesn't devour him whole. Instead it amplifies his presence, accentuating every line of his sturdy frame.

His white shirtsleeves are rolled halfway up his arms. Ink swirls on his arms too, up to his neck, as if he's made of the very essence of darkness. The sharpness of his jaw calls attention to his perfectly kissable lips before his piercing, ghostly blue eyes draw me in.

Every inch of him screams power and control, and it unnerves me more than I'd care to admit.

His steps are deliberate and calculated, as if he's on a mission. I press my body closer to the wall, bracing myself for whatever this daredevil, the prince of the Inferno Consortium, has in mind.

"Julian . . . what do you want?"

He arches his brow, assessing the rise and fall of my chest before trailing his eyes down my curves. The action heats my skin.

Oh, help!

I can't afford myself any distractions now. Not when Adrian has just finished with his own dose of snooping around.

"Can't I come over to say hello?" The corner of his mouth turns up and my heart amps to a hammering state, betraying the calm façade I'm so desperately trying to maintain.

He wants to just . . . come over and say hello after ten years?

"Since when have you ever cared about pleasantries?" I raise my chin slightly as I look up at him. "Don't think your charms will work on me anymore."

"Anymore, huh? Who said anything about charm?" He leans in closer. A strand of jet-black hair falls over his eye. "I'm just curious what's got you so worked up." He plays with a strand of my hair, and my eyes widen as the shock of his ice-cold touch sends shivers down my spine.

The silence I was craving is punctuated by the sound of my racing heart and his slow, measured breathing. In a second I'm transported back to the old days, when his touch was a certainty.

It's the night before my first day of high school. He's lying on my bed, one arm behind his head, as he follows my fretful figure while I pace back and forth across my room trying to choose what to wear for the occasion. You only get one first day of high school, and I want it to be special.

He's supposed to be helping me, but all he does is stare, the corner of his plump lips curving ever so slightly whenever a grunt of frustration leaves mine. He looks lost in thought, someplace else, until something flickers in his eyes, and he calls me over to him. His long arm lifts, and I crawl into the nook beneath it.

He plays with the strands of my messy hair before whispering how good red looks on me.

So I wear red . . .

The day he started ignoring me I wore red. Like the blood that seeped out of the cracks he made in my heart.

"Nothing." I hold in the gasp that threatens to leave my lips at how good his body feels up against mine. "Now leave me alone."

I can almost taste the heat radiating from his body. His intense gaze is becoming more difficult to hold without flinching away.

"Or what?" His eyes fall to my lips before he grips my chin between his fingers, brushing his thumb over my lower lip. "What will you do, Aurelia? Run to Adrian for protection?"

The way my name sounds coming from his lips sends a shiver down my spine. Could be the fact it's been years since he last called me by my name, or that this is the longest conversation we've had since I started dating Adrian ten years ago.

"Oh, please. Jealousy is beneath even someone like you."

Then I shove him back.

Even with all the force I put into it he doesn't move much, only enough to get his hands away from me.

He chuckles, the sound so foreign for someone I've known most of my life. His eyes glint, and I think he might be laughing for a different reason.

"Talk," I spit.

"Not yet."

He steps back into my personal space, forcing me to crane my neck to maintain eye contact as he towers over me.

"What are you waiting for?" My voice loses strength as I fall deep into his eyes.

As the confines of the corridor seem to shrink even more around us, my nerves start to unravel.

"Patience, golden one," he murmurs. "You'll find out soon enough."

I ball my hands into fists as I do my best to prevent my body from reacting to his closeness. "Stop playing games, Julian," I hiss through gritted teeth. "I don't have time for this."

His icy eyes darken, the specks of white between the cerulean ocean swallowed by his dilating pupils. His features take on a predatory air that makes my pulse quicken despite myself.

"Tell me, Aurelia." He leans in, our noses almost touching as he cages me in.

I try to angle my face away from his, but having him this close clouds my reasoning, and now I want him closer.

"What's going on between you and my brother? You two seemed awfully . . . intimate earlier."

"Adrian and I were just talking."

Why do I feel like this isn't the first time I've been in this situation, with the need to reach out and touch him? To lose myself in his warm embrace.

What the hell is going on with me?

"Really?" he challenges, brushing his finger over my pulse. "Because it looked like more than just talking from where I was standing."

"And why were you looking, Julian?"

His gaze flickers down to my mouth, then to the rise and fall of my chest, lingering there awhile before returning to my eyes. "Maybe because I think there's something you're not telling me."

"Oh yeah?" I feign interest. "Maybe. Maybe not." Closing the small distance between us, I look deep into his eyes as I grit, "Either way, it's none of your business."

His other hand moves over my waist before he tightens his grip and pins me in place. His touch is addictive, like the sensation of burning alive—I crave for more to burn faster.

"It is my business when you haven't exactly been around lately. Who knows what you've been up to?"

Me? *Me?* I want to scream it at his smug face. He was the one who ruined our friendship my freshman year of high school and then acted like an absolute asshole the whole time I dated Adrian!

God, he needs to leave before I either claw out his eyes or do worse. *Far worse.*

"Like I said, it's none of your business." My voice wavers slightly under the weight of my growing anger. "Now, can we drop this?"

"No."

I lose it. "Why do you even care? You haven't cared about me for *years* and now you suddenly decide to? No. You don't get to play hot-and-cold. So stop caring now!"

I'm heaving by the time the last word gushes out of my mouth. I stayed quiet all these years. *Why?* God, I don't even know myself. Maybe I thought hearing how bored he was would hurt me more. Maybe because in the silence I could still hope.

"You're right." Julian's hushed words slither out like needles to the skin. His expression is impossible to read. "I don't give a fuck about you. Never have and never will. Yet I can't help but wonder which pretty little mask you're hiding behind."

As he grips my chin, all the hatred I feel for him boils within me.

"You can't stand the thought of him knowing something you don't," I spit, relishing in the way his expression sharpens at my words. "Adrian always gets better than you, and you can't stand it."

He clenches his jaw—hard—eyes narrowing. But just when I thought I hit him where it hurt the most, a smirk stretches his lips. "Maybe you're right. What will you do about it, golden one?"

"Don't call me that."

"And what will you give me in return?"

Do I want something from him?

The real question is, can I get what I want from him?

Then, just when I least expect it, he licks the bare skin of my collarbone, all the way to my earlobe. "I'm waiting, *golden one*."

I bite down on my lower lip, suppressing the gasp that tries to escape. "Is that the best you can do, Julian? You'll have to try harder than that if you want to get under my skin."

"Trust me," he murmurs, leaning closer to me until I can taste his warmth on my lips. "Getting under your skin isn't deep enough."

His eyes follow the movement of my tongue as it dampens my parched lips, wetting his lips in the process.

And then he takes a step back. So fast his loss leaves a chill over my flushed skin.

His hands are back in his pockets, far away from touching me, as his eyes roll down the silver gown tightly caressing my curves. Then they roam back up, stopping at my breasts.

I cross my arms defensively on instinct, bouncing my breasts farther out in the process.

But his focus isn't on my body—it's on something else entirely.

"Is that blood?"

"What? Where?" I stammer, my eyes darting down to where he's looking.

And right there, just above the low neckline of my dress, on my breast, is a small droplet of blood.

DeMarco's blood.

Before I can react, Julian reaches out and gently wipes away the droplet with his fingertip. He holds it up between us, clearly displaying the crimson stain, before doing something that sends a bolt of shock through my entire body.

He licks the blood off his finger. His gaze doesn't leave mine the whole time.

"Julian! What are you doing?" Feeling both repulsed and inexplicably drawn to him at once, I watch him suck it clean.

"Interesting," he says, unfazed by my reaction. "It doesn't taste like yours."

"Wh-what—?"

"Your little secret," he whispers, his voice taking on a dark, dangerous edge. "I'm going to find out what it is . . . one way or another."

CHAPTER FOUR
AURELIA

Has Julian always been such a psycho?

The encounter with him still lingers on my skin like an unwanted ghostly touch, his whispered promise ingrained in my mind. He tasted DeMarco's blood without second-guessing it. God. I can feel the two glasses of champagne I drank earlier threatening to come up.

Liar. You liked it. His depravity lures you in, my inner voice reprimands me.

Turning my head to the side, I give myself a once-over in the entryway mirror of my apartment. My cheeks and my neck are now an oxblood color—an embarrassing contrast to my pale complexion.

Julian isn't here, but simply the memory of tonight makes my hands tremble. At least I know he can't reach me now. Well, he could. I'm only an elevator ride away from his penthouse.

I dart my gaze around the small living room, searching for Valentine, but all I find is the empty green velvet couch and the TV turned off. The lamp next to the couch is off too.

The only source of light comes from the small, rusted gold sconce above the irregular oval mirror in my entryway. My own restless face stares back at me.

My hair is luckily still pinned behind my shoulders, although some strands have escaped, thanks to Julian's playful fingers. A few more strands cling to my neck, while others spring on alert like I just came back from war.

And I might as well have.

I hate how easily he gets to me even despite my best efforts to remain calm. If he wants me to feel a certain way, he always gets what he wants.

He's had this power over me ever since we were seven.

Couldn't I just remain a distant memory to you?

What an idiot I was back then to complain when he stopped giving me attention.

I let out a deep grunt before straightening up and walking into the narrow corridor connecting the living room to the kitchen. A sense of relief immediately rushes through me at the familiar surroundings. White picture frames are scattered across the wall, containing photos of my youth. Most of them are photos of myself smiling at Valentine behind the camera, but there are also some of Julian and me.

Every time I walk past them I'm overcome with the thought that sometimes the pain of losing people is worth it for the memories you have with them.

I take a deep breath, inhaling the burned scent of

vanilla coming from the curved green diffuser on the light wooden console table. I bought it for Valentine last Christmas. He's a coffee addict, and the smell is starting to linger to the point of being nauseating.

Just like what happened with Adrian and Julian tonight. The memory picks at my nerves.

I guess the scent of vanilla can't soothe everything.

"God, I need a drink." I sigh, massaging my temples with my fingers.

"Rough night?"

I head into the kitchen to find Valentine sitting at the table sipping a cup of black coffee—his nightly ritual.

"Is it that obvious?" I collapse onto the chair next to his.

He doesn't even need to study me up close to know there's something wrong. He's the right hand of the Harrow family; he already did that the moment I walked through the door.

"Your cheeks are flushed, and you look like you've been through hell." His shaved dark hair, peppered with strands of gray, is all I can see due to the size of his mug.

Collecting large mugs has been Valentine's hobby for the past two years. Half of the kitchen cabinets are full of them, along with different coffee beans.

Valentine is in command of day-to-day operations in the Harrow business. *Both* of the Harrow businesses, the Inferno Consortium being one of them. He's an intimidating, solid wall of muscle, clad in his usual attire: a black T-shirt and black pants. But underneath it all, there's a warmth he reserves only for me. It's in the way his eyes narrow the slightest amount, or how the corner of his mouth jerks up when he looks at me.

He doesn't see the orphan girl, but someone he raised as his own.

He's never told me much about my mother, only that he was working for the Harrows when she was alive. Now I know about her past, it makes complete sense he decided not to tell a little girl her dead mother was a sex slave. However, he does like to remind me—*always*—how he didn't really have a choice in adopting me, because the moment he saw my big, round eyes he was forced to take me in.

Without going into detail, I mutter, "Julian Harrow," before asking, "Is this your first cup of the night?"

"Third," Valentine states bluntly. "Ah, so it's Julian this time, not Adrian." He gives a knowing smirk.

"Adrian is a whole other issue." I sigh, massaging my temples again. "But yeah, tonight was all about Julian. Wait—did you say 'third'? You know what the doctor said. No more than three a day!"

Valentine suffers from mild hypertension, and the doctor advised him not to be excessive with his coffee intake, but Valentine is stubborn. If he wants his coffee, he'll have it. I like to think my resilience comes from his stubbornness.

His forehead crinkles. Resting his elbow on the table, he gives me his full attention. "You need to be careful around them, especially Julian. He's dangerous and unpredictable. Stay as far away from them as possible."

I don't even have the opportunity to answer, because he adds, "You know how dangerous the Harrows can be."

He's completely ignoring my comment about his well-being. I wouldn't be surprised if he's doing it on purpose, steering the conversation in another direction.

"I'm aware. I won't let them stand in my way."

Valentine arches a brow, waiting.

"And I'll be careful. I promise," I huff.

Satisfied, he nods before returning to his coffee.

We stay there for a moment, silence between us, as I stare at the man who gave me a chance.

My thoughts drift back to my mother's diary. I've had it for a few months, since the day Valentine decided to give it to me, yet the details of the horrors she went through still eat at my insides every time I read them. The way her handwriting changes depending on her emotions, on what she went through each night at the hands of powerful families. Families like the Harrows.

"Thanks for always being there for me, Valentine. I don't know what I'd do without you," I whisper, breaking the silence with my wavering voice.

His eyes twinkle with warmth as he looks up at me. "Anything for you, kid."

Then, like any other time when things get a little emotional, he asks, "Do we need to go cut some onions?"

I can't help but chuckle, and the faintest smile stretches his lips.

We haven't cut onions since I was ten. We always used to, whenever my little heart couldn't handle the emotions storming inside of me. Since Valentine is the worst person to go to for comfort, he'd make us cut onions in the kitchen. He said this way, I could cry my emotions out without having to talk about them.

"No need. Save them for another time."

"All right." He clears his throat. "Now, go get some rest. You've got a big day ahead of you tomorrow."

"Got something for me?"

"You just wait and see."

Nodding, I make my way to my bedroom.

The moment I open the door, the mellow shade of cool teal greets me. Next are the various pieces of art I've painted over the years—some bold and vibrant, others dark and moody, just how I like them.

My bedroom is my cozy refuge from the chaos outside.

A console bookcase, which I painted white with scattered green leaves, stands against three walls of my room, overflowing with new and well-worn books, while some shelves are occupied by cherished mementos.

There's a small vanity table that I still need to paint facing the floor-to-ceiling windows.

The view outside is just like one of the art pieces adorning the wall: a sky full of twinkling stars.

In the center of the room, far from the four walls, is my sanctuary: my bed, with its plush duvet and collection of colorful pillows. There's no headboard—I decided to throw it away, wanting an unobstructed view of all my artwork while lying down. Some of the pieces on the wall behind my bed were purposely painted to be looked at upside down.

I plop down onto it, positioning the pillows to hold my back as I get comfortable. Brushing my fingers over the softness of the duvet, I lift the diary off the nightstand and open it.

The persisting scent of old paper and . . . lilies fills the air before my mom's secrets are whispered back to life.

This is all I have of her. This book is a bridge between us; a connection that transcends time and death.

The more I read it, the more I get to know her.

Her fears, hopes, and dreams are all faded ink now. This is all that's left of her.

I clutch the diary tighter, my knuckles turning white.

This, right here, is my mission. My purpose.

I was born from the ashes of my mother's suffering. The least I can do is avenge her name.

Skimming the pages, I flip through the last entries. An ache spreads in my chest as her emotions seep from the inked words and surround me, making me feel like I'm there with her.

June 21st

They treat us like animals. They rotate us depending on the day and their twisted desires. But as time passes, the more I'm requested to be out of my room and in theirs.

They use me as an object. They see me as a soulless person.

The things they do to us . . . the way they make me feel.

I must endure it. Now more than ever—for my daughter, for the hope that one day she'll be free from this hell.

The words blur as my fingers, holding the diary, tremble.

Five months after this entry I was born. My mother must have only just found out about me. Maybe, just maybe, I gave her the last remaining strength to fight for us.

I continue reading the words I've read a hundred times already. Each entry boils my blood.

These powerful families . . . these monsters have been hurting and manipulating people for far too long. They hide behind their power and wealth, but I see right through them. I see their weakness and I'll use it against them.

The Inferno Consortium will learn what pain feels like. And how powerful someone they've wronged really is.

July 15th

> *Today they tried to break me.*
>
> *They tried and succeeded, but I didn't let them see it.*
>
> *Lady Marlowe decided to use my naked body as it pleased her the most. She made me crawl on all fours around the room, for all the guests to see. And when that wasn't entertaining to her anymore, she burned me with her cigarettes.*
>
> *But she didn't touch my belly. My Aurelia. She didn't touch her.*

Tears sting my eyes before falling down my cheeks as images of my mother's torment fog my vision. How her dignity was stripped away with each cigarette butt that touched her skin. How they laughed as she suffered.

In this moment I swear to myself, I won't just kill them. I'll make them suffer, just as they did to her.

July 15th

    I can still hear her raucous laugh as she stood over me. The sizzling sound as she stubbed out her cigarette on my naked back. The overwhelming pain and the metallic taste of blood as I bit down on my lip to stifle my cries.

August 2nd

    They didn't call me today. They left me alone in my room, and it's the only moment I've had to imagine my beautiful Aurelia. How her laugh will sound or if she'll have my vibrant red hair.

    She'll be brilliant. A bundle of life. I'll make sure of it.

    She's my purpose, my strength to keep fighting.

    She's going to make a wonderful woman.

Her determination and hope intertwines with mine, igniting a fire in my core—a burning desire to ensure her dreams weren't in vain.

With each word my resolve grows stronger.

I will not let her down.

September 17th

    They think I'm weak. They think they can break me.

    But I'll never give up. No matter how much pain I have to endure, I'll go through it for my daughter.

    I want to see her smile. I want to hold her and promise her everything will be all right. That her life will be full of joy and love.

    I will endure anything for her sake.

October 8th

If there is one thing I have learned through all this, it's that love is not just a fleeting emotion or a simple connection between two people. It is a force powerful enough to withstand any heartbreak. Any cruelty. And it is that love which sustains me now, as I hold onto the hope that one day, no matter how faraway it may seem, Aurelia and I will be together against all this.

October 19th

How much longer can I survive this?

The days are shorter now. The sun doesn't shine as brightly as it once did.

But I have to be strong. For my Aurelia. For the love she gives me, even if she's not here yet.

For the hope that she will one day live the life I dreamed of.

November 21st

Today I made a promise. I looked into those green orbs and promised her I'd fight for us.

I'll make sure they all pay for their sins. For each time I cried alone in bed; for each time they touched me.

I'll fight for my old self, and for my daughter.

This one is her final entry, written the day I was born, just four days before she was found hanging in her room. Something happened in those days. Something that shredded to pieces what little resolve she had left.

Whatever it was doesn't matter. I know who did it.

Now, all I have to do is retaliate. For her, for myself, and for every other victim of these monsters.

Hours pass me by as I read through the pages. My eyes start to flutter closed as sleep threatens to pull me in. The diary slips from my hands and I'm plunged into a restless sleep.

I find myself in a dream, a consuming blackness, with my mother's words sketched in big, bold letters everywhere.

"If there is one thing I have learned through all this, it is that love is not just a fleeting emotion or a simple connection between two people . . ."

"I won't let your pain be for nothing," I whisper into the darkness.

The dream changes shape, and I find myself standing at the edge of a cliff with Seattle no more than dots of light below me. Wind picks up, and it whips around me, tugging at my hair and my clothes as it pushes me closer to the precipice.

In an instant the wind takes shape as a figure, standing behind me, hissing, "Look at them, Aurelia."

My gaze focuses on the world below.

"They think they're untouchable, that their sins will never catch up to them."

I dart around, expecting to come face-to-face with the source of the voice. But no one is there.

Only darkness surrounds me. And yet the voice sounds familiar. I've heard it before, but the more I force myself to pinpoint it, the harsher the headache pounds at my head.

"Who are you?" I yell into the pitch-blackness.

"Does it matter?" the voice replies from somewhere above me. "What matters is that you know what must be done."

I twist around, but there's still nothing there.

"Say it," the voice purrs.

And without being told what I need to say, the words flow from my mouth.

"They'll pay for what they did to my mother," I vow. "Every single one of them."

"Good," the voice says, sounding satisfied. "You know what needs to be done, Aurelia. Don't hesitate. Don't falter."

"I won't," I say into the abyss surrounding me. "They will feel the same pain and humiliation they inflicted upon her—I swear it."

The voice shifts, sounding different as it warns, "Remember, the path you walk is a dangerous one. Trust no one."

"I won't."

Whoever this entity is, they don't need to tell me twice.

"Especially not him."

The moment the last words reach me, the image of Julian appears in front of my eyes.

He's standing tall and proud, his eyes filled with the same darkness that taints the atmosphere.

"I'll never trust him," I breathe.

"Good." The voice breaks, fading back into the wind as the dream shifts.

And I find myself in yet another nightmare.

I'm back at tonight's fundraiser. Both Julian and

Adrian are standing frozen in front of me. Their gazes scorch every part of my body as they stare at me.

But there's something else lurking beneath the surface. Something I can't quite identify. Something that freezes me to the spot.

Valentine's earlier words echo next. *"Stay away from them, Aurelia. You don't know what you're getting yourself into."*

Maybe I do.

CHAPTER FIVE
AURELIA

I step into the Harrows' penthouse, looking for Valentine, and immediately sense something is off.

I've spent most of my life in this place. When I was younger, it was because Valentine couldn't—or rather, wouldn't—trust a babysitter to look after me, so he took me wherever he went. Since his work consists of being at arm's length from the Harrows at any given moment, we were here a lot. Then, when I grew older, it was because of Julian. Later, it became because of Adrian.

Whatever the reason, this penthouse has become a second house to me. Not home—there's no warmth here.

The place is usually pristine. Its dullness is the reason I get goose bumps whenever I come here. There's no personality, no color. That's how I know something must be happening.

This is an unusual form of unsettling.

Petals are scattered on the marble floor, the vase the flowers were in now lying on its side on the round table in the center of the foyer. With a gust of wind it could roll off, meeting the petals with a crash.

I make my way to the formal living room and freeze.

Something is seriously wrong!

Papers fall from between the hands of the scattering guards as they hurry in different directions. But no one makes a sound.

It's like sitting front-row at a silent play. No one dares to speak. Their expressions are enough to convey the disarray. If I had to guess, I'd think they were afraid to attract Lucian's anger.

If there's one thing I've learned in my years spent here, it's that Lucian hates turmoil. Especially when he isn't the instigator of it.

"Hey!" I shout at a passing guard. "What's going on?"

"Vincent DeMarco is dead," he pants, recoiling at his own words. "The Consortium's in chaos."

A thrill spikes through me, but I feign shock.

I wounded the Inferno Consortium with just one kill. Imagine what will happen when more die.

Is this what Valentine was talking about last night? Could this be an opening for me to slither in and cause more damage?

I need to find him.

"Thanks."

Nodding, he disappears down the corridor.

"Looking for someone?" A smooth yet sharp voice stops me, stirring whatever he awakened within me at the fundraiser.

I steel myself as I turn to face him.

Guards rush past him and he remains unbothered,

leaning against the wall as his gaze darkens. Julian's features sharpen as he stares at me, making it impossible for me to understand what's going on in that head of his.

"Valentine." I cut to the chase. The less time I spend here with him, the better it'll be.

"Right," he drawls, hands in his pockets. "Our little chat at the fundraiser last night must have left you longing for more civilized company." The faintest of grins stretches his lips.

I press my lips together, my heart squeezing. Memories of the way his touch felt as it molded to my curves, held me obedient, flood back in.

But it's the way he's staring at me now that makes my blood turn cold. Not hot, but a chilling emptiness. Because it only serves to remind me of the void he left in me the moment he decided I wasn't worth his time, attention, or affection.

Julian Harrow and I need to keep to our separate paths. Just like we have done for the past ten years.

"Hardly." I scoff. "I just need to talk to him."

"Of course." He pushes off the wall and takes small, deliberate steps toward me. The depth in his eyes locks me into place. "But if you ever get bored of tasting the same old—"

"Julian!" A sharp voice interrupts him.

A woman with legs half my height stands at the far end of the foyer. Her eyes are the darkest black I've ever seen, and she has long brown hair. A white knitted dress is draped elegantly over her figure.

That's a *Rabanne* chain-detailed midi dress. I'd recognize it with my eyes closed. Eleanora spoke about it maybe ten to twenty times last Friday when we met at her place for what she loves to call "pamper Friday." She's always had an eye for fashion, and with her family's wealth she's able to indulge in the latest trends. She says her extensive knowledge of fashion is a means of survival, because in a world like ours, the masks we choose to wear say more about our character than we'd like.

I guess that's why I dress to catch the eye. I don't want to cower away like they expect me to. I'm the odd one out, but that doesn't mean I need to play the part.

"Your father needs you in his office."

"Thank you, Lady Marlowe." He gives me one last glance before turning to follow her.

Lady Marlowe.

My mind races with the probability that this is the same Lady Marlowe from my mother's diary.

It's impossible.

It can't be the same Lady Marlowe.

Then again, the families who are a part of the Inferno Consortium span generations. No one else is called Marlowe if not a Marlowe.

But this woman is young. Her face doesn't carry the weight of all her wrongdoings. Not yet at least.

She must be the daughter. Or a niece.

Whoever she is doesn't take away from the fact she is a Marlowe. She may not have inflicted pain directly onto my mother, but she's no saint. Not if she's a member of the Inferno Consortium.

I need to find Valentine and ask him to tell me everything he knows about this Lady Marlowe and her connection to the Harrows.

I need answers, and I need them fast.

Determined, I make my way through the corridor opposite the one Julian and Lady Marlowe disappeared down. With each step I take, questions assault my thoughts.

How long have the Harrows and the Marlowes been doing business for? Yes, they're both members of the Inferno Consortium, but that doesn't mean their front companies have to interconnect.

How am I going to play my way deep into Lady Marlowe to destroy her?

And most importantly, since when was Julian this involved in the family business?

Thinking of him doing the disgusting things I read in my mother's diary leaves dread crawling up my spine. Could he have changed this much?

My pulse races. I hope not.

Why? Because seeing him again stirred up old feelings? Because I foolishly think we can just erase ten years and pick up where we left off?

Stupid.

Stupidly hopeful.

I need to stop thinking of Julian Harrow. But when I think back to Lady Marlowe, he invades my thoughts again.

How deep does Julian's connection with Lady Marlowe go?

I can't help but to dig deeper.

What if targeting Lady Marlowe will hurt Julian too?

I let him take root in my heart, where he once was and never left.

Why do I suddenly care about him?

Did I ever stop?

His recent interest in me is already complicating things. He's finally talking to me after ignoring me for years, and I suddenly feel obliged to consider him when planning my next move.

He could throw everything to shit.

Or maybe, just maybe, he's a blessing in disguise.

Can I use their friendship to bring her down?

I bite my lower lip, tasting the peach lip oil.

I don't know anything about Lady Marlowe or her role in the Inferno Consortium, but if she's here at the penthouse, talking directly with Lucian, then she's ranked highly. Too highly for me to just ignore. I need to get close to her and learn her secrets, her weaknesses. Playing nice could be my best weapon—at least until I have more intel on her.

I'm about to get lost in the labyrinth of light gray walls, black-and-white marble floors, and the occasional abstract expressionist artwork, when I spot her sitting on the white cushions of the couch.

She must have escorted Julian to his father's office and then headed through the adjoining corridor on the east side to get here before me.

Valentine can wait. When will I get another opportunity like this?

"Lady Marlowe?" I approach her with a confident stride even though my heart could give out at any second. "It's a pleasure to meet you. My name's Aurelia Draven."

As I sit down next to her, every nerve in my body spikes, on high alert. I subtly scan the room in my peripheral for any potential intruders who might divert her attention from our conversation or cast a shadow of suspicion over me.

It's no secret that my relationship with the Harrow brothers is complicated at best and lethal at worst. Me being at the penthouse isn't weird since Valentine works here, the boss to every single one of these panicked guards, but if anyone finds me speaking to a member of the Inferno Consortium without Adrian or Julian by my side, their suspicions could arise. Especially now that another empire has just crumbled.

But I'm not too worried.

I'm ready to deflect any intrusion with a distracting comment about the latest society gossip, or with a charming smile. I'm not blind to the way the guards look at me.

"Ah, you must be the golden one." Her words slither down my body. "You're quite the entertainment around here."

Her voice pitches high on the last three words, carrying a sense of superiority that makes my teeth grind. Sharp black eyes sweep over me like scorching coal, making my gut instincts scream.

Danger, danger. You know nothing about her.

Ignoring it, I stand tall, chin jutted out, as I refuse to let my unease ruin this precious chance. Instead I evaluate her too, picking up every detail about her that could become a potential clue—a weapon to use or avoid.

Her long, chocolate-brown hair is pinned behind her shoulders, not even a strand out of place. The expensive *Rabanne* dress hugs her petite frame as she crosses her long legs.

She projects power and wealth.

Yet there's something else that makes my heart thunder in my chest. Whatever lurks behind those vacant eyes, I recognize it all too well.

Calculating intelligence mixed with ruthless determination.

It's like looking in a mirror. My own self is reflected in her gaze.

"I've heard about you."

I force a smile onto my face. *The fakest of smiles.* "Only good things, I hope."

I hope I look more confident than I feel.

"Depends on who you ask." She glances at her immaculate bloodred nails. Each one is filed into a sharp point. The nail polish is such a deep shade of red it's almost black. The cut of Lady Marlowe's dress emphasizes the sharpness of her collarbone and the thinness of her arms.

A cruel elegance radiates from her. Like heat from a flame.

"Tell me, what brings you to mingle among our kind?"

Our kind. I try to let it slide, yet it burns along my skin.

"Curiosity, mostly. Your name is quite popular in certain circles too."

"Is that so?" She raises an eyebrow. "Well, curiosity can be a dangerous thing, especially around here."

"Sometimes danger is half the fun." I notice the corner of her lips twitching in an almost-smile. "Besides, who doesn't like a little excitement now and then?"

She hums in agreement. "But too much excitement can lead to trouble."

"Trouble can be . . . interesting."

"Perhaps," she concedes, sweeping her fingers in front of her, letting the brightness of the long drop ceiling light bounce off her diamond rings, "if you have your family's name to deal with incoming threats."

"How resourceful!"

"It is." Her expression softens ever so slightly at my sweetened words. "In fact, I'd wager there isn't a situation we couldn't handle if need be."

"Your confidence is inspiring."

Someone please take me now and choke me to death.

I have a feeling she's too preoccupied with basking in the compliment to catch the fakeness in my voice.

"Thank you, Aurelia," she responds, finally calling me by my name. "You're quite the enigma, aren't you? But I think I like you."

"Likewise, Lady Marlowe."

"Please, call me Victoria," she insists.

Bingo.

That was way easier than I anticipated.

Tilting her body, she turns to face me. "Tell me, how did you come to know Julian?"

The implication in her question is obvious: How does an orphan girl, daughter of a whore, befriend the prince of the Harrow family—of the Inferno Consortium?

"Ah, Julian," I muse, thinking quickly about what to say. "We met through mutual friends. He's quite the charmer, isn't he?"

I leave out how we used to be childhood best friends before he decided to act like a dick and throw away years of friendship.

"He is," she agrees, chuckling. Her eyes shine with mischief. "He always did know how to make an impression."

"How long have you known him for?" I try my luck, my voice dripping with honeyed sweetness.

She narrows her coal eyes on me, leaving a trail of chills creeping over my body as I wait for her next move.

I try to remain at ease as I wait for her answer.

Then, when the seconds seem to stretch out, she lets out a giggle.

"Well, you see, our connection goes back several generations. My great-grandfather and Julian's great-great-grandfather were close friends and partners in business, building new possibilities to . . . branch out. Let's just say, their bond was passed down through the years." She seems to hesitate for a moment, weighing her words before adding, "My mother and Lady Harrow were quite good friends when my mother was still alive."

There's no doubt now that she's the daughter of the Lady Marlowe my mother mentioned in her diary.

"Partners in business? What kind of business?"

My mother's diary gave me a different perspective

into their world, but I'm Valentine's daughter: I hear and see things.

"Various ventures," she replies vaguely before going back to checking her nails. "Some more successful than others."

"So Julian has been integral to your family's success?"

"Absolutely." She smiles as my blood turns cold. "He's always had a keen mind for strategy and negotiation. In fact, he recently helped us secure a deal that has greatly expanded our influence."

Ignoring the unfamiliar ache spreading inside of me, I dig deeper. "A deal, huh? Well, that doesn't sound like Julian at all."

Victoria feeds on the skepticism in my voice. She'd do anything to make her life, this included, seem interesting in the eyes of someone like me.

She cracks a smile. One that leaves me uneasy. "I'm not at liberty to discuss the details. But let's just say, it's been very profitable."

This isn't exactly what I wanted. Not even close. But at least I've answered one of my questions: I can use their relationship to my advantage. I can use Julian without feeling any guilt. Especially now that I know how tainted he is by the Inferno Consortium.

"Well, I must say, I'm impressed by Julian's abilities."

She hums in agreement. "I have no doubt he'll continue to be an invaluable asset to both our families."

I force a smile.

Something subtle but intrusive cracks inside of me, snapping, molding into something different. Something unrecognizable. Maybe I was still holding onto hope, onto that version of Julian I trusted with my naïve heart. But I should have stopped long ago. I should have tossed all hope the moment he trashed everything we were. When he decided I no longer mattered.

I shouldn't have hoped for a viper to be nonvenomous.

The Inferno Consortium takes and takes, leaving a shell of a human in return. Leaving a hungry man willing to do anything to fill that void again.

And Julian Harrow? *He's ravenous.*

"I'm in quite a generous mood today. Almost forgot about that hopeless case of a man dying." Her eyes gleam when they take me in. "I'm hosting an intimate gathering at my cabin tonight. I'd be delighted if you could . . . join us."

"I'd love to. Thank you, Victoria."

This is exactly the opportunity I need. Attending this party will allow me to start mapping out Victoria's routine, finding the cracks in her curated façade. I have to be ready. I need to be two steps ahead of her, predicting each of her actions before she even considers them.

This party is my chance to strike.

"Excellent." Her smile widens. "And you'll be attending with Julian, of course. After all, you guys are friends."

"Of course," I echo. *Great.*

He's the one person who could sabotage everything and he's already suspicious of me. How will I get him off my back in there?

Maybe if I tell him to meet me there, I can arrive a bit earlier and use the extra time to snoop around and talk to people.

I'll need to be good at getting closer to Victoria while keeping Julian in the dark about my true intentions.

"Perfect!" She claps her hands as she gets up to leave. "I'll let him know the details," she says from over her shoulder, her voice fading as she rounds the corner. "It's sure to be a memorable evening."

What?

"Wait, Victoria—"

But it's too late. She's already gone.

"Perfect," I huff, sinking down between the cushions . . .

And the doomed realization there is no escaping Julian Harrow.

CHAPTER SIX
JULIAN

The nauseating scent of a Cuban cigar whirls around me. Lucian's office is covered in a thick layer of smoke, hiding the gold leaf on the mahogany bookshelves from my eyes.

I'm standing in front of his desk, yet his presence towers over me. I shuffle my feet on the plush Persian rug with the pestering need to leave this place.

No one knows how much standing here is killing me.

It's the middle of the day and the sun is shining outside, but the curtains are drawn. Long shadows are cast across the waxed surface of Lucian's desk from the torchiere lamp in the far corner of the room.

The tension between us is palpable.

Adrian is at his side, looking as composed as ever.

The smug bastard.

"DeMarco is dead," Lucian growls. "We need to find out who did this." His hands twitch, a tangible echo to his seething rage.

The room seems to shrink under the weight of his anger. It hangs heavy in the room.

But Lucian's anger isn't anything new. Nothing unexpected for me.

It's an old friend.

The way his jawline sharpens as he grinds his teeth together. The way his eyes darken, boring into me. The way his vein throbs in his forehead, threatening to burst at any moment.

I'm all too familiar with how much his own wrath dominates him.

The sight wrenches something within me. Not out of fear but recognition.

The man in front of me is the same one who haunts my mother at night, unleashing his fury upon her, punch after punch.

The familiar frosty glint in his eyes—the same color as mine—as he lifts his hand to her. The same protruding tendon tightening along his forearm like a steel cable. The same cruel curl of his lips after each blow meets its mark.

The man in front of me is an uncanny reflection of that monster. And just like in a nightmare, all I can do is stand by helplessly and watch the darkness lurk within him.

"Of course, Father." Like the perfect obedient son he is, Adrian doesn't waste any time in pleasing him. "We'll do whatever it takes to find the person responsible."

I let a chuckle filter through. Thorough and heavy. Intentional.

"I expect you to put your shit aside and focus on the task at hand," Lucian snaps, slamming his fist down on the desk. "DeMarco's death has caused a significant disturbance within the Inferno Consortium. This cannot go unpunished."

"Understood."

The truth is, I don't give a damn about DeMarco or the Consortium, and they know that. I've been making it obvious since the day I learned to talk. But then the years passed, and the longer I went against his orders, the more Lucian beat my mother. Things changed. Aurelia was no longer in my life and my mother needed me more than ever, so I learned to keep my opinions to myself and do Lucian's dirty work for him.

Lucian breaks eye contact. "From what we've gathered,"—he stands from his chair and leisurely walks to the bookshelf, making a scene of scanning the shelves—"we believe one of those filthy whores killed him. He was found in his hotel room with an open bottle of champagne, his glass full, and another glass missing from the set."

"Are we sure about that?" Adrian asks.

"Positive. It's always the fucking whores," Lucian spits before laughing, the raucous sound a cruel joke to the ears. "Just like your mother, eh, Julian?"

Darkness gathers in my sight at the mention of my mother. My nails, unyielding, dig into the soft flesh of my palm as I clench them. The urge to punch the bastard right then and there itches under my skin, a tantalizing temptation dancing at the edges of my restraint.

But for her . . . for my mother's sake, I hold back.

Last time I lost control she paid the price with two broken ribs.

Lucian has always been cunning at sniffing out vulnerability. Like a bloodhound on a hunt, he found mine in her—our mother. He uses her to manipulate me into taking part in the family business.

Adrian, on the other hand, doesn't need Lucian to control him. He fell in love with the family business at first sight. His one true love.

He cares about our mother, but never before the business.

"Leave her out of this, you piece of shit."

"Watch it," he warns.

Then, just like that, he shifts gears with practiced ease, his disregard for anything but power evident. Not even his own wife is more important.

"We need to find the whore who killed DeMarco, and we need to do it now."

I listen to my brother as he goes through the file containing every girl who was working that night. He states their name and their hour stamp before coming up with a list of five suspects.

While I remain with only one.

The blood staining her breast. Her flushed state. Her late arrival.

The details of DeMarco's death flood my mind as I try to make sense of it. How did she manage to do it? To watch the life drain from a man's eyes is no simple task.

I can't believe she did it, but that unexplained bloodstain on her breast haunts me. Taunts me. And then DeMarco dies? There's no such thing as a coincidence. Not when it has something to do with her.

What is her motive? Why did she want DeMarco dead?

The more I think, the more unanswered questions I have.

"Julian."

Lucian's harsh voice snaps me out of my thoughts. He's looking at me like he would kill me if I weren't his son.

"I need you and Adrian to handle the fallout from DeMarco's death."

"Understood," I reply tersely, a headache forming at the front of my head.

"Adrian, you're dismissed."

Lucian waves a hand at him and Adrian nods, leaving me alone with the sperm donor.

"And you, Julian." His cold stare turns to me. "How are things going with Lady Marlowe? You know how important it is that we maintain a good relationship with her family."

"Everything's fine," I lie.

In truth, I've been doing everything I can to avoid Victoria. Just the sound of her irritating voice is enough to shrink my dick.

"See that it stays that way," he warns. "The Marlowes are too valuable an ally to lose because of your foolishness."

"Of course."

"Good. Now go."

Just as I'm stepping out of his office, Victoria saunters in.

She's the epitome of the classic Inferno Consortium daughter. Her chin juts out defiantly as if challenging the world to knock her down a peg. Her spine is rigidly straight.

Every inch of her screams power. She knows her worth and she doesn't shy from showing it, imposing it, on others.

Emotions? They're nowhere to be found on her face. She's stoic. A smooth, unreadable statue.

She is who Lucian wanted me to be. And I guess this is why I hate her more than I should.

"Julian," she purrs while my patience evaporates, "I was just coming to invite you to my party tonight. It's going to be quite the event." She leaves the nature of the party hanging in the air like a ghostly secret. But I know all too well what her parties look like.

Lucian does too, more than anyone else here. He used to attend them every time, but now he prefers to host them.

The unspoken promise of decadence and debauchery is a familiar tune to my ears.

Her black eyes sparkle as they trail up and down my navy hoodie and jeans. I could be wearing a clown suit and her eyes would still fucking sparkle.

Turning around, I slowly smirk at Lucian. "As tempting as that sounds, I have other plans tonight," I tell her as I stare at him, my voice dropping an octave.

"Are you sure?" She takes a step closer before running her fingers down my arm. "It's going to be a night to remember."

"Positive," I say flatly, brushing her hand off me. I walk past her, leaning close to her ear to whisper, "I'm not Emeric. My dick doesn't just get hard for anything that walks. So cut the shit."

Her eyes widen at my words, the sparkle gone.

Good.

Without waiting for a response, I move to leave my father's office. I'm about to step over the threshold, relieved not to be forced to look at their faces for another second, when her tight voice cuts through the silence.

Loud enough for Lucian to hear.

"What a shame. I guess the golden one—what's her name again? Oh right, *Aurelia*—will be left alone tonight."

I stop dead in my tracks. "I'm not in the mood, Victoria."

"And I'm not one for jokes." She laughs, her gaze jumping to my father's as his attention zeroes in on us. "At least she had the decency to show appreciation for the invite."

Bullshit. Aurelia has never attended any of the Inferno Consortium events—why would she now?

Because she isn't dating Adrian and he isn't keeping her from attending anymore, the voice in the back of my head taunts.

Images of Aurelia among them, vulnerable and exposed, flood my thoughts.

Vulnerable and exposed for you, the voice echoes.

"Fine," I say through gritted teeth. "I'll be there."

"Great!" she exclaims. "The party is at nine at my cabin. You remember the dress code. Be a gentleman and let her know?"

I grunt in response, leaving the room with her nagging voice trailing behind me.

Tonight I'll go to the party. Tonight I'll find out whatever secret Aurelia is hiding. Tonight I'll play with her. Tonight . . .

She'll be mine.

The sun is setting on the horizon, bathing Seattle in glowing hues of orange.

I'm standing outside Aurelia's apartment. The walls of the corridor, lined with floor-to-ceiling windows, showcase the breathtaking contrast between the city skyline and the fiery background as they capture the essence of the sunset hour.

My shadow stretches long and thin on the marble beneath me as I pick at the lock of her apartment door. The smell of freshly brewed coffee wafts from beneath the door, mingling with the subtle hint of fresh laundry. Or maybe . . . vanilla?

I know she's the one who killed DeMarco. I don't have concrete proof yet, but I know she did it.

I haven't been able to shake the thought all day.

That's why I'm picking at the lock and slipping inside.

I need to find proof.

Without making any noise, I make my way through the short corridor to the living room before heading upstairs to her bedroom.

I know every inch of this apartment, every turn and every wall an echo of my past, a maze I could walk through with my eyes closed after the countless nights I snuck through these corridors in pitch-darkness.

Valentine knew about my break-ins. He never said or did anything about them. After all, it was his teaching that turned me into a lock-picking expert.

I still remember that sun-drenched afternoon he spent with me outside his apartment, where he told me, "The world doesn't leave any door open for you. You've got to break yourself in."

New pictures decorate the white walls now. Memories I wasn't a part of. But there are also whispered stories of our unforgotten shared past.

A chill creeps over my body as I let the familiar surroundings wash over me.

Each corner holds a memory that tugs something deep within.

How long has it been since I last set foot in here?

Pushing open her bedroom door, I step inside. My legs go weak as everything that's changed crashes down on me.

Her honey perfume still clings to the air. At least that much hasn't changed. Its sweet scent sends a shiver down my spine. It reminds me of the summer nights she would lay her head on my chest and I would play with her curls, our laughter ringing wild as we counted the stars.

Shaking off the haunting memories, I give the room a quick scan.

Everything has changed.

Her room is no longer a space containing the best memories of my life. Her room is now a stark reminder that she's no longer mine. That we're once again strangers.

This isn't the same room I visit in my dreams. This isn't the same room I was in last time, years ago.

There are no pink stripes on the walls. Instead they're a cold shade of teal, covered with artwork I've never seen before.

I feel like an outsider, a stranger heading to meet the woman Aurelia grew up to be.

I feel like she slammed a door on our past.

Shaking off the burning need to get to know this new version of her, I search every inch of the room for what I came here to find.

I look under her bed. Behind the stack of papers hiding the books displayed on the white wooden bookshelf. My fingers graze the small bottles on the vanity table and the softness of her honey-scented bedspread.

But all I find is her.

She is everywhere. In every little figurine adorning her desk. In every paintbrush lying on the floor. In every colorful notebook with strings of material and paperclips peeking out of it.

I'm picking up the notebooks, skimming through them, when a leather-bound book hidden beneath a pile catches my attention.

This one looks worn out, less vibrant than the others.

I know whatever I'm searching for is written in these pages.

I flip it open, and torn pages stare back at me. I'm about to flip to the next one when her voice drifts toward me.

"My lingerie drawer is over there, creep."

A smirk curves my lips, and I turn around to look at her.

There she stands, leaning against the doorframe, her arms crossed defensively over her chest. The gesture pushes her cleavage further up, calling for my attention.

Tempting. But all of her is. Always has been.

Every inch of her calls for my gaze to linger over it.

Her curves are wrapped in a pair of emerald sweatpants. The color makes her green eyes pop, flecks of burned honey catching the light. A black tank top hugs her stomach, accentuating each dip of her body. A faint strip of her lower belly is bare.

Her inviting lips, the color of ripe summer peaches, curl into an insufferable smirk that sends a jolt straight to my dick. She's clearly amused by my intrusion. Or she hopes to give that impression. Hopes I won't notice the way her eyes keep calling to the diary still in my hand.

"Now, why would I go through all this trouble for some lingerie?" I ask, taking a step toward her.

Her hair's in a messy bun on top of her head. My heart thuds heavily in my chest as I take in the sight of her this close up.

From the smattering of freckles dusting her nose to the soft flush on her neck down to her chest, she's painfully beautiful. The only kind of agony I'd endure for life.

"No," I continue slowly. My eyes travel leisurely down the expanse of her body, catching the invisible shiver I leave behind. "I want something . . . more."

Something worth my time. Something worth the time I lost.

"Say it, Julian."

"Why did you kill Vincent DeMarco?"

When I heard of DeMarco's death, the only proof I needed was in the flustered way she was acting that night, DeMarco's mysterious disappearance, and the bloodstain on her skin. Something inside of me screamed she did it. Or maybe it was only my hope that she was as tainted as me.

"Really?" She scoffs, walking toward me. "Do you really see me as a murderer, Julian?"

"I see you as someone who's hiding something," I retort, holding the diary up between us. "What's in here that's so important? Are you afraid I'll find out the truth?"

She doesn't waste time and snatches the diary from my grasp. I let her, amused at the lines that form in the middle of her brow as she tightens it against her chest. Her nose wrinkles ever so slightly.

"Sometimes people like to have an ounce of privacy. I have a diary, just like half of the population." Her green eyes blaze with anger. "I didn't kill DeMarco. And I didn't write it in my diary. I may be secretive, but I'm not stupid."

"Then what are you hiding?" I close the last remaining space between us and lower my gaze to her.

Too fucking little to be this lethal.

"None of your damn business," she hisses, taking a step back.

She's smart. She's not running away.

"Everything is my business when it comes to you,

Aurelia," I growl, my headache mounting. "Especially when it involves you attending tonight's party."

"Ah, so that's what this is really about." She lets out a hollow laugh. "Afraid I'll have too much fun without you?"

"Oh, you don't have to worry about that. If it's not with me, I'll still be there to watch."

She has no clue what she's getting herself into. The question is, why?

"What were you doing in that hotel room?" I ask.

She raises a brow. Her gaze falls behind my shoulder. "Who says I was even there?" she continues, her eyes narrowing to slits like the cuts of a gemstone. "You're grasping at straws here, Julian. Just admit you don't have any proof and move on."

"If you won't tell me, then give me the diary."

"Absolutely not." She clutches the book even tighter to her chest.

It's cute, the way she thinks I won't be able to take it from her with little to no force. But she knows me. She knows I don't use force to get what I want. I prefer to use . . . different means.

"Do you know what you've caused?" I ask, taking a step closer to her. "The Inferno Consortium wants retaliation. They won't grant you the same mercy you gave DeMarco. They will rip your soul. You'll wish you were dead."

"Your precious Consortium, huh?" She scoffs, her lips pulling downward as she tilts her chin up, her gaze frozen on mine. "You really think I give a damn about that cesspool of corruption and crime? If you're so worried about me attending Victoria's party, maybe you should be more concerned with what kind of people you associate with."

"Cut the shit, golden one. You can't seriously be shocked that I'm involved in my family's business."

"Don't call me that."

"No?" I move an inch closer.

Her neck strains to maintain eye contact.

"What should I call you then? The orphan? The motherless bitch? Or I could call you what some of my father's guards call you. Wasted rat's cum."

The depths of her eyes blaze with untamed fury. Her body tenses to support the onslaught of emotion. Then, in a swift movement, her hand connects with my cheek in a piercing slap.

It's strong enough to turn my face to the side and reach whatever softness I have left in me, cracking it.

"I may be the daughter of a whore," she breathes, low and thunderous, "but at least I'm no son of a merciless killer who would watch you *die* before his empire." Her voice is low but harsh enough to cut. "I may be mother-less, but so are you, by your mother's choice." She stands on her toes, close enough for me to taste her words. "I may be wasted rat's cum, but I live among you." She smiles. "Now tell me, how fucking beneath you am I really?"

"Not even close enough for what I want."

Her lips part, eyebrows mirroring mine as they meet in the middle.

Why does she want to attend tonight's party? It doesn't add up. It reeks of danger. Makes anger simmer inside of me. If I can't convince her to stay away from Victoria's party, then I need to steel myself for whatever chaos awaits us.

I need to be there too. Not because of Victoria, but for Aurelia. I need to shadow her steps. Shield her from unseen threats.

And maybe, while I'm at it . . . dig deeper into the secrets she's keeping from me. Learn the reason why she did what she did.

"I'll pick you up at eight." I force myself to take a step back.

Striding over to her dresser, I yank open the top drawer. I'm already dreading what Victoria has in store for everyone. If Aurelia is so determined to attend, then she'll do it in the correct way. But fuck, the last thing I want is to watch her get eye-fucked.

Rummaging through Aurelia's delicate garments, I pick the first set of lingerie that fits the dress code but won't reveal too much to the old scumbags.

"Here." I toss the black lace teddy at her. "Wear this. You want to go to Victoria's party? This is the kind of shit she expects her guests to wear."

Aurelia catches the lingerie, and when she looks down at it, her cheeks turn a light shade of red. "You're unbelievable, Julian," she hisses. "I can't believe you think I'd actually wear something like this just because Victoria fucking Marlowe says so."

"Welcome to our world." My voice drips with sarcasm. "You wanted to go to the party? *That's* the price of admission. If you don't like it, stay home."

"Nice try. But I'm going with or without you." She glares up at me, her eyes blazing with defiance.

"Please, don't let me stop you." I fix her with a hard stare, hoping to convey just how serious I am.

There's no doubt in my mind that she's hiding something from me. Something that has to do with DeMarco's death. From the moment she walked into that ballroom to the moment she rushed away from Adrian, I never took my eyes off her.

There's no other explanation for that goddamn bloodstain.

I know she killed him.

What I want to know is, why? Why did she kill DeMarco? What is their connection? What other secrets is she keeping from me? And how far will she go to protect those secrets?

If she's really behind DeMarco's death, I need to find out why she killed him before Adrian or the Inferno Consortium catch wind, otherwise there won't be anything left of her.

Whatever pushed her to kill DeMarco had better be worth it. Because she's five steps to hell. The devil's right behind her.

And like fuck will I let her go through this alone.

"I hate you, Julian Harrow."

"That's too much of a compliment even for you, golden one."

CHAPTER SEVEN
AURELIA

*W*here the hell is he?

I pace the perimeter of the living room, glancing at the clock for what feels like the hundredth time. The hands seem to mock me, ticking away. Each second is another testimony of how truly distant we've become.

He lied to me.

An hour. Sixty agonizing minutes have passed since 8 p.m., the time Julian was supposed to pick me up for Victoria's party. Impatience bubbles inside of me. The silence of his absence echoes in my ears.

Where is he!

I adjust the belt of my brown trench coat, pulling it tighter around me as if it will somehow distract me from the ever-growing anticipation. When I look at myself in the mirror, frustration stares back. It's etched in every line of my face. I fiddle with an invisible strand of hair peeking from the high ponytail, pursing my red lips together in a futile attempt at smoothing out any smudged lines.

But nothing I do will make the detrimental realization that he isn't coming disappear.

"Damn him," I mutter under my breath.

Exasperated, I plop down onto the couch. I feel defeated. This is not how tonight was supposed to go.

His absence feels like a slap in the face, a wake-up call that I shouldn't trust the boy who pushed me into this abyss of solitude in the first place.

It stings, this form of betrayal. But beneath it, there's an unexpected sense of . . . relief. Because with Julian out of the picture, tonight has become an easier opportunity for me.

Well-fucking-played, asshole. You just turned tonight into a very enticing, unmissable event.

Standing, I pick up my phone, its screen lighting up as I scroll through the list of names. My thumb pauses briefly over Valentine. He probably knows where Victoria's cabin is located. But calling him will mean having him tag along, and the thought of having his gruff voice dictate how I should go through with the plan is not something I'm in the mood for.

I should have gotten my driver's license with Eleanora the moment I turned sixteen.

But of course, I didn't see any use for it until now. Why drive if you have people to drive you all the time? Adrian always drove me places.

My gaze falls to the "VV" contact.

After I broke up with him, Eleanora begged me to change Adrian's name to "VV"—short for "vapid vampire." That's what she's been calling him since the very first day we started dating. She says he's dull and draining, and after my second martini I didn't have the strength to snatch my phone out of her grasp as she typed out his new contact name.

I don't know why I haven't changed it yet. Anyway, vampires are cute.

A sense of familiarity washes over me as I stare down at his number. He was there for me when Julian wasn't. If anyone knows where Victoria's cabin is, it'll be him.

Taking a deep breath, I dial his number and wait.

If Julian doesn't want to give me a ride, I'll just have to find another way to get to the party.

He picks up within seconds.

"Aurelia?"

"Adrian, do you know where Victoria's cabin is?"

There's a pause before he asks, "Why?"

He doesn't sound surprised, yet there is something off about the way he drags the word out. Maybe he's just irritated at me for disturbing his Wednesday night at the office.

"I need your help." I choose my words carefully. I know how to get to him—how to get him to help me. "Julian was supposed to pick me up for the party, but he never showed up. Would you mind giving me a ride?"

Adrian goes silent again. "I'm not sure that's a good idea, Aurelia."

He was always cautious about taking me to these kinds of events when we were dating, so I don't blame him for not agreeing right away.

"Come on, Adrian." I taste his name on my lips, dragging out the words. The same way I'd tease him in bed. "I've been looking forward to this party for weeks," I lie. Like I always did in bed. "It will really piss Julian off if *you* take me instead."

He sighs heavily, clearly not thrilled at the prospect of going to a party instead of making his father proud.

Silence engulfs us once more, and I'm cautious of his train of thought as he mulls over my offer.

"All right, fine."

I know I shouldn't be wondering why he accepted and just be glad he did, yet I can't help but question it.

"For old times' sake," he adds. "But you'd better be ready to go when I get there."

"Trust me, I am more than ready."

A few minutes later, there's a sharp knock at my door.

Adrian's broad figure fills the doorframe. He's dressed in a crisp black suit that clings to his lean form, accentuating his muscles. The seriousness in his expression showcases how much he already regrets this.

His wavy hair is combed back meticulously—though he probably threaded his fingers through it several times beforehand. He always does that whenever he's lost in thought.

Shadows fall on his face from the city lights coming through the window behind him, intensifying his dark ocean eyes. Regret shines behind them. It's as if he's already mourning the decision to accompany me.

But why?

"We should go, or we'll be late," I say, walking past him to make my way to the underground parking lot where all the Harrows' cars are parked. They have their own parking floor, while us *commoners* have to park one floor lower, if we're lucky.

We make the journey in silence. The longer we drive, the more trees surround us. The scent of pine settles my nerves, filtering in on the chilled August night air streaming through his open window.

I can't wait to see Julian's face when he sees me arriving with Adrian.

Settling comfortably on the leather seat of Adrian's Cullinan, I glance out the window. The destination—a cabin close to the Teanaway Community Forest—simply screams "undisturbed private party." It'll take us about an hour or so to get there, so I might as well relax before the long night ahead.

When we finally pull up to the cabin, I can't help but freeze in awe.

Towering trees cocoon the cabin, hiding it from peering eyes as they cast eerie shadows over the log-built cabin. Some of the moonlight breaks through the branches, bathing it in a graceful glow. It reflects off the large glass windows that seem to be tinted black, obscuring any outsider's view of whatever is happening inside.

A haunted beauty in the middle of nowhere.

"This place is incredible," I breathe.

Bloodcurdlingly beautiful.

Adrian parks the Cullinan on a gravel driveway next

to a sleek sports car. A few other vehicles are parked haphazardly around the driveway, as if the guests couldn't wait any longer to get to the party.

We step out of the car, and Adrian leads me down the stone-paved pathway lined with flowers the color of night.

"Wait until you see the inside," he says, still not so thrilled about being coerced into coming here.

"Thanks again for bringing me, Adrian." I give him a sincere smile in the hope of warming him up a little.

"Let's just get inside." Without looking at me, he leads the way to the front door.

The faint thud coming from the music extends to our ears as we approach the door. But it's not until we step inside that the complete contrast from the serene exterior strikes me.

Chatter booms, along with the low bass. The cabin is buzzing with people, the music thumping loudly and echoing off the walls.

The atmosphere is intoxicating and charged with a hint of . . . sweat.

The dim red lights cast an almost sinful glow over the guests scattered throughout the space.

Turning to look at Adrian, I catch him unbuttoning his white shirt.

"What are you doing?" My hands extend on their own to stop him.

"Look around, Aurelia." He tilts his chin at the other guests, and I follow his line of sight, only now noticing how everyone is dressed—or rather, undressed.

Nearly every guest is almost bare.

The guys are wearing nothing but black pants, while the girls are clad in black lingerie, some topless with only nipple covers adorning their chests.

And they're all wearing masks, making it impossible to identify them.

The outfit Julian picked out for me is starting to make a lot more sense.

Slowly I shrug off the trench coat, revealing the lingerie set I'm wearing. A more revealing choice than the modest black lace teddy Julian picked out for me.

If he wanted me to be discreet and obedient, he should have showed up.

Adrian's eyes linger on my body, taking in the intricate lace design of petals covering my nipples, down to the intersecting thin strips of satin that form two X's: a big one at the navel, and a smaller one closer to my midriff.

But my favorite part is the sheer gauze—the same color as my skin—that leaves little to the imagination.

"Come on." He finally breaks the silence, eyes back on the guests. "Let's get this night over with."

I feel exposed yet oddly confident.

Eleanora won't believe me when I tell her about tonight. Especially the part about me going to this kind of party with Adrian.

Swaying my hips with every step I take, I follow him further into the party.

I scan the faces of the masked guests, searching for any hint of familiarity—or even just someone willing to help me blend in by lending me a mask.

Why didn't Julian tell me about this part of the dress

code? I would have brought one. Especially since I have to go unnoticed while I search around the place.

Although, the deeper I navigate through the sea of naked bodies, the more I notice how everyone is too busy grinding on one another to notice me.

This strange sense of exhilaration mixes with my uneasiness.

This party is a far cry from the usual high-society events I've attended in the past. Despite my determination to see my plan through, I can't help but feel the intoxicating air affecting my senses.

No.

Stick to the plan.

I need to find a mask, then I need to find a way to leave Adrian behind for a little while. Just enough time for me to look around.

With my thoughts cleared, I follow Adrian as he parts the crowd, sneaking a peek here and there at the people around me.

"Look who decided to join us," a voice purrs from behind us.

Victoria.

Turning around, I watch her approach. Her eyes rake over me with a mixture of surprise and something else.

"I must say, golden one, you're full of surprises."

"And you certainly know how to throw a party."

"Of course." Her gaze flicks between Adrian and me. "I must admit, I expected to see you with Julian, not his brother. Has the other brother bored you already?"

Adrian stiffens beside me at her words, but he remains silent, taking us in. This is the first time he's seen us talking, but from our easy exchange, he can probably deduce this isn't our first conversation.

Now he knows Julian didn't invite me to the party, but Victoria did. Personally.

"Adrian was kind enough to give me a ride," I counter coolly.

"Adrian." Victoria's plump lips stretch as she greets him.

"Victoria."

Tension travels between us as their gazes remain locked on one another. I'm about to ask how long they've known each other, so I can learn more about their family ties, when Victoria breaks their silent duel.

"Well, I'm glad you made it regardless." She looks back to me. Her eyes narrow as she takes in my appearance. "Although it seems you've come unprepared. You're not wearing a mask."

"Julian didn't mention it."

"Typical!" Victoria sighs dramatically before disappearing into another room. A moment later she returns with a golden mask and hands it to me. "Here, put this on. We wouldn't want you to stand out too much."

"Thanks." I slip the mask over my face, while Adrian slips one out from his pocket, putting it on.

We wouldn't want you to stand out too much—and yet she gave me a mask the color of my nickname.

I try to let the choice of mask wash over me.

We aren't friends. I'm planning to bring her empire to the ground, to kill her, so Victoria picking a gold mask for me is nothing but childish spite in comparison.

"Go on then," she says dismissively, gesturing

around the room once our identity is hidden behind the masks. "Mingle, explore, do whatever it is you came here to do. I've got other guests to attend to."

I watch her sashay away. Taking in a deep breath, I try to clear my mind.

I can't afford to get too caught up in this event. It's my alibi; I'm not here to sample the lascivious side of the Inferno Consortium.

Squaring my shoulders, I begin to weave my way through the crowd with one goal in mind: to gather as much information as needed, no matter what challenges lie ahead.

But first I need to get Adrian off my back.

We make our way further into the cabin. Red lights cast shadows of desire on the bodies of people as an alluring blend of scents fills the air. It's a mixture of expensive perfume, sweat, and desire.

The first room we enter is filled with people writhing together on red cushioned mats, the loud beat of the music muffling their moans as they taste each other. Yet I can still make out their desires. The way their mouths form an "O," or the marks on their skin from violently needing more.

My heart beats fast as I take them in. Until a solitary figure catches my attention.

A man wearing a badger mask stands there observing, but I can't tell if it's me he's looking at or the bodies of the people between us. His stillness in such a charged room feels like chaos in contrast. My attention falls solely on him as unsettling shivers snake their way down my spine.

But it doesn't last long—not with Adrian's impatience evident in the way he grabs my arm and steers me forward.

The next room contains an arrangement of BDSM equipment, everything from whips and chains to intricate leather harnesses. A woman wearing nothing but thigh-high stockings is bound to a St. Andrew's cross. A man in black pants and a green mask prowls around her, flogging her each time her panting starts to lessen.

Her face contorts in pure bliss.

"How's our little saint feeling right now?" Adrian mocks, observing my reaction to the view in front of us. "Horrified enough? Want me to take you home?" There's a hint of mockery in his tone.

My eyes zero in on the girl.

Each time the leather hits her skin, her mouth pulls in, choking on the pleasurable sensation of needing the pain to feel alive. Each whip is followed by a cry for more.

And more.

Her neck stretches skyward, eyes squeezed shut.

"Aurelia?"

I can't seem to look elsewhere.

A barely noticeable breeze caresses my bare skin. My nipples harden into tight peaks as I feel her pleasure as my own.

One last whip and—

"Are you even listening to me?"

The sound of Adrian's voice filters in, but it's his massive body blocking the girl that shatters whatever trance I was in.

"What?"

He shakes his head and goes to the next room. Without a second thought I follow him, my eyes trailing behind me at the girl being held by the flogger as he takes her someplace faraway.

My teeth sink into my lower lip as I try to shake the feeling sizzling through my body, burying the jealous sting of wanting to be her.

I follow Adrian into the next room and gasp.

A large circular bed is situated in the center of the room. Mirrors surround it on every wall, allowing the participants' reflections to be watched from various angles.

"Exhibitionists," Adrian says. "They get turned on by the knowledge they're being watched. Something you hate, if I recall correctly. Since the craziest thing we ever did was reach first base in my car."

And yet I've never felt anything like this before. Watching their raw display is awakening something within me, as if a hidden door to my desire has been thrown open.

Adrian's right: I've never gone this far before. I've had sex before, but in the comfort of our bedrooms. Sex in public areas was off-limits. And in front of people? Wouldn't even dare to consider it. But as I stand here, only allowed to watch, hunger consumes me. The reason I came is slowly being obscured by this need for *more*.

More touching.

More tasting.

More feeling.

I rush outside the room, hot to the touch as I brace my hands on my hips, the feeling of bare skin a reminder of how deep in this world I truly am right now. Physically, but emotionally too.

This party is overwhelming, stripping me bare layer by layer, each room a mirror of my hidden desires.

Adrian steps up next to me, his eyes taking in my flushed state.

"Have you been to many of her parties before?" I dare to ask him. But I'm not daring enough to look at him as he answers.

"More than I can count."

My next words scratch at the back of my parched throat. "And when we were dating?"

I already know the answer. We started dating when I was fifteen and he was nineteen. He may have attended Victoria's parties before then, but there's no doubt he came here all throughout his twenties too.

When he doesn't answer I raise my gaze to his.

"Yes."

I nod up at him. "Right." I try to shake off the repulsion forming in the pit of my stomach. "We should find something to drink. Watching all that has made me thirsty."

We move down the corridor, bypassing other rooms, each one hosting a variety of sexual activities. Bondage, role-playing, orgies—all catering to different fantasies.

I can feel Adrian close by, his words taunting our breakup and what little love he felt throughout our relationship. God, how pathetic am I to feel dirty at his expense?

The low buzz of the bass filters in as we part ways in

the room. "I'll go get us something to drink," he says and leaves.

Deciding enough time has passed, I focus on what truly matters.

I need to be quick before he comes back with our drinks.

This new room looks lifeless compared to the others. It's still packed with people, but where the other rooms provided the guests with something to use, this one sets them free with only their bodies. This feels a lot like the parties I attended with Eleanora: just drunk people doing what they do best.

I'm making my way deeper in when I feel a pair of eyes on me.

Searching for the source of my unease, I spot a guy watching me intently from across the room. His gaze is unwavering, almost predatory, and it sends a shiver down my spine.

Yet I can't help but stare back.

His dark hair falls messily over the silver mask he's wearing. Ink adorns his whole chest, stretching to his arms. I can't see his face, but the weight of his stare is impossible to ignore.

For a moment I consider approaching him, but I've wasted enough time already. Adrian will be back soon.

I try to ignore the nagging feeling of being watched and instead focus on talking with the guests until the right opportunity appears for me to sneak away and snoop around Victoria's cabin, starting with her bedroom. I'd go now, but Adrian will be back soon. I need to do it at the right moment, and this isn't it.

I attempt to engage in small talk, but my senses are overwhelmed by the shared lust tainting the atmosphere, making it hard for me to concentrate.

And I can't shake the sense that the man's piercing gaze means trouble.

Or how his eyes are still boring into me.

I scan the room, trying to find someplace where I won't feel the weight of his intense gaze.

But without wanting to, my eyes fall on him again.

This time I notice the two skeletal snakes intertwining in the middle of his chest—and the hands of two barely dressed girls, both vying for his attention.

Yet he seems completely disinterested in their advances.

His focus is solely on me.

Who are you? And what do you want from me?

He's intriguing yet annoying all at once. Can't he just . . . I don't know, have fun with those two deprived girls and leave me the hell alone?

He's lounging on a plush couch, the two girls draped over him. Their hands roam his defined body as they whisper in his ear, giggling at whatever he tells them.

The overwhelming need to trace those intricate patterns with my fingertips devours me whole as we stare at one another. He's wearing a silver mask, but his smoldering eyes are exposed enough for me to see.

Movement to his right catches my attention, and I see another guy sitting on a chair next to him, legs spread open, drink dangling from his hand. He's dressed similarly, but with no tattoos etched onto his brown skin. His purple mask conceals his identity as well.

But there's something about his posture and the way he observes the scene around him that reeks of familiarity.

I try to shake the feeling of unease his attention is giving me, but no matter which corner of the room I occupy, the tattooed man's piercing stare is still there.

It's unnerving.

Several minutes go by with me feeling like hunted prey, and irritation finally gets the better of me. I square my shoulders and cross the crowded room, clenching my hands so hard that half-moons become engraved on the skin.

I stop before the couch where he's reclining, two girls under his arms.

"Can I help you?" The words slip from between my gritted teeth, my voice dripping with annoyance.

He doesn't answer immediately. Instead he takes his time, roaming his gaze up and down my body before finally meeting my eye again. The action alights something inside of me. It's like a signal, as if I'm used to this person's attention. No—*as if I crave it.*

The two black holes where his eyes are hold me captive, but something around his wrist makes my heart skip a beat. Not just anything. A unique black hair tie, with a black bead in the shape of a raven.

Sadness floods my senses, mingling with bitter anger.

"Julian?" My voice is barely above a whisper as I stare into the eyes of the man who once meant everything to me.

"Ah, so you recognize me," he drawls, an amused smirk playing at the corners of his lips.

Without thinking, I grab the drink from the other guy's hand and throw it straight at Julian's face. The liquid splashes across his skin, dampening his dark hair and causing the two girls to shriek in surprise.

And Julian simply chuckles.

CHAPTER EIGHT

AURELIA

"Well, that was refreshing," Julian coos, fixing his sticky hair.

"That was for never showing up." I glare at his amused face. "Now, stop. Staring. At. Me," I say through gritted teeth.

In the blink of an eye he stands from the couch, his body crushing mine. "I don't think so," he growls in my ear. "You were made to be watched by me."

Taking a small step backward, he glances intently at the curves of my body before his eyes settle back on my face.

Heat rises in my cheeks, and I curse myself for blushing so easily around him.

"Aurelia," he says in a measured manner. "Why aren't you wearing what I told you to?" A hint of disapproval laces his words.

"You like it? It's *Bordelle*."

His eyes flick back and forth between mine. "You didn't follow my orders."

"And you didn't pick me up."

His lips twitch. "That's a bit immature, don't you think?"

My mouth parts, so close—*so damn close*—to smiling.

"I had some unexpected business to attend to," he adds.

"I can see that." My gaze falls to the two girls sprawled on the couch behind him. "Luckily, your brother was kind enough to help when you couldn't."

On cue, Adrian approaches us with drinks in hand. "Is everything okay over here?"

"Everything's fine, Brother," Julian replies. "Aurelia was just telling me how she's going to meet up with me once she's done sucking your dick."

His gaze sends a challenging thrill down my body.

"Now that I think about it, there's a lot Adrian and I need to catch up on. It might take all night," I drawl as I brush my finger over the rim of the black-tinted cup.

"Right, right." Julian feigns a pause. "It always did take you hours to finish."

The purple masked guy sitting next to Julian bursts out laughing.

"What the fuck?" Adrian's eyes narrow as he looks at his brother. He grabs for my arm to steer me away, and I let him.

But before he does, I add, "I think Adrian can make me come much faster than you ever did."

Julian arches his brow at me as if to ask, "Is that a challenge?"

Maybe it is. I smirk at him.

Mischief glints in his eyes. "Show me just how much

fun you can have, golden one. I dare you," I hear him say as Adrian seats me on a vacant couch not too far from Julian's. The contents of the cup spill onto it slightly.

I cross my legs and take a big sip of the drink.

From where I'm sitting I have a perfect view of him. And so does he of me.

One of the girls caresses the length of his chest, while the other speaks sweet nothings into his ear as he sits. Her hand heads an inch closer to his dick, yet his blue eyes are on mine. Daring.

"I swear I should just let our father beat the shit out of him."

"Huh?" I turn to look at Adrian.

"That will teach him to stop running his mouth." He shakes his head, taking a sip from his cup.

I'm about to ask him what he means by that when the blonde in front of me, tucked into Julian's side, moans. One of his hands tangles in her curls while he devours her. Anger prickles over me as she grinds on his leg.

Having had enough, I whisper, "Adrian?" and lean in close.

My mind races as I consider what having Julian wrapped around my finger would feel like. If he sees me with Adrian, will it ignite something within him? Will he see me as more than just an object?

I should feel disgust. I should laugh at how desperate the girl looks. And yet all I feel is an eagerness to prove him wrong.

Adrian hums before I curl my hands around his neck, pulling him toward me. His hand instantly wraps around my waist, squeezing hard, before pushing me further away from his heated body.

His eyes flicker back and forth between mine. Contemplating. Assessing the situation.

I lick my bottom lip, letting the movement drag out as I watch his stare darken, his thoughts flooding with my lips—with my taste.

We've broken up. He's not mine anymore, and I'm not his . . . So how far can two exes go before crossing the line?

"Do you think we could . . .?"

"I don't know," he murmurs as I move my hand through his short hair. "I'm not really thinking right now."

With that, he crashes his lips to mine. Tilting his neck, he deepens the kiss.

When I'm begging for air, he presses soft kisses along my neck before going back up to my lips. His fingers ghost over my inner thigh, and I spread my legs for him.

Each touch sends shivers down my spine, but not because of him. Instead it's the intensity of Julian's gaze that sets my heart racing. The thought of him watching, seething with jealousy, makes every caress from Adrian feel electric.

Across the room we watch each other. Taste each other through other people.

The hands of the other girl with short brown hair glide over Julian's chest and arms, her lips grazing his tattooed skin. And I crave to taste him. Taste his depravity.

He grabs the blonde, letting her straddle his legs,

which are covered in black sweatpants. My breath hitches as his large hands grip the bare skin of her ass.

Meanwhile Adrian pushes me against the back of the couch, getting between my legs as his hand hooks around the strings of my lacy underwear.

My nipples harden, poking through the material, as his other hand plays with them, pinching then soothing. My body arcs at his touch, head lolling backward as he licks the skin between my neck and my shoulder.

I bite my lips, half-lidded eyes taking in Julian as he kisses the neck of the blonde, brushing her hair to the side and pulling her body to his while she grinds on top of him.

As she feels the effect I'm having on him.

His hair is all over the place from her fingers running through it. Black strands fall down his face, and even with the mask hiding him, I can still feel his carnal look at seeing Adrian's hands dip inside my underwear.

He slaps her right ass cheek, and my body aches for her. A wave of pleasure rocks through me. He slaps her left ass cheek, and Adrian's finger flicks over my clit, making me cry out, eyes slipping shut.

Adrian growls, biting down on my neck. I try to resist the need to fall into complete submission at the pleasure. To let Julian have power over my body without even touching me with one finger. But I'm so dangerously close to losing control, to giving in to the lust threatening to consume me.

How fucked-up am I, to be fantasizing about my ex-boyfriend's brother's touch while getting fingered by said ex-boyfriend?

I suck in a sharp gasp. *Too fucked-up. A lost cause.* A moan threatens to escape as I feel the intrusion of Adrian's finger.

My body tenses. I'm so close. So deliciously close—

A pair of hands pulls me away.

"What the fuck!" Adrian yells as I'm yanked from his grasp.

"Shh," a familiar voice whispers in my ear, his breath hot against my skin. "If you come, it'll be on my fingers, not my brother's."

Frustration mixes with the arousal still building in me.

Julian doesn't give me a chance to protest as his hand clamps around my throat. His fingers press into the soft skin with a force that will leave me bruised tomorrow. My pulse shoots up, and I know he can feel the beat as it caresses his fingers. I know he loves it.

I shoot him a glare, looking up at his towering frame. From this close I can see his piercing eyes behind the mask, flickering back and forth.

A sigh leaves his lips, and in one swift motion he releases my throat, only to sling me over his shoulder and guide us through the throngs of people.

The position, coupled with the dim red lights, confuses my senses as I try to grasp a sense of direction. *Where are we going? Where is he taking me?*

I'm seeing everything upside down when I catch the eye of a familiar face in the crowd. Victoria stands at a distance, her view of me unobscured. She keeps her eyes glued to me, her head tilted slightly as her lips curl into an uneasy smirk, the tips of her fingers brushing over them.

In an instant Julian turns around a corner and she disappears from view.

A thud hits my ears before he puts me down, my back connecting with the wall of a softly lit room.

At least now I can think of something else other than her disturbing stare.

"Julian . . ."

His finger strokes my lips, silencing me. "Quiet."

I'm still trying to adjust my eyes to the darkness when his body cages me in. He grazes his teeth over the bare skin of my neck, making me see only him.

"Should we tell my brother this was all for me?" He drags his finger over my drenched underwear.

Embarrassment washes over me as I struggle to keep my body from betraying me. I try to push him away, but my hands scratch at his skin instead, and I sigh for more.

And more.

His lips leave a feverous trail as they descend toward the swell of my breasts.

"He should see how fast you come for me." He cups my left breast, teeth piercing the flesh, before he tears the material off.

I cry out, but my protests die in my throat.

I don't have the time to feel the cool air, because his teeth sink into my nipple. Sucking, his tongue soothes the pain away, leaving me wanting more.

I can't—

I need to—

I can't let him—

I can't make this easy for him. He just decided one day that I was worth his time, and now he's between my legs without even putting in any work?

Threading my fingers through the back of his hair, I pull his mouth away from my breast. Searching his eyes, I pant, "In your fucking dreams."

His lips spread. A devilish smirk greets me. "You already are."

I'm lifted from the floor before I can get a word out, and I squeal as he throws us onto the bed, his body pressing me down. The hard length of him digs into my stomach as I contain myself from grinding my body, succumbing to the desire he's ignited in me.

His fingers trace their way down my waist, teasing the sensitive skin beneath my waistband.

A shiver covers my body, and before he hooks his finger to shed my underwear—my remaining dignity—I push him away, using my legs to throw him onto the bed.

Pressing him under me.

He growls deep in his throat as I make a scene of settling on his hard dick. Grabbing his wrists away from the dip of my hips, I pin them above his head.

We both fucking know it would take him less than a second to throw me under him, toss my underwear to the side, and thrust in.

And he would make it *hurt*.

Addictively so.

"You like me at your mercy, golden one?" He grins at me, eyes flicking between mine and my exposed breasts.

"I'd like it if you called me by my name," I say, scanning the room for something to tie him up with.

"You didn't that night," he breathes, just as I spot a pair of handcuffs on the shelf atop the headrest.

The shelf is filled with an assortment of sex toys and other pleasure devices—some familiar, others foreign and vaguely intimidating.

I lean in, delicately skimming my lips over his, but not enough to fall for the taste of them. I can't afford to let Julian consume me.

Holding his wrists with just one hand, my fingers inch above us, catching the handcuffs without making a sound. The feathery touch is a consolation for what I'm about to do.

"Remember," I murmur, unlatching the cuffs. "You asked for this."

He hesitates for a moment, his gaze narrowing. Only when the metallic click of the handcuffs echoes in the silent room does he understand.

"Aurelia . . ."

"Sorry, Julian." I watch as he struggles against his restraints. "But I have a party to attend."

"Unlock these cuffs right now, Aurelia!" he snarls, tugging at the handcuffs attached to the bedpost, but I ignore his orders.

Instead I take the red velvet blindfold from the shelf and tie it over my breasts as a makeshift bra since Julian tore mine to scraps.

Opening the door, I stop midway. Taking a deep breath, I close my eyes and remind myself of the reason I came to this damn party. Tonight isn't about pleasure. Tonight is about finding out secrets.

"You'll regret this when I find you." His low voice sends shivers down my spine.

"Promise?" I smile back at him.

With one final look at him bound to the bed, I shut the door behind me. My heart races with adrenaline and the remnant effects of being edged.

Without giving myself time to register what just happened or how things escalated so quickly, I weave through the sea of writhing bodies.

It's time to focus on my mission.

I need to find something—anything—against the Marlowe family.

As thrilling as it was to have Julian at my mercy, I can't allow myself to be distracted any longer.

The party is still raging on, the sexual energy in the air thick and suffocating as I head to the west wing of the cabin, hoping for some luck in finding Victoria's office or her bedroom.

The more I walk, the fewer people are around. The urge to push forward is stronger with the last person I pass. The music is still loud enough to reach this side of the cabin, but it's only faint in here.

I spot a dark green double door at the far end of the corridor. It's either another private room like the one I left Julian in, or maybe, just maybe, it's what I was searching for.

I quicken my steps. The click of my heels echoes through the corridor, but the sound of a door closing stops me.

"Hey," a voice calls out.

Flinching at the intrusion, I turn to see a man dressed in all-black, his face obscured by a mask in the shape of a badger. The same man from the red room. I guess he *was* staring at me then.

"You're Aurelia, right?"

"Who's asking?" I hesitate.

He's wearing a shirt. Is this his first time here too? No. It can't be—he's wearing a mask.

"My name's Damien," he answers, extending a hand. "I've got some information you might be interested in."

I give his hand a skeptical look and cut right to the chase. "Really?" I raise a brow, trying to gauge his true intentions. "And what would I be interested in?"

He shifts in place, and I catch the maroon folder clutched in his hand.

"I think what I have in here will be of great use to you," Damien says cryptically.

He takes a step closer, and I mirror him, taking one back. I tilt my chin up, making it clear I don't trust him.

"We can't talk here," he adds.

Without further explanation, he crosses the corridor and disappears behind those double doors.

"Why do they always have to be so mysterious?" I grumble under my breath before following him.

"Let's not waste more time. What's in the envelope?" I say, pushing open the door.

Heat wraps around me, the only light coming from the fireplace. The walls are all lined with shelves of leather-bound books, an intimate sanctuary of knowledge.

This might be the coziest library I've ever been in.

"Over here," he calls from the shadows.

He's standing in the depths of the room, away from any windows or doors.

"Who are you?" I approach him cautiously. "How do you know me? And what's inside there?"

Damien chuckles, purposely moving the envelope from one hand to the other. "Why don't you take a look for yourself?"

He hands me the thick folder overflowing with papers, and I take it from him. As I flip through the pages, each one reveals a missing piece of the story I've been following like a silent prayer. The difference between these pages and the ones in the diary strike me, stealing all the air from my lungs.

My eyes widen as my muscles stiffen at the defeating realization I had it all wrong. All fucking wrong.

My throat thickens as disjointed phrases leap off the pages at me.

"Master is back . . . Master says I'm pretty . . . Master doesn't like it when I cry . . . Master says he loves me."

My hands shake as I scan the pages.

"Master doesn't like it when I call him by his name."

Written in my mother's handwriting.

"Lucian wants me dead."

CHAPTER NINE
AURELIA

"Lucian Harrow," I say under my breath. His name tastes like poison on my tongue. "What did you do to her?"

The words inked on the worn pages spiral in the backs of my eyes while my fingers tremble, holding onto the truth as it unfolds. The maroon folder Damien handed to me discreetly earlier now lies abandoned on the mahogany shelves nearby.

These are the missing pages from my mother's diary, and the secrets hidden within them threaten to shatter everything I thought I knew about her death.

Full of dread, I read the words scrawled across the page. Words that suggest Lucian Harrow was involved in her suicide.

An uninvited memory washes over me.

Lucian's blue eyes are vacant as he looks down at me from his towering height. A height so high for a little girl of only eight years old. A smirk tugs at his lips as he toys with one of his smelly cigars.

The sun shines over us, yet no light can reach us. No— only darkness is present. That heavy, slimy kind of darkness that suffocates the naïve mind of a child; shatters their perception of life.

"Remember your place, golden one," he says. "You're nothing more than an orphan who got lucky."

His friends laugh, a raucous sound, as I flinch.

Why can they laugh? Why is it that when I do he gets mad?

This day is the day I'll slowly learn who I'm meant to be . . . before learning who I really am.

The memory fades, and my stomach twists into a knot at the thought that my mother might not have taken her own life but was killed by one of the most powerful men in Seattle.

My thoughts race, trying to piece together the puzzle of my mother's tragic past, when I notice something.

Damien is gone.

I didn't even hear him leave the room.

Panic claws its way up my throat, making it difficult to breathe.

Standing here alone, with the weight of my mother's darkest secrets in my hands, leaves me feeling vulnerable and exposed.

"Damien?" I call out hesitantly.

No response comes, and the silence seems to mock my growing alarm.

The walls of the library close in around me. Shadows

dance ominously across the rows of books, cast by the flickering fireplace.

I can't shake the feeling someone is watching me, lurking just beyond my line of sight.

Because I'm not alone. The ghosts of the sins inflicted on my mother are within reach.

Shaking the thought, I force myself to focus on my mother's words. I finally have the missing pages of her diary—of her life.

The pages continue to paint a horrifying picture of Lucian Harrow's depravity, and the more I read, the more certain I am that he played a bigger role in my mother's death.

I try to ignore the cold dread pooling in the pit of my stomach as I absorb each harrowing detail, but the emptiness of the library gnaws at me. The silence becomes deafening as I strain to hear any sign of Damien's return.

My discomfort is palpable, and it clings to me like a second skin, making it impossible to shake the sense of impending danger.

I lift my gaze as the dullest sound reaches my ears, whispered from the void. I stare at my empty surroundings, hoping against hope it's Damien miraculously reappearing. But the library remains engulfed in silence, offering no comfort or reassurance.

So I continue to read. I can feel my mother's pain, her shame and her fear, bleeding through the words.

"*Master,*" she wrote, describing her complete submission to him. But as the entries go on, her feelings for Lucian begin to evolve. "*I thought he loved me. That I was his little gift. That's what he called me when I pleasured him right,"* she confesses in one passage. *"But now I see the monster he truly is."*

The change in her perception of him is chilling, and it only serves to fuel my growing hatred for the man who took my mother away from me.

I want answers, justice, and most of all, I want Lucian Harrow to pay for what he did.

But these are just some of the pages in the envelope.

Maybe he didn't kill my mother. Either way, from what I've read, he deserves to suffer at my hands, just as much as she suffered at his.

"Found you," a voice growls behind me, warming my nape and startling me out of my thoughts.

As I turn toward the voice, the pages slip from my grip, fluttering to the floor like fragile leaves caught on a gust of wind.

"Julian." The word whooshes out of my mouth, and my heart gets stuck in my throat as I scramble to pick up the letters.

I feel exposed under his piercing gaze—*the same color as Lucian's.*

"Do you know the difference between me and you?" he whispers, stalking around me, his towering height forcing me to tilt my head up to maintain eye contact. "I'd chain you to keep you."

I glance down at the red marks around his wrists.

"And once I do, I intend to exploit your body like an altar. *Day and night.*"

His last words slither down my body, goose bumps erupting in their wake.

I glare at him, my anger momentarily overpowering the ghastly effect of my mother's words. "So what? You'll pray for me?" I ask, clutching the letters tightly to my chest as if they're a shield against his promises. But then I think better of it and swiftly hide them behind me, in the hem of my underwear.

"I'll *worship* you. On my fucking knees."

I hear the shuffle of feet and spot Emeric Grimward, Julian's best friend and the son of one of the Inferno Consortium families. The purple mask he was wearing before is now clutched in his grip. He's standing a few steps behind Julian, arms crossed over his chest.

Julian doesn't need to follow my line of sight to know who I'm looking at.

"I brought reinforcements in case you decide not to cooperate."

His lips stretch at the way my eyes round.

Before I can react, his long fingers wrap around my arm like iron bands, yanking me toward him with a force that makes me gasp.

"But before we can have our fun, you need to be punished," he growls.

In one swift motion he hoists me over his shoulder. I kick my legs uselessly in the air as I struggle to break free.

"Put me down, you arrogant creep!" I pound my fists against his broad back in a futile attempt to make him loosen his grip.

Even Emeric seems surprised by Julian's sudden hostility. To my annoyance, he doesn't make any move to intervene.

"Keep it up," Julian drawls. "I always did enjoy a challenge."

His words only serve to fuel my anger, and I redouble my efforts to escape.

I twist and squirm in his grip like a wild animal caught in a trap. But Julian is relentless, his hold on me unwavering as he carries me through the corridors of Victoria's cabin. The murmur of distant voices and moans provides a haunting soundtrack to my humiliation.

"Let go of me!" My voice cracks with desperation, my nails clawing at Julian's unyielding grip. "You have no right to treat me like this!"

"Tell me what you're hiding, and maybe I'll consider it," he shoots back. "Until then, you're going to listen to me whether you like it or not."

A rising tide of panic gnaws away at me.

It could be the rush of blood going to my head, or maybe my mother's words haven't really left my mind yet, but I swear his voice morphs into a deep, aged tone.

The voice of a monster.

I feel a dull ache in my chest, blood pounding in my ears.

"Master says I'm a good girl when I listen to him."

"Master says I'm his little gift, and that gifts must be shared around. He likes sharing me a lot."

"Master likes it more when I scream. So I scream. And I scream."

"Master punished me today because I didn't feel too well. He says punishments are necessary for stray girls like me."

I draw in a sharp breath. A mask of blank terror blinds my vision.

I can feel the stares of onlookers as we pass through the crowded rooms. Their whispers only add to my growing sense of helplessness.

"Please," I whisper. My voice is barely audible even to myself as tears threaten to spill over. "Please, just let me go."

"Give me a reason." His tone is cold. Unforgiving. "Give me one good reason why I shouldn't drag you back home and tell Lucian you're responsible for DeMarco's death."

Dread crawls up my spine as my gut churns at the implication.

"Because I didn't kill him, Julian." The words taste like bile in my mouth. "I had nothing to do with it."

"Then prove it," he demands. "Tell me what you're doing here tonight. Why you had someone else's blood on you."

But as much as I *long* for him to let me go, for the chance to breathe without feeling the crushing weight of Julian Harrow, I know I can't give him what he wants.

Because I killed DeMarco.

And now more than ever, I want to kill his father.

"Julian, please," I beg. "Please don't do this."

"Sorry, love, but you've left me no choice."

And with those chilling words, I know there is no more escaping the Harrows.

This has become a game of chance. I'll either die at his hands or his father's.

The chilly night air greets me like a slap in the face as

Julian dumps me abruptly onto the damp forest floor. My tears and my sorrow reach a boiling point, and I push myself up. My hands slip slightly on the wet leaves covering the ground as I glare up at him with all the anger I can muster.

"Are you done throwing me around like a rag doll?"

The forest is eerily silent. The shadows swallow us whole as we stand among the trees.

"Start talking." Icy blue eyes fix on me with an intensity that makes it feel like he's peering straight into my soul. "Why did you kill DeMarco?"

"Julian, I told you, I'm not—"

He cuts me off with a snarl. "Let's try this one last time." His voice echoes through the darkness. Jaw clenching, his hand snakes behind my back, untangling the knot of the makeshift bra and leaving me naked as he ties my hands with it instead, knotting the blindfold behind my back.

The material bites at my skin. I fight the urge to plead for the other version of Julian—the one whose mouth was tasting every dip of my body just half an hour ago.

"You think I don't know what's going on? You think I can't see how you've wormed your way into this part of our lives?" His hand gathers my ponytail and he pulls, tilting my neck at an uncomfortable angle.

My neck's bare, inviting his teeth to mark the unmarred skin.

"Julian, please, just let me explain," I try again, but the cold, hard look in his eyes tells me any attempt at reasoning with him will be futile.

He's too far gone, consumed by the darkness that has

always lurked beneath the surface of his carefully crafted façade.

"Explain?" he scoffs, pulling my face closer to his. "How do you explain getting a party invitation from the daughter of the Inferno Consortium? How do you explain DeMarco dying of poison, his body found with dried blood coughed out all over his thousand-dollar suit—and a drop on this very spot?" His finger travels up from my waist to my breast, flicking past my nipple. He pinches the skin above it, leaving a red mark resembling the bead of blood. "What the hell were you hoping to achieve by killing him?"

"Nothing!" I cry out, feeling the weight of his gaze bearing down on me like a physical force. "Because I did not fucking kill him!"

"Don't test me, Aurelia."

I refuse to let him break me. I've come too far, sacrificed too much, to give up now.

I meet his gaze defiantly, refusing to back down. "We can go on all night," I spit.

A sudden flash of black catches my attention—something familiar on his wrist—and I remember the hair tie I saw on him earlier tonight. Something inside me snaps, and I lose myself amidst all the pain and anger I've been struggling to contain.

He doesn't expect it. Yet his reflexes are fast. His hand falls from my hair and stops my knee from meeting his groin.

"Is this supposed to be some kind of sick joke?" My voice trembles with rage. "Wearing that tonight, of all nights?"

"What are you talking about?"

"The hair tie!" I push my knee up again, aiming for his dick in the hope of getting a hit.

But he stops me just in time. Then he flips me around, my back against his chest as he holds me still, his hand wrapped around my hair to pull my head back so he can look down at me.

"Why are you wearing it now?" I screech. "You bastard! What were you trying to obtain? Did you hope things would go back the way they were if I saw you with it?"

"Believe it or not, Aurelia, not everything is about you," he retorts.

But there's a hint of something in his voice that makes me pause.

"I never took it off."

"Never?" The word comes out as a whisper.

My eyes glaze over as I think back to one of those tedious social events we were forced to attend when I was seven and he was ten.

We find comfort in each other's silent company—well, I find comfort in Julian's. I'm far from silent. All I do is chatter about Valentine disagreeing with me buying another doll. I've tried telling him how the dolls I already have need friends—a big group of friends, so they never feel lonely—but he just shakes his head and changes the subject. Julian, on the other hand, agrees with his lack of words—or so I'm choosing to believe.

I don't have many friends. The guards who work for the Harrows prefer to keep their families as far from this world as possible, and the Harrow brothers are never around when I sneak up to their apartment. So to be finally sitting next to someone close to my age feels like a dream come true.

Between all my complaining, Julian turns to me and says, "I'll buy you all the dolls in Magic Mouse Toys."

My big eyes widen, giggles erupting at the exciting news. Magic Mouse Toys is the biggest toy store I've ever been in!

"Really? You promise?"

"I don't need to." He scoffs, seemingly offended.

"Okay then." I nod, noticing how similar he is to Mr. Grumble from my book. Then I let out a gasp, the realization hitting me. "But we aren't even friends! We need to be friends to give each other gifts."

His brow arches as he watches me bite my lower lip in concentration. Then I slip my favorite black hair tie, embellished with a raven, off my wrist and onto Julian's.

Valentine gave me the hair tie as a memento of my mother. He believes ravens share her personality.

"Here." I clap my hands clean, satisfied with my ability to problem-solve quickly. "Now we're forever friends."

"Julian, I—"

My words are cut off by the sound of snapping twigs and heavy breathing. Adrian appears in front of us, his face a mask of urgency.

"I've been searching everywhere for you. We need to leave now. Father needs us," he says between breaths.

"Can't it wait?" Julian snaps, his gaze still locked on

mine, so he doesn't notice the way Adrian's face contorts when he looks at him.

If possible, Adrian's dark eyes darken even more, eyebrows meeting in the middle and jaw clenched tightly. His nostrils flare as he catches long breaths from running to us.

"No. It's urgent," he insists. "Both of you need to come with me. And fucking cover her up, will you?"

"It's nothing you haven't seen before," Julian says.

I shiver as my dignity takes the hit once again.

Julian tears his eyes away from mine, taking a step back to create more distance between us. Much as I want to feel relief at the interruption, I don't know if I'll be able to face Lucian Harrow tonight.

What could he possibly want from me?

Julian unties me in less than a second and slaps the blindfold onto my chest. I catch it before it falls and cover my nakedness. He's looking everywhere else but at me, his eyes filled with uncertainty. But I can't understand what for.

"Let's go," Adrian calls out, gesturing for us to follow him as he turns to leave.

Julian hesitates for a moment. Something flickers behind his eyes before he turns to follow his brother.

I stare after them, mind reeling from everything that just happened. The realization that Julian never took off the hair tie weighs heavily on me, adding another layer to the already complicated emotions swirling inside of me.

"Move that perky ass, Aurelia, or do you want me to put you over my shoulder again?" Julian calls back.

"What a gentleman," I mutter, forcing my legs to move.

I follow the Harrow brothers through the dark forest as they exchange heated, hushed words with one another. I could try harder to listen to their conversation, but my thoughts are too consumed by other matters.

Julian is so close to putting all the pieces together. What if his father is five steps ahead of him? What if he knows about me?

We arrive at the place where Adrian parked his car. Julian came with Emeric tonight, so he's driving back with us.

Adrian gets behind the wheel, leaving us alone for a fraction of a second. Before Julian can get in, I let the one question pestering my thoughts out.

"Julian," I whisper, taking a hesitant step toward him. "What's going to happen now?"

The words I don't say stay locked inside of me: What's going to happen now *with Lucian? With us?*

Without even turning to me, he replies. "Whatever needs to happen for me to protect my family."

And then he shuts the door.

The weight of his words settles around me like a shroud. Suffocating and inescapable.

He may be wearing my hair tie, but his heart and his loyalty are elsewhere.

———————————

I'm sitting in the back seat, the air thick with tension,

as our silence gets interrupted only by the crunch of the gravel road.

It feels like the entire world is holding its breath, waiting for all hell to break loose.

The missing pages burn a hole in my skin.

I won't be so lucky next time. I need to be more careful. With my hands tied, Julian could have grabbed them from the hem of my underwear effortlessly.

Why didn't he?

"Would you two care to explain why we're being summoned by your father as if we're his personal pawns?" I snap, my frustration getting the better of me.

"If you didn't want to be treated like a pawn, you shouldn't have gotten involved with our family," Julian growls, not bothering to look at me.

"Involved?" I scoff. "You mean like when your brother seduced me and dated me to then fuck other girls at parties like this one? Or do you mean when you showed up and started treating me like your personal plaything?"

"Enough," Adrian interjects. "We can argue about this later. Right now we need to focus on getting to Father before he loses his temper."

"Whatever," I mutter, seething with anger.

As we continue through the forest, the moonlight creates eerie shadows of the trees, casting an unsettling atmosphere over the road.

An hour or so later I see the ominous outline of the Harrow penthouse looming in the distance. Its dark windows stare back at me like the empty eyes of a predator.

I shudder involuntarily. I feel like I'm walking straight into the lion's den.

Adrian turns us down the underground passage into the parking lot, the black metal gate opening automatically when it catches the sensor in Adrian's car.

And we're in. No escaping now.

We get out and head to the elevator. A lick of fear goes up my spine in anticipation of what could be waiting for me.

We arrive at their floor in record time. I'm one step away from the imposing door when Julian grabs my arm.

"Stay close," he warns.

I nod, swallowing the lump in my throat as I fall into step behind him.

Adrian leads us down the candlelit hallway. The art pieces framing the walls look like living nightmares in the scarce lighting, nothing like the happy picture frames in our home. I feel increasingly out of place in this cold, posh tomb.

"We'll find out soon." Julian's hand brushes against mine for a brief moment, sending a bolt of electricity up my arm. I glance up at him, feeling the striking difference between the Julian of now and the one of just an hour ago, in the forest.

We reach a set of double doors guarded by two burly men.

"We're expected," Julian says.

The guards exchange a glance before stepping aside, allowing us to enter Lucian Harrow's inner sanctum.

As the doors swing open I brace myself for whatever lies ahead, knowing my life is hanging in the balance.

"Ah, there you are." Lucian's voice drips with disdain as he looks up at his sons from behind his massive oak desk. "I was beginning to think you'd lost your way."

"Sorry to disappoint," Julian replies icily, his gaze frozen on his father, assessing every small movement. Mine moves toward Valentine's stoic stare—frozen with undetected worry. I can see it in the crinkling lines around his eyes and the stiffness in his shoulders.

He's warning me.

"Enough with the pleasantries," Adrian interjects, giving Julian a sizzling stare—one that seems to resonate with Julian as they share unspoken words with one another. Then he continues. "Father, tell us, why did you call us here?" His tone shifts the moment he addresses Lucian.

"Because it's time we had a little chat." Lucian leans back in his chair, his hands clasped together in front of him.

His eyes flick to me.

"All of us."

CHAPTER TEN

JULIAN

Aurelia's tension radiates like heat from a fire at my father's words.

My eyes trail from him to her, catching every short breath that leaves her parted lips. Her hands are frozen by her sides, but her fingers twitch involuntarily as if they're calling for a weapon to form between them.

She doesn't need one. I'm seconds away from reaching for the gun in my back pocket, body coiled like a spring. If even one of her perfect red strands touches the ground, his head will be next.

I'm not the only one to notice the thickness in the air between us. Adrian follows closely, his eyes trained on Lucian, trying to decipher the reason for this sudden call and why it involves Aurelia.

"Sit down." Lucian gestures to the chairs in front of his desk.

Adrian immediately complies, taking a seat with a

straight back, attentive. I hesitate, unwilling to put any distance between myself and Aurelia.

She glances at me, her wide green eyes filled with uncertainty.

"Julian." Lucian's voice is sharp. Commanding.

Reluctantly, I take a seat next to Adrian, Aurelia on my other side.

I keep my body angled toward her, ready to leap if the bastard decides to shift his attention onto her. And I'm not the only one. Valentine stands as silent as stone at the far end of the room, close to Lucian, his full attention on her.

They share a look—not just any look but one filled with years of bonding. He speaks to her through it, and she listens, trusting him fully. It's subtle enough not to attract attention, but since I can't keep my eyes away from her, I notice it.

Her presence is like a magnet, drawing me in even when I know it's dangerous. And despite the uncertainty we're in, I can't help but take in the details of her appearance.

I catch the way her red lips contrast perfectly against her pale skin. The shapes of the freckles dusting her nose. The stubborn tilt of her chin that tells me she won't be broken easily. The shade of her green eyes—how there are two spots of brown in the left eye and just one in the right.

But I also see the fear lurking behind her brave façade. The tremble in her foot that she tries to hide by crossing one tightly over the other.

I hate seeing her like this.

Something inside of me roars for me to take action. To comfort her. To make her feel safe again. Yet I know any unexpected reaction from me would only draw more attention to her, putting her in danger. It's already a miracle Lucian didn't comment on her barely-there outfit.

Seeing a half-naked girl is nothing out of the ordinary for him. And yet his eyes run hungrily up and down her body as if she's a piece of art he's contemplating adding to his collection.

Fucking pervert.

Did he call her here just to have a good look?

Something simmers deep within me.

Or maybe he somehow found out about Aurelia's involvement in DeMarco's death. If that's the case, things are about to get far more dangerous.

If only she trusted me enough to tell me *why* she did it, I could have prevented this inconvenience.

Not only that, but she decided to handcuff me and leave me alone in bed.

God, I'll forever hear the taunting giggles that erupted from Emeric when he found me. The prick took pictures before untying me.

"Your friend here is quite beautiful, don't you think?" Lucian's eyes are still lingering on Aurelia. There's a predatory glint in them that makes me want to put myself between them, but I control myself. Even as disgust churns within me.

"Her beauty is not the reason you called us in here," I say with false self-control, "so cut the shit and tell us."

"Ah, always straight to the point, aren't you, Julian?"

He leans back in his chair, fingers clenching together as he continues to praise Aurelia. "You see, I've been thinking about how best to utilize the golden one here. She has certain . . . talents after all."

Aurelia stiffens beside me. She glances at Valentine, and he subtly shakes his head.

Is this it? Has he discovered her secret?

I swallow the lump forming in my dry throat, my hand centimeters away from the gun's trigger.

I take a deep breath and focus on every single movement Lucian makes. I have a clear aim of his head from here—I could kill him before he could even take in his last breath. It would save Aurelia from his wrath, leaving me to take my brother's bullet.

But she'd be safe.

Lies. The voice in my head mocks. *With you gone, who'd protect her from the rest of the Inferno Consortium? Who would keep the demons at bay?*

Lucian's eyes narrow as he studies us, his gaze lingering on Aurelia for a moment longer. "Adrian," he says, breaking the silence. "Leave us."

Adrian hesitates, casting a worried glance in our direction before nodding stiffly. "As you wish, Father." With that, he disappears through the door, leaving the four of us alone in the room.

No brother, no bullet to the heart. I might survive this after all.

"The girl has relied on our wealth—on the Inferno Consortium—for quite some time now," Lucian starts, the words oozing from his mouth like venom. "It's only fitting that she starts to prove her worth, don't you think?"

Aurelia may have been adopted by Valentine, but that might as well be a misfortune, because in doing so he kept her close to us. Kept her part of the Inferno Consortium and close to Lucian.

She isn't a lady. She's a girl, and girls of the Inferno Consortium get used.

I grit my teeth, forcing myself to keep my anger in check as I feel Aurelia's fingers digging into my arm. Her grip is desperate, a silent plea for me to remain calm despite the storm brewing inside of me.

"Aurelia is more than capable of standing on her own. She doesn't need to prove anything," I say with a tight jaw.

"Ah, but that's where you're wrong, Julian." He leans forward, his gaze never leaving Aurelia's face. It's as if he's trying to dissect her with his eyes alone. "Now that she's old enough, she must learn to contribute to our world."

"Your world?" Aurelia spits, finally finding her voice after what seemed like an eternity of silence. "The world of corruption and violence? I'm not interested in being a part of it."

"Unfortunately, my dear, you don't have a choice," Lucian replies. "You've already taken the benefits that come with this life, whether you wanted to or not. Now the only way out is to become useful."

Aurelia remains silent, her eyes wide, with something I can't describe flickering in them. I can almost feel the weight of her dread pressing against me, suffocating us both.

As much as I don't want her to take part in this fucked-up, twisted world I live in, there's no denying the truth in Lucian's words.

"If you want her to become useful, she'll need guidance. I'll help her, but on my terms." My voice strains with the effort of holding back. The less I piss him off, the faster we can get out of here.

"Your terms?" Lucian raises his brows. A smirk pulls at the corners of his lips. "Very well. I will allow you to oversee the girl's . . . integration into our world. But remember, she is ultimately my responsibility. Do not forget who you answer to."

She is ultimately my responsibility. The pig.

"Of course."

"Perfect."

I hear my muscles strain as he looks at her.

"Now let's get down to business."

Lucian begins to outline his latest conquest, taking pride in the way Aurelia's revulsion taints her expression. She's a fighter, but even she has her breaking point. And it seems we're rapidly approaching it.

I don't blame her. I puked too the first time I heard Lucian's detailed description of the woman he and his friends had fucked before carving their initials into her skin and hanging her as trophy art in one of our living rooms, leaving her to rot.

And then I fainted when he took me to see her.

I was only six.

"Is there a problem, golden one?" His voice drips with sarcasm. "You look as if you're about to be sick."

Aurelia swallows hard, throat bobbing.

Then her eyes dart between me and him before she lifts her chin, a dare shining in her gaze.

"I'm fine." Her voice picks up strength. "Let's just get this over with."

His expression drops all trace of friendliness. "Remember, you are here because I've allowed it. Your life, your very existence, is dependent on your usefulness to me. Don't forget that."

A strange heaviness forms in my chest at seeing Aurelia's freckles dull in color, the way her chest is suspended in the moment, as if she drifted someplace else before being forced back down into this hell.

She had the same reaction her first day of high school, when she stopped at my locker, a plate of star cookies in her hands—my favorite. I love eating the angles before digging into the middle. But I pushed right past her as if she didn't exist.

Like my heart wasn't fucking screaming to go back to her.

"Now, enough with the pleasantries—we have more important matters to discuss. Victoria Marlowe has informed me she's grown quite fond of you." His eyes stain her with his vileness.

Tensing, I contemplate his next words.

"Your task is simple," Lucian continues, informing Aurelia of what she's to do. "You will work together with Julian to ensure Victoria's happiness and satisfaction. This will secure our alliance with the Marlowe family and keep the peace after the chaos of DeMarco's death."

"Father," I say, my voice steady despite the need to gag at calling him that, "you can't seriously want her to get involved in something this delicate. She will blow everything up. Victoria's needs are being taken care of. She's *satisfied*."

Aurelia crosses her arms and huffs.

"Do not test me, boy," he snarls. "If you refuse to do as I say, I'll make sure your mother pays the price."

I know he isn't bluffing.

He's done it before to keep me in line. But this time something inside of me snaps. I can't let him hurt my mother, but I also can't sacrifice Aurelia for it.

Lucian notices, because at the lack of a response from me, he says, "Her pussy must be gold if you'd give your mother to me to save her. It must be so if she's being tossed between you and your brother. Since we're keeping it in the family, maybe it's time for my turn. What do you say?"

Aurelia stiffens next to me at his words. Her eyes round as she tries to mask the faint tremble of her body. A boiling fire ignites within me at seeing her like this.

Clenching my fists, I'm barely able to keep my bitterness in check. "You will not lay a finger on her."

Lucian laughs—a cruel, mocking sound that echoes throughout the room. "Fine." The amusement is clear in his voice. "You'd best do as you're told, or I'll be taking her to bed with me next."

With that, he dismisses us from his presence.

Without needing to be told twice, we leave.

The air in the corridor is cold as we step outside, the chill settling into my bones. But it's better than staying in the smothering heat of his office.

I glance at Aurelia, noticing how her body seems to tremble ever so slightly. Her eyes are wide, her lips pressed into a thin line.

"Julian . . ." Her voice is barely above a whisper. "How long has your mother been getting hit by your father?"

The question catches me off-guard.

I can't ignore the genuine concern shining in her eyes. I hesitate for a moment, my throat tightening as I find the words.

"Since I was old enough to understand what bruises were. And that Mommy screaming wasn't because they were playing tickle," I say, my voice rough, borderline calloused. "He uses it to control me—to keep me in line."

Tears shine in her eyes, and she reaches out to touch my arm. "I can't let you choose me over your mother, Julian. I'll help you with the Marlowe situation."

Her words hit me like a punch to the gut, and I struggle to find the right thing to say.

How can I protect her if she refuses to stay out of harm's way?

The truth is, I don't want her involved in any of this—not with the Marlowes, and not with my family. But what choice do I have? She's determined. And if I try to protect her, I'll only be putting her in more danger. Plus, she got herself into this mess to begin with by killing DeMarco.

"Fine," I concede, my voice straining. "But you need to understand that getting involved in my job means crossing lines you might not be ready to cross. Are you prepared for that?"

Like a knife digging into my flesh, I feel a sharpness bleeding me dry as all my past failed attempts at protecting my mom flood my vision. All the phone calls to the police, worthless when they were getting paid off the books by the Inferno Consortium; all the times I stood up for her; all the times I sought help from relatives and friends; all the times I begged Adrian to do something—anything.

Worthless.

"I've tried to shield my mother before," I hear myself admit. "And it's always ended badly."

She hesitates, and for a moment I think she might back down.

But then she looks up at me, her eyes filled with determination.

"I can handle it, Julian. Trust me."

Oh, I know you can, little one.

It's not her I need to prepare. It's me.

The thought of her getting caught up in the dark underbelly of the Inferno Consortium makes me sick with fear.

If anything happens to her, I'll never forgive myself.

But you can't even protect your own blood . . .

I lean in closer, our faces mere inches apart as I whisper my warning. "Just remember, though, if you're going to get involved in my life, I won't hesitate to get involved in yours. And I will find out the truth no matter what it takes."

It's a threat but also an invitation, a challenge for her to rise to.

She shivers at the proximity, her body tense yet oddly inviting. It's clear she isn't afraid of me—not in the way she should be, considering what we just went through.

As I pull away I study her face, trying to discern what's going on in that little head of hers. But she remains unreadable.

"Is this another promise?" Her voice is tinged with something that sounds a lot like excitement. "You still have another promise to uphold." She lightly bites down on her lower lip.

My dick stirs.

I still need to punish her, and lucky for her, I keep my promises.

"It's a guarantee," I say. "But no handcuffs this time."

"Deal." A smile tugs at the corner of her plump lips.

CHAPTER ELEVEN

AURELIA

"Are you sure about this?" Eleanora asks, her eyes narrowing. "I've told you a million times, I don't trust the Harrow brothers. Especially Julian."

I'm standing in front of the mirror at Eleanora's house, applying a thick layer of red lipstick to match the color of my *Valentino Garavani* silk wool mini dress. Adrian gifted it to me on our second anniversary. It's too pretty to throw away, so I still wear it sometimes.

I frown at her mention of Julian. It's been two days since the meeting with Lucian Harrow, and I haven't heard from him since.

"Trust me." I glance over at her as she carefully curls her long black hair. "I feel the same way. But I need to blow off some steam, and Julian's club has the best booze. Plus, I can't spend another pamper Friday stuck at home watching 'The Sweetest Thing' one more time."

Eleanora rolls her eyes, their amber color striking, and sighs in agreement. "Fine. But don't come crying to me when Julian goes celebrating his victory with one of those skanks, breaking your heart again."

"Please." I scoff, giving myself a once-over in the mirror. "As if I'd let someone like him mess with my heart. Besides, you can't talk. Last time I checked, your relationship with Emeric wasn't all sunshine and roses."

I'd never let Julian mess with my heart? Liar. He already has.

Eleanora and I became friends during our freshman year of high school, right after she found me crying my eyes out in the girls' bathroom because Julian had pushed past me, ignoring my very existence, in front of his friends. She dried my tears and offered me some wise words on how to make him regret ever treating me that way while she munched on the star cookies I'd baked for him.

Her confidence and independence—and my lack of both—were what brought us closer together. She taught me how to believe in my own strength, while I taught her to let her sensitive side take over occasionally.

It's funny how Eleanora helped me to become this version of myself who stands up for herself and the ones she loves—who isn't scared of killing the people who wronged her mother—more than she knows.

"Exactly," she says, "because there is *no* relationship. We aren't dating. We just have fun."

"Whatever you say, Eleanora."

She and Emeric are fuck buddies. She insists she likes it this way, but I know she's secretly harboring feelings for him.

As we make our way to the Den, a place where predators gather to watch their own kind battle it out, I think back to how self-controlled I was in Lucian's studio while my insides were screaming.

He was so relaxed as depravities left his mouth. The things he talked about crawled all over my skin. I wanted to end his life there and then. I was so tempted.

Instead I kept my cool and agreed to work with Julian on entertaining Victoria—whatever that means. It's a risky move, but it'll get me closer to my goal. And once the Marlowe family goes down, Lucian will be left vulnerable and exposed for me to kill him.

The fight club is packed when we arrive. The atmosphere is electric with anticipation. Glancing around the gloomy navy venue, I watch the crowd jitter with excitement for tonight's fight. Two weeks have passed since the last one.

I feel my pulse quicken to the beat of the music as we move through the crowd. Even if the people here are all ironically dressed formally, this place remains tainted with danger, exciting me in ways I can't fully understand.

"Look at us." Eleanora's voice strains above the blaring music. "We look like femme fatales, ready to break hearts and take names."

I grin at her, feeling confidence surge in me with the way people are staring.

Eleanora looks stunning, dressed in a form-fitting dark purple leather dress that showcases her long legs. We decided to wear a matching set of black combat boots. The contrast between them and the red mini dress with bows is exactly what I was aiming for: formal but edgy.

"Let's hope so." I scan the room for Julian. Tonight I need to make sure he sees how much time has passed since we were friends. I want him to see how much I've changed. He needs to know I'm not the same naïve little girl he discarded. And maybe I want him to want me. Just a little . . . just for fun.

We take our positions near the front, close to the boxing ring in the middle of the room, as the crowd cheers and jeers, signaling that the fight is about to begin.

Julian will soon step into the ring.

Tonight the winner of the last fight will be up against him, vying for the title of the Most Ruthless Fighter in Seattle. A title Julian has held for three years now, ever since he opened the Den at twenty-five.

These tournaments happen every two weeks, drawing in people from all backgrounds who crave the adrenaline rush of watching the brutal fights—or participating in them.

This isn't a closed-door event like the ones of the Inferno Consortium. Everyone is welcome here.

Eleanora shouts, "Are you ready for this?"

"Ready as I'll ever be."

Watching Julian fight has always had a weird effect on me. It's the push and pull of seeing him bleed that makes me both worried and captivated.

Valentine didn't approve of me attending university, so I had to settle for taking Fine Art classes in the safety of our home.

One day I overheard two of the Harrows' guards discussing Lucian's disappointment in Julian for spending thousands of dollars on an underground fight club instead of focusing on the family business. That conversation ignited something within me—a desire to break free from my sheltered existence and experience the same reckless abandon Julian seemed to embody.

Yet I've never dared to defy Valentine's wishes. Not after he took me in and treated me as his own.

Besides, there was always something deeply satisfying about the moments when he would hang my artwork on our kitchen walls—a daily ritual we both cherished. I couldn't give that up back then. And I guess he couldn't either, because he still asks for them from time to time. In his typical, detached manner—but he misses my drawings nonetheless.

I never stopped painting; I just keep my art to myself. The first time I read my mother's diary, something shifted inside of me. My artwork portrays the dark turmoil in my head now, and I don't want him—or anyone, for that matter—to see it.

A guy double my size—no, triple—enters the ring.

Shaking off the memory, I turn my attention back to the present and the guy going up against Julian. The crowd's reaction is mixed as he steps in, with some cheering and others remaining silent, waiting for their fighter to make his appearance.

The guy—Fury, the announcer calls him—does some jabs in the middle of the ring, making a little show of it. His face is painted with streaks of red and orange as if he's on fire, and he wears red shorts and matching shoes. He isn't wearing any MMA gloves. Julian hates not feeling his opponents' skin breaking under impact, so he abolished them. The club is his, so he makes the rules.

"God, this is ridiculous. Do they seriously not know how to dress for the occasion? That shade of red is *not* his color," Eleanora complains, her voice barely audible above the roar of the crowd.

"Introducing the reigning champion, the Ripper!" the announcer bellows, whipping the crowd into a frenzy.

Julian steps through the crowd, his muscular body, adorned with tattoos, straining as he jumps into the ring. He's wearing black shorts and matching shoes. My heart skips a beat as his eyes, almost silver under this light, catch me in the audience.

A skeleton is painted on his lower face, and he smirks at me before turning and opening his arms, calling for the audience to go feral.

"Well . . ." Eleanora begins, but I slap her on the arm before she can continue, rolling my eyes at her drooling for him. He's undeniably attractive, but I'll die before admitting that—or having my best friend admit it for me.

The bell rings and Julian stalks forward. His fists are clenched, knuckles white, his muscles flexing under the bright lights as he takes his stance, dark eyes fixed on his target.

They circle each other like predators, their movements calculated and precise.

The sound of fists hitting flesh echoes through the arena as they exchange blows. Julian seems to anticipate his opponent's every move, countering with swift strikes that leave the other guy reeling.

I can't tear my eyes away from the brutal dance unfolding before me. My heart races with adrenaline as I watch Julian dominate the fight with ruthless ability.

"Hey, I'm going to grab something to drink," Eleanora shouts over the noise. "Want anything?"

"Don't worry about it," I yell back, masking my eagerness to escape the crowd's intensity for a moment. "I can get it for us."

"Are you sure? You'll miss the rest of the fight."

"It's fine. Julian will win like he always does. I won't miss anything new."

I tear my gaze from the entrancing sight of him dominating his opponent in the ring and head toward the bar, weaving through the crowd.

When I finally reach the other side of the room, the bar is packed with people ordering while watching the fight. I squeeze between two men in suits and lean against the counter, trying to get the bartender's attention.

The atmosphere is thick with thrill and a hint of sweat, leaving me feeling intoxicated despite not having had a drop of alcohol yet.

The sleek, polished counter of the bar gleams in a rich navy-blue hue, catching the light and reflecting it back in a mesmerizing dance. The shelves behind the counter are lined with endless rows of bottles, reaching all the way up to the high ceiling. A large mirror hangs on the wall behind the bar, adding depth to the already spacious room.

"Hey there, gorgeous," a deep voice purrs in my ear.

I turn to see a tall, lean man leaning casually against the counter next to me. His light hair is perfectly tousled, and his smoldering eyes seem to hold an invitation for sinful things.

"Hi." I give him a small smile. "What'll it be?" I ask him, and confusion clouds his face until I tilt my chin toward the bartender waiting to take his order.

His eyes roam over my body before he shakes his head. He orders a Jack and Coke, and I notice his gaze falling back down my body like a predator sizing up its prey.

I order my drinks next and wait for the bartender. Glancing over my shoulder, I see Julian's fists connecting with his opponent's face over and over again.

I'm not missing anything new. Although the way his muscles dip and bulge . . . that is *very* new and not at all like the boy I knew ten years ago. I subconsciously bite down on my lower lip.

"Feeling brave enough to step into the ring yourself?" the guy asks, his voice dripping with innuendo. "I bet you'd put on quite a show."

"Thanks, but I think I'll leave the fighting to the professionals," I shoot back. My tone turns icy as I try to create some distance between us. But if he notices, he doesn't show it.

Instead his hand suddenly grips my arm tightly, and he pulls me closer.

"Come on, don't be like that," he murmurs, his breath hot on my neck as his other hand slides around my waist.

Panic rises within me, along with a fierce surge of anger.

How dare he touch me like this?

"Get your hands off me," I snarl before shoving him away with all my strength. The force of my push catches him off-guard, and he stumbles.

"You fucking bitch," he hisses, his breath putrid as it engulfs me.

In a second his hand connects with my face in a vicious slap that sends me stumbling backward.

The crowd cheers with madness as Julian deals a blow to his opponent's temple. Everyone is too high on adrenaline and other substances to notice my predicament.

Before I can regain my senses, the man grabs onto my arm with a bruising grip and pulls me away from the crowded bar. His fingers dig into my skin, leaving red marks in their wake as he leads me into a corner, hiding us from prying eyes.

The shadows seem to close in around us as I try to pull away, but his grip only tightens, trapping me in this secluded space alone with him.

"Let go of me!" I shout. But my voice gets lost in the cacophony of the crowd as I struggle to break free.

He's too strong, and he knows it, as he presses me against the wall. His hot, alcohol-laced breath traces my neck as he whispers, "With this little dress, you are just asking for it, aren't you, baby?"

I grunt in frustration, pushing with all my strength at his chest. But he doesn't budge.

"Such a pretty little thing." He sneers, his fingers

digging into my flesh as he starts to tug at the hem of my dress. "Look at you squirming for it. You are making my dick so fucking hard."

"Stop it!" My insides tighten as his intention becomes horrifyingly clear.

"Quiet. I'll make it quick. You'll beg me for more afterward."

His clammy hand covers my breast and he squeezes in delight. Air tickles my inner thighs, and I know he's seconds away from touching my center. The sound of his belt unbuckling is enough to wake me from the fear.

I remember the knife I brought with me, concealed in my combat boot.

Searching for it, my fingers tremble as I lift my leg and feel the hilt in my palm. In one swift movement I free it, pointing it at his chest—but something flashes beside us, catching my eye, and the guy gets yanked away from me.

"Touch her again and I'll rip your fucking throat out."

I hear Julian's deep growl rip through the air before he stands over the man. Anger seeps out of his pores. He can barely contain himself. His light eyes are now a pool of intense darkness, matching his body, which is covered in blood from the fight that ended seconds ago.

The metallic scent of iron fills the air, mixing with the tang of sweat and adrenaline, as Julian's muscles tense and ripple beneath his stained skin.

Then the sickening crunch of bone echoes through the air as Julian's fist connects with the man's face, sending him crumpling to the floor, unconscious.

Just one punch. And the bastard is now lying on the ground. Where he belongs.

"Are you all right?" Julian turns to me with concern etched across his bruised and battered features. "Did he touch you?"

"Yes," I manage to choke out. My throat squeezes shut with all the emotions brewing inside of me, threatening to overwhelm me.

Yes, I'm all right? Yes, he touched me? Yes what?

"He didn't . . . he didn't get far."

Relief washes over Julian's face, but it gets quickly replaced by a dark, wrathful expression.

"Show me where he touched you."

I hesitate for a moment, unsure of what he wants, but I comply anyway, pointing to the place on my breast where the guy's hands violated me.

Shame and anger rush out as I relive the helplessness I felt just seconds ago. I lift my gaze to Julian's and wait.

His eyes bore into the spot. "Where else? I want you to show me everywhere he touched." His voice is low, the anger from before still visible as he struggles to control it.

Nodding, I feel my throat scratch as I try to swallow. Mouth parched, I move my fingers down to my inner thigh, then right up under my ass.

"No, not like that." He grabs the knife I forgot I was clutching. "Show me with this."

"Wh-what?"

"On me."

A fierce protectiveness shines in his molten blue gaze. A need to make things right. And so, with trembling

145

fingers, I take the knife back and press the tip to each spot on Julian's body that mirrors my own violated parts.

"Here," I whisper each time, my voice barely audible over the pounding of my heart.

And each time, Julian nods with determination before forcing my hand to drive the knife into his flesh, leaving angry red marks that weep blood.

"Remember this," he tells me, pointing at the crimson dripping to the floor. "Your body is mine. Your soul is mine. Whatever happens to you happens to me. Especially when I should have been preventing it."

I stare at him, bloodied and battered, and I can't help but feel a strange sense of gratitude mixed with raw fear.

"This is what I mean when I say you are mine," he growls.

Movement calls for our attention as the bastard whimpers on the floor, groaning in agony as he tries to regain consciousness.

Julian's eyes light up with a twisted gleam, and he turns to me, his wicked smile stretching wide. "He's waking up, love."

My anger for the bastard comes rushing back, and a copy of Julian's twisted grin appears on my lips. "He looked better when he was unmoving."

Julian swears under his breath, his eyes darkening as they sink to me. He licks his lips, leaving a trail of red. "Fuck, you're something else," he whispers.

I don't respond, my attention fixed on the molester as he struggles to get back onto his feet. I can feel Julian's intense gaze burning into me. He's itching to kill him, but as much as he wants to, he wants me to take the lead. Wants me to make the asshole regret what he did.

The air is thick with tension. Every muscle in my body is coiled and ready to strike.

"There's no point in telling you not to treat a girl like that again . . ." I take a step closer to him, and he staggers, hitting his back against the wall. "Because there won't be a second time." I smile as I plunge the knife into his stomach.

He roars in pain, clutching at the wound in shock. His eyes round as he chokes on air. He felt so powerful just a few seconds ago, but only now does he understand he's skin and bone, no different from me.

He went for my body; I'll go for his soul.

Without hesitation, I stab him one more time—straight through his neck.

Blood spurts everywhere, and he crumples to the floor.

Dead.

A rush of adrenaline courses through me. Relief and satisfaction next.

Julian entwines our bloodied fingers, squeezing my hand ever so slightly before leading me out of the grimy corner and toward his matte-black *Ducati* parked outside.

The sleek machine seems to purr with anticipation as Julian straddles it before extending a helmet to me. I hesitate, my hand frozen in midair as I stare at it.

The events of the night are still swirling through my mind—the bastard's hands on me, the taste of fear as he violated me, the visceral satisfaction of exacting my revenge.

"Hey." Julian softly breaks the spell, offering me his bloodstained hand.

I look at him and see the same pain, anger, and determination mirrored in his eyes.

For a brief second I allow myself to forget about the guy and what he did to me. I place my trembling hand, soaked with blood, in his crimson one and feel a strange sense of comfort at his touch.

In one swift motion I slip on the helmet and climb onto the bike behind him. I shoot a quick text to Eleanora to let her know I'm heading back home with Julian without giving too many details. I'll let her imagination explore what might have happened tonight. I don't want to worry her . . . or tell her I killed someone.

As we speed through the Seattle night, the wind whipping through my hair and the city lights blurring together, I cling to Julian, feeling more alive than ever before.

Because despite everything, I know we're similar in so many ways. Bloodied, broken, but still fighting.

CHAPTER TWELVE

JULIAN

The moment we enter my penthouse the heavy silence of the night surrounds us.

Aurelia stops in her tracks, her eyes darting around the place as if she's a trapped animal. "Maybe I should just go home . . ."

A heavy feeling hammers in my chest. The thought of leaving her alone tonight gnaws at me. She's been through enough, and I wasn't there to prevent it from happening . . . I just need to have my eyes on her for the rest of the night.

"No." The word comes out harsher than intended. "You're staying here tonight. You're not going anywhere."

Her eyes lock with mine, and I can see the defiance in them. But she doesn't argue back. Instead she chooses to follow me through the penthouse.

That's my good girl.

We reach my bedroom, and I flick on the lights,

revealing the king-size bed with its black silk sheets and the floor-to-ceiling windows that offer an unbeatable view of the Seattle skyline. A large abstract painting hangs on one wall, its vibrant colors and distorted shapes challenging the viewer's perception. That's why I love abstract paintings. I could lie in bed and stare at them for hours.

But it's the pinboard next to it that truly tells a story, adorned with a collection of my favorite book quotes and various trinkets I've collected over the years. Each one holds a special memory. They're more than just objects; these are fragments of my past. That's why I didn't add anything to remind me of Aurelia. Categorizing her as something that happened once and no longer exists would be wrong. That's not her. She's still a part of my present, something I refuse to let go of.

My eyes fall to the poem I pinned to the board, "The Chrysophilist" by Theodore Montclair. I read it every night before falling asleep, to the point I now know it by heart. Like a religion. A prayer.

Like a sinful spell for the heart.

"The Chrysophilist

It shines,
calling to you the first time you see it.
Never rusts,
but it does with your heart.
It gleams,
telling you it's all you need.
Never wavers,
but it does with your judgment.

You can't resist its call,
like a siren to a sailor.
But this time it's different;
you're not the only one being lured in.
The shine fades,
the rust takes over your body and soul.
Its weight drags you down into an abyss of greed and
corruption.
And when you finally touch rock bottom,
there will be gold to cushion your fall."

If we were at school, I'd know how to analyze the shit out of it.

It's a sick joke. Theodore Montclair and I share the same fate, but while he knew how to express himself with words, I prefer fists.

"Wait here," I tell her, my tone softer this time.

Aurelia hesitates for a moment before nodding, and I leave her alone in the bedroom while I go into the connected bathroom to prepare a bath for her.

I turn the faucet and it groans to life. I watch the water fill the tub, the sound a soothing, steady harmony as it echoes off the bathroom tile. I turn the faucet further to the side and let warmer water stream down. Steam fills the air, sticking to my already damp skin.

Memories of tonight at the Den flood my mind.

The first image to appear is that son of a bitch who dared to put his filthy hands on her. But then guilt overpowers the memory and I start to feel like shit for being fucking blind to it all.

I was fighting in the ring when I saw Aurelia disappear with that piece of shit. In that moment I couldn't care less about the thunderous cheer of the crowd or defending my title of Most Ruthless Fighter in Seattle. All that mattered was finding her and making sure she was safe.

With a vicious punch, I knocked my opponent out cold, giving the crowd one last opportunity to roar as I raced after her.

I found them just in time, but the anger and guilt still burn within me. Anger at him for touching her, and anger at myself for letting it happen.

But more than anger, the guilt is relentless.

All the punches I throw and all the victories I claim mean nothing if I can't protect her.

I'm already failing at protecting someone else in my life —I can't fail at protecting her too.

"Julian?" Aurelia's voice startles me, pulling me out of my thoughts.

I turn to face the door, my jaw clenching. "I'm almost done in here."

"Okay."

I hear her steps echo next as she walks around my room.

She's probably taking in how much my room has changed since the last time she was here. Just like I did when I walked into hers.

With a final glance at the now full bathtub, I shut off the water and walk back to my room.

"It's ready."

Startled by my voice, her body jolts a little. She turns toward me and away from the poem she was reading.

"Thank you," she whispers, eyes zeroing in on mine for just a second, enough to leave me wanting more of her attention. Those big green eyes are like a portal to a world of everlasting spring. It makes my chest tighten every single time I stare at them.

Forcing myself to focus on her, and not on the way she awakens my whole body, I follow her into the bathroom.

I can't help but watch her, taking in the way the light plays on her fiery red hair and the curve of her hips as she moves. Despite everything that's happened between us, she is still the most beautiful thing I've ever seen.

But I have to remind myself that tonight isn't about lust or desire. It's about taking care of her and making sure she feels safe.

"Is that . . . my favorite honey bodywash I smell?"

Apivita Royal Honey. After being in her room the other day, I couldn't shake her smell, so I went and bought it. Simple.

If I had to be haunted by it, might as well make it right. Plus, it seriously leaves the skin smooth. Emeric wanted to buy himself a bottle, but I punched the guy. Fuck if I want my best friend to smell like the girl of my dreams.

"Come here," is all I say in response, ignoring her question.

She steps closer to me, her gaze hesitant but trusting.

As tempting as it is to let my hands wander over her body, I remain focused on the task at hand.

"What are you doing?" Her voice wavers slightly as I reach for the hem of her dress. Yet she doesn't distance herself. Trust shines in her inquiring eyes, feeding me into oblivion.

"Taking care of you," I reply, keeping my tone gentle yet firm.

Slowly I lift the material, exposing her skin inch by tantalizing inch. My breath catches in my throat as I take in the sight of her: the smooth expanse of her pale stomach, the delicate curve of her waist, the way her chest rises and falls with each shallow breath.

God, she is perfect.

"Julian . . ." she whispers, a hint of vulnerability lacing her voice.

The way she says my name could shatter my resolve if I let it. But I can't allow myself to be distracted. This is about her, not us.

"Relax," I murmur, pulling her dress up and over her head, leaving her standing before me in just her lingerie.

My fingers itch to trace every line and curve of her body. To explore every inch of her until I know her better than I know myself. But instead I continue undressing her, carefully sliding the cream mesh thong down her legs.

"Step out," I instruct softly, and she obeys without hesitation, kicking the thong aside. All that remains now is her smooth silk satin bra.

The cream material barely contains the swell of her breasts.

"Turn around."

As she does, I reach for the clasp, my fingers brushing against the warm skin of her back. I can't help but let out a silent groan at the contact, my body aching with need for her.

"Julian, I don't . . ." she says, but I cut her off.

"Trust me," is all I say as I unhook her bra and let it fall to the floor, leaving her completely exposed to my ravenous gaze.

She turns around and my eyes roam her body hungrily, taking in her rosy nipples peaking at the cool temperature, the curve of her hips, the soft triangle of hair between her thighs. She is flawless, an ethereal goddess standing before me in all her naked glory.

"Into the tub," I instruct gently, guiding her toward the steaming water. As I help her step in I let warm water cascade over her hair and her shoulders, careful to avoid her eyes.

She looks up at me then, her eyes searching mine for reassurance.

"Shouldn't you be the one taking a bath?" she asks softly, gesturing toward my body. "You're the one who's covered in the most blood."

"Shh."

Silently, I squeeze some soap onto the sponge and lather her body, starting with her feet.

She shivers as I take each foot in turn, massaging and cleaning them with tender precision.

My touch is gentle as I move to her legs, working my way up to her inner thighs, which elicits a soft moan from her lips. God, the sound she makes is like a siren call, beckoning me closer to the edge of control.

"You can't resist its call,
like a siren to a sailor."

Her eyes flutter closed. The stiffness of her muscles gradually fades as she lets me take full care of her body, trusting me to make her feel good. Safe.

As I continue to wash her I mentally trace the cuts and bruises on my own body, using them as a guide for where I need to pay extra attention to hers. I don't want her to have to relive the horrific experience by asking her where she was touched; I want her to relax and forget about everything that happened, if only for a little while.

"Is this okay?" I ask as I move to her breasts, washing them gently but thoroughly.

She nods in response, her eyes fluttering closed as I move on to the next spot.

I'm finishing rinsing her body when she whispers my name. Her voice is filled with a tenderness that threatens to break me.

"Thank you."

"You don't have to thank me, golden one." I step back and give her some space.

Something moves behind her eyes at hearing the nickname. That tenderness falters.

I grab the towel and envelop her in it.

I know I've done what I set out to do—taken care of her and helped her feel safe, like I failed to do at the Den —but it doesn't make it any easier to walk away from her. Especially when all I want is to be close to her; to hold her in my arms and lose myself in her warmth.

But I can't. Not yet.

I gently dry every crevice of her body before my fingers find their way to her wet locks of hair. The soft, damp strands feel like silk between my fingers, and I can't help but marvel at how vibrant and beautiful they are.

"Your hair," I hear myself murmur as I run my fingers through it again.

Aurelia chuckles softly, catching me off-guard with the unexpected sound. "You've seen it before, you know."

"Never like this," I admit, letting my fingers linger in her curls for just a moment longer.

Memories of all the times I'd watch her hair bounce whenever she burst into laughter, or the way it curled perfectly around my fingers when I played with it while she slept, flood my mind.

"It's been years since I've seen it so . . . alive."

She looks at me then, her eyes shining with something I can't quite place.

There's no denying the unspoken words that dance in the air as we stare at one another. This push and pull, it's a dangerous game, and one day it will all come crashing down on us. That's why I pushed her away . . . although now all I want is to pull her in.

"And when you finally touch rock bottom,
there will be gold to cushion your fall."

But not tonight.

Tonight she needs me to be strong for her, to help her forget the horrors of the night and find some semblance of peace.

"Come on," I say, leading her over to the large mirror on the wall.

She looks puzzled as I reach into the cabinet and pull out a hair diffuser, and I grin as I plug it in and gesture for her to sit down.

"Let me handle this."

"Wait—you have a hair diffuser? And you actually know how to use it?" Aurelia raises a brow in disbelief. "Is that curling gel?" Her eyes round as she spots the pink bottle on the counter.

"Of course," I reply with a smirk. "I'm full of surprises."

"Clearly," she mutters, still looking somewhat baffled by the situation. "But really, I can do it. You don't have to—"

"No," I insist, cutting her off. "I want to. I want you to keep your natural curls and not straighten them." I meet her gaze in the mirror, my eyes softening as I add, "They're beautiful."

Just like you.

Aurelia hesitates for a moment but ultimately relents, allowing me to take control of the situation and dry her hair. She sits quietly, watching me in the mirror as I carefully manipulate the diffuser, coaxing her curls into a voluminous, fiery crown that seems to defy gravity itself.

My movements are precise, yet it takes me longer than I'd like to admit as I try to grab hold of her hair, making sure to dry every strand.

When I'm finished I step back to admire my handiwork, feeling a strange sense of pride swell within me.

It only took me nine or ten late nights spent watching tutorials to finally master it.

I know she hates her hair from all the meaningless, hurtful comments members of the Inferno Consortium have made. The ladies make their remarks out of jealousy, because of her youth, while their husbands do so out of pure boredom.

Aurelia's stubborn. She'll never style it like this. But I'm relentless, and if she won't do it, then I'll do it for her. I want her to love every inch of herself like I do; I want her to stop hiding behind the version of her they created.

Or maybe, just maybe, I want her to look like she did before I sent everything to shit.

"There," I say, giving her a small smile. "Perfect."

"Thank you." Her voice is barely above a whisper as she reaches up to touch her hair, brushing the soft curls, lost in thought. "It's been so long since I've seen it like this."

"Then wear it like this more often," I tell her, my voice gentle yet firm. "You should never be ashamed of who you are, Aurelia."

She looks at me then, her green eyes shimmering with unshed tears, and for a moment I think she might break down. But she doesn't. Instead she nods, accepting my words as truth even if she doesn't quite believe them herself. Not after all those years of verbal assault she went through because of her mother or her looks.

"Here." I give her one of my shirts. "Put this on and get some rest. You've had a long night."

As she slips my long-sleeve shirt on over her head, I can't help but notice how big it is on her. The hem falls close to her knees, and the sleeves almost completely cover her hands. It's strangely endearing, and I find myself fighting back a smile.

She's mine, I lie to myself. *She looks beautiful as mine.*

"Shut up." She swats at me before crossing her arms over her chest.

"I didn't say anything." The corner of my lips threatens to pull upward, revealing the smile I'm trying to hide.

"You didn't have to." She looks down at herself with a hint of amusement.

"But if I did," I say, my voice low, "I'd say how there's something incredibly sexy about a woman wearing nothing but a man's shirt."

Aurelia blushes at my words, and I allow myself to bask in the view.

"Come on." I guide her toward the bed.

She hesitates for a moment, looking almost nervous at the prospect of sharing a bed with me. I can't blame her, given everything that happened tonight.

"Relax," I tell her. "I promise I won't bite . . . unless you ask me to, of course."

Her cheeks flush pink, and I can't help but fucking love it when she blushes like that. It makes her seem so innocent. When she really isn't.

"Fine," she mutters, still blushing as she climbs into my bed, pulling the covers up around her.

God, she looks absolutely perfect lying there in my shirt, her curls spilling over my pillow.

I have to remind myself that tonight has nothing to

do with satisfying our desires, and everything to do with her.

"Are you coming to bed?" she asks, her voice soft and unsure as she glances back at me.

Fuck.

"Not until you fall asleep." I try to sound casual even though my dick is rock-solid, straining against the confinement of my shorts.

The need to stretch out beside her and feel her body against mine is distressing; the urge to trace her curves with my fingers destructive.

I know if I lie down beside her, the temptation to touch her, taste her, will be too strong to resist. And while I may be many things—a liar, a criminal, a killer—I am not the kind of man who takes advantage of a woman when she's vulnerable.

At least not tonight.

"Okay," she says, still watching me with those big green eyes that seem to see right through me. "Just . . . don't stay up all night because of me, all right?"

I give her a reassuring smile, stepping away from the bed and settling into a nearby chair, where I can keep watch over her as she sleeps.

My eyes never leave her figure as she snuggles down into my bed. She looks at me with mock confusion, knowing full well why I chose to sit here instead of joining her.

"Good night, Julian." She smiles with her eyes closed.

"Good night, golden one," I whisper back.

Seconds pass, and she's fast asleep.

I stay in the corner of the room, my body tense from

the earlier fight and the dreadfulness that came over me the moment I saw the fucker's hands on her.

I keep my eyes on her. Steady. Like I'm scared something or someone could hurt her again.

She looks so peaceful as her chest softly rises and falls. Peaceful, but not at peace. Just like me, she has this entity raging inside of her, eating at her with each passing day.

I stare at her, and I can't help but think of how this silence surrounding us only serves as a false sense of serenity. We aren't normal people, and there's no simple life waiting for us once the sun rises.

We aren't the kids we used to be.

And yet as she sleeps, caressed by the moonlight, she looks just like she did the first time I saw her. Just like that little girl blinded by her surroundings as she giggled to herself, running through the green field, trying to catch up to the blue butterfly that was on her nose seconds ago.

They call her the golden one, the lucky girl who survived the life she was born into. The chosen one. They call her this *in mockery*. Because she's an orphan, gilded by our lifestyle.

But I decided to call her the golden one because in that moment, when I turned toward the erupting giggles, I finally saw a person living. Truly living; truly happy.

A girl with red hair, kissed by the sun's rays.

A girl with red hair, kissed by life.

And when you grow up to be a reaper, you can't help but become obsessed.

Obsessed to the point of killing her.

But within that lies the irony, because if she dies, I lose my purpose to live.

And God, all I ever wished for before her was just that.

To die.

CHAPTER THIRTEEN

JULIAN

T he up and down movement of Aurelia's chest lulls me all night. Not even sleep is as restful as losing myself to the sight of her.

I can't bring myself to leave this chair, to stop watching her sleep so peacefully in my bed. The sight of her lost in the serenity of sleep chains me in place.

But as the morning sun creeps into the room, casting golden rays across her beautiful face, I know I have to get up.

Yet I stay still a second longer.

A second longer to feel the echo of guilt as the idea of Aurelia being involved in DeMarco's death scratches at my insides.

Is it my fault? If I hadn't pushed her away all those years ago, would she still have done it?

With a heavy sigh, I carefully get up. I take a quick shower, washing the paint off my face and the dried blood from my body. Once the water turns cold, I slip out and dry myself off. I take a new pair of sweatpants and walk silently out of the room.

Why did she do it?

Why can't she trust me?

Because she's no fool. Because you took her trust for granted, the voice in the back of my mind whispers.

Padding silently through the hallway, I reach the kitchen. I rub my eyes, which feel heavy as my eyelids drag closed. Like sandpaper, their dryness cuts with each blink.

It must be 5 a.m. Too early for the household to be awake, but right on time with my usual schedule.

That's why, when I round the corner, I'm surprised to find Adrian already there, sipping his coffee and perusing the morning paper. He's already dressed in his usual crisp white shirt and dark blue trousers—a sight for sore eyes this early in the morning.

Now that I think about it, when was the last time I saw him wearing anything but his usual annoyingly formal attire?

He glances up at me with a smirk, clearly taking note of my disheveled appearance—the opposite of his pristine one.

"Rough night?" He raises his brow.

"Something like that."

I pour myself a cup of coffee, trying to ignore his hawk eyes.

"Speaking of last night, I've got some new information on DeMarco's killer," Adrian says, setting down his newspaper.

I try to keep my expression neutral as I lean against

the counter sipping my coffee. I hope against hope he hasn't figured out Aurelia's involvement in his death.

"Really? What'd you find?"

"Well." He rests his elbows on the table. "It seems we have a new player in the game. Someone who's been keeping a low profile but has recently made quite the entrance."

No.

"Go on," I urge, my stomach twisting into knots as I brace myself for what he might say next.

"Turns out our mystery man has connections to the criminal underworld. Seems he's been making moves to consolidate power and take out the competition. But here's the interesting part," Adrian continues, pausing for dramatic effect. *Dickhead.* "He doesn't seem to have any connection to the Inferno Consortium."

Wait . . .

Man. He said man.

Momentary relief washes over me, but it's quickly replaced by an even greater sense of dread. What if this guy is involved with Aurelia? Maybe he helped her kill DeMarco. And most importantly, how long will it be before he leads Adrian to her?

"Are you sure?"

"Positive," Adrian replies confidently, finishing off his coffee with a satisfying gulp. "This guy's been on our radar for a while now, but he only recently stepped into the spotlight. I'm convinced he's the one behind DeMarco's murder."

"All right," I say slowly, mind racing as I try to

process this new information. "So what's our next move?"

"We need to find him and take him down." His eyes darken with determination. "No one messes with the Harrow family and gets away with it."

"Do we have anything to go by? A name, maybe?"

Adrian shakes his head. "All we know is that he . . . doesn't exist."

"What the fuck are you talking about?"

"The Consortium is searching for him." Adrian looks me dead in the eye. "Has been for years, and they still haven't caught the man."

"No one is invisible." I take a long sip of my coffee, the liquid burning down my throat. "Did he ever kill anyone before DeMarco?"

"That's the thing. If he ever did, no one knew."

"Until now." I echo his thoughts.

This guy isn't DeMarco's killer. His killer is sleeping cuddled up under my sheets right now. But it won't hurt for Lucian to think he's found him. It'll give me some time to crack Aurelia open before they figure everything out. Plus, this guy deserves some fair play.

After all, karma doesn't exist in this life. It's just a playing card people use to their own advantage.

I'm playing mine on him now.

"Julian?"

Aurelia's voice rings out from my bedroom down the hall, startling both me and Adrian.

"Is that . . . ?" Adrian's eyes widen with disbelief.

"None other," I reply, feigning nonchalance as I lean

against the kitchen counter. I can't help but smirk at the look on Adrian's face. "She stayed over last night."

"Stayed . . . over?" Adrian echoes, his expression a mixture of shock and anger. He studies me for a moment as if trying to determine if I'm telling the truth. "Are you telling me Aurelia spent the night here, with you?"

"Yep," I confirm, taking another sip of my coffee. "We slept together."

My words hang heavy in the air, and I can practically feel Adrian's rage growing by the second. It's not like I'm lying. Although she did all the sleeping while I just stared.

"Julian, don't you dare—" he starts, but I cut him off, knowing exactly where this is going.

"Relax, brother." I wave a dismissive hand. "It's not like it's the first time."

"Stay away from her," he bites out, clenching his fists at his side. "She's not a pawn for you to play with."

Annoyance flickers in my chest, but I ignore it, keeping my expression cool and indifferent. "And since when did you become her personal bodyguard?"

"Since she started acting suspiciously." He narrows his eyes at me. "Did you know she was desperate to go to Victoria's party? I've been keeping tabs on her since then. She's definitely hiding something."

I freeze on the spot.

Fucking hell, can this morning give me a break?

My mind races with thoughts of Aurelia's secret. It's not surprising that Adrian noticed her strange behavior, but hearing him confirm it sends a shiver down my spine. He's always been more observant than most give him credit for.

His gaze doesn't waver from mine, searching for a hint of anything. "There's something going on with her, Julian. She's not the same girl she used to be."

"None of us are the same people we used to be."

"Look, I don't know what game you're playing." His voice is low and intense. "But I won't let you drag her deeper into our world. Not when I don't know what she's hiding."

"Who says I want to drag her into anything?" I retort, anger finally bubbling to the surface. "Maybe I just want her."

"Then you're a bigger fool than I thought," he snaps.

I don't respond, letting his words hang heavy in the air between us.

"Stay away from her, Julian," Adrian repeats, his voice softer now but no less insistent.

As he storms out of the kitchen I bite back a thousand retorts, knowing they won't change anything.

The moment his footsteps finish echoing down the hall, Aurelia appears in the doorway. Her hair is tousled, and her cheeks are flushed.

Her eyes flick toward Adrian's retreating figure before settling on me. She arches a brow in a silent question.

I can tell she overheard our conversation from where she was hiding behind the kitchen door, and I relish in the fact she knows Adrian believes we've been intimate.

"Good morning, beautiful." I ignore the daggers forming behind her eyes. "Sleep well?"

"Slept better," she hums, trying to sound casual as she crosses the room to pour herself a cup of coffee.

I can't help but stare at her as she moves. Her hips sway with a confidence that seems so natural, so innate, it's hard to believe this is the same girl who blushed every time we fought; whose vulnerability shone through when she thought no one was watching.

"Is everything okay with Adrian?" she asks, taking a sip of her coffee and grimacing at the taste.

The sugar jar is right there on her left. I know she sees it. But I guess adding some sugar proves her vulnerability? Fuck knows.

I don't answer her. My thoughts are still caught up in the conversation I just had with my brother. His suspicions about her, his warnings for me to stay away from her—it all feels like a giant weight pressing down on my chest, making it hard to breathe.

He is so close. *Too* damn close.

He'll soon smell the blood staining her hands.

"Julian?" Aurelia's voice breaks through the fog in my mind, pulling me back to the present. "You look . . . I don't know, worried. Did something happen?"

I shake my head, not trusting myself to speak. Not that there's anything to say when she has so much more to reveal first.

"Forget it." I turn away from her and focus on my own cup of coffee, its nauseating smell a stark reminder of how things usually turn out.

How much longer can I keep pretending everything is fine when it so clearly isn't?

With that, she turns her attention to making herself some breakfast.

She moves around the kitchen with practiced ease, opening cabinets and drawers without hesitation. It's obvious she's been in this kitchen many times before, back when she was dating Adrian and would spend the night in his room.

Those were the days I conveniently allowed myself an extra-long lie-in. It was either that or bash Adrian's head on the counter every time she blinked her big eyes up at him.

The thought vanishes as I watch Aurelia toast a bagel and spread cream cheese on it, her every gesture familiar and yet somehow new. There's something both comforting and unsettling about the way she fits so seamlessly into our lives, as though she belongs here more than I do.

But then I remember Adrian's words—his warnings, his suspicions—and I know I can't afford to let my guard down. Not now. Not ever. Because no matter how much I want to believe otherwise, there's a darkness lurking beneath her surface. A secret that threatens to destroy her—along with me.

Because I'll be fucked if I ever let her go *anywhere* I am not.

Aurelia finishes preparing her breakfast, adding some smoked salmon, and as she takes a bite of her bagel I admire the way her eyes sparkle with life. She always has been a beacon of light. Whenever I find myself immersed in my thoughts, she'll be there for me to turn to, brighter than the city lights.

I want to reach out and touch her, to lose myself in her warmth and forget about the darkness threatening to consume us both, but I know I can't. Not when there's so much at stake.

"Julian," she sighs, pivoting on the spot as she looks at me. Her voice breaks the silence between us. It seems she was debating whether to push further or not and decided to just go for it. "What's going on with Adrian? You two seemed tense earlier."

When all I do is gulp down the last remaining dregs of my coffee, she eyes me skeptically. Then she takes another bite of her bagel and presses further.

"Come on, Julian. I know you better than anyone. You're hiding something from me."

I'm hiding something from *her*?

I lose it.

"You have got to be fucking kidding me!" I meet her gaze head-on despite the turmoil raging within me. "I'm not the one who killed a man and is now buried beneath his carcass." The words slither out, vibrating on my last nerve. "Adrian is just concerned about some things. And he has his reasons to be."

"Oh, for God's sake. I didn't kill DeMarco!" she heaves out, body vibrating with the force she puts into playing the part of the misunderstood victim. Then something switches inside of her. She registers what else I've said and asks, "Concerned?" A hint of annoyance creeps into her voice. "What does that even mean?"

"Let's just say, he's been paying closer attention to certain people than you may have realized. And he's starting to put some pieces together."

Aurelia's eyes narrow, and she sets her bagel down on her plate, her appetite seemingly forgotten. "Are you saying he's been spying on me?"

"Maybe."

Aurelia slams her palm on the kitchen counter, her face a mixture of hurt and something else. "I can't believe this! What gives him the right to invade my privacy like that? And why are you defending him?"

"Because he's my brother!" I snap, my own temper flaring in response to her accusation.

And because you. Don't. Trust. Me.

"And because I know he's only doing it to protect our family," I add instead.

"Even if it means treating me like a criminal?" Her eyes blaze with indignation. "I thought we were past all that, Julian. I thought we were . . . closer than that."

It's like a punch to the gut, hearing her voice crack with disappointment. But even as my heart freezes over, I know I can't afford to let my emotions cloud my judgment.

"Sometimes, golden one," I say, struggling to keep my anger steady, "we have to make hard choices for the people we care about."

She thinks I'm still talking about Adrian. If only she knew how deeply I've thrust myself into this shithole she created; how I'm talking about her and not him. But why give her the satisfaction when she keeps lying to me?

"Is that what this is then?" Her expression hardens slightly as she searches my face for answers. "Just another hard choice for you to make?"

I witness the slow change in her gaze. The spark that

was there a minute ago ignites, burning everything softly, leaving only the jagged edge now staring back at me.

"You're running out of time." My voice is low and heavy with the weight of my certainty. "Sooner or later, either Adrian or I will uncover your secret, and when that happens . . ."

I trail off, unable to finish the thought. Because deep down I know there is no good outcome to this situation. No scenario where we all walk away unscathed. We're past that now. The clock has been ticking for far too long.

"Is that a threat?" She stares at me with wild eyes.

"Consider it a warning." My heart pounds in my chest, freezing as I take a step back from the precipice of our shared destruction. "Because I honestly don't know which is worse."

And with that, I grab the half-eaten bagel from her plate and take a bite, the stale taste a stark contrast to the sweetness present last night.

I turn and leave her standing in the kitchen, alone— just how she likes it.

For now.

CHAPTER FOURTEEN
JULIAN

The gym is my sanctuary.

It's the place where I can release all the anger and frustration building up inside of me day after day. Hour after hour.

My shadow dances in the afternoon sunrays as I pound away at the brown punching bag hanging from the ceiling. My fists pulse in time with each thud against the heavy leather, while sweat drips down my face, soaking into the waistband of my sweatpants.

All the rage I feel toward Aurelia and her stubborn refusal to tell me why she killed DeMarco oozes out of me.

Slowly. One punch after the other.

"Fuck," I mutter under my breath, gritting my teeth.

She's just as stubborn as I am, and it drives me insane.

I know what she's hiding . . . but goddamn it, I just want her to trust me enough to tell me herself. I'm not asking too much.

I'm five punches into my set when I hear the irritating voice of my best friend.

"Oi." Emeric saunters in, beaming his thanks for whoever was latched around his dick this morning. "You're really giving that bag a beating, mate. What's got you so riled up?"

Panting, I stop my assault on the punching bag and grab the towel I left on the floor, dabbing at the beads of sweat trailing down my neck.

Sometimes I forget how irritatingly perceptive this asshole can be. He's always able to guess when something is upsetting me. I take it that's what makes a best friend, but even if we weren't friends, I know he'd be able to read me like a book. We're each other's missing piece.

That sounds like a cliché, but I don't give a fuck. This guy is my right-hand man. We've been friends since we were in diapers.

Emeric's family moved here from Manchester, England, seeking a new life as members of the Inferno Consortium. His father wanted to expand his wine business, Grimward Manor Vineyards, in ways that couldn't be achieved without getting his hands dirty.

But I have my mother to thank for our friendship, because it's thanks to her and Lady Grimward that I got to meet this shithead. Emeric isn't just my best friend; he's closer than blood could ever make us.

He knows about the way Lucian treats my mother—treats *me*. He's been by my side through everything, the closest thing I have to a brother outside of Adrian.

He is family. More so than my actual family.

"Adrian and Aurelia this morning." I throw the towel

back to the floor and go for the water bottle instead. "They are driving me insane."

"Ah yes, the lovely Aurelia." He leans against the wall, and a devilish glint appears in his eyes as he asks, "How's your little game with her going? Still trying to break down her walls?"

"Did some damage here and there." I smirk at him even though the muscles in my neck strain at hearing her name. I have a lot to do this morning, with my father breathing his orders down my neck, yet I'll need to throw some punches for a few more hours to ease my nerves.

I clench my fingers around my bottle and spray some water over my face, combing my hair back with my fingers. "How are things going with Eleanora? You should have her teach Aurelia some of her tricks."

Emeric's face darkens slightly at my words. I swear I love the guy deep down.

"Don't worry about me, mate," he says dismissively before averting the conversation from my little comment, knowing damn well it would be useless to go at it. "I'm just enjoying our time together for however long it lasts."

I narrow my eyes at him. "Come on, Emeric," I drawl, enjoying the way his cheeks redden, jaw clenching. "Everyone can see you're smitten with her, *mate*."

"Really, Julian?" He scoffs. Emeric hates it when I talk back in British. He thinks I do it to mess with him. He's right. "We're fuck buddies, nothing more."

Ah, come on.

"Really?" is all I say, not quite believing him. "Anyone with two eyes can see the tension brewing between you two." I throw the bottle at his chest, and he catches it, a chuckle reverberating around the gym.

Emeric hesitates—a rare occurrence for someone as talkative as him. He looks around the room, anywhere but at me, before silently admitting, "It doesn't matter . . ." He presses his lips together, contemplating his next words. No—more like digging them deep within him before pushing them out. "Even if there was . . . even if there was more to this,"—he looks me dead in the eye—"it wouldn't change anything."

I stay quiet, my brow furrowing as I wait for him to continue. I know if I push him for answers, it'll only take him longer to tell me.

"Her parents have arranged for her to marry some Italian prick next year, so whatever this is between us, it'll be over soon enough."

"What? Eleanora's getting married? To who?"

"Some rich family from Rome. Can't remember his name, but it's all been settled." His gaze flicks to the side, and I can tell this is bothering him more than he wants to admit.

"Fuck . . ." I mutter.

Eleanora and Emeric's "love story" has been ongoing for years. They may like this little arrangement they have going on, but I know it's cutting at him.

The thought that things might be ending stings even the strongest of people. No one likes change. Especially change that is permanent.

I'm not too close to Eleanora, but I still feel somewhat sorry for her too. She deserves better than a loveless marriage built on business connections.

Everyone does.

"Anyway." Emeric clears his throat, changing the subject once again. "I found something that night at Victoria's cabin that might interest you."

My curiosity piqued, I raise a brow. "What was it?"

He hands me a worn out piece of paper. "This."

I flip the paper between my fingers. It looks like it's been torn from somewhere. A book, maybe? No. It's handwritten. Perhaps a diary?

"Where did you say you found this?"

"It fell from Aurelia's hand when we entered the library," he says, a smile creeping out.

I flick my eyes from the piece of paper to him and back. "What the fuck am I supposed to do with this? It's old and"—I wrinkle my nose—"smells like death mixed with sex."

"Would you just bloody read it, mate?" he snaps, pushing the hand holding the paper closer to my face.

I do as he says and scan the crumpled paper. With the smudged ink, it takes me longer to decipher what the messy handwriting says, but as I read on, I feel this growing sense of disgust and confusion in the pit of my stomach.

"*Master says I must be more obedient*," the writing says. "*He tells me I am not allowed to disobey him again, or else I will be punished. I don't know what I did wrong, but I promise. I promise to be better. For him.*"

"Who the fuck wrote this?" I lift my eyes to meet Emeric's expectant gaze. The smug expression he had before is now long gone, replaced by something far more serious.

"Keep reading." Nodding his chin toward the paper, he urges me to continue.

Even if I don't want to, I return my attention to the disturbing words as my stomach turns in on itself.

"Master says I cannot speak to anyone unless spoken to first. He tells me I am too opinionated and that I need to learn my place."

"Master says he will teach me where I belong."

"Jesus Christ," I breathe, looking up at Emeric again. "What the hell is this?"

"Like I said, Aurelia dropped it when you practically dragged her out of the library like a caveman claiming his prize."

My grip tightens on the paper, crumpling it even more. I stare at him. "This is fucked-up, Emeric."

Why was Aurelia reading this? Did she write it?

"This isn't all of it." He closes the distance between us, dragging his finger over the page still clutched in my hands, bypassing sentences that send chills down my spine. "I was confused too when I was reading it. But it was here"—he points to a specific line—"that everything made a little more sense."

"Lucian wants me dead."

My chest constricts as the words slam into me at full force, and my mind starts to race with a million questions.

What the hell is going on? Who does Lucian want dead? Is it Aurelia?

Dread creeps up my spine, wrapping itself around my heart. The thought of Lucian putting his filthy hands on her twists my insides; tortures me in the slowest of ways.

If I'm not able to protect her after everything I've done and sacrificed . . .

Fuck.

Without wasting any more time, I march out of the gym. I need to find Aurelia, and this time she'd better give me some answers.

I'm done being—*acting*—patient.

"Not even a kiss goodbye?" Emeric fakes a pout at my retreating form.

I don't even bother to reply.

I'm outside my apartment in seconds. I don't even consider the security guards nodding my way as I pass them. Storming down the corridor, I opt for the stairs, jumping down three at a time to get there faster.

My heart pounds in my chest, matching the frantic rhythm of my breath as it heaves between gritted teeth.

"Lucian wants me dead."

Those four words taunt me, haunting the depths of my mind as I reach her apartment.

I pick the lock of her door and sprint toward the stairs up to her bedroom.

As if the house itself is holding its breath, the whole place is in an eerie silence, anticipating the confrontation to come.

I reach her bedroom and slam the door open. The knob leaves a small dent on her teal wall.

But she isn't here.

The room is empty, devoid of what I'm searching for. My fists clench, impatience twisting into knots inside of me.

I am so tired of having to wait for that stubborn girl

to come clean about DeMarco's death. It's well past time for me to get the words rolling out of that tight little mouth.

How is my dad involved in all this? Why?

Stepping back into the hallway, I strain my ears for any sound that might give away where she is. Not that this place isn't too big for me to just barge into every room.

As if on cue a faint humming reaches my ears. I turn my head to the left, my gaze falling to the bathroom on the far side of the hallway. The only bathroom in this house. My pulse quickens. As if I'm walking in slow-motion, with each step closer to her my anticipation worsens, going feral for me to be faster.

The door is slightly ajar, and I silently peer through the gap.

There she is.

I lose sense of my anger, robbed to the bones of it.

Aurelia is standing in front of a full mirror, steam swirling around her figure. Her bare skin glistens, while the other half of her is wrapped in a towel. A towel I so want to hook my fingers around and throw to the ground.

I trail my gaze over the same curves that haunt my dreams. The towel leaves little to the imagination. It's just a tease. A little disturbance.

Her lips part slightly as she hums softly, following the tune of the song playing through her phone. The sound makes my dick twitch, but the images that rush behind my eyes next are what undo me.

"Please," she moans in my ear, tongue darting out to flick my earlobe.

Her thighs squeeze my waist, a small roll of her hips as she grinds over my pants. The black skirt she's wearing rides up as my hands roam the length of her thighs, up to her hips.

"Aurelia . . . I can't—" I groan as her fingers thread through the hair at the back of my neck, pulling back so hard I see the darkness in her eyes.

My fingers squeeze lower on her ass, and I bite at her skin to give back the same pain.

But she likes it.

Her eyes narrow just a little. Just enough.

Her tongue peeks out from her pink lips, and she gives one last roll of her hips. "Please." Lips pulling up in a smirk at my hiss, her hands fall down my chest, hook around the hem of my pants, and dip inside. "I want to feel you."

But her hand isn't reaching for my dick right now. No—it's going for a flat iron instead. And just as fast, the anger from before storms back in at full force.

She is defiant to the very end.

My teeth grind together as I watch her straighten a strand. She knows how much I love those curls, and yet here she is, erasing a part of herself I adore. But this isn't the only thing that boils my blood. It's the realization that even when she's alone she finds the need to hide behind a mask.

Cautious, I push the door open just enough that I can slip through without her noticing me. She's standing in front of the full-length mirror on the right side of the bathroom, meaning I'm out of her line of sight.

I creep further in, my eyes frozen on her every movement. She lets the long strand fall and goes to straighten another one.

She seems so at ease, unaware of the havoc I'm about to unleash.

I take one last step. I'm right behind her. Her perfume tugs at my dick, but I ignore the surging feeling that overtakes my body.

I inhale her addictive scent one more time. Then I let my prey know she's not alone.

CHAPTER FIFTEEN

AURELIA

I let the straightened strand of hair fall from my fingers as I move on to the next one. Drops of water from the steam roll down the full-length mirror as I peek at my reflection. My cheeks are red from the hot shower I just took, my freckles dancing wild on my shoulders and my chest. They're always more visible whenever I blush or warm up.

I returned from Julian's apartment this morning to find Valentine secretly swinging his hips to some eighties R&B song. He said he was just itching from the new pants he was wearing . . . I don't know why he can't just admit to having a bad sense of rhythm.

Humming along to the notes of the same song now, I try to clear my mind of the news Valentine shared. News that gets me so eager my feet jiggle with pent-up energy.

He informed me Marcus Whitman will be in town for the week, meeting with the Inferno Consortium to discuss some delicate details regarding DeMarco's death.

That old scumbag is proving very useful lately, helping me from the grave.

First Victoria, and now Marcus. If he hadn't taken part in my mother's suicide, I might even be grateful.

If she did *kill herself . . .*

The flat iron glides through my hair, and I begin plotting ways I can take Marcus down. The reminder of how I'll feel once I kill him—that sense of satisfaction—surges through my body.

I bet the rich get off on money just as much as I get off on vengeance.

I'm so lost in thought, looking at the shelves and my reflection, that I don't notice Julian's presence until I feel his breath on my neck.

"That's *two*, golden one."

His growling words send a shiver down my spine, and a sharp bolt of panic makes me drop the flat iron in surprise. The sound of it clattering loudly against the tile floor is all the response he gets.

My body stiffens, and I stare at him through the reflection in the mirror, mind blank as I level my racing heart.

He takes a step closer, tilting his head as he says, "Two times." His voice is low and smooth, like velvet on my skin. "You've disobeyed me twice now. You should be more careful."

I can't help but glare at him through the mirror. *Is he kidding me?*

"Disobeyed you?" I scoff in complete disbelief, tightening the towel around my body. "Spare me the melodrama, Julian. Just tell me what you want."

His vacant blue eyes bore into mine. "Answers, Aurelia."

He steps to my side, his body now on full display for me to look at. He's wearing the same training shoes as Adrian. They've always been kind of freaks with their indoor gym, and . . .

Breath whooshes out of me as I trail my eyes up his bare, glistening chest.

He isn't wearing a shirt, and the sight of his tattoos leaves me hypnotized. Up close I can see that everything etched into his skin looks decayed: two skeletal snakes, a butterfly flying on his left collarbone, petals on the right side of his torso. The snakes even swirl down to the tattoos on his arms.

The only normal-looking one is the Latin sentence "UBI TU, IBI EGO" etched vertically between the petals on the right side of his torso.

I remember Valentine watching a documentary on TV about the Romans, where they mentioned these marriage vows, while Julian and I hung around the living room. We were around nine years old then.

"UBI TU GAIA, IBI EGO GAIUS." *As you are Gaia, I am Gaius.*

But another interpretation is, "Where you are, there I am."

Why does he have the Roman marriage vows, which a husband pronounces on his wedding day, etched into his skin?

At my lack of response he adds, "I'm tired of your games. I want the truth."

Swallowing hard, I rack my brain for some semblance

of a plan to put an end to all this. I know what he wants. But I can't give it to him.

"The truth?" is all I say to buy me some time.

A cold chuckle leaves his lips as he kneels to grab the flat iron from the floor.

Confusion grows within me at every cryptic move Julian makes. He surveys the flat iron in his hand as my eyes remain locked on his through the mirror, which is slowly drying from the steam.

"What a shame," he murmurs next. His tone of voice sets my teeth on edge. But it isn't until he snaps the flat iron in half that my breath hitches.

"What the fuck, Julian! Are you crazy? What is wrong with you?" My gaze moves from the broken half dangling by the wires, still intact, to the manic reflection in his eyes.

He circles around me as he brushes the outer side of the flat iron over my exposed skin. "Why are you straightening your hair, Aurelia?"

He doesn't answer my question; instead asks me one in return. As if this is his game and he makes the rules.

There's something chilling in the way he uses my name. I think I prefer it more when he calls me by that denigrating nickname.

My eyes roll of their own accord. "Is that what this is about? Really, Julian?" I huff.

When all he does is just stare at me expectantly, I relent and add, "I like it straight, okay?"

As the words leave my mouth, memories from my childhood resurface at the forefront of my mind. The way those entitled kids I grew up with would always find a way to make me feel like the odd one out, the orphan girl with no family name or fortune to call her own. And when that became last season's mockery, they picked on my curly red hair.

I remember those endless jokes. How their voices always dripped with cruel taunts. How all they did was point and laugh.

The humiliation was unbearable.

Valentine bought me a flat iron as a gift two days before my first day of high school. As soon as he did, I learned how to straighten my hair, all too eager to embrace the change.

With time it grew on me, and I came to love the sleek, straightened look. It made me feel powerful, like a soldier wearing armor: it didn't make me look weak. It made me look ready for war.

"Happy now?" My voice is pinched with irony, irritation seeping into my voice.

A sardonic smile twists his lips. "Very. It's just a pity you feel the need to hide who you really are."

"Who I am is none of your damn business," I snap as I follow his fruitless teasing.

He moves the flat iron from my back to my arms, then across my chest, making a scene of slowing down when it brushes over the swell of my breasts.

When he's behind me again, his gaze lingering on mine, he counters, "Maybe it should be." The hand holding the flat iron drops to his side, seemingly forgotten. "Because right now, I'm the only person standing between you and the consequences of your actions."

Anger flares within me. "Is that supposed to be a threat?"

We stare at each other for a beat, the tension in the room palpable, with neither of us willing to back down.

Then the sensation of the flat iron slipping beneath my towel breaks the moment. Bursts it as it edges closer to the sensitive flesh between my thighs.

I'm caught off-guard.

He's still watching me through the mirror as a soft moan escapes my lips. The flat iron flickers over my clit, the sensation stopping me *dead*. Not alive. Fucking dead.

"What are you doing?" I pant, unable to control my breathing as I lose it with each tantalizing touch.

He continues to tease me, circling around my clit. "Consider this a punishment."

I'm delirious. I must be, because I laugh at his words. Then I choke back the sound as the flat iron grazes my clit. I bite my lower lip.

"This doesn't really feel like a punishment." Desire builds inside of me, but I try to suppress it.

It's useless.

I tilt my head back just a little as I run my eyes hungrily over Julian's body.

His dark hair is combed back. One strand falls over his ghostly eyes. Veins protrude from his forearm, mingling with the snake tattoo, as his hand moves beneath the towel.

And this raw need to run my nails down his toned chest invades my mind. I want to hear him hiss with pleasure. I want his hands on me instead of the metal circling my clit.

My focus shifts the moment heat appears between my legs. But this isn't caused by my arousal. This is something else. This is—

My eyes dart to the plug still connected to the wall. All the feelings and sensations stemming from him, fogging my reasoning, vanish. Reality settles deep within me. He may have broken it in half, but the thing is still functioning. The inner part of the flat iron is still scorching-hot.

Panic surges through me as I try to take a step away from him. But Julian anticipates my move, snaking his arm around my waist and pulling me back tight against his chest, leaving me feeling trapped, defeated, and *wet* for him.

"Going somewhere?" His lips graze the shell of my ear. "Master says you must be more obedient."

I lose sense of time.

I swear I'm choking on air.

"Good little gift." Julian whispers venom.

My mother's words jab at my insides. *"I thought he loved me. That I was his little gift. That's what he called me when I pleasured him right."*

"Now, answer me, who is Master? Why were you holding onto that page at Victoria's cabin? Why did you kill DeMarco?"

How did he get the page?

How much does he already know?

I force myself to remember what's written on that specific page, but the panic eating at me is too strong.

His grip around my waist tightens. "The run's over. No more lies." The heat from the flat iron grows more intense where it lingers between my thighs. "Tell me, golden one." His voice is soft. A creepy kind of soft. "Tell me everything."

I'm losing time. How much longer can I evade his questions?

I take a deep breath, the flat iron an impending threat. In no time I'll feel its seething burn. But I'm not scared. I'll welcome the pain. I'll do anything to prevent him from finding out the truth.

His eyes move to the rise of my chest. Then he tsks.

And my body grows cold.

His breath is hot against my ear. "Such a paradox." The hand between my thigh twitches. "A killer who cares about other people's suffering."

Something pokes at my back.

His dick is as hard as stone. *Fucking psycho.*

You are dripping-wet, the voice in my head says. *He could bend you down and slide his dick right in*, it slurs. *You aren't so different from him.*

I nearly lose the strength in my legs.

He must know, because he tightens his arm, preventing me from falling to my knees in front of him. I know the sadistic bastard would love nothing more.

As if reading my thoughts he says, "We're both fucked in the head. We have the same affliction. We're hooked on pain."

I squeeze my eyes closed, bracing myself for the inevitable burn.

But instead all I smell is burning skin. No pain.

I snap my eyes open and gasp at what I see.

Julian is pressing the heated flat iron against his

lower abdomen. His expression is blank through it all, gaze locked with mine as if daring *me* to react to his pain.

I twist to my right, hand reaching for the burning iron. "Julian, stop!"

I'm inches away from reaching it when he pulls it away. A faint hiss, more delight than pain, is all that comes out of him.

"Who is Master? Why were you holding onto that page at Victoria's cabin? Why did you kill DeMarco?" he asks me again, his tone unwavering, unaffected by the red patch of raw skin on his stomach.

Wh-what just happened?

I stare at him, wide-eyed.

Words evade me.

Did he just . . .? Why would he do that to himself?

One second.

Two.

At my lack of an answer, he lowers the flat iron to sear the flesh of his right pec. The skin sizzles as my stomach flips. *And his lips twitch.* In sick pleasure.

That's when it hits me. The realization he is so far gone. So out of his awful mind.

He deserves it, and yet . . . I can't stand to see him hurt himself. Even if he enjoys it. Because there must be something far worse going on with him if he does.

It's my weakness. *He* is my weakness.

"Please stop!" I scream, the force scratching at my throat, eyes welling up.

At the sound of my voice he hesitates, then he pulls the flat iron away. Even with the rawness of my expression he watches me expectantly. Waiting.

I know this is it. Even if I make it out of here without spilling my secret to him, he'll find another opportunity to do far worse.

Maybe this is the day I die.

It would feel better to die than to live with the failure of disgracing my mother's memory.

His hand moves higher, until it's just a breath away from his neck.

"Okay!" I grab his arm. "I'll talk."

"Good fucking girl." His voice is hoarse.

I clutch his arm around my waist. "Let me just—" I look at the marked patches of skin. "Please."

Something flashes behind his eyes at the word. The plea.

He takes a step back and gives me space to reach the bathroom cabinet under the sink. Kneeling, I gather everything I might need to disinfect and treat his burns. When I turn back to him I guide him to the countertop, and when he doesn't sit on top of it I raise an eyebrow.

He flicks his eyes all over my face and then hikes himself up, allowing me to tend to his self-inflicted injuries.

I gently clean and dress each burn, my hands shaking slightly with the pent-up anger I feel at his stupidity— and the fear he might be more hurt than he's making out.

All I can feel is this buzz in my mind. My mouth moves, answering all his questions, pouring my heart out for him. But I don't hear myself speak. I'm caged in someplace else, hiding in wait for him to act on my words.

"I . . . There's a lot you don't know. It's about my mom . . ."

I tell him about my mother's suicide, her diary, and every monster mentioned in it. I tell him how Valentine is the only other person who knows what I've been up to. How he's been helping me with this quest for vengeance. Then I tell him about the mysterious guy at Victoria's party and the missing pages of the diary.

And about Lucian.

How I'm not sure anymore that what killed my mom was suicide. That maybe his father killed her once he was done with her. That maybe once he found out his pet had gotten pregnant by one of his friends he decided to move on to someone younger. Untainted. Pure.

I don't tell him how one of those friends I'm killing off could be my father. Or how the thought leaves a sour aftertaste.

My hands are shaking once I finish tending to his skin. The truth lingers between us, heavy and tangible enough to be sliced by our silence.

I just shared the darkest corners of my soul.

There's no turning back now.

"Are you going to kill Lucian?" is all he says.

Our eyes lock onto one another's, the intensity setting my heart racing.

There's no point denying it now.

I nod, swallowing hard.

A wicked grin slowly spreads across his face. "Torture the bastard first. Play with him. That sack of balls hates it."

CHAPTER SIXTEEN

AURELIA

I button up my *Maje* knitted black minidress, adjusting the material clinging to my body.

White details adorn the dress, one long strip in the middle accompanying the buttons, and four strips where the faux pockets are located—two on the chest and two on the hips. The hemline falls dangerously close to the thigh, leaving a hint of skin, but with the way the neckline wraps up and over the collarbone, this is a perfectly classy dress for the occasion.

Tonight, death is within my grasp, and I'll be playing it like strings, making Marcus Whitman dance to his demise. I can hardly contain my excitement. My heart races eagerly, my fingers shaking slightly as I secure the last button of the dress.

Inhaling a steady breath through my nose, I try to regain control.

Tonight is nothing out of the ordinary. It's just another night spent as a killer.

A killer, the voice inside my head haunts. *Tonight you'll have more blood dripping from your hands.*

"God, you're unbelievably sexy when you're preparing for murder."

Julian's voice drops a note as it drifts to me from the bed, where he's lying with one leg bent at the knee, fingers laced behind his head as he watches me intently. Not a care in the world, just my body as his sole focus. Not what I'm about to do tonight.

Maybe being a part of the Inferno Consortium from a young age shaped his perception, making murder seem like an inevitable occurrence in life.

I feel my neck up to my cheeks heating. I'm blushing undeniably at his words, the red in perfect contrast to my pale complexion.

I hate how easily he can affect me. With just a few sweet words he gets my body responding to him.

"Wish I could join you tonight. Nothing like a good kill to get the blood pumping, right?" he adds, a lopsided smile stretching his lips.

I try to ignore the piercing heat on my skin, reminding me—no, reminding *him*—of how pliable I am at his meager compliments.

"Focus. You have your own business to take care of." I twist and turn, checking to make sure the dress is ready to be worn outside.

Am I telling him to focus, or myself?

"True, but it doesn't mean I can't appreciate the view."

My gaze flicks to his through the mirror, and I catch his eyes roaming the length of me. Slowly. Torturously.

Shaking off the effects, I slip on my shiny black pumps from *Amina Mauddi*. They're Eleanora's. I wore them once and then *forgot* to give them back . . . But all things considered, that's what best friends are for, right?

Four days have passed since our bathroom encounter. I expected Julian to go running to his father, or better yet, to kill me with his bare hands. Instead he's been the most helpful.

He arranged tonight's *event*. Being my eyes and ears, he managed to find out where Marcus was having dinner. The guy's a busy man, and with only a week for me to do what I need to do, it's been hard to find a free slot in his agenda.

8 p.m. sharp. Table reserved for two at Sulawesi Spice down in Pioneer Square.

He's going there with some colleagues. And all I have to do is kill him.

Sounds laughably simple, if you take away the sixty reserved tables and the staff. Oh, and his bodyguards, of course.

Arranging my hair, I style it in a half-updo, leaving two pieces to frame the light makeup around my eyes. I'm smoothing down some rebellious strands with gel when I hear the mattress dip.

Standing from the bed, Julian joins me by the mirror. "Put this on," he murmurs.

Our eyes meet in the reflection. Before his usual cocky grin can stretch those soft lips, something vulnerable flashes behind his cold eyes. But just as quickly as it appears, it's gone.

"It's perfect for Sulawesi Spice. Trust me, you'll have

every man's eyes on you . . . including Marcus Whitman's."

He hands me the dress. Our fingers brush together, and I try not to show the surge of emotion that courses through my body at the touch.

My fingers run smoothly over the black bodice of lace, down to the long satin skirt. I peek inside at the tag, and when I read *"Alessandra Rich"* I eye Julian skeptically.

"I gather this wasn't just lying around your room, was it?"

"Are you implying I don't have girls leaving things for me to find?"

I cross my arms. "A whole dress? What, did they leave your room naked?"

"And satisfied," the asshole adds.

I push the dress back at him. "I can't accept this." Turning to face the mirror, I give him my back.

"Aurelia," he murmurs down my neck. "Accept the gift."

"No, thank you." I lift my chin.

"Stefanie will be very hurt when she hears about this," he pushes, knowing exactly what to say.

"Stefanie?" I can't control the way my voice pinches. "You went to her? Why?"

Stefanie is Lady Harrow's private stylist.

A chuckle leaves his lips. "Isn't it obvious?"

He bought me a dress . . .

He bought me a dress.

Why?

"Fine." I sigh, trying my best not to let his attentive stare catch the gratitude spreading into a blush over my cheeks. "But don't think I'm wearing this for your benefit."

He grins. "Of course not."

He doesn't make a show of turning the other way while I change into his dress. I know what thoughts invade his mind while he trails my movements, but it's the subtle change in his gaze that makes me wonder what really lies behind his mask of lust.

Am I just another body to him?

What does he really think about when I'm on his mind?

His childhood best friend? A killer? A body to check off the list?

How different is he from his father? From the Inferno Consortium?

I adjust the straps of the dress as Julian checks his watch. His expression turns stony.

"I need to head out. There's some business I have to take care of with the Inferno Consortium. You're sure Eleanora is joining you tonight?"

Right. Whatever he needs to take care of is too much of a burden for me to know. I spilled my guts to him, but he can't even tell me one thing about tonight.

Classic.

I nod at his question. Eleanora has something to take care of with her family before the dinner, so I'll meet her there.

"How am I supposed to kill Marcus without her noticing?" My fingers automatically land on my lips as I remember the pale pink lip gloss adorning them.

"Don't worry about it," he reassures me as he shoots

off a quick text. "I told Emeric about his 'little toy' being at the restaurant tonight. He'll make sure to keep her busy."

"Did you tell him about me?"

About me killing people.

"No." He puts his phone back in his pocket, blue eyes clashing with mine. "He doesn't need to know."

"Thank you." I give him a small smile, relieved no one knows about me.

Yet.

Julian takes a step closer to me, and just when I thought things couldn't get any weirder, he presses a soft kiss to my forehead, freezing me with the action.

"Knock 'em dead." He grins sheepishly. Then he leaves.

Only he can find humor in the most unusual of situations.

I watch him turn the corner and disappear, unable to suppress the smile tugging at the corner of my lips.

"Have you tried their Rendang before?" Eleanora asks. Her tongue peeks out to lick at her lips as her eyes roam the faux-leather menu. "I heard it's absolutely divine!" Her eyes twinkle with excitement as she peeks up at me.

Soft lights glow from above us, adding a hazy vibe to the biomorphic restaurant. Plants crawl over every wall, and sets of booming flowers sit on each circular wooden table. Red chairs hold the customers as they chatter away, matching the ceiling-height red curtains at the entrance.

The whole restaurant is packed, leaving me with a sense of dread at the thought of having to kill someone in a place so crowded without being noticed. But this is the most upscale Indonesian restaurant in downtown Seattle, so I should have expected some obstacles.

"Can't say I have," I reply, eyes darting around the space to find Marcus Whitman.

He's sitting five tables away from us. From where I'm seated, I can see his side profile as he discusses something with the other three men dressed in suits. His bodyguards are pressed against the wall close by, their eyes like a hawk's, scanning the perimeter.

"Then we should definitely order that!" Eleanora's voice fills the room with her enthusiasm. "Oh, and the Nasi Goreng too! I've been craving it all week."

"Sounds delicious," I murmur.

The aroma from the dishes being served at the tables next to ours digs a hole in my stomach, making it growl with indescribable hunger. My mind may be elsewhere, but those dishes do sound delicious.

Placing the menu down on the table, Eleanora's brows knit, meeting in the middle. "Is everything okay?" Her lips, painted a deep burgundy color, curve at the corners. "You seem a bit . . . distracted."

Her long black hair is braided to the side, daisies and irises pinned here and there, decorating the hairstyle. They're the perfect complement to the lilac *Carolina Herrera* dress with black tulle peeking out from below. Its square neckline showcases the shining pearls around her neck.

Assuring her, I place my hand over hers. "Everything's fine. It's just been a long day, that's all."

Humming, she lifts a brow and inclines her chin toward me. "Did you go shopping without me?"

Confusion pinches my features. Then I remember about the dress I'm wearing. "Of course not! Julian gifted me the dress." I all but whisper the admission.

"He *what*?" Her hand falls to her chest. "My God. The guy knows how it's done," she says, more to herself. "Well, *four thousand dollars* has never looked better on anyone else."

Nearly choking on the cool water I've been sipping on, I try to quash the realization Julian spent so much money on me.

What the hell is going on in that head of his?

The waitress, dressed all in white, jots down our drink order, tells us she'll come back for us to order food in a bit, and leaves us in a comfortable silence I appreciate.

I glance at Marcus every now and then, but Eleanora, blind to my ulterior motive, detests the silence. We've shared each other's company in silence many times before, but she loves to chat, and a date at Sulawesi Spice practically screams for conversation.

"Did you see that new art exhibit at the gallery down the street?" Eleanora's question breaks me out of the spell that is Julian Harrow. "The paintings were so full of color, yet they seemed so . . . so *dead*. I could've spent hours there."

"Really?" I place my menu on top of hers on the table, my attention drifting between her and Marcus. "I haven't had the chance to check it out yet."

"We could go together sometime this week!" The light speckles of honey in her eyes shine at the idea.

I could honestly benefit from some time with her. Time where I'm not planning a murder.

"Sure."

Laughter from one of the other tables filters in, and I flick my gaze back to Marcus. He's laughing at something one of the sullen-looking men said. His relaxed demeanor irks every fiber of my being.

Time stops. Everything but him blurs, and you'd think I was the protagonist of a romcom with the way my heart beats out of my chest. I might as well be—

Madly in love with the thought of killing him.

"Earth to Aurelia!" A snapping of fingers follows Eleanora's words. "Are you with me?"

"Sorry." I force a sheepish grin.

There's movement to my right, and I notice the waitress leaving our table. Eleanora follows my gaze and says, "I took the liberty of ordering for you too."

"Fair enough." I laugh, this time focusing my attention on what my best friend has to say.

Hours pass us by. Our food arrives, and I surprise myself, eating everything presented to me without a second thought. I guess killing doesn't make me squeamish.

I look at my friend. The way her nose wrinkles as she laughs herself away. I wish I could tell her the truth. Everything. But I can't risk putting her in danger. Her life is already messed up as it is. I can't pile more shit on her plate.

Her family just informed her of the man they've arranged for her to marry. A young man or an old man, we have no idea what age he could be. I don't know if she's intentionally keeping the details of her soon-to-be spouse close to her chest or if she seriously has no intention of knowing more about him.

Swirling my wine around the glass, I sneak a peek over her shoulder to where Marcus is now ordering dessert. Time is ticking by. I need to put the plan into action.

Each second is a hammer against my skull. I can feel my blood boiling relentlessly as it flows through me.

"Isn't this place just perfect?" she gushes, patting her lips with the satin napkin. "I could eat here every day!"

Mumbling my response, I make a mental note of my next steps.

"Oh, did you hear what happened to that couple down the street from where I live?" Eleanora starts. "Apparently—"

"Evening, ladies." A soothing voice lands in the middle of our conversation, and I spot Emeric sauntering up to our table wearing a playful smirk reserved just for Eleanora. "Mind if I join you?"

Thank you, Emeric.

"Absolutely—"

"Not!" Eleanora spits out, dark brows looming over her venomous eyes as she glares at Emeric. "This is a girls-only night out. You can find yourself another table. Or better yet, another restaurant."

Seeming unbothered by her, Emeric takes a chair from the table next to ours, giving the old lady dining by herself one of his signature smiles, then sits.

I swear, the lady blushes. Or maybe she's suffering from a severe allergic reaction, because her skin is furiously reddening.

"Are you not listening to me?"

He shrugs at her. "I've been told I have selective hearing."

"Oh, I'm sure you do," she mumbles, taking a generous sip from her glass of Sauvignon. "Why are you here, Emeric?"

He takes his time, glancing around the restaurant before a smile plays on his lips. He looks back at a fuming Eleanora. "Just thought I'd grace you ladies with my charming presence. Plus, I couldn't resist the chance to see the lovely Aurelia."

I try to contain my laughter as Eleanora lets out a derisive snort.

"You aren't welcome here. So leave." She narrows her eyes and pushes her body forward, locking her gaze with his on the other side of the table.

"Ah, come on, love. Don't be like this." He gives her a lopsided smile. "I promise to behave," he whispers.

I watch them as everything outside of themselves seems to fade away. This may be the best chance I'll get to steal away without worrying Eleanora.

Julian was right: Emeric knows how to distract her well.

I slip down the corridor, quickening my steps as their loud voices fade. My breath catches in my throat when I spot the waiter carrying Marcus's dessert. I know it's his, because Julian was kind enough to inform me this is Marcus's favorite restaurant, and he always asks them to make a specific off-the-menu dessert.

I clench the vial in my hand, skillfully opening it as I pass by the waiter. With one step to my left, I bump shoulders with him, careful enough not to make him drop the food, but hard enough to blur the action of me pouring the contents of the vial into the dessert.

"Oh, I am so sorry!" I quickly grab for his arm, forcing eye contact with him as the white powder mixes with the meringue topping.

Three seconds.

That's how long it takes to change the course of a life. That's how long it takes me to set Marcus's demise into motion.

The waiter apologizes too, then he delivers my gift to Marcus on a silver platter. Literally.

I wait in the shadows, watching carefully for him to take a spoonful of his beloved dessert: Key lime pie. *Pathetic.* But before he can, one of his bodyguards steps forward. He leans over and takes a spoonful in his place, his lips sealing the dessert in his mouth as a bullet of panic rises in my throat.

He's testing the food before Marcus eats it. How did I not notice this during the dinner? *He has a food tester.*

I draw in a sharp breath, my stomach churning. This could fuck up the whole plan.

Without moving an inch, I stay waiting, my eyes glued to both of them.

It doesn't take long for the effects to take place. Just

when my feet are starting to cramp in the heels, the sound of silverware clattering reaches me.

Marcus is about to excuse himself from the table when the bodyguard whispers in his ear and bolts out of the restaurant. Not to the bathroom, where Marcus's fast steps are taking him.

Thank God.

The weight of all the unease and anticipation finally lifts. I was so certain they'd both go to the restroom together, but lucky for me, Marcus is a traditional boss: the employee and the employer can't share the same restroom.

Poor man. He's probably running around the street searching for a public restroom right now.

Marcus rushes past me, and I lean closer to the wall, making sure he doesn't see me. But I can see him perfectly—the way his face is a shade paler and how his hand clutches at his lower belly. His steps are clumsier the more he hurries.

When the restroom door closes I follow behind him, making sure no eyes are on me. Slipping through, I lock the door behind us.

He's inside one of the stalls. Grunts fill the otherwise silent room while I lean against the sink and wait.

I stretch my fingers, cracking them at the knuckles.

Spiking the Key lime pie with laxatives was a bit childish, but God, how exhilarating it is to know I've humiliated him. Sometimes death feels like the easy way out. And having him found with shit in his pants? That's priceless. Fitting, really. Especially for dirt like him.

The stall door opens, and the shadow of a tall figure

falls over me. His thick eyebrows wrinkle as he gives me a once-over.

"Can I help you?"

"I think you can." I place a hand on my hip, the action pulling at the corner of his mouth. His eyes sparkle with something close to hunger.

Disgust pushes its way up my stomach. *He thinks I'm willingly flirting with him.*

He couldn't be more wrong.

"Have we met before?" He takes a step closer to me.

Then, as if remembering what he just did, he steals a fast look over his shoulder. Maybe he's checking to see if he left a mess, or perhaps he's just sniffing to decide if I can figure out what he did from the smell.

The answer is yes.

When he turns back to me he scratches his chin. "You seem familiar."

Deciding to play with him a bit, I say, "Maybe I remind you of yourself, Dad."

I laugh at the way his face contorts.

"Or maybe you remember my mother—*Lucian's little gift*?"

His face lights up before crumbling to the pit of the earth.

Oh, he remembers her well.

I let a wide smile curve across my face. "You never thought you'd see her again, did you?"

Realization creeps into his expression.

"Were you relieved to learn she killed herself? Why was that? Was she not good enough for your sick games?" I shake my head. "It doesn't matter. Because now I'm here in her place, ready to make you pay for all the suffering you caused her." I pull out the gun, with the silencer in place. "Lost for words? Let me help you with that."

I don't even attempt to aim. Instead I squeeze the trigger. The bullet passes through his left knee. And just like I promised, the bastard heaves out a pained scream.

"That's better, don't you think, Marcus?"

The sound of his body collapsing to the floor follows next, hands stained red as he clutches his now shattered knee.

As the pain courses through him, every indent of his face contorts, stretching toward the ground. He turns around, putting all his weight onto his good knee as he tries to crawl toward the bathroom door, leaving a trail of blood behind him.

Excitement surges, and my lips twitch as I step forward to kick him in the stomach, putting a stop to his pathetic attempt.

He looks up at me with mercy shining in his bulging eyes. But I have none to give, just like he had no mercy for my mother when she was alive.

"Are the things you did to my mom flashing back to you, huh?" I shout at him as rage overcomes me, and I shoot him in his right shoulder. "All those disgusting, degrading things you made her do—did to her!"

This time nothing comes out of his mouth, only short gasps for air.

The sight's a sweet caress to my tortured soul.

His sweating hand struggles as it pats his pants pocket, trying to get something out of it. The object gleams in his hand, and in one swift movement I kick the phone from his grip.

"Don't even think about it," I say through clenched teeth, my patience slowly evaporating.

"G-go to h-hell," he hisses, using all his remaining energy to spit those three words at me through gritted teeth.

I beam down at him. "After you."

And I shoot him in the center of the forehead.

I watch his unmoving body for three seconds—that's how long it takes to change the course of a life—before the smell of feces hits my nostrils. Not the smell of blood but the flood of brown liquid leaking from his trousers.

It's disgusting. Borderline nauseating. But I can't not revel in his humiliation.

I didn't even need him to strip. It's obvious he died covered in his own filth.

Before leaving the bathroom, this time I double-check there's no blood on me. When I'm happy with how I look, I return to Eleanora and Emeric, who are closer to one another than they were before.

Emeric must have worked his magic, because the furious Eleanora that I left behind is nowhere in sight. Or she's playing him. You can never really tell with these two.

I pour myself some wine and swallow it down in one breath.

"Ugh." Eleanora's face scrunches up. Looking around the restaurant, she asks, "What is that awful smell?"

Twirling my finger over the rim of the glass, I mumble in amusement, "Smells like a coup to me."

CHAPTER SEVENTEEN

JULIAN

"Please . . . P-please, I b-beg you . . ." The gasped words stammer out of his mouth, blood dripping down his chin.

I circle the bruised man tied to the chair in the middle of boxing ring at the Den. The stains on the floor suit the place, giving it that extra touch of violence. I should consider telling the cleaning company to leave them there.

I created the Den to escape the violent life Lucian raised me into. Ironic, really. Yet the type of violence that happens here is an art form, a way to release built-up tension. A way for me to retaliate since I can't at home.

Yet right now, as I punch the asshole to death, I can feel the way Lucian was able to taint my sacred place without even having to take a step inside. Should I stop, or should I keep going—use his face the way I can't Lucian's?

The latter should be exciting.

Swollen eyes plead at me. "It wasn't m-me. I s-swear!"

I choke down a laugh. How stupid does he think I am? I saw the surveillance footage of him breaking into Lucian's office at Harrow Enterprise. I fucking saw that disgusting face twist with pleasure as he forced himself onto Marison, Lucian's secretary, before hacking Lucian's computer with a flash drive and stealing important information.

He couldn't resist, could he?

Lucian sent me here to teach him a lesson: Don't steal from the rich. But in truth? I'm only doing this for Marison.

Like they say, greed gets you killed.

"Let's see if that small head of yours understood . . ." I inch closer to his face from behind his chair. With my hand resting heavily on his shoulder, I wait expectantly for him to repeat the words I instructed him to say earlier.

"I-I'm a—I didn't do it!" He cuts himself off, voice booming through the empty place.

Grunting, I straighten up, my jaw clenching while my lips twitch with excitement at what awaits him. "Very well," I drawl before throwing a punch to the side of his temple. The crack of bone vibrates down my spine, awakening something inside of me. "How about now? Are you over your bullshit yet?"

Blood splatters out, raining down on the floor, and I feel like a painter creating his next masterpiece.

The idiot's head snaps back, eyes rolling upward in pain as I stare down at him.

He worked as an intern in the North America sales division. I know the pay wasn't the highest, but it sure was more than he would have gotten working anywhere else. Someone must have put him up to this. There's no way a guy like him would have come up with the plan alone. Then again, he did rape Marison.

He isn't as innocent as he makes himself out to be.

I'm staring at him, head inclined to the side, when the earpiece I'm wearing crackles to life.

Her voice appears next.

"Lost for words? Let me help you with that," I hear her say. My dick stirs, jaw clenching with all the venom she spits at Marcus.

Fuck.

And when I hear the unmistakable sound of gunfire I grunt with pain. A different kind of pain from the one Marcus is undoubtedly experiencing right now.

I planted a bug in the dress I gifted Aurelia tonight. Not because I don't trust her, but because I couldn't deal with the thought of missing out on witnessing this kind of rage coming from her. There is nothing hotter than a woman who doesn't mind getting dirty to achieve what she wants.

There is nothing sexier than feminine rage.

When she told me about her mother I felt a weight fall on me. It was all too familiar. The treatment she went through is nothing uncommon in the Inferno Consortium—something even my own mother can't run away from.

But Aurelia's mom wasn't treated like a human being for even a moment. It was only in those last seconds of her life that she was finally a person. That she finally lived to die.

"Are the things you did to my mom flashing back to you, huh?" Aurelia shouts.

Blood rushes through my body, and I see black.

My hands ball into fists, and I hear the sickening crunch echoing around me as I rain punch after punch down on his face. My rhythm is in sync with her anger—with her hard breathing as she relives what her mother must have felt. Everything, until Aurelia becomes her, letting all her injustice out through the wounds she inflicts on the guilty.

"Julian, please have mercy!" he whimpers through each punch.

But I only hear her instead. "All those disgusting, degrading things you made her do—did to her!"

An image of my mother flashes behind my eyes, her bruised body and defeated soul as she came to my room to read me bedtime stories even after what Lucian did to her. Even while she bled she put on a smile for my eyes only.

Her soft voice as she read each happily ever after. How her eyes shone even behind the makeup concealing the truth.

I hear Aurelia seething at Marcus, and I know she's close to killing him. "Keep going, golden one," I say under my breath even if she can't hear me.

My fist connects with his face. Over and over again.

"No-no. Please . . . I'm sorry. I'm sorry," he softly pleads, so faint I hardly hear it. Panic rushes over his features.

Then a gunshot rings out, and I grin like a madman as I hold the gun to his forehead, my shot matching the one coming from the earpiece.

Like two halves of one soul, both of us are silent as our panting encircles us, each with a dead body in front of us.

I step away from the dead man. His eyes are still open, staring blankly at where I was standing. I drop the gun to the floor and wipe my hands clean on his shirt. Then I send a quick text to Valentine to come clean up this mess.

Heading outside, I put my helmet on and turn my bike back to life. I need to go home and tell Lucian that everything has been taken care of. Then I need to find Aurelia.

There's one perk of buying her the dress . . .

Since I bought it, I get to rip it off.

The corridor is pitch-black except for the artificial fireflies of the city lights at night glowing outside the windows.

I'm heading toward Lucian's office, leaving behind a trail of bloodied footprints on the marble floor. The squish of my leather boots is the only sound as I turn the corner.

I need to be quick. The noises that came from her lips through the earpiece are now forever stuck in the crevices of my brain. I can't unhear them. And the more I wait, the more my dick strains against my jeans.

Much as I like a little pain mixed with pleasure, this is a new level of torture.

I'm done being a patient guy. I have been for ten years. *If you don't count that night.* And I don't count that night.

I stretch my neck, combing a hand through my hair as I push away the memory . . .

The taste of her lips . . . The feel of her curves . . . The smell of her hair . . . The look on her face when she came.

Well, fuck. I didn't even make it a second without falling into the trap.

A warm golden light filters out from under the imposing doors of Lucian's office, but my mind is elsewhere. My lips stretch upward as that defiant little look Aurelia gets crosses my mind.

Ironic, isn't it? The woman who breathes life into me is the same one stealing it away from others.

My hand is a millimeter away from the doorknob, eager to get this over with as quickly as possible, when a deafening shriek reaches my ears.

A scream I recognize all too well.

Bursting through the double doors, I search frantically for her as everything inside of me slowly decays. Whatever warmth was spreading through my chest is now replaced with a cold wash of dread.

"Mom!" I hear myself exclaim. She's standing across the room, with her hair twisted around the fist of a man as his other hand roams every single inch of her.

A frown twists my features, legs trembling with pure rage. "What the fuck are you doing?" I roar, and the asshole leers, his meaty hand groping my mom's breast.

I flinch to the side and crush Lucian with my gaze. He's standing behind his desk, gratification playing in the sinister smile he sports.

"Ah, Julian, I was wondering when you were going to show up." He rounds the desk, taking a step toward me. "I'm just doing what every dutiful husband does: exploiting what belongs to me." He answers my question mockingly, hands outstretched as if to prove his innocence. As if what he's doing is acceptable and I'm the insane one for questioning it.

That only fuels my anger.

"You sick bastard!" My voice is thick. I clench my fists and aim for his smug face. My elbow's rising when my mom's plea halts me.

"Please, Julian . . . don't." Her voice wobbles. Tracks of tears run down her cheeks, and my face contorts as I watch her.

Why are you letting him treat you this way? I ask her through the sadness flitting across my face. *Why aren't you fighting back?*

"See how weak you are, boy?" Lucian's raucous laughter prickles my skin. "Just like your mother."

I keep my stare trained on my mom. Her eyes beg me not to fall for his jeers as a wave of helplessness begins to swallow me whole.

Inhaling a deep breath, I tune myself as far out as I can get. But something must be leaking inside of me tonight, because when Lucian says, "Go ahead—have your fun with her," I lose it.

One fragment after another. An agonizing pain.

Buttons from my mom's blouse fly everywhere as the man rips it open. Her whimper rings in my ears.

I clench my jaw. I try—I *try*—to do nothing like she wants me to.

I lower my gaze, but it's pointless. Lucian grips my chin and forces it up. Forces me to witness my mom being degraded.

No. Lucian isn't the one forcing me to do anything. It's *her*. She forced me to when she begged me not to get involved, to do nothing.

"Look at her, Julian." Lucian's putrid breath slithers down my nape. "This is the price of your weakness."

I feel my bones break, an ache pushing its way through my heart.

I want to push the man away from her. But I know if I do, she'll be the one to suffer for it. Much as it kills me, if I do anything, she'll be the one to die.

"Oh, grow some balls!" His hand falls to my groin, and he squeezes, his fingers tightening their grip on my chin.

Bile rises in my throat—not so much from his touch, but for how worthless it makes me feel to watch my mom being violated. To be nothing but a spectator to his vulgar display of power.

If only the bastard would find his pleasure someplace else. I'd give my body for hers to go untouched.

His laughter fills the room, accompanied by my mother's grunts as she tries to wrench herself free, finally deciding to fight back. But he's too strong for her. She's using all her strength to get his hold off her hair while he unbuttons her pants with ease.

The action surges something within me, and I twist around, slamming my fist into Lucian's face with all my force. The sound of his bones breaking temporarily soothes the wounds he carved into me.

I think all this is over.

How can I be panting? Why do I feel like I've exhausted all my energy with just one punch?

"Julian!" Mom screams at the top of her lungs, the word choking out of her.

Blood is trickling down Lucian's nose when he looks back at me, the smug smile still frozen on his lips.

"That will cost her a lot, son." He nods his chin to the guy, silently ordering him.

I fucked up.

A pit forms in my stomach as the man delivers a brutal punch to my mother's beautiful face. The action mirrors the punch I left on the right side of Lucian's face.

My vision blurs.

She falls to the ground, sobs wrenching from her dry lips, and I feel my body fall alongside her, heavy with the guilt I feel as it pulls on me.

I try to go to her—to comfort her, to hold her—but I can't bring myself to move. I try to speak, but nothing comes out.

All I can do is stare as my whole body shakes. And shakes. And shakes.

I'm sorry, Mom. I'm sorry. I'm sorry.

The words remain trapped, unheard by her—by anyone but me.

Then hands grab my shoulders, and I'm pulled back to my feet. Salt coats my lips.

"Why the fuck are you so soft for her?" Lucian questions. His brow furrows as he studies me. "Is it because you want to fuck her?"

His question shrouds my vision as a hollowness rips apart my insides.

He can't be serious. This can't be happening.

He shakes me hard. "Answer me!"

I blink the mist away from my vision and glance at him. "Fuck. You." I spit each word at his face.

Something seems to flash behind his cold stare before he chuckles like I've just told the funniest joke. He pats my shoulder and says, "You think she's worth anything? Look at her. She's just a vessel for my seed. A plaything for men like us."

"I am *nothing* like you."

He hums, scratching his chin in thought. "You're right. I'm not a pathetic excuse for a man."

His comment falls flat as I hear my mom grunt in protest at her pants being pulled down her legs. The man's grip is unwavering as he gets closer to having his way with her.

I look back at Lucian. "Let her go," I demand. "She's not part of this. It's between you and me."

His blue eyes frost my insides as we stare at one another, two sides of the same coin.

He whistles to the man, whose face is deep on my mother's throat, and signals for him to leave. The grown-ass man whines and pushes her away before leaving the three of us alone in the room.

"Everything is always between you and me." He sits back in his chair. "Next time I come to hear you're spending your time on the golden one instead of doing what I asked of you, I'll have you watch as your mother takes it from the whole Inferno Consortium."

I fist my hands, itching to unleash my wrath upon him, but my mom collapses to the floor now that no one is holding her up, and my full attention falls to her. Her chest rises and falls in hastening movements.

"Clean yourself up," Lucian commands as he looks down his nose at her. "And you." He points a finger at me. "Start acting like the son of the most powerful man in Seattle. Heir, after your brother, to a criminal empire."

I kneel beside her and dry her tears with my finger. Then I cradle her shaking body in my arms and whisper reassuring words in her ear out of Lucian's earshot.

I share some strength with her as she looks at me, color gradually reappearing in her skin. Without hesitation, I pull her up with me and out of the room.

You know what happens to the kids you imprison? They grow up to build cages.

How can I want to live when my mom taught me the only way out is death?

Sometimes I wonder if the golden one will save me or if she's already too late.

CHAPTER EIGHTEEN
AURELIA

I smile at the guards stationed outside the Harrows' penthouse and make my way toward Julian's bedroom.

After leaving the restaurant and saying goodbye to Eleanora and Emeric as they ventured off into the night together, I couldn't shake the need coursing through me to share what I did with Julian.

Having someone besides Valentine to talk to about this hidden side of my life feels exhilarating. I want to see Julian's face when I tell him how I left Marcus lying on the floor in his feces.

Julian and I planned for me to kill Marcus in the bathroom with the silenced gun, and to make it quick: in, shoot, out. But I couldn't make it so easy for Marcus to pay for his sins. I needed more than to just make him bleed.

I needed to humiliate him. The laxative—that part of the plan was my own little touch.

The silent hallways seem to stretch out. I can almost hear my own heartbeat with how quiet it is.

It's not surprising. This place has always been eerie. Elegant, but fucking terrifying. And not because of the monsters residing in it, but because they always seem to be goading me with stories of my mother.

These walls witnessed her undoing.

If only they could speak.

Dusting off invisible lint from my outfit, I'm opening his bedroom door without knocking when a piercing scream tears through the penthouse. My breath gets stuck in my throat, the sudden sound startling me as I whirl around.

I peek back through the hallway, but it's deserted.

No guards running around. Nothing.

Deciding to check it out, I give the bedroom a quick glimpse too, making sure Julian isn't in there. Then, with hesitant steps, I search for the owner of such an icy howl. I could almost make out the scream calling Julian's name, but I'm not so sure. The voice was too distorted as it echoed down the halls.

What if the voice did scream Julian's name? What if he's in danger? What if he needs me?

I quicken my pace, head turning left and right.

Fear threatens to consume me as I speed through the corridor. Images of Julian, hurt, overtake me. As much as I try not to let it, this dreaded feeling takes root inside of me, flooding my mind with worst-case scenarios.

I need to find him now and make sure he's all right.

He can't be hurt . . . he just can't be.

The kitchen is empty, the only light coming from the

city skyline. Appliances are lined up on the counter ready for tomorrow's breakfast, stacks of oranges piled one on top of the other. The room emits serenity, nothing like the scream I just heard.

I inhale a ragged breath.

Maybe I heard wrong. Maybe Julian's fine and isn't home yet. Maybe, just maybe, I was wrong.

Even with the new mantra I keep repeating to myself, I can't shake the terrible feeling something is wrong.

God, why did I think it was best to stop at my apartment and leave the gun there before coming here? The one time I might need it to do good and I don't have it with me.

I'm turning the corner when I catch a faint light coming from the end of the corridor. Like a beacon warning me.

Drawing closer, I feel the air in the atmosphere shift. The closer I get, the heavier the air gets. It's not until the double doors are in front of me that I remember the last time I was in Lucian's office.

Fear. It's so palpable I could choke on it.

What if Julian isn't the one in need of help? What if it's someone else? Someone like my mom . . .

I creep closer. The scream is on repeat in my mind. With each one I hear, the voice distorts, becoming more haunted. More tortured.

I just need to find out what's going on.

The door to Lucian's office is slightly ajar, enough for me to see Julian's fist in the air as it aims for his father's face. Enough for me to see Lady Harrow's body getting touched by a man I've never seen before as he holds her with a hand in her hair, pulling her head toward his chest. Her body arches as she tries not to touch him, but this only causes him to see it as an invitation to touch more. And more.

My throat swells, hand clutching my chest to remind myself to breathe.

Even with everything happening to her, she pleads with Julian to do nothing. To just stand there and let whatever they have in mind happen.

She pleads with him with tears running down her cheeks, the word "help" shining in her eyes.

Why are you letting him treat you this way? Why aren't you fighting back?

"See how weak you are, boy?" Lucian tells him. "Just like your mother."

But Julian isn't weak. He doesn't look it as he forces himself to stay still. Forces himself to follow his mom's wishes and maintain control.

He looks the opposite of weak. Even with the dullness in his eyes and the paleness of his sheer skin, he is not *weak*.

"Go ahead—have your fun with her."

Then the buttons of Lady Harrow's blouse fly all over the place as the man rips it off her. His hands, greedy to explore, roam her now bare skin.

Squeezing, scratching, bruising her.

I can't . . . I can't just stare and do nothing.

My hand falls on the doorknob, twisting it for support, but a weight pulls me back. Before I can make a move, a firm arm wraps around my chest and a hand claps over my mouth.

"If you care about Julian, don't interfere. If our father learns he cares about someone else too, he'll start using you against him," Adrian whispers in my ear.

Tears pool in the gap between my face and his hand, blurring my vision as his words sink in.

"Look at her, Julian. This is the price of your weakness," I hear Lucian say as I struggle to breathe through my nose.

I feel a shiver run up my spine from the way Adrian's body trembles against my back. He clenches his arm around me, holding me closer to him. I know he isn't doing this to console me, but to use me as a shield to protect himself.

"Oh, grow some balls!" Lucian's hand falls over Julian's groin, and he squeezes, feeling him as he drives his point home. Adrian winces behind me—slightly, but enough for me to notice.

A breath hiccups out of me, silenced by Adrian's hand as I feel a pulsing form at my temple.

Stop! Don't fucking touch him! I want to scream. I want to throw myself in there and make him stop.

"Please," I choke, my voice muffled by his hand.

"Trust me, I want to help them as much as you do, but we can't risk making things worse," is all Adrian says. It sounds like he's suppressing his emotions about what's happening before our eyes.

I keep my gaze on Julian, spotting the way his whole demeanor shifts when he twists around and punches his father in the face.

"Julian!" Lady Harrow screams.

Adrian's hold on me tightens, almost to the point of

cutting off my air supply—except I'm already holding my breath. He's clearly startled by Julian's unexpected reaction too, anticipating the consequences.

"That will cost her a lot, son." Lucian turns to him, a crooked, bloodied smile in place.

Shock coils around my heart, and I flinch back into Adrian, suppressing a scream as Lady Harrow gets punched in the face. She falls to the ground, sobs wrenching from her wobbling lips.

I can feel Adrian's muscles stiffening as he watches his mother on the ground, defeated. His breathing is labored, his chest rising and falling in sync with my quickened heartbeat.

Nausea coils its way up. Julian falls to the floor alongside her, and I feel my legs give out too. If not for Adrian holding me, I'd be on my knees with him. I'd be by his side, lending him the strength he needs to fight back. To stop his father once and for all.

To help Lady Harrow.

To kill these psychos, like I'm doing with my mother's demons.

My vision blurs with fresh tears as I watch Julian's body shake.

And shake.

And shake.

His eyes are glued to his mom, mine on the boy I love as he crumbles in despair.

I can almost hear his shredded apologies.

I'm sorry. I'm sorry. I'm sorry.

His silent words reach me. I hear him despite the

deafening chaos of the room. All I want is to go to him, hold him, give him hope.

Then Lucian's hands land on Julian's shoulder and he pulls him back to his feet.

"Why the fuck are you so soft for her?" he asks him, nose scrunching. "Is it because you want to fuck her?"

I fight back the noise that threatens to come out of me. With trembling fingers, I grip Adrian's arm for support instead, feeling his pulse throb under my fingertips.

His hand around my mouth slips a little with all the tears rolling down my cheeks. Or maybe from his weakening resolve to remain in place and not help.

"Answer me!"

I flinch in Julian's place. How can a father say something like that? How can any of this be happening right now?

How is Adrian just standing here witnessing it all without doing something?

"Fuck. You," Julian spits back at him.

A chuckle leaves Lucian's lips, and I blink a few times to make sure I'm seeing correctly. Lady Harrow's pants are being unbuttoned as she thrashes around. The blouse she was wearing before now lies on the floor, wrinkled and forgotten.

I don't think I can do it anymore. I start to shake too, my body begging me to run inside.

"You think she's worth anything? Look at her. She's just a vessel for my seed. A plaything for men like us."

My nails dig into Adrian's arm at his words. Red stains his pristine skin as I dig harder. Something inside of me breaks, shattering as it mixes with pure rage and hopelessness.

"I am *nothing* like you."

I don't hear anything else. Not when I'm fighting to keep myself from crashing.

Something boils in me to the point of utter defeat, as if everything Julian is feeling is getting sucked out of him and stored in me. I'm paralyzed as I watch him seethe at his father for the way he treats his mother, while his mother loses parts of herself she'll never get back.

Is this what being a child is like? Is this what having parents looks like?

Valentine isn't my real dad, but he would punch anyone who dared touch me. Not the other way around.

They gave him life just to play with it. *Why?*

The man pushes Lady Harrow away, making her stumble on her feet and fall to the floor, before heading toward us.

In a second Adrian has me shuffling on my feet to keep up with him as he maneuvers me with his hand clutched around my wrist.

We pass by the framed art on the walls, but all I see are the images swirling in red from the office, Lucian's words taunting in bold letters as they dance around Julian and Lady Harrow's faces.

Blinded by the memory of what happened not even five minutes ago, I don't notice where Adrian is guiding me until I find myself in the middle of one of the three living rooms—the one farthest from Lucian's office.

Shoving Adrian in the chest, I free myself from his grip. "What is wrong with you?" I pant, my hands furiously rubbing at the new set of fresh tears as they roll down, smudging my mascara even further. "How could you just stand there and do nothing?" I shout, voice trembling with suppressed sobs.

His lips are parted, breath held, as he stares at me, seconds away from losing it . . .

And he does. The composed, calculated Adrian finally loses control. His hands ruin his perfectly styled hair as he pulls at the strands. Different emotions flash behind his eyes at me.

He tugs his tie loose and then sinks onto the couch, hanging his head between his shoulders as his leg bounces up and down, up and down.

"You don't understand."

"Then make me understand!"

He lifts his head. I expect there to be anger at the tone I used, but instead he looks wrecked.

"You want to know why I didn't help them?" His voice gets louder, jaw clenching slightly. "Because the only way to protect them is by staying out of it. You think what you saw in there is bad?" He shakes his head. "Imagine what he'd do to you, knowing you mean something to Julian."

"That's it? You're protecting them by doing nothing?" I cross my arms over my chest, needing the smallest sense of comfort.

Adrian stands, circling the perimeter of the room as he says, "It's not that simple. There's so much more going on than what you saw tonight."

My voice finally breaks. "Then tell me!" I cry out.

He glares at me, hating me for pulling the next words out of him.

"Our father has always treated our mother like crap," Adrian begins while he walks up and down the room, glancing my way here and there when he loses control over his words, spilling everything to me. "He never saw her as anything more than a *thing* he could use. He would use her to secure new business ties. He would . . . share her with other men."

He hesitates for a moment, tracking the tears silently falling down my eyes. "Their marriage was arranged, but I don't think my mother ever expected it to be this bad. I even think she loved him once, but that must have lasted a week."

"And Julian?" My voice trembles as I push further.

He swallows hard, his hands clenching. "Julian has always stood up for our mother, ever since he was a little kid, and our father hates him for it. I learned early on that if I wanted to help her, I needed to stay quiet, but Julian could never do that. He would always get between them, even if it meant getting himself hurt. Then, one year, Julian started throwing punches back, and since Lucian couldn't get to Julian with force, he started using our mother in retaliation, hurting her when Julian defied him."

"We need to stop him, Adrian." I take a step toward him, hoping he understands how important it is that we do. "We can't let this continue."

It feels like he's about to agree with me; like something's switched inside of him.

But then darkness pools in his eyes, his brows

meeting in the middle, and he says, "Stay away from Julian. From this family."

A bitter laugh escapes me. I feel disgusted at how easily he can pretend like everything is okay, changing the focus of this conversation onto me.

"It's a little too late for that, don't you think? This is the closest fucked-up thing to a family I have."

"You're going to get yourself killed."

I can't tell if it's a warning or a promise.

"I don't fear death." My expression hardens.

He cracks a smile as he flicks his gaze to the side before steadily saying, "You're going to get *him* killed."

My heart freezes, muscles going taut at the thought of something happening to Julian.

I don't think I could forgive myself.

At my silence Adrian turns to leave, but I call out one last thing, not yet done with the conversation.

"That's where you have it wrong."

He looks at me over his shoulder.

"I can't kill someone who's been slowly dying all this time."

His shoulder muscles twitch. So I thrust the knife deeper.

"You see, Adrian, your brother's been dying every day that you've let this mistreatment go on."

This time I'm the one to leave.

I don't even check to see if I might run into Lucian. All I care about is finding Julian. But when I reach his room and open the door, I don't find him there.

Where are you?

Murmuring reaches my ears. Knowing he must be

nearby, I follow the voices. The closer I get, the more I can make out Julian's voice, soft and soothing.

I reach Lady Harrow's bedroom and see him gently brushing his mother's hair as she sits in front of her vanity.

"Everything is all right now," he reassures her as he untangles the hair from the mess the man made before attempting to braid its short length. "I'm always going to be here for you."

Julian gives her a hand, and she reaches for it, standing up. He helps her take some pills before bed. They exchange more whispered words, then he caresses the top of her head, eyes watchful over her as she drifts off into a deep sleep.

It feels strange seeing him like this.

So gentle. So tender.

The Ripper who cuts throats . . . he looks nothing like the intimidating Julian Harrow everyone fears.

After a while he makes his way back to his room, and I hide in the shadows. I don't want him to see me. I don't know how he'd react if he knew what I saw happen tonight.

He enters his room, and without bothering to take a shower or change his clothes, he collapses onto his bed.

And he stays like that, surrounded by darkness, unmoving on his bed, for hours.

You take care of her, but who takes care of you?

CHAPTER NINETEEN
AURELIA

Click, click.

At the muffled sound my hand freezes in the air. Head tilting toward the entrance door, I hold my breath as I strain my ears.

The door creaks open, and a set of piercing eyes crash with mine.

"Still not over your bad habits?" I raise a brow, clutching the black beaded *Jacquemus* shoulder bag Eleanora gifted me for my twenty-fifth birthday. "You know you can knock, right?"

Julian rests his body sideways against the doorframe, arms crossed over his chest, creasing his black shirt. He's wearing all-black today, and I can't help but feel like it's an omen of how things are going to be from now on after last night.

"Knocking is for strangers."

His voice is a delicate frost to the skin: pleasant on the surface, but painful once it reaches past your layers. I truly listen to it, hearing those icy undertones caused by a night of suffering at the hands he should expect an embrace from.

He's good at masking.

How many times has he hid behind a wall of indifference? How many times did I not see what was really going on inside of him?

"We need to leave." He makes a scene of checking his clock before adding, "Now."

"What? Why?" I frown.

"Doesn't matter. We only have half an—"

"Excuse me!" I all but scoff. "*We* aren't going anywhere. *I* have a date with Eleanora. So if you'll excuse me—"

He stares at me, expressionless, like I never cut him off. ". . . hour to get there, and at this hour, the streets will be jammed. Grab your things, and let's go."

So I play him at his own game.

"If you'll excuse me, she is expecting me." I grab the keys to the apartment and twirl them around my finger.

"Eleanora won't be joining your little tea party tonight," he says casually, closing the space between us until he's towering over me. "She'll be too busy sucking Emeric's dick."

My cheeks burn up at his words, heat spreading to my belly, my whole body betrayed by the desire he just plunged into me with those three little words.

I shouldn't be so affected. Even if the words swirled around his mouth before reaching my ears in the form of velvet.

His finger dances on my skin as he tracks the pink staining my cheeks, my neck, and my chest. "Little fox," he whispers, reading the expansion of my pupils perfectly. Noticing the hitch of my breath.

I raise a brow at the unexpected nickname before my eyes flick down to his lips. So damn close. If I detested myself—and I do—it would take me a second to taste them. To press all my wants and needs onto the tip of his tongue.

I want him to thrust into me with enough force to make me forget all those years he ignored me. I want him to match the scars he left inside of me, on my bare skin. I want to feel every single emotion he ever caused me, even the bad ones, because those will taste sweeter than honey once I remind myself how all the shit he put me through brought me here.

Julian breaks the moment, taking a step away from me. The dark circles under his eyes are the same shade as his hair, holding my gaze captive as images of last night flood my mind.

He notices the way I'm studying him and in a second turns around, heading for the door. I watch his lean yet muscular figure retreat, and all I can think of is the way those muscles strain when he fights.

Now I know why he fights. Now I understand the Den a little more.

A hollowness grows in the pit of my belly—it's been growing there since I saw Lucian's enjoyment reflected in Julian and Lady Harrow's pained eyes.

I hear him sigh as he halts on the threshold. His head tilts back as if he's tired of all this. Then he turns around fully and stalks back toward me.

Without even allowing me time to react, he wraps his

strong arms around my waist, and in one swift motion he throws me over his shoulder.

"Julian!" Blood floods my mind. "Put me down!" I bang my fists on his back, using all my force, hoping to leave a mark or two.

Air swirls around my bare leg, up under my denim skirt, as his hand squeezes me in place at the crease of my ass.

I think I'm flashing the whole body of guards. Valentine is going to kill me for this.

We arrive at the underground garage. Julian opens the door to a black SUV and sets me down. He buckles my seat belt as I shake off the confusion. Then he rounds the car and sits next to me.

"Let's go," he orders the driver, gaze fixed out the window.

"Why aren't we taking your bike?"

The car roars to life.

Without turning to look at me, he says, "Because I won't be able to drive it later tonight when we need to get back."

His words hang in the air between us, their underlying heaviness weighing on my mind as it races back to his dark circles and sour mood. His gaze remains fixed out the window on the city outside, while I can't take mine away from him.

The tension in his shoulders is impossible to miss—the way his fingers twitch, like he's reliving memories even his own muscles haven't had time to forget.

He could mean anything with that cryptic comment, but somehow the only thing I can think of is that tonight he wants to forget about yesterday. And tonight he'll need me to do it.

Needles jab my skin at the thought. I don't know what he has in store, but I'll do anything to help him the way I couldn't yesterday.

Seattle comes to life as the sun sets, the streets overflowing with people eager to get home to their loved ones, while groups of pedestrians mingle around before going to their destination for the night.

It may be Thursday, but the August summer air screams for the night not to go to waste. Though it's chillier here than in other states, when you deal with snowy winters like ours, this is paradise.

Especially for someone like me, who hates the snow.

I've never understood the excitement of celebrating something that conceals everything of its beauty. That kills with its faux fragility. Maybe it's because I was born on November 21, the month snow begins to cover the city. *The month my mother died.*

I hate snow. Nothing good comes from it.

Fifteen minutes pass, and I turn to Julian. "Where are we going again?"

I've been on this side of town a lot with Eleanora, but no specific place comes to mind that Julian would want to take me to.

He seems lost in thought, but at the sound of my voice he snaps out of it. His eyelids are drooping—not from physical tiredness but mental exhaustion.

"We're attending an Inferno Consortium new member event. It's like an open evening. Victoria will be there."

Her name leaves an acrid taste in my mouth. I'd forgotten about her. Between Marcus and last night, my priorities have been completely misplaced. I guess my attendance tonight isn't because Julian needs me to help him forget about his father but because I have a job to complete. Victoria is the one who needs my entertainment. Well, ours.

I glance down at my short light-wash denim skirt, tight black T-shirt, light-wash denim jacket, and black high-heeled boots. Black sunglasses push my hair away from my face. This outfit screams "unsuitable for a night with the Inferno Consortium."

"Julian?"

He hums his response.

"I don't think my outfit is appropriate for where we're going."

He gives me a slow once-over before a smirk greets me. "Don't worry. No one will even notice."

The SUV comes to a sudden halt, and the car behind us honks while Julian exits, leaving me to scramble quickly out behind him. His words circle back and forth.

I'm out of the car when I spot a neon purple sign reading "Lavish Eden" glowing down at me, and I immediately understand what Julian meant by "no one will even notice." This isn't one of those typical posh restaurants.

Julian is the first to walk inside, and I'm just behind him, hyperaware of the guards as they look me up and down. Maybe I underestimated this place . . .

As we push through the curtains, low purple lights blind me.

Oh, I definitely underestimated this place.

Different shades of purple adorn every inch of the club. Long velvet couches and sleek glass tables with matching drapes frame the stage, where poles are fixed to the ceiling, stretching to the floor.

I can almost taste the sensual atmosphere. Feel the expensive furnishings.

On the right is a row of doors. I guess those are the private booths for when someone pays extra for a moment of intimacy.

Lavish Eden is a stunning strip club. The opposite of tacky.

The excessive purple could put anyone off, but there are soft lights casting shadows all over the place, leaving it dark, mysterious and exciting.

This isn't a kid's dream. This is an adult's fantasy.

Eleanora would love this place.

A crowd is already forming at the far end of the room. Everyone is dressed in their own way, all very formal, but not in the dress code typically expected of an Inferno Consortium function.

"Welcome, everyone, to Lavish Eden!"

We all turn toward the voice onstage.

A guy the same age as Adrian, twenty-nine or so, stands with his hands in his black pants. His face is slightly concealed by the shadows dancing across it, but I can see the sharp line of his jaw and the playful smirk stretching his lips.

"Is that the new member?" I murmur to Julian.

He narrows his eyes a little as he tries to see the guy's

face. "Yeah. He arrived last night. We still haven't been introduced."

Last night? He set up a business from afar?

"Impressive."

"Aurelia," Julian breathes. "Don't provoke me."

My lips part as I feel his words caressing the side of my neck. The act leaves a confused sensation in my stomach, and I ache at just the thought.

"Tonight," the new member continues, "we celebrate the opening of our newest location, Lavish Eden. I invite you all to indulge. Let the night be filled with your wildest fantasies!"

The crowd erupts into cheers. Everyone applauds as the curtains drape closed and the night finally begins.

I smile at his words, the cheering of the crowd leaving me excited for Lavish Eden to bring *my* wildest fantasies to life. If I knew what those looked like.

My attention flickers to Julian. *I know who it involves.*

"Let me know when you find Victoria," Julian says, then he leaves me for a conversation with a group of Lucian's friends.

"What? I thought we were doing this together."

It's useless—he's already gone before I can finish my complaining.

I scan the room once more in the hope of finding Victoria. *Is she even here yet?*

Cheering from behind startles me, and I turn to find a pair of guests clinking their glasses together as waitresses and waiters weave their way through the crowd.

Trays overflow with drinks, food, and a variety of drugs to choose from. But what catches my attention is the pink netting covering the staff's faces and their thin purple lingerie. Stripes of bold pink paint their skin, glittering whenever light shines on them.

The mysterious new member of the Inferno Consortium was right: this is a wild fantasy.

Dancers start to spread through the room, each one taking their place on the stage. I'm entranced by the swaying moves of one of them when a soft weight falls on my shoulders, trailing down my arms. Sending shivers down my whole body.

I tilt my face to the right as the dancer's fingers move to my waist. She encircles me, hands leaving scorching trails over my body. Then, as fast as she appeared, she leaves for the stage. A sultry smile is playing on her lips when she looks back at me.

I know I'm heating up. I know my cheeks must be the color of lava, and that my chest is moving up and down too quickly to be defined as normal.

She swirls around the pole, one hand gripping it.

Her body is completely covered in deep purple. She's naked, aside from a barely-there thong. Her hips sway in sync with the music, her eyes never leaving mine as she arches her back against the pole, one leg anchoring her in place as she spins down it.

A giggle erupts from my lips as I admire her talent.

I can feel Julian's eyes on me. I know he saw the way she played with me before she went onstage. I dare a glance at where he's standing—

He arches his brow.

And I smirk.

People are talking to him, but he's too preoccupied with observing me.

"You've made quite the impression," an upbeat voice whispers from behind me.

"Victoria!" I feign surprise. "I didn't know you'd be here."

Her hair is pinned to fall over one of her shoulders, red-stained lips matching the underside of her black heels, and a black suit clings to her curves. On her neck a diamond necklace disappears between her cleavage.

Relief floods through me to know she found me.

This time I don't have a plan. Because this time I can't kill her. I was sent here to entertain her as Lucian wants me to.

But even if I can't kill her, I can still use this opportunity to get closer to her, establishing my usefulness for the next time, when I'll be following my revenge plan instead.

"Of course." She brushes invisible lint off her sleeves. Her fingernails are painted a deep red, long and pointed. They could carve an eyeball out. "It's not every day one gets to attend an event like this. I wouldn't miss it for the world."

A waiter saunters past us, and before they can move to the rest of the people, Victoria plucks two vodka shots from the pale pink tray. Clinking her glass with mine, she gives me a stretched look, waiting to see what kind of partier I am.

I take the shot.

My eyes squeeze shut, a grimace etched onto my features as I swallow the burning liquid down.

I fucking love vodka.

Shaking my face a little, I feel my muscles tighten with excitement before the inevitable moment where life feels as light as a feather.

When I open my eyes again, it's to Victoria holding two new shots in her hands. This time I don't wait for her to offer it. Instead I hold mine up in salute and swallow it down.

"I knew I liked you for a reason." She beams.

We continue to drink and drink, one shot after the other, until one becomes five and I can't feel my legs anymore. But whoever gave two shits about feeling their legs when their mind felt like a cloud? You could spill my life's darkest secrets and I wouldn't even bat an eye.

I'm starting to hate the idea of entertaining Victoria even less.

Sweat glides down my back, hair sticking out in every direction from the countless hours of dancing. Or maybe it was just forty-five minutes. I can't really tell with the tinted windows.

Yet Victoria looks pristine. Only her bloodshot eyes reveal the amount of alcohol she's consumed—and her uncontrollable giggling anytime one of the waiters gets close to an elderly couple. I thought old people lost their sight once they reached a certain age, but that woman sure knows how to appreciate a man with just her eyes.

And the husband *hates* it.

"Another round!" Victoria cheers, and in an instant, two shots appear in her hands.

"Woohoo!" I throw my head back, swallowing down the burning liquid as the room starts to spin.

"Hey." Victoria rests her hand on my shoulder. A playful smirk stretches her lips as she glances toward the dancers. "I dare you to go up there and join them."

A hiccup leaves my lips. Shaking my head, I feel my movements slow down. "No way. I can't dance like they do!"

The dancers sway their hips as the soft lights caress their tempting curves. Their movements are calculated, professional. I'd make a fool out of myself if I attempted to do the same.

Victoria leans her lips on my ear, her voice honeyed as she says, "Come on. Just for a bit."

The words send chills over my heated body with all the alcohol coursing through it. I feel the dainty touch of her fingers as they find the hem of my shirt, and she caresses the bare skin there. My breath hitches, a spark trailing through every drunken part of my body.

"Please?"

There's something different about Victoria right now as she coaxes me gently, almost like her words are hiding something from me. Her vulnerability, maybe? No . . . she may be drunk, and her words are sweeter than they usually are, but her eyes are as sharp as a blade.

She wants to see if I'll loosen up and give in to the night—to the ways of the Inferno Consortium. She's suspicious of me, testing how far I'm willing to take it.

Not only that, but this will deepen our bond.

The closer I can get to her, the closer I'll get to killing her.

My teeth sink into my lower lip, and I glance sideways, locking eyes with Julian. He hasn't stopped looking at me, and the thought of him seeing me strip in a room full of people sends a pulsing ache down to the space between my legs.

"Fine. But only if you count to ten." I give her a serious look. "That's how long I'll be up there. Not a second more."

"Deal!"

I make my way toward the stage on wobbly legs. The dancer steps to the side, giving me a long smirk before gesturing for me to come up and take her place.

I can only hear the click of my heels as I ascend the stairs, heartbeat pulsing wildly as I try to catch the rhythm of the song playing out.

Stumbling a little, I grab the pole for support. My back is to the audience, and when I turn toward them, giggling to myself, I freeze.

Then Victoria decides to whistle at me, calling for everyone's attention.

Swallowing to wet my dry mouth, I focus my attention on one person. The reason I chose to do this in the first place.

His piercing eyes wait patiently, and I sway my hips. Slowly at first, not giving too much too soon. I take my jacket off, making a show of waving it in the air and throwing it at the crowd.

One.

"Yes!" Victoria cheers. "Give us more."

The bass of the song pounds in my ear, the beat calming me down, allowing my body to sway smoothly as I brush my hands from my hips to the ceiling. My neck stretches to the side as I brush my hair away, showing the audience—showing *him*—where I'd like him to sink his teeth.

The cool metal bites at my fingertips. The feeling against my heated skin makes me delirious.

Two.

I step in front of the pole, pressing my back against it like the dancer did. I arch my back and let my head fall as I roll my hips. The hardness of the pole against my ass causes a gasp to part my lips.

Julian tilts his head to the side, his eyes the darkest shade of blue, the dirtiest smirk on his lips.

He knows. The cocky bastard knows I'm thinking of him as I grind on the pole.

Three.

Moving forward with my chin held high, I turn to the side, bend my upper body forward a little, and unbutton my skirt. I push the material down my legs. Slowly. Heavily. Making sure it *pops* as it passes my ass then drops at my feet.

I think the crowd cheers. Their voices filter in one ear and out the other.

The stage lights cast a glow over my body, the pearl-white thong I'm wearing contrasting with the rich room.

Four.

Circling around the pole, I give him a complete view of me. My arm is propped over my head, hand slipping along the pole.

Someone is now standing next to Julian, but I can't see who from here. Whoever it is, they're not important enough to make him take his eyes off me.

The thought makes me smile.

Big, bad Julian Harrow, and *I* have him wrapped around my little finger.

I continue to circle the pole, the click of my heels getting swallowed by the crescendo of the song.

Five.

Hooking my fingers around the hem of my shirt, I throw it over my head and into the crowd.

Victoria catches it and swings it in the air. Then *smells* it.

I shake my head a bit, eyes glassy from the shots of vodka. I think the alcohol is making me see things.

CHAPTER TWENTY

JULIAN

"Five," I count.

I'm giving her ten seconds up there before I put a stop to this little show.

I can't drag my gaze away from her body. The way it sways, catching the neon lights, and how delicate her skin seems—it's all too much for me, enough to make me forget about last night.

The dips of her hips scream at me to dig my fingers in, to squeeze the indents as I pound my dick between those soft legs.

Five more seconds. I can watch, but not all night.

I need her. Like I've never needed anything else in my life.

Her fingers pull at the hem of her shirt, and in no time, white lace greets my eyes, daring for me to get up there and take her for myself.

"Six."

I've been watching her the whole night. I saw the way Victoria cornered her the moment she set foot in this place. She spoke sweet words to her and managed to get her drunk. Then up there.

But I know the reason she's up there isn't because of Victoria or the alcohol coursing through her veins. She's brave enough to stand on a stage half-naked for one simple reason . . .

Aurelia's shirt gets tossed to the crowd and is caught between Victoria's claws. She lets everyone know how euphoric she is at catching it by pressing her nose into the material, inhaling it with such desperation I can see it from where I'm standing.

"Seven," I growl, jaw clenching.

"Are you talking to yourself, mate?" Emeric's annoying voice appears by my side. "You are such a weirdo—ooh!" He notices Aurelia. "Quite the show, huh?"

I barely spare him any attention. Next time I'll refrain from telling him where I'm headed for the night.

He didn't text me much after our arrival, only mentioning how Eleanora flaked on him. Eleanora hasn't texted Aurelia since then—I've watched her the whole time to be sure.

I wonder how Emeric doesn't go insane with how secretive that girl can be.

"Eleanora would love this place." He turns on the spot, admiring the club. "She's always had a thing for the color purple."

"Sure," I mutter, not really listening to what he's saying.

Aurelia is grinding her perky ass on the pole. She arches her body, arms locked around the upper part of the pole above her head. She's wearing nothing but her lingerie and black boots.

She knows what she's doing.

"Fuck," Emeric breathes.

And I smirk.

"Yeah, Emeric. Take her all in."

There's nothing I love more than when others appreciate her beauty—as long as they keep their hands to themselves.

In one swift movement she gives us her back. Her legs are slightly parted, so fucking inviting. She peeks over her shoulder, her lips curving to the side as she gives me a daring look.

She laces her fingers over her back, reaching for her bra clip.

She's about to push the boundaries she *knows* I've established in my mind.

"Eight, nine, ten." The last three seconds are up. "Looks like you're mine now."

In a heartbeat I step forward and up the stairs. She's unclipping her bra and letting it fall to the floor as I move behind her. I'm blocking the crowd's view of her breasts when she turns to them.

I hear the crowd boo at me, but I don't care. She's so close right now I can smell her sweet perfume—so different from the provocative act she's putting on—but most importantly, I can see the smirk she's wearing.

This is the reaction she was hoping for.

"Show's over, golden one."

Her gaze is intoxicating, her plump lower lip getting

stuck between her teeth as she looks up at me. "Finally," she almost purrs.

I don't waste another second. I reach for her arm and throw her over my shoulder. The action gets a giggle out of her that constricts around my hardening dick.

Weaving through the crowd, I search for a private room.

I know there are numerous private rooms here, but with the amount of alcohol being passed around, there won't be any available by now. And I don't have time to waste.

I need a different kind of private room. Any will suffice as long as I'm buried deep inside of her.

A waitress passes by, and I snatch the tray of cocaine from her hands, then I head toward the row of closed doors.

Aurelia is still giggling as she sends soft punches to my back without effort. If she's trying to make me believe she isn't dripping-wet from the way I manhandled her, she's in for a rude awakening.

I walk down the corridor until a sign catches my attention: "Employees Only." I try the doorknob and shake my head when I hear it click open. *If you don't want someone to enter, you should lock the door.*

Although that's never stopped me.

I stretch my fingers across the wall, searching until I feel the little switch and flip it. A light flickers on, making the same sound mosquitoes make when they get fried by those bug zappers.

"Julian . . ." Aurelia giggles before a hint of worry

strains her voice. "I-I think I might puke if you don't put me down."

The doors lead to what appears to be a basement. When we reach the bottom, I put Aurelia down as I contain the chuckle threatening to come out at the way her hands jump to cover her breasts from my prying stare.

Like she wasn't just stripping naked in front of one hundred sets of eyes.

"Bit late for modesty, don't you think?"

She doesn't answer me. She's too busy glancing around.

We aren't in a storage unit like I anticipated. This is an old indoor theme park under renovation. Which makes my skin crawl.

There are barrier planks outside a semi-deflated bounce house. Dust and flakes of dried paint cover most of the floor. Big, dull cartoon statues smile with crooked teeth, and there's a jungle gym missing most of its monkey bars.

This place is—

"Creepy." Aurelia breaks the silence. A shiver runs down her body.

This place is dry and cold, but I know that shiver came from the eerie ghosts of people laughing and having fun in this room.

"This place is like something out of a horror movie. Why would they have an abandoned indoor theme park?"

"They're renovating." I tilt my chin toward the equipment. "It could get turned into anything."

She squeezes her arms tighter. The movement pushes her breasts higher up, and I see the pinks of her nipples peeking between her fingers.

"So why did you bring me down here? Just to comment on my lack of modesty?"

Ah, so she did hear me.

"Partly." I smirk then place the tray of cocaine on the yellow seat of a spring horse, taking out the pocketknife to arrange the powder. "And partly to talk about your little striptease upstairs. Victoria dared you to do it, didn't she?"

"I don't see any harm in it."

I scoff. "Of course Victoria dared you."

Aurelia narrows her eyes.

Carefully, I separate the powder into long lines, licking the remnants off the blade. "I saw her sniff your shirt. She wants you." I peer up at her to catch her reaction.

Did she already figure it out?

Her eyes widen, two emerald gems peeking out at me.

I guess she didn't.

"You can use that to your advantage, you know," I tell her.

"I . . ." She chews on her lip then falters when she sees what I'm doing. "What are you doing!" Her voice rises.

"Isn't it obvious?"

"You don't even know where that came from! And besides, this place is . . . sad. It's just sad to do it in a place like this." She wiggles her shoulders as a way of pointing to our surroundings since her arms are preoccupied with covering what's mine from me.

Sad? How can a well-loved playground be sad? There's nothing sad about a place full of memories; a place that once was useful. "Sad" is something that remains the same through time.

"Doesn't mean we can't have some fun with it."

I steadily stand up from my crouched position. With the knife twirling between my fingers, I tilt my head to the side, deciding which part of her I want to scar first.

A little game—a taste before I get to feast on my meal.

Her steps mimic mine. I take one forward; she takes one back. She can't escape me. And truthfully? I don't think she wants to.

She may be scared, but she's savoring it. Just as much as I am.

The back of her legs collide with a ping-pong table, putting a stop to her sad attempt to escape. Her hands spring up, slamming on my chest as I chuckle and push forward, curving her body until she lets her back fall on the flat surface.

I cage her under my body and flick her nipple with the tip of the blade, growing hungry at the little sounds escaping from those rosy lips.

"Open your eyes," I order.

Her eyelashes flutter open on command, and my dick stirs at her compliance.

"Now don't move."

I retrieve the tray of cocaine. Trapping her back against the table, I use the knife to collect the powder and place it on her body, this time in shorter lines so I can take more of it.

I'm turning her into my own personal canvas. A perverse form of body art.

"Thanks for the fantastic idea," I mock. "This already feels way less sad."

"You're a psychopath," she breathes, breath hitching when I prick the skin with the point of the blade, mixing her blood with the coke.

"Keep the insults coming, love." I lean down next to her ear and whisper, "They only turn me on more." Then I take the first line of cocaine from her collarbone, nose burning as I incline my head and ride the first hit.

Not enough.

Moving down her body, I lick the line of her breast, sucking on the skin once the powder is gone until it turns red. She threads her fingers through my hair, and before she gets to pull me away from her, I pin her hands over her head.

I lick every part of her, sucking until the powder disappears and I'm desperate for more.

"*Please*," she moans. Begs.

And I lose control.

Images from the last time she pleaded with me penetrate my mind.

"God, this wouldn't hit as hard without your body to taste," I groan.

This isn't enough.

"Fuck it." I brush the last lines off her body and onto the floor. "This." I bite the underside of her breast, and she squeals. "This is my drug."

I bite, lick, taste every inch of her.

Her heavy breathing and rising moans are all I can hear as I spread my tongue down her navel until I reach the only patch of material still on her body.

Her body arcs, following my touch.

Needy. Desperate. Mine.

But there's something I need to do first. Before I can indulge in her.

"Lucian is having a party tomorrow night." I kiss around the hem of her underwear. "You need to be there. It's an order."

She tries to speak, but only shaky breaths reach my ears as I let my tongue run over the material, teeth delicately latching onto her clit before I do it again.

I free her arms and play with her nipple, making her body tremble. Her fingers find my hair in no time, and she tugs, failing to pull me from her.

"C-can't, s-sorry," she breathes.

I groan before bringing my lips back between her legs. This time I bite, making her scream as her head rolls backward and she pulls me *closer* with her fingers. I grab her hands away from my hair, pinning them back above her head.

If she wants me, she'll have to beg for it.

I'm back on top of her, and I stare down at her, so needy for me. "Tell me what you want." I watch her shiver beneath me. "Beg for it."

When she doesn't speak I grind into her.

Her body twitches. She arches her back and draws me closer. "Please fuck me." Eyes burning with fire, she doesn't even blink as she looks at me, waiting to see how far I'll take it.

"You can do better than that." I grab her chin in a tight grip.

Her lips brush with mine as she whispers against them, "I want you to spread me open. I want you to make me come until I can't think of anyone else but you. I want you to brand me."

My dick is so fucking hard. I don't know how much longer I can stare at those green eyes without going insane.

"Tell me what you are." I yank her underwear to the side and thrust a finger in, finding her needy for me. She soaks my finger as I slide deeper, and when I flick my thumb over her clit, her hips buck.

"Julian," she gasps.

"What are you, golden one?" My thumb strokes while I pump in and out of her. The slick sounds intertwine with her hastened breaths, and I think I could come with just this view.

She's spread open, eager for my touch as she begs for release.

Her lips part.

"Tell me," I groan.

Her body twitches, taunting, as her eyes close.

I tsk, pulling my finger out of her when she closes her legs too, preventing my hand from leaving her aching core.

"Please." Her voice is raw, cheeks red.

"I'll let you come if you tell me what you are."

She nods then pushes my fingers back between her

legs. We both groan at the sensation. When I don't move, her hips buck, grinding on my hand, and I let her as I curl my fingers, touching her sweet spot, then circle her clit.

"Julian?" she pants.

"Yes, golden one?"

I feel her pulse around my finger. "I-I'm yours."

And she screams. Her body clenches, head lolling back as her breath gets stuck inside. Her orgasm washes over her, and I'm over the edge with her.

Only, I don't come. The need to bite down on her throat overcomes me, but I crush her lips with mine instead. She tastes of damnation. Like sweet death. In a blink she could ruin me.

Her lips part, inviting me in, and I dart my tongue inside. She spreads her hands over my chest before she's ripping the buttons open, nails raking over my skin. Biting, scratching. Leaving me souvenirs of the night.

My mouth's hungry for her. I bite her lip, sucking it in before letting it go with a pop. Not even a second later, her lips are back, locked with mine, our tongues dancing as her moans get swallowed down.

"Be at the party tomorrow," I order between kisses.

"No," she whispers before biting my lower lip. Her tongue pokes out to lick the raw skin.

"Stubborn girl."

I pull away from her intoxicating lips and shift my attention onto her neck, sinking my teeth into her delicate skin.

I bite her hard. Enough to leave a mark. She shrieks, eyes widening as she looks up at me before instinctively wrapping her hand around the spot.

Standing up, I put some distance between us. She does the same, scrambling back on her legs, chest rising and falling.

Tension radiates between us, dense enough to be felt. My patience is running thin, and if making her feel good doesn't get me the response I want, there's only one other way.

Our gazes lock for a long, stretched-out heartbeat before I break the silence with one single word.

"Run."

CHAPTER TWENTY-ONE

AURELIA

H e doesn't smile.

No twitch of his muscles. No tilt of his head. No twirl of his knife between his fingers.

"I said *run*, golden one."

His dangerous tone startles me, and I take a step back.

I don't want to run. I don't want to put distance between us. But his eyes turn into pits of rawness. This starving need to punish me. He looks unhinged. His rigid expression screams resolve—I'm not going to change his mind. I can't even find words after the way he made me come three seconds ago.

My steps are small yet deafening as I race deeper into this haunted place. I would have opted for sneakers, had I known I was going to get chased like an animal, *naked*, in an abandoned indoor theme park.

I can't hear him behind me, but I feel him, with the

way the hairs on the back of my neck stand on end. I don't see him, but I can feel his gaze. He's far away. Yet he could reach me in no time.

He's giving me time. No . . .

He's having his fun.

A mountain of rocks in the far corner of the room catches my attention, and I sprint toward it. There's a slide incorporated on one side and a wall for rock climbing on the other, with the entrance to what appears to be a cavern in the middle, hidden by some plastic vines.

If I confuse him by running in a different direction, he'll miss me entering it. I can stay hidden for a while and then dash for the entrance.

Why are you trying to escape him? the voice inside my head questions.

I don't have an answer.

I'm crouching behind the semi-deflated bounce house, straining my ear to hear if he's close while I take off my shoes, discarding them for this next phase of the plan. I can't let him know I'm in the cave because he heard my heels.

When I'm certain he didn't see me, I bolt. My bare feet pad on the cold floor as I enter the cave. My breathing is heavy, heart pounding loudly in my ears.

"What the fuck?" I breathe out, eyes scanning the light blue kitchen inside the cave. A family of mannequins has been placed to look like they're baking together, the little girl and the little boy laughing as they throw flour at one another. The mother, dressed in a lilac apron, holds a wooden spoon as she smiles down at them, the father hugging her side with a look of admiration.

My gaze flickers over every detail as a dreaded sense of resentfulness spreads inside of me. The way they've been positioned, it's all a lie. No family is that happy . . . carefree. At least none of the families I've met.

Yet as I stand motionless in front of the mannequins, I can't help but feel a spike of jealousy coursing through my bones.

I could have had this with my mom. We could have been this happy and carefree.

Then I hear his voice from outside.

"You could've been the good girl you said you were and accepted my order to attend Lucian's party."

And my mind changes direction. I don't feel a sense of jealousy; I feel disgust.

Hearing Lucian's name freezes my blood. Every revolting touch he left on Julian's body last night filters in, and it's like I can feel him on me.

How can he act with such indifference? Does he seriously want me to attend a party after his father had the nerve to have his wife molested by another man?

What even is there to celebrate?

My fists clench at my sides.

"Victoria is attending, and you remember what Lucian wants us to do, don't you? Or should he remind us?"

Oh, do my insides twist at the underlying meaning in his words.

If I don't go, his father will punish him.

I can't let that happen.

Maybe I can use the opportunity to ask Victoria out on a date. If what Julian said is true, she'll eagerly accept my invitation, and once I have her alone, I can finally exact my revenge for her mother's sins.

"Found you," he whispers darkly in my ear, and a thrill goes through me. His arm snakes across my waist from behind and prevents me from moving away. "I'll always find you." The cold steel of his knife traces my neck, across my chest, and down my hips.

I feel so small, vulnerable, in his grip.

The blade reaches the hem of my underwear and in a swift movement slices the material in half. I gasp at the sudden loss of it, feeling my last shred of decency pooling at my feet.

If he moves his hand a little closer, he'll be able to tell how wet I am. Despite my better judgment, I can't help but ache for him—to chase this feeling he's infusing within me.

"You're so fucking tempting, golden one." He nestles his nose in the crook of my neck while moving the knife higher up my body. With a flick of his wrist, he brushes the blade against my nipple before moving to the other one.

The more he does it, the harder they grow, and I grow wetter.

"You like this?" He licks the expanse of my neck. "Imagine what else I could do to you with this knife."

His taunt sends waves of pleasure down my body, and an ache forms between my legs. I clench them together. But the moment I do, I feel how good it is to have something rubbing at my swollen clit, and I can't seem to stop.

I don't notice the blade reaching my neck until it draws blood, and Julian bends down, sucking me dry. My head lolls back on his shoulder as I let him feast on me.

Gasps and moans echo in the silent human-size dollhouse.

Pressure builds between my legs. My own friction isn't enough.

"Such pretty sounds you're making."

My eyes close, body arcing toward the heat radiating from his body. Something hard and cold parts my legs, circling my swollen clit and making me jump at its sensitivity.

"But I bet it's nothing compared to the noises you'll make when I really give you what you want."

The handle of the knife thrusts hard into me, and I lose strength from the intrusion, legs wobbling as a scream rips from my lips.

Julian's arm keeps me from falling, while the other one holds the knife he's fucking me with. Drops of crimson fall down his wrist to the floor as he clenches the blade in his fist.

He angles the knife, and the handle pounds on the spot that turns my screams into moans, my vision blurring as I lose myself to the fullness he's creating inside of me.

"That's it." He thrusts the slick handle in and out, brushing his finger over my sensitive clit and making my breath hitch. "Do you feel how wet you are for me? How much you want me?" he asked huskily, biting teasingly on my shoulder.

I whimper. *"Yes."*

I grip his hair, pulling his mouth back to my skin. His erection presses into my back, and I can't stop thinking about having it inside of me. Filling me.

More, more, more, is all I can think.

Lost in bliss, my other hand latches around his, and I quicken his thrusts, squeezing at the building sensation.

Julian groans, and I remember about the blade, but I can't stop. His dick twitches behind me, and I know he doesn't want me to stop either. He's as sick as me, in love with the pain. So I keep guiding his hand in fast thrusts. Our breathing becomes labored, filled with moans and growls.

"Remember this punishment." He licks my earlobe.

My legs give in as the orgasm builds.

"Next time I tell you to do something, you'd better fucking obey."

He tightens his arm around me and drives the knife faster. Harsher. Deeper, not caring that the blade's tearing his skin.

My lips part, an ache spreading to my core. I'm on the brink of an orgasm when he suddenly stops, pulling the knife out of me and tossing it to the ground.

The steel clangs, bouncing, and I stare at it as it slides to the other side of the room, away from where it was about to make me scream with pleasure.

Julian brushes a lock of my hair to the side. "Didn't think I'd let you come that easily, did you?"

He spins me around and presses my front harder into

the wall. Then I hear the metal clink of his belt buckle as he unfastens it.

I'm struggling in his grip, about to protest, when he slams into me and I see stars. A guttural cry escapes my lips.

"Fuck!" I scream.

My chest heaves as he pounds into me mercilessly. His hand grips my hips, and he pulls me against him every time he thrusts, guiding himself deeper.

My fingers claw at the wall, flakes of blue paint wedged between my fingernails. We're destroying the picture-perfect family of mannequins, tainting them with our sick pleasure.

He tangles my hair in his fist and yanks my upper body against his chest. "You feel so fucking good wrapped around my cock."

His words make me moan, but it's his bloodied hand wrapping around my neck and constricting my airways that makes me pull him into a hungry kiss.

My core tightens as we swallow each other's moans. His fingers push into the back of my hair, pulling me closer to him as something subtle yet undeniable shifts between us.

He turns me to face him and lifts me in his arms, pushing my back against the wall as I wrap my legs around him for more support, to have him closer. His thrusts become longer, deeper, more deliberate, as he savors every second of this moment.

Blue eyes pierce my soul as I lose myself in their white speckles. His pupils dilate, and I know he's close when I feel the familiar pressure building within me too.

We rest our foreheads on one another's. We aren't kissing anymore, yet a warmth still spreads to my chest.

"So"—*thrust*—"fucking"—*thrust*—"beautiful."

His voice fills with awe as a growl heaves out, matching the moan separating my lips.

Julian captures my lips again, and we both ride wave after wave of pleasure together, locked in each other's embrace.

My body trembles a little, light blinding me as my body becomes weightless, and I cling desperately to him for support.

He's still inside of me, his head resting on my shoulder as he gasps for air. His body cages me against the wall, preventing me from collapsing to the floor. I thread my fingers in his hair and realization hits me that I just had sex with Julian Harrow. With my former best friend.

What is he now? What are we now?

He carefully pulls out, and I feel empty. Like we were supposed to stay in each other's arms. Like he just stabbed me in the chest and is now tugging the knife away.

When my feet are back on the ground, reality back in check, I wobble. My hands reach for the wall so I won't make a fool of myself, but I don't need the support, because his arms dart out and wrap me close to his chest.

"Didn't realize I went so hard." He speaks from the top of my head, chin resting on my hair, and I instantly close my eyes, wishing I could encapsulate the comfort he gives me.

My heart is made of steel because I was taught to

guard it. But deep down I'm still that little girl who needed love. I'm still that little girl who wondered why her friends had a mother, but she didn't. I'm still that little girl who dreamed of being held in someone's arms.

And sometimes I dream of being that little girl. Not the killer they made of me.

"Neither did I," I joke. Despite everything, I can't help but let out a little chuckle. I can't help but feel happy.

A wave of tiredness washes over me, and I involuntarily close my eyes.

I can rest here for a little while, can't I?

Fingers stroke my hair while words are whispered, but I can't hear what Julian says.

Then something is being draped around my shoulders and strong arms are lifting me. I snuggle my head in the crook of his neck and inhale his cologne: a mixture of cedarwood and . . . *home*.

Julian carries me away from the dollhouse and back upstairs to the ongoing celebration. Everything around me is hazy, forgettable, as I try to bask in this sensation of vulnerability.

People usually hate feeling like this. They work hard to achieve the opposite; to feel protected. But I don't need to feel protected. I can take care of myself. I want to feel vulnerable, utterly raw. Because once I do, whoever I'm in the presence of is the only person I can truly be myself with. The only person I can really trust.

And it seems that person is Julian.

But I'm not surprised. He was my best friend for a reason. That connection never disappeared—we just had to search for it between the mess of years we spent not talking.

"Where are you taking me?" I manage to ask.

"Where do you want to go?"

"Nowhere. I want to stay right here."

"Then we'll go nowhere together," he murmurs.

Nowhere together. I think I like the sound of that.

CHAPTER TWENTY-TWO

JULIAN

Rain drizzles down the windows and traffic clogs the roads, mimicking the chaos inside our house as the maids scurry around completing their tasks. The clacking of their ballerina shoes against the marble floor and the sound of their hushed words echoes down the corridor to where I'm standing in the kitchen.

Tonight's party is hours away, but the house looks prepared already. Yet knowing my mother, she's having everyone triple-check every single detail, leaving no chance for Lucian to complain.

But Lucian *will* find a way to punish her tonight in front of the guests. He always does.

"The vase! Yes, that one." My mom's voice carries into the kitchen from where she's scolding a maid in the corridor. "Can't you see how it clashes with the table-cloth? Put it next to Pollock's 'Number 30'!"

Pouring myself some coffee, I shake my head at her tone. As if the maid would have a clue putting the vase in the wrong position will earn my mother three spanks. Or that adding more than five ashtrays to each table will result in a day without food and water.

The maid might know—if my mother didn't hire new staff every week. Coincidentally, always before they start linking her increase in makeup to the constant screaming and crying coming from Lucian's office.

"Julian?" She waves a hand in front of my face, calling my attention away from my running thoughts. "You haven't listened to a word I've said, have you?"

I lean against the cabinet taking a sip of the bitter coffee, the taste guiding me back from the hell that is Lucian. "Sorry, Mom. What is it?"

Her brows move slightly, trying to appear like a frown but failing with the amount of work she's had done. "Is everything ready for tonight?"

The same blue of my eyes scans down my chest, paying particular attention to the fingernails carved into my skin. Aurelia made her mark on me last night when she was screaming my name.

I don't usually walk around half-naked, but today caffeine is a necessity, right after my morning workout and before heading for a shower.

Mom's tired gaze connects with mine. "You know how your father gets when things aren't perfect." There's concern laced in her voice.

I hate seeing her like this, slowly fading.

"Everything's under control."

She gives me a soft nod before tracing her fingertips over the scratches on my chest. "Make sure to keep an eye on her tonight, Julian. You know how these parties can turn out to be."

Her words make me pause. A nod is all I manage.

Mom reaches up and brushes a stray hair away from my face, the action igniting her radiant smile. "She's so lucky to have you," she says tenderly.

Her words feel like a stab to the heart. The meaning behind them is crystal-clear. Not only that, but the longing shining in her eyes for something better—something Lucian could never give her—is enough to let me know she wishes she was as lucky as me and Aurelia in her marriage.

She wishes her husband wasn't the abusive piece of shit he is.

I grab her hand and give it a squeeze, letting her know she has me too.

"Who's so lucky to have him?" Adrian appears in the kitchen, heading straight for the plate of tuna canapés.

"Don't." Mom slaps his hand away. The soft expression that was on her face seconds ago is now replaced by something sterner. "Instead of eating the guests' food, why don't you give us a hand? There's still plenty to do before the party starts."

She doesn't wait for him to answer, because she isn't asking. She's demanding.

I watch her go, her small figure retreating to scold the maids, leaving behind a silent Adrian, who just stares after her.

My mother has never shared the same warmth with Adrian as she does with me. She never was the same mother to him. And I know it's because she resents him for all the times he never stepped up to protect her. Instead he let her battle with Lucian's wrath on her own.

"What the fuck happened to you?" he asks when he turns back to me, gaze sweeping over the scratches on my chest.

I smirk. "Shouldn't you recognize the pattern?"

He narrows his eyes, waiting to hear more.

"I would have bet you'd be able to recognize the way she scratches when you make her come . . . or maybe you never got that far."

"You're fucking her?" There's a storm looming in his glacial glare.

"Isn't it obvious?" I take a sip from the mug.

He groans, elbows resting on the table as he drops his head between his shoulders. "One thing, Julian. Stay away from her. You couldn't even do that?"

I fucking lose it.

As I slam the mug on the counter, it shatters into millions of pieces.

"I did as you said. I stayed away from her for ten years!" I fume.

Ten. Years.

One.

Two.

Three.

Four.

Five.

Six.

Seven.

Eight.

Nine.

Ten.

Not hours, days, or months. *Years.*

A decade of my life spent without her. He can't ask me for more.

His head snaps at the sound of the ceramic shattering, the warm liquid dripping down the counter to the floor. Its scent wraps around us, a comfort before the chaos.

"Getting involved with her makes everything we did until now meaningless!" His rough voice cuts through the hushed silence the maids are trying to maintain.

"Adrian." I clench my jaw—something I've been doing more frequently when talking with him. "This was your idea. If it doesn't work, that's on you." I look him dead in the eye. "You told me until the end of high school, yet you stayed with her for seven more years!"

All the pain I felt during those years comes crashing back down on me. The resentment that shone in her eyes whenever she looked at me. The way the green of her eyes lost the glint it once had. How slowly, torturously, I became a ghost to her. Nothing but a shadow of the past.

"So if Father hurts her, it's my fault?" A bitter laugh leaves his lips, tainting the sweet smell of the apricot crumble cooking in the oven. "No. I think that'll be on you."

Tension radiates between us.

I am so fed up with him telling me what I can and can't do. I listened to him back then because he gave me a deadline. I won't stay away from her forever.

I can't live a life without her in it.

What if Lucian hurts her? the deep voice in my mind slurs. *What if she dies? She'll be gone forever.*

Scoffing, I say, "Lucian doesn't want to hurt her, and he probably never did back then either."

Who am I really saying this to? Him or me?

I continue. "You were the only one who noticed his interest in Aurelia and came up with the brilliant plan to fake-date her."

I still remember the way he appeared in my room, hair disheveled, going on and on about how he'd caught Lucian licking his lips while watching Aurelia's ass saunter away. I remember how his eyes went round when the idea popped into his head: *"If I date her, Father won't look at her anymore. He's never shown any interest in the girls I've dated. But if you keep showing him she's your friend—or more—he might do something."*

"You really think that?" He shakes his head, looking almost hurt. "She's a beautiful girl, Julian, I won't lie to you. But it was still hard as shit dating someone I didn't love for ten fucking years.

"I did that for you—and for her. I grew up with Aurelia too, you know. I couldn't just watch Father put his hands on her. I could do something this time. I could help her."

I could help her the way I couldn't help Mom. I can hear him thinking it.

But then he adds, "Maybe you should show me some gratitude for what I did."

"Gratitude?" I clench my fists. "You think I should be grateful for having to watch you date the woman I *love*?" I spit. "I should be grateful for watching you take all her firsts—*our* firsts?" I'm seething by this point. "You think I should be grateful for watching her look at you the way she used to look at me?"

"You weren't there, Julian!" he shouts. "You didn't notice the way Father would eye-fuck her. It got progressively worse as she got older. He'd look at her like he was seeing a long-lost prize appearing again."

Of course he did. She reminded him of her mother. *Fuck.*

Adrian was just trying to help, and I'm being a dick about it.

But I need him to understand.

"I was young and naïve back then. I can protect her now."

"Like you're doing with Mom?" he scoffs.

"Yes." I grind my teeth.

"Julian." He takes a step closer. The ocean blue of his eyes ripples with emotion. "You haven't been protecting Mom. You've just been sharing the pain together."

His hands capture my face, framing it, as he closes the distance between us, pieces of broken ceramic cracking under his foot. Our eyes lock onto one another's.

I can't remember the last time he was tender with me.

"You need to stop getting in the way of Father's anger." His voice is grave, low. "Compared to Mom and Aurelia, you're disposable to him. He would never kill Mother, because she brings joy to his sickness, but you? You're nothing but a thorn in his side. One day, he'll pluck you out." He whispers, "And I don't think I'll be able to survive seeing you go. Do you understand that?"

Adrian shakes me.

My throat's dry, a lump forming in the middle of it.

I've never seen Adrian stripped raw before now. But I can't. I can't do what he's asking me to do. Maybe it's selfish. Maybe I'm the shittiest brother in the whole world.

But I'd prefer for Lucian to kill me with his bare hands than to face a life without the girl I've loved for my entire life, or one where my mother continues to slowly die with each finger he lays on her.

Last time he played smart. He brought someone else in to do the touching while he focused solely on me. But next time . . . Well, there won't be a next time, but if there is, it might be the day I finally let Emeric join in and punch the man to death.

I nod as I watch the faintest smile curve Adrian's lips.

It's a lie. A white lie that will let him sleep at night.

It's the least I can do.

He takes a step away from me, and just as he's about to leave, he places a folder on the table, tapping it with his index finger. "The information you asked me for on the owner of Lavish Eden."

With a heavy sigh, I open the folder and skim through it.

There's no real reason why I asked Adrian for information on the new member of the Inferno Consortium. I don't know the guy, but I loved using his club. Without it, I wouldn't have felt Aurelia's body writhing beneath mine.

I flip over the pages.

Lorenzo Mancini.

There's a full biography on the guy, but no picture. Nothing interesting. He's lived a pretty normal life—if you consider being a billionaire normal.

He's the son of the Mancini family. I've heard of them before. They're the richest family in Italy, owners of various hotel chains, some of which the Inferno Consortium uses for business events.

Lorenzo, on the other hand, seems to own a series of strip clubs and restaurants across Italy, France, Spain, and Norway. And since he just opened one here in Seattle, I guess he's expanding his empire in the United States too.

And he's achieved that by joining the Inferno Consortium.

They offered to make him a member for free in exchange for the use of his estates for meetings or dealings, and he got the green light to open his business in our territory.

I close the folder.

Reading about every single meeting he had with the Inferno Consortium and my father is making me nauseated.

Heading back to my room, I close the door behind me and throw the folder onto my bed, moving to the bathroom to take a shower. I'm stripping off my pants when I catch sight of the art piece Aurelia left on my chest last night.

So much has changed. I still can't wrap my head around the fact she kills people. I always knew she was special, a missing piece of my soul. And if my soul is dark and depraved, then she can't be sunshine and rainbows.

But the truth is, we made her the way she is today. My family did.

Lucian did.

The thought jolts me to realize, through the havoc of these past few days, I forgot to ask her how it went with Marcus Whitman. Not how she killed him or if she did, because I heard every symphony she sucked out of him, but how it all turned out afterward.

Grabbing my phone, I send a quick message to Valentine.

He responds immediately.

Valentine: *They don't know about her.*

I turn on the shower while I type out, "What does Lucian know about the kill?" and click send.

Valentine: *They think the guy that killed DeMarco killed Whitman too.*

Another text arrives quickly.

Valentine: *Since he was at the restaurant that night. What the fuck?*

Blood rushes away from my face, my heart pounding in the backs of my ears.

I don't waste another second; I hit Valentine's number and wait for his voice to break the irritating ringing tone.

When he finally picks up, making a scene of letting it ring for a while like he wasn't holding his phone when I called, I impatiently ask, "What was he doing there?"

"Hello to you too, Julian," he drawls in mockery.

Funny. Did he grow a sense of humor in the past few hours?

"Cut the shit and tell me what you know about the guy."

Who is he really? What does he want from Aurelia? Does he know about her?

A sigh greets me from the other end of the line. "Adrian spotted him through the restaurant's CCTV cameras. Before you ask, I edited the videos, cutting Aurelia entering and leaving the bathroom, before I gave the recordings to Adrian."

The bastard is good at what he does, I'll give him that.

He continues. "He was easy to notice, because he was the only one dining alone, wearing nothing but a black hoodie."

How did Aurelia not see him?

"Were you able to capture his face?"

"No." Valentine is quiet for a beat, then I hear shuffling on the other end of the line before he adds in a low voice, "He walked into the bathroom right after Aurelia left—"

Loud talking echoes through the line, cutting off Valentine. He speaks to someone else, grumbling here and there, while my patience sizzles.

"Valentine."

There's more grumbling before he manages to continue. "He left a raven's feather on the body. Do you have any idea what it could mean?"

I rack my brain for an explanation but come up empty-handed. Why did he let Aurelia kill Whitman without getting involved? Who is this guy, and what does he want from her?

Then the most dreadful thought digs a hole in my stomach.

What if he hasn't told anyone about what Aurelia did because he wants to use it to his advantage? What if he'll use her to get back at me for pinning DeMarco's death on him?

"The invisible man," that's what Adrian called him. Fuck, I wish he'd stayed invisible a bit longer.

Then, before I can ask the one question pestering my mind, Valentine answers it.

"No, Julian. Aurelia isn't working with him," he says. "Actually, she has no idea anyone was there to know she killed Whitman. I'd like for us to keep it that way."

He wants me to lie to her. I would have thought he'd be the one to teach me to never lie to a woman, but I guess he can't be any different from the men of the Inferno Consortium.

What's another lie to add to the pile? It's better this way, for her own good. If she knows, havoc will rain down. And the Inferno Consortium will notice her involvement.

"Fine."

"I've got it under control," Valentine says. "Trust me."

"Keep me in the loop if anything new emerges."

"Will do."

I hang up and stare at my reflection in the steaming mirror.

I look a fucking mess.

Dark, puffy bags under my eyes, glaring red scratches

on my chest, hair sticking out in every direction, hands clenching the edge of the sink.

And still, it's the happiest I've felt in ten years.

CHAPTER TWENTY-THREE
AURELIA

ing.

P The numbers on the elevator screen gradually increase.

Valentine is standing by my side. Only the hum of the elevator accompanies us while we wait to reach the Harrows' floor. The party starts at 11 p.m.—an unusual time for a party. A bit late, if you ask me, but it doesn't seem to bother anyone else.

"Are you sure you want to go tonight?" Valentine peeks down at me out of the corner of his eye.

This is the second time he's asked me in the span of minutes.

"I don't have much of a choice, do I?" I sigh. "Victoria will be there, and Lucian wants Julian and me to entertain her."

I fidget at the idea of having to entertain her and what that might imply now I know she could be interested in me.

"Has Julian told you what these parties are like?"

I brush my hands over the peony-pink satin dress, then I plaster a reassuring smile on my face. "No, but it's not my first Inferno Consortium party. I think I can handle it."

Valentine doesn't seem convinced. *What has gotten into him?*

The doors of the elevator open, and he walks out in silence. Pulling something from his jacket, he places it on his face. It takes me a few peeps to spot the badger mask.

"Nice mask," I snicker. Half of it is normal, while the other is a striking red, as if the badger's skin has been skinned off. "Did you bring one for me too? I had no idea we needed them."

"You should know. The Harrows host this party every two months." His voice is muffled from the mask.

I try not to let his dark tone leave an uneasy trail down my body, but it's useless. It's as if the moment the mask slid onto his face, someone else overtook him.

"The Hunt is one of the Inferno Consortium's favorite events. Not only for the leading families but also for the girls working at Lucian's brothels."

My brow furrows in confusion as I try to make sense of what he's telling me. His steps are long and unwavering as I try to keep up with him.

"It's their way to *upgrade* from an average sex worker to an escort, but it's also a gift for the Inferno Consortium families, who enjoy selecting their preferred girl in a . . . primal way."

The air between us grows dark with the implication of what awaits me tonight.

"Lucian . . . he likes variety. But the truth is, he

changes the girls at his brothels because the Consortium members from New York need somewhere to keep the girls who didn't get bought in the annual auction."

I stumble at his words. The revelation slides out of his mouth with ease. I thought I knew enough about the Inferno Consortium, yet the deeper I dig into this sinister world, the more I want to run as far away from here as I can.

"Annual auction . . . Are the girls participating of their free will?"

It doesn't even seem like he heard me. He continues to walk straight ahead, reaching for the two guards outside the door.

"Valentine!" I hurry my steps to keep pace with him.

The guard doesn't even look up from the clipboard in his hand as Valentine walks past him and inside.

"You won't need one," he tosses over his shoulder, answering my previous question about the mask, so gently spoken I would have missed his words if I weren't trailing behind him.

My brows deepen at his sudden cold attitude and the way he just dodged my question about the girls.

I'm intending to ask what's going on when an arm springs out, blocking my path. Looking down at it, I gape at the guard who isn't even blessing me with his attention.

"Name?" he hisses.

I freeze at the question. After twenty-five years of being known as the golden one, of having every pair of eyes on me, hearing this question doesn't make me feel good like I thought it would.

The guard knows who I am. They all know me as Valentine's daughter—their boss's daughter—so why is he asking me my name . . . and why isn't he looking me in the eye?

"Aurelia," I reply, a bitter taste in my mouth. "Draven."

He doesn't react to the name. Nothing, not a blink of an eye or a slight glance in my direction. Instead he scans the clipboard with the tip of his pen before tapping on a specific spot. Then he grabs a pin and a white ribbon from the bowl next to him.

"Wear this around your neck."

"Why do I need to—?"

He waves a hand, dismissing me, before the guard next to him gives me a terse push, urging me inside.

I stumble in my heels, grabbing onto the wall for balance. I gape at how different the place looks. The Harrows' penthouse has been stripped of its usual austere appearance. In its place is this mysterious, gloomy, pitch-black hole.

The floor-to-ceiling windows have been obscured. The only source of light comes from the dancing flames of the candles, which have been strategically placed to illuminate the adjoining pieces of art. Yet that's not all they're shining their light on.

The penthouse has been turned into something unrecognizable, as if stripped bare of all pretenses. The true Harrow family reflects off the polished surfaces, from the ominous portraits of Lucian now hanging on the corridor walls to the smell of cigar present in every corner of the house.

He isn't locked in his studio anymore; he is now the sole presence in this home. Anyone walking through that door will feel his chilling eyes on them as they make their way to one of the living rooms. It's an act of power. He's showcasing his dominance, reminding everyone who the leader is.

Tying the ribbon around my neck, I make a bow with the extra material then delicately fix the pin to my dress without ruining it.

Glancing around me, I notice we're in the same living room where I first spoke with Victoria, only now there is no white couch, just big rosebushes in black vases and long tables holding drinks at the far ends of the room, leaving a lot of space in the middle . . .

Now that I think about it, almost all the furniture is gone.

I search for Valentine but can't seem to find him. I thought he was going to be here somewhere waiting for me to enter.

A man with a badger mask walks past me, and I immediately call out to him.

"Valentine?"

The man turns, and when he does, I catch how his mask lacks the red half like Valentine's.

"Sorry, I thought you were someone else."

Everyone seems to be wearing a mask. Well, mostly men. There are badger masks, but also piercing, deep red fox masks, and there are far more foxes in the room.

Chills erupt all over my body as I think back to what Valentine told me about this party. The Hunt. Are they wearing masks so we can't identify them or to stoke the sick pleasure they feel from chasing down girls like predators?

Something feels off. Even Victoria's party didn't make me this uncomfortable . . . this uncertain. Like I just unknowingly walked into a party I don't belong at.

I should find Valentine or Julian right away. I don't think walking around the place alone is a good idea.

I nibble on my lower lip as I glance around the room again. I don't think I'll be able to spot Julian in a sea of masked people . . .

At least it's pretty obvious who I am. He'll soon come for me.

I fill my fidgeting hands with a glass of sparkling wine and stroll aimlessly deeper inside. Everyone seems to be divided into groups of their designated mask. Heads turn my way, and I give a sweet smile at whoever hides behind them.

I'm sipping from my almost empty glass when a giggling reaches my ears. It doesn't take long for me to find the source. A group of girls, bare of masks, isn't hard to miss. Maybe they could help me make sense of this weird night.

My glossy lips stretch to the side as I approach them with the friendliest smile. "Hey there."

Their heads snap toward me.

"I'm Aurelia," I greet them before gesturing toward our bare faces with a light chuckle. "Seems we're the only ones without masks here, huh? Any idea why?"

One of them snorts, placing a hand over her mouth to prevent a laugh. The one closer to me steps forward, her chocolate eyes narrowing as they fall down my body and back up.

"You think you're cute?" She crosses her arms over her bursting cleavage. "You may have that whole pure-girl act going on, but I can see how used and trashy you really are. No guy here will want you, and if you try to steal our men . . . well, I'll personally make sure you pay for it."

My lips part, words forming, but she flips her long hair and leaves. The others follow right behind her, and I watch them saunter away, at a loss for words.

I gulp down the remaining contents of my glass and hunt for some more. I'll need a lot to drink if I want to survive the night.

It takes me a while to find something else to drink. The tables only hold empty glasses by the time I reach them, and there may be a lot of staff members scurrying around the place, but they're all dressed in black, with matching masks covering their faces, so under the dim lights they're easy to miss as they blend in seamlessly with the surroundings.

Pulling out my phone, I scroll down my contacts list until Julian's name appears. He still didn't find me, and staying alone in this place gives me the creeps.

Clicking on his name, I let it ring until it reaches voice mail, over and over again.

Why is he not answering his phone?

I dial again.

No answer.

My finger hovers over his name, but I refrain from clicking it again.

"Thank you all for being here."

The voice booms through the room, its crudeness calling everyone to fall silent, the chatter and clinking of glasses stopping instantly. Everyone turns their attention toward the man wearing a gold fox mask, standing on a makeshift stage at the far end of the room, where the big windows showcasing the starlit city once were.

The stale smell of cigar intensifies, burning my nostrils, and my breathing shallows at the same moment as something clicks into place and I start to remember.

"I ran so fast. My hair was slapping at my face, and he was right behind me, his gold mask with black holes for eyes grating at my deepest, most carnal self." My mother's words flood my mind. *"Catch me. Catch me and do with me what you will."*

The messy handwriting inked on the very first pages of her diary comes crashing down on me. I remember those were the only moments she seemed happy. Anytime I read those pages, it felt like her soul would appear in front of my eyes with the brightest of smiles as she recalled the time she left home and found herself here.

Oh, how I ache to tell her to never set foot in this house.

To run. Far, far away.

"Rule number one," the man wearing the gold mask —*Lucian*—states. "No unmasking until the end of the night."

Her words accompany his.

"The moment his teeth sank into me I knew I was losing myself. But gosh, how exhilarating it felt to finally have

someone treat me with hands that dealt with need instead of politeness."

"Rule number two. The rabbits can run for however long they please, but once they get captured, they need to fully submit."

"He illustrated power. The kind I was used to, the kind I hated, but he didn't treat me like they did at home. He seemed to see more than just my skin. He wanted to carve the depths of it."

"Rule number three. Consent is taken, not given. Remember, foxes." He smirks, and the crowd goes into a frenzy, cheering loudly. But my mother's voice is louder.

"He broke the first rule, and call me romantic, but that did it for me. The mask was off, and he was breathtaking. With deep blue eyes and the palest of skin, like snow. I thought that was a sign. I love snow."

My throat constricts, mouth as dry as a desert as my vision blurs.

"Rule number four. You are allowed to do whatever you want to your prey. As long as you let us know where you do so, so we can deep-clean afterward."

"He was harsh. It hurt in the beginning, but then he gave me soft kisses all over my shoulders and my cheeks and the pain faded into intoxicating pleasure."

"And rule number five." Lucian stills, waits a second, then shouts, "Enjoy yourselves!" He claps his hands, signaling for the game to begin.

Now I understand why Valentine didn't seem convinced about letting me join in tonight. Why didn't he tell me my mother was once at a party just like this one? That she was *one of the girls.*

I shouldn't have come. I can't . . . I can't just stay here and let whatever happened to my mother happen to me too. Screw Julian and Victoria.

For fuck's sake, screw Lucian Harrow.

Laughter erupts, and I jump at the unexpected sound. A girl without a mask is giggling as a fox chases her through the corridor. He makes menacing noises that seem to fuel her giggles even more. Goose bumps cover my whole body at the view.

They've all lost their minds. I shake my head in disbelief as my body shakes with horror.

"Run," a voice whispers in my ear from behind, and I all but scream.

Fuck these lunatics.

Turning around, I raise my hand, ready to slap the last remaining brain cell out of them, when the man wearing a fox mask dodges it with no effort. His hands are in his pockets while he stands still, unaffected.

"Run," he repeats, "or you'll be easy prey. You don't want to be caught by the wrong fox."

I don't recognize his voice. Or his nonchalant demeanor.

He reaches for the pin before I can back away and brushes his thumb over it. "The royal rabbit. They've already staked their claim."

"What do you mean?" My eyes bore into his. "Staked their claim? I'm not an object! No one can claim me!"

His laugh is velvet, a slimy caress to my tense nerves. It deepens my unease.

"Oh, but they already have."

"Who are you?" My stomach churns.

"Does it matter?" The black holes where his eyes are lock with mine. "All that matters is that you need to hide —now."

I stare at the shades of red in his mask, how they play with the scarce light of the candle. If I squint my eyes, the fox appears to be moving. Alive and vigilant.

"Do we know each other?" Attempting to catch a glimpse of him, I take a step around him. Waves of dark golden hair, almost like burned honey, frame the red mask as a few strands fall over it. I try to move a tad to the left. This way, the candlelight can cast more light over him, and I'll be able to see more of him.

But he's a fox. Intuitive, intelligent, and playful. And at my imperceptible movement, he blows on the candle.

Destroying the only way I had to learn more about him.

Leaving me between the claws of the shadows.

"Wait!" Urgency taints my voice, but it still comes just below a whisper.

"Hide in the Harrows' walk-in closet," he urges. "Behind Lady Harrow's winter coats is a concave wall, where you can wait until the end of the party at exactly three in the morning."

"How do you—?"

"It's where your mother hid."

His words stab me like a thousand knives, leaving me stumbling on the spot. My vision blurs even more, hands tingling.

"Wha—?"

Screaming cuts me off mid-sentence.

A girl—the one who was holding in her laughter

earlier—is caged between the arms of a fox, his mouth latched onto her neck as he rips the ribbon with his teeth. From where I'm standing, it looks like a fox biting into its prey, killing it.

He spits the ribbon onto the floor and goes back for more.

Then I see her thrust at his chest, her body trembling even more, until a piercing shriek splits the silence.

Panic blinds me as I see her throwing punches at him.

He doesn't flinch. Instead he remains in the same spot, with his mouth on her neck.

I think I'm truly seeing a fox devour a rabbit.

She screams, and I recoil. Her voice wobbles as it turns into despair, wailing.

The more strangled sounds she makes, the more I'm ravaged with despair.

I can't seem to move. I want to help. Push him away from her—from leaving another mark on her skin.

But I can't move.

My heart is thundering, but I can't move.

Her knees buckle until her body slumps into his arms. Obedient, compliant, now she's lost her senses. The fox lifts her in his arms. Her head tips back, and I see the mark he left with his teeth. The crimson dripping down her fair skin. *The consequences of my weakness.* And a suppressed scream leaves my mouth.

I frantically look around me for someone to share my reaction. Instead I come face-to-face with Lucian still onstage, and I finally notice the two golden foxes behind him—how they stand unmoving. Observant.

The Harrow brothers are staring at me. Their father too.

Lucian remains still, and the fox on his left copies him, detached, with his hands in his suit pockets. Yet his stare is scorching-hot on my skin, making me want to peel every layer of it off me. His posture screams of control—the kind that has his hands fisting in his pockets. Like he wants to do something but can't. Like he's the opposite of in control.

Then my eyes move to the right, where the other fox stands tall, his hands visible with all his built-up emotion. Julian's face may be covered, but I can picture the tautness of his brow and the way his lips are crooked in a sinister smile.

I know that's him . . . but I'm even more certain the moment he tilts his head.

Ravenous.

CHAPTER TWENTY-FOUR

AURELIA

I push my legs, running with all my strength through the corridor.

My heart pounds in sync with the sound of my heels. Figures shift form in the shadows as I pass them in a blur. One of the gold foxes is following me—maybe all three of them. All I know is that I can't let fear deliver me into their arms without a fight. I'm not easy prey like my mother was. I have claws, and I intend to scratch back.

I breathe through my nose, my legs threatening to buckle under me, but I force myself onward, using the memory of my mother to sharpen my resolve. Her pain blocks any surfacing doubt.

The mysterious guy with the red fox mask gave me a hiding spot, and I'll use it. Just not now. Right now I need to get to the kitchen and procure a weapon.

I round the corner and see the kitchen door looming ahead. Sprinting, I head toward it, but a vase perched on a small table catches my attention. Without hesitation I throw it behind me, sending it crashing down onto whoever is following me, hopefully slowing them down and giving me enough time to search for a knife.

They probably hid every dangerous utensil for the party . . . or maybe not. After all, what fun would it be for their twisted games if they couldn't play a little?

Yanking open the drawer closest to me, air whooshes from my lips at the sight of glinting blades. *Of course they didn't put the knives away.* They want the foxes to have some fun.

I wrap my fingers around the handle just as a body slams into me from the side. Air gets knocked out of me along with the knife as it slides from my grasp. Cold tile stings my cheeks next as I land with a hard thud.

"Let go!" I shout as desperation fuels me to get myself free.

Wrestling, I struggle against the mass of the body pinning me down. But it's futile. Whoever is above me knows how to restrain a body. The thought leaves a lingering sense of dread as adrenaline surges within me. I throw my elbow behind me in a haphazard manner and hit something hard. The painful grunt that follows confirms I got the asshole in the face.

He pushes himself off my back, distracted by the unexpected blow, and I use the opportunity to roll onto my side and push him further away, until I'm free to drag myself toward the knife.

"Get back here!"

I'm too busy stretching my fingers toward the blade to identify who he is, let alone to follow his orders. I feel my nails break with the pressure I'm putting them under as I claw at the floor, trying anything to reach the knife faster.

"You little bitch," I hear him snarl.

My fingers are inches away from the knife—so close that when his hand latches onto my ankle and yanks me away I scratch my skin on the blade as I make one last futile attempt at grasping it.

I kick my legs wildly. "Get off me!" My voice is raw as I shout.

Then a hollowness spreads in my stomach at the feel of his cold hand climbing up my bare leg, under my dress.

"Don't fucking touch me," I say from between clenched teeth.

Twisting, I try to put some distance between the sickening feeling of his hand and my body. But the closer he gets between my legs, the more his grip turns to iron. He is stronger than me. I need to find another way to fight him. If not with my body, then with my words, like Valentine taught me. I'll need to use this fucker's lust against him if I have any chance of escaping.

"Is this the best you can do?" My heart thuds at the back of my throat as I try not to show how weak I sound. "Don't you want to look at me?"

Silence.

I shut my eyes, praying he falls for it.

Please, please, please.

"Don't you want me to look at you?"

Acid burns up my throat at what I'm about to say. "If you take me from the back, I can picture whoever I like . . ."

A groan greets my ears, and then I'm being turned onto my back, no grace in the movement as I match his groan with one of my own. Pain radiates from the back of my head as it meets the icy tile.

At least the plan worked. Now I'm face-to-face with him.

And an old, polished fox mask.

He laughs, parting my legs with his lower body and pressing his erection between them, making me hiss at the sensation. My hands get pinned above my head as I feel a hopelessness like I've never felt before.

"You little sluts always squirm, don't you? Always trying to free yourselves, but you fail to understand you're just making us harder." He leans in. "And harder."

Then a stinging sensation spreads across my right cheek. His hand's midair after having slapped me hard. My vision blurs, and a metallic taste swims in my mouth from biting my lip.

"Rule number two. The rabbits can run for however long they please, but once they get captured, they need to fully submit," he repeats, almost scolding me. "Tell me you'll be thinking about someone else again and I'll make the whole Inferno Consortium fuck you into unconsciousness. You'll wish it were just me."

A heaviness tightens in my chest at identifying his voice.

My mouth dries at his words, because I know how much truth they hold. He isn't just talking. He means the threat. He did the same with my mother, passed her around like a hand-me-down.

"You look just like her." He skims his nose over the side of my face, sniffing in my perfume.

I think I'm dying.

Slowly. Painfully.

Lucian brushes his finger from a strand of hair, down my cheek, leaving a trail of burning skin in his wake. "Red like a child's favorite crayon. Red like the flowers butterflies pick. Red like sacrifice and passion." He grips my chin and tilts my head up, forcing me to stare into his eyes behind the mask. "Red like blood. Red like fire. Red like war. Red like *mistakes*."

I flinch as his breath tickles my face. His eyes bore into mine, making my skin crawl with the intensity.

"Your mother was so beautiful. On a day just like this, I captured her for myself." He hums to himself. "So docile and *needy*." He laughs.

I stare at him with a straight face, but a tear rolls down from the corner of my eye, betraying me. Another one follows, hot against my pale skin.

"So full of life. A little bird just learning to fly after a life spent behind bars." The bastard smiles.

He smiles.

"She was finally free, but she flew to me, and I had to cage her in. I couldn't let her go. I couldn't lose all the light she brought with her."

So you sucked it all out of her.

"She was mine. My personal escape in the middle of the night. She was happy to be mine." Then his tone shifts, and he slams me against the floor, hard enough that the hatred in his next words sinks in better. "But you started to intoxicate her, poisoning her against me," he snarls, anger growing with each word he spits at me. "You took away my gift!"

He shakes me again, this time knocking my head hard on the tile, and I see stars. My lips part, but I don't have the energy to moan in pain.

"You took her away from me." His panting caresses my cheek. Growling, he whispers, "So I'll use you in her place."

Lucian leans down and bites the ribbon around my neck, sinking his teeth into my skin. Pain shoots through my body, and I scream, waking up from the daze he put me in with his words. It's like everything washes over me and I finally feel.

Everything.

Swinging my legs up, I use my newfound determination and the years of training Valentine drilled into me to deliver a harsh kick to his hip, pushing him off me even if it means tearing my skin open.

Lucian stumbles backward, glancing down at me with my blood tainting his lips, and I use the opportunity to hook my hands around his face, shoving my thumbs into his eyes, allowing for his screams to tickle my soul. I dig my nails a little harder into his skin, deciding to match his blood with mine.

"I should rip your eyes out right now." I push my thumb in, and he shouts in agony. "But I want you to see me when I finally take down everything you care about."

He seizes my wrists, but the more he pulls, the more I fucking push.

"You pathetic, useless girl," he gasps. "I don't have anything I care about."

"You're wrong."

In his show of dominance he's revealed his Achilles' heel.

Me.

"I'm all you have left of her." I let out a giggle that turns into a hysterical laugh. "I'll take her away from you again."

My laughter dies as the unease that persists in me comes back and I remember he's the reason my mom isn't here with me now. My mouth turns down in anger, and I clench my jaw.

Nose wrinkling in disgust, I throw a punch to his neck, stealing the air away from him. He falls onto his back, choking from the pain as his hands try to get some air back into his lungs.

Standing on wobbly legs, I run for my life.

I run and run and run.

An ache spreads from my legs up to my torso as if I've been running for hours, but I haven't moved much. The kitchen isn't in my peripheral vision anymore, but Lucian could catch up to me at any moment.

I'm not safe. I don't feel safe in my own skin.

My chest tightens, lips tingling before numbing completely.

I keep pushing forward. *Just one more step*, I repeat to myself.

One more ste—

My breathing quickens, too fast for me to catch a breath. I'm choking on too much air.

I can't breathe!

A stinging sensation spreads across my chest, down

my arms, until all I want to do is peel off my skin. A vortex of searing numbness consumes me. I'm feeling so much of nothing that I'm left staggering on my feet. I collapse onto my side, pressing all of my weight into the wall as I struggle not to fall. But it's no use. I may be standing, but my insides are turning in on themselves.

I clutch my hand to my chest, trying to calm my rapid heart and the searing panic attack, but my hand falls to the pin still there, and the corridor starts to swirl around me. I'm ripping it off before I can control myself. The metal sound it makes as it bounces on the floor rings in my ears.

But it's not enough.

Broken sobs break out of my mouth as an unbearable tension grows in my head, and I fear I might implode. I shut my eyes, but the darkness awaiting behind them only feeds this pounding sense of loneliness.

I feel so utterly alone in all of this. *She left me alone with the heavy burden of her vengeance.*

Loathing spreads through my veins as my arms and my legs begin to tingle uncontrollably. I hate her for coming here. I hate her for loving Lucian, even if short-lived. And I hate her for leaving me.

I'm heaving by the time those thoughts take shape in my mind, sweat dripping down my temples to my neck, when the consuming sensation of guilt washes over me and I let out the most gut-wrenching scream.

I wish she never had me. I wish she let Lucian kill me like he wanted to. I wish she didn't love me so profoundly.

Warmth touches my cheeks, delicately, and my eyes

spring open, gaze colliding with worried eyes. Julian's warm hands frame my face as he observes me. He isn't wearing his mask, and I can see all the lines of concern etched into his expression.

Help me. Please help me.

My eyes plead with his, but rasping is the only sound that comes out of me as I dig my nails into his hands, clinging to him in the hope he won't disappear.

"Look at me," he urges. "What happened?" He sweeps his eyes over me as he searches for the answer.

I move my hand to my neck and tap there, under the wound Lucian gave me. My vision is blurring with tears, but I still catch the way his eyes darken the moment he sees.

"I-I can't b-breathe."

"Did Lucian do this to you?" he demands, the veins in his neck announcing the rage coursing through him.

More tears get soaked in his hands as I nod my head. I try to tell him everything, but my voice wavers between sobs and hiccups. Nothing coherent manages to come out.

His eyes flick back and forth between mine before a veil falls over his expression. He lifts me into his arms and leads me to his bedroom. The stroke of his fingers on my back pulls some of the weight off my chest, but the sense of hopelessness persists.

I don't think it'll ever leave.

We arrive at his bedroom, and he gently places me on his bed before locking his bedroom door. I don't feel trapped in this room; I feel trapped inside my own skin.

Julian falls to his knees and moves between my legs,

leveling his stare with mine while he cautiously covers my eyes with his hands.

"Wh-what are you doing?" Panic slowly rises as I'm left alone with my thoughts. "Julian?" I move my head back, but he doesn't take his hands away.

"What do you see?"

I see Lucian's mouth arching into a menacing laugh. I see my mother crying on the floor. I see her body hanging from the ceiling or trembling at his feet. I see her holding a little version of me in her arms. Then I see her regrets as they become mine.

"Aurelia." Julian's voice brings me back. "What do you see?"

I see black. I see nothing.

"N-nothing," I voice.

"Good," he murmurs, thumb stroking my cheeks. "Now, what do you hear?"

"Only you," I whisper.

He removes his hands and I collide with celestial blue eyes. And a realization that I've lived a similar moment before.

"Whenever you need to escape this place, you cover your eyes, okay?"

"Julian . . ."

His brows twitch as he studies my expression, capturing the words I can't find the strength to say out loud. "You forgot about that night, didn't you?"

The memory of Emeric's party, a few months before I broke things off with Adrian, comes crashing down on me. Eleanora invited me to it. Emeric hosted the party at his place to celebrate finally getting a promotion in his family's wine business after years of convincing his father he was ready for a more influential position.

I've already had too much to drink when Eleanora has the brilliant idea of stealing a bottle of wine to spite Emeric for choosing a job that will see him traveling overseas more often. She coaxes me to share it with her, until my head's swimming with the effects of the alcohol and my bladder's fit to burst.

"I need to find a bathroom," I tell her, my drunken words slurred, but even as I get up to leave I don't think she hears me, too lost in her own alcohol-induced haze as she rants on about Emeric in between bursts of tears.

Yet she swears she's not that into him.

"I'll be back in a sec," I hear myself say on some far-off level of consciousness as I walk out on her mid-rant. It's probably for the best. She'll only deny everything she's saying when I bring it up again in the morning.

The Grimwards' three-story mansion is like a maze, and I'm tripping over things and stumbling into walls, pretty sure I'm lost forever and will never find my way back to the party, when I hear glass breaking farther along the corridor.

I don't know where I am. There doesn't seem to be anyone else in this part of the house.

Following the sound, I find myself on the threshold of a guest bedroom in ruins.

And there in the center of the room . . .

Julian.

He's brutally unplugging the bedside lamp, his breathing ragged, hair tousled, as he yanks and yanks at it.

When the lamp finally gives up, he throws it against the wall and lets out a guttural scream.

He doesn't notice me.

But I'm watching him.

He's on a rampage, his emotions in tatters, losing all self-control as he unleashes his anger on the room. I've never seen him like this before. I can't put a name to the feeling that washes over me as I watch him. I'm simply frozen in place, a captivated viewer.

Until he looks at me finally.

And for some reason, whether it's because I'm drunk and not thinking straight or something else, I decide to pretend all those years he ignored me don't exist. Pretend we're still best friends and that I'm not dating his brother.

What I didn't know back then was that Julian was having a panic attack, and I was going to help him get through it the same way he did with me tonight.

I also didn't know I was going to straddle his hips and beg him to fuck me when he forced his lips onto mine.

Or that I was going to forget about it.

"Until now."

CHAPTER TWENTY-FIVE

AURELIA

"What do you want?" Julian heaves, his chest rising and falling as his body remains unmoving in the center of the room. "Leave. Now." His eyes narrow the longer I take to follow his order.

I take a step forward, closing the door behind me as I sway on my legs. Bracing myself on the doorknob, I giggle before slapping a hand over my mouth and glancing back at him.

"I need to use the bathroom." I clear my throat, straightening up.

"You're drunk," he says, massaging his chest.

I cross my arms. "No."

He's gulping in air now.

"Julian?"

"The bathroom"—the muscles of his arm strain as he tightens his hand over his chest—"is at the end of the corridor."

When I don't move he spins to face me, and that's when I

see the bleeding cut on his right cheekbone. Did he get into a fight? *It wasn't at the Den—his fight is next week. I glance down at the hand clutching his chest, but I don't see any sign of torn or bruised skin.*

Julian always fights back . . . so why does it look like this fight was one-sided?

The muscles in his neck strain with the way his jaw is clenched tightly. He looks like a ticking time bomb about to explode, and when his turbulent blue eyes notice my resolve not to leave, he shouts, "Leave!"

But his eyes, they plead for help.

Stay.

The silent word is deafening in the way his eyes have softened, contrasting with the sharpness of his expression. The only part of his body he can't tame; a window into the turmoil inside of him. I can't ignore it. After years behind a solid wall, there's finally a crack.

Maybe I'm too drunk—or just idiotic—but I want in. I want him to share his pain with mine. Mix them together until they become one infernal mess.

He staggers back, hitting the bed and falling onto it. The hand over his chest is now pulling at his shirt, a sob breaking through his gasps.

"Julian?" *I'm at his side in an instant.* "Julian!"

He doesn't look up. He doesn't move.

He seems elsewhere as his body trembles.

Instinctively, I straddle his hips and cup his face before tilting it towards me. The position helps me break the spell he's under.

"What happened?"

Sadness clouds his features. Tears shimmer in his eyes before falling to soak my skin.

He doesn't answer me.

He doesn't try.

He doesn't even see me.

So I cover his eyes with my hands. He doesn't flinch away from my touch; instead he leans closer. He feels warm, his body strong under my legs. I try to refrain from touching every inch of him, but I can't control my mind from wondering how he feels.

"There's only me," I whisper, hoping to repel whatever thought is haunting him. "There's only me." I repeat it until his breathing calms and the silent sobs fade away.

I feel his body slowly uncoil with each uttered syllable, calming under the steadiness of my voice as it copies my tempo.

"You," he finally says in a brittle voice. "There's only you."

I uncover his eyes, feeling him blink against the sudden light. "Only me."

Color comes back into those blue eyes of his, and my lips curve into the ghost of a smile. Something shines in his eyes now. Like he's done waiting. Like everything is going to be different.

It's been ten years since the last time he looked *at me.*

He ignored me for years . . . Now I'm all he sees.

I jolt awake, taking in the familiar surroundings of my bedroom.

A shudder ripples through me at the memory of his

touch, how starved it felt; how he pulled me closer like he couldn't get enough—like he'd waited years to do it.

Kicking the bedsheets away from my sweaty body, I turn to the side and squish my face into the cool pillow, hoping the smooth linen will smother the flush spreading across my cheeks. The smell of the clean pillowcase and my honey perfume invades my nostrils, drowning out the lingering scent of Julian from my dream. But it doesn't last long. His scent is ingrained in me. I'd smell it anywhere if I just closed my eyes and focused on him.

I glance at the thick curtains. The sunrays are filtering in, and dust specks fly lazily around the room. It must be noon. Then I hear banging in the kitchen, and I know I'm correct. Valentine is deliberately making loud noises to wake me up, but I don't want to get out of bed today. Not after last night.

I need a break from the Harrows. I need a break from life and my plan.

At the mention of him, the memory of his lips branding my skin resurfaces. The way his hand would ever so lightly squeeze my hips, or how he'd bite me whenever I moaned too loud, just to make me moan even louder.

It's like I can see that night so vividly now. The veil of the alcohol has been lifted and every single detail is inked into the backs of my eyes.

The muscles of his arms going taut as he guided me up and down.

The veins in his neck when he clenched his jaw,

tilting his head back, anytime I swayed my hips in a figure eight.

The way light reflected in his eyes when he looked at me—even though it was the middle of the night and there was no light shining on us.

How was I able to forget all of that?

I bury my face in my pillow, grunting all my frustration away, but the material grazes the soreness on my neck, eliciting a hiss out of me. I instinctively cover it with my hand, the fresh wound pulsing uncontrollably.

Lucian's bite floods my mind, burying any memory of that night with Julian, and I feel like getting sucked in by the comfort of my bed for the rest of the day.

The exaggerated noises coming from the kitchen cease. I hear footsteps echoing next before the creaking of the door.

Valentine appears in the doorway, his tall frame filling the whole space as he scans my disheveled appearance, judgment etched in his features.

"You can't avoid life forever," he says in his signature gravelly voice.

Sitting up, I pull the covers around me, up to my neck, careful to hide Lucian's bite. "Easy for you to say," I mumble.

If I want to leave my bedroom, I'll need to get washed and ready first, and to do that, I'll need to go into the bathroom and come face-to-face with myself in the mirror—with *his* teeth engraved on my skin, making me feel everything again.

Making me sick.

I think Valentine rolls his eyes at me. "Here." He pulls

out an onion from his back pocket, extending it to me. "I thought about bringing the knife, but considering your current state, I figured it was best not to."

"Ha-ha, very funny." I play a little with the onion, rolling it from one hand to the other as I try to contain the smile that curves my lips at the gesture. "I could always just peel it."

"Don't expect me to stay," he huffs. "The years of me crying in front of anyone are long gone."

His words pull a warm-hearted chuckle out of me, leaving me weightless enough to appreciate all those years of him taking care of me.

He gave me a father when I lost a mother. He gave me a home when I was never granted one.

He picked me up and hasn't dropped me since.

"How's your plan coming along?" He ambles around the perimeter of my bedroom, his hands locked behind his back as he waits for an answer. "Tell me about your progress."

I'm so thankful he isn't asking me about last night. There's so much I want to ask him, but if I do, then he'll ask questions back, and I don't think I can stomach telling him about Lucian.

I will tell him eventually . . . Well, maybe. What will it get me in return? It's not like he can go against his own boss. Or maybe he would, but the thought of Lucian killing another person I care about is too dark for me to entertain.

"Victoria is next on the list. I'll invite her out to a secluded location and then strike."

He hums, his eyebrows meeting in the middle, but he doesn't stop walking.

I read his confusion and clarify, "Her mother played a part in her death." I pause, weighing up my next words. "She used her as a living ashtray, Valentine. Made her crawl naked in a room full of people. She used and degraded her."

"And her daughter will pay for her sins . . ."

I sit up straighter. "She's a member of the Inferno Consortium. Don't insult me by trying to get me to believe she didn't do fucked-up things."

His lack of an answer is an answer in itself.

He knows what vile things those people do. His job involves preventing the things they do from leaving their circle. Cleaning up any traceable evidence.

"Don't forget, there's more at stake here than just vengeance. Victoria's family is currently very valuable to the Harrows. Killing her could leave their business in serious trouble. Are you sure you want to do that to Julian?"

I want to do that to Lucian. I'm so very fucking sure.

"He knows what her family did to my mom. I'm sure he'll want to give me a hand."

He wants nothing more than to kill his father. At the very least, to make Lucian's life a living hell. He won't mind leaving me to have my fun with Victoria.

"All right, let's discuss the plan." He rolls a map of Seattle out on my lap, making a scene of pressing down the wrinkles on the paper.

"You know digital maps have been invented, right?"

He levels me with his gaze. "You'll need to choose a

secluded spot to lure Victoria to. But not so off-the-grid that it won't be as easy to pin the crime on someone else." He taps on an area in Downtown Seattle. "Something like this place."

A wooded area near the outskirts of the city, with a few stores here and there.

"I have a better idea." I can't just invite her to an unfamiliar location like that. I need her to think she's the one in control. "Do you still have that guy's contact? The one who edited me out of the CCTV footage of Sulawesi Spice?"

"What do you have in mind?"

Picking up my phone, I scroll through our chat until I find Victoria's phone number. "Can he erase any trace of text messages?"

"Of course he can. He gets paid for it—he can do anything I want him to."

"Peeerfect." I smile as I hit send.

He peeks at the screen. "What did you do?"

"I just invited her out for drinks."

"And you think that will work?"

The phone pings, and I smirk at the screen.

Victoria: *Ah, the golden girl . . . Meet me tomorrow night at the Cascade Grand Hotel. I have some things to take care of before then, but the rest of my night is free.*

Another message arrives.

Victoria: *I still have unfinished business with you after the way you disappeared from Lavish Eden.*

I glance up at Valentine, basking in the way his eyebrows rise in disbelief. "She deserves to die with that stupidity."

He shakes his head, rolling the map back into its original form and leaving the onion with me. "Remember, you have to be convincing."

"I know."

"Make her believe you're attracted to her."

Won't be too hard. I may like guys, but the girl is gorgeous. The power she radiates lures you in even if you don't want it to.

That's what happened to me that night at Lavish Eden. As much as I hate to admit it, I didn't really choose to get drunk; I just lost track of everything and allowed her to steer me around.

"Trust me, I can be very persuasive when I want to be."

He heads for the door, hand on the doorknob as he tells me firmly, "Your plan had better work. We can't afford any mistakes."

"I know," I whisper back. The more distance he puts between us, the more the heaviness from before weighs on me. "I won't let you down."

"Good." He fixes his stare on me. "Because if you fail, there will be no coming back from this. The Inferno Consortium may think they've found their target, but it wouldn't take much for it to get redirected onto you."

And what will Lucian do to me this time? He won't go easy on me. He won't kill me. He'll do far worse.

He'll turn me into my mother.

"Then let's make sure I don't fail," I reply steadily.

He nods, the lower side of his lips twitching.

That has always been his way of showing me he's proud.

"Before I go and leave you moping—"

"I am not moping!"

"Do you want me to keep Julian informed about what we discussed?"

My scowl eases a little at hearing his name.

"Yes. I think he'll enjoy knowing her days are numbered."

CHAPTER TWENTY-SIX

JULIAN

"Y ou're not fucking killing her."

The door slams shut behind me as I barge into Aurelia's bedroom, the abrupt noise echoing in the silence of her room. The only sound is the ragged rhythm of my breath as it matches the pounding in my head.

I was lying in bed unable to sleep when Valentine called to inform me of Aurelia's plan with Victoria. Without even needing to get dressed, I rushed here.

She's lying in bed, blinking the fogginess from her eyes. "What time is it?" She squints up at me, a sleepy frown stretching her features.

A pillow is trapped between her legs as she hugs it to her side. A long shirt covers her body, leaving her bare thighs on full display.

I pause for a second. That looks a lot like my shirt. The one I gave her the night she slept at my place.

She looks so vulnerable right now.

So tempting.

"Three in the morning," I reply, standing at the foot of her bed to hover over her delicate body. Her bedsheets are long forgotten.

She rubs at her eyes. "Have you lost your mind?"

Sitting straighter, she rolls her neck, massaging the base of it. The soft glow of the bedside lamp captures the bite Lucian left on her, and all the frustration I was feeling seconds ago turns into pure anger.

Maybe it's the tick of my jaw or the way my demeanor shifts, but she notices and quickly hides it with her hair. It looks like embarrassment is evident in her gaze.

She feels embarrassed?

If I didn't already have a million reasons to kill the bastard, this one would be enough.

He managed to make her feel ashamed of herself. Of her strength.

I wish she knew how easy it is to bruise when you fight back.

And she fought back.

"You can't kill Victoria," I let out before I forget why I came here, forcing the anger fuming inside of me out of my voice.

The green speckles in her eyes turn warm with the gold light caressing the side of her face. Her scowl from before deepens as she says, "Is that why you're here—to tell me what I can or can't do?"

"There are consequences to your actions. You don't know what you're getting yourself into."

"Neither do you, Julian."

I don't know if I want to marry the girl for how stubborn she is or fuck her. Either way, I can't seem to not want her when she makes it so difficult for me to convince her. Maybe I want her to challenge me for the rest of my life, or maybe I want to see if I can fuck the stubbornness out of her.

I like a good fight. Especially when it's with her.

"You can't kill Victoria, because the Inferno Consortium needs her help right now." The next words to leave my mouth have an acrid taste. "Especially my family."

Asking her not to kill Victoria to benefit Lucian's business is like asking her to let him win. Again.

Her laughter fills the room, her chest jerking with the movement, and my shirt slips down her left shoulder. "That's exactly why I need to kill her, Julian. She's part of the reason all these terrible things are happening." She glares up at me.

Somehow I don't care if she takes me for an idiot. Not when I'm fighting with myself not to push her down on the bed, open her legs, and taste her. Her exposed skin is too tempting as it radiates all her softness, a perfect contrast to her sharp attitude.

I'm trying to save our heads. *But I can't stop thinking about giving her head.*

"Aurelia." I try to reason with her. Or more with myself, really. "You can kill Victoria. I can help you do it, just not so soon." I grit my teeth as she rolls her eyes. "We need her for now."

"Is that so?" She crosses her arms over her chest, climbing onto her knees on the bed to level our stares. At least she tries to. She still needs to tilt her head up to stare into my eyes. "I didn't tell you about my plans so you could intervene, Julian. This is my mission, and I won't let you or anyone else stand in my way."

"Do you think you're some kind of superhero out to save the day? You're going to get yourself killed, and then what? What will be the point of all this?"

"Maybe it's worth dying for!" Her gaze blazes with determination. "Maybe there's more at stake here than just your precious business deals." Her voice turns condescending with the last few words.

Your precious business deals.

She knows my only business is the Den. Nothing else.

"I know you want to avenge your mother. I understand that more than anyone." My voice turns dangerously calm. "But if you go after Victoria now, you could bring everything crashing down on our heads. The Inferno Consortium needs her alive, her business going strong."

"Maybe that's what needs to happen."

She doesn't mean it. She's just a committed, stubborn girl—

"Maybe this whole twisted world we live in needs to burn so something better can rise from the ashes," she seethes in all seriousness.

Fish are born in water, so they don't fear swimming. Birds are born in trees, so they don't fear flying. Bats are born in darkness, so they don't fear the night. So I'm not surprised that a girl born from death doesn't fear it either. That a girl born from selfishness doesn't fear altruism, and that a girl born nameless doesn't fear being alone.

But it doesn't mean I get to accept it.

A boy born of abuse doesn't fear fighting for affection.

"Damn it, Aurelia!" I shout. "You're not thinking clearly! You can't just go around killing people without knowing the consequences! You can't just give yourself away so easily!"

She inches closer. "Watch me." Her voice holds chilling resolve as she stares at me, daring me to stop her.

We taint the surrounding air with anger. It's palpable between us as we feed it to one another. Her opposition is only fueling me, and as I stare down at her, green eyes blinking up at me, I can't help but drown in how fucking beautiful she looks.

There's something admirable about the trust, the strength, she puts in herself.

At my silence she adds, "I'm going to do whatever it takes to make things right." Her eyes narrow. "And there's nothing you can do to stop me."

"I don't think so."

At my calmness she snaps, grabbing the nearest pillow and hurling it at my face. It hits me square in the nose.

I'm too stunned to react.

Her eyes round as she remains frozen, perched on the bed. Waiting.

Did she just . . . throw a pillow at my face?

In a second I'm lunging forward on the bed to get a hold of her. Anticipating my move, she leaps off and darts to the other side of the room, as far away from me as possible.

"Come on, Julian!" she laughs.

She grabs a plush elephant toy from a nearby shelf and doesn't hesitate, throwing it in my direction. This time I dodge it.

"Is that the best you can do?" she jeers.

Did I just create a monster? Maybe I shouldn't have woken her up. Isn't 3 a.m. the devil's hour or some shit?

"What? You've lost your words?" She snatches anything her little fingers touch and throws it at me.

A navy book first.

"Aren't you going to tell me what a bad girl I am?"

Pink and yellow pencils follow next.

"*You can't kill Victoria, Aurelia.*" She mocks me by trying—but failing—to copy my voice.

Then erasers in the shape of little watermelons hit me in the chest, and I just stand there incredulous as I watch them hit the floor.

"I'm going to have so much fun slitting her throat." She punctuates each word, making sure I catch every single one before tossing rolled-up socks toward me.

I move my hand quickly and stop the collision midair. Snatching the pair for myself, I throw them back at her, hitting her right in the face.

Time seems to stop, and we both stare at one another, panting and wide-eyed. She glances down at the pillow and then back at me before bursting into laughter. And despite everything, I can't help but feel a smirk tugging at the corner of my own lips.

It's been so long since the last time I heard her laugh.

No—that's a lie. I heard her laugh a lot of times with Adrian. Too many times. But it's been so long since she last laughed with me.

It only took her throwing a pillow at me to make her laugh. I'd let her suffocate me with them if it'd keep that serene, genuine look on her face.

"All right." I close the distance between us. "You think you can just run around doing whatever the hell you want? Let's see how you like this."

Without leaving her time to react, I yank her against me, trapping her wrists behind her back with my hand. She cranes her neck back as I force her to look up at me, her chin pressing on my pecs.

Her laughter dies.

"Let me go, Julian," she hisses, squirming as she tries to loosen my grip. But the more she brushes her body over mine, the more I don't want to let go.

I tighten my hold on her.

"You're going to listen to me." I lean closer. "You're not going to kill Victoria tomorrow night. If you try, you'll have me to deal with."

Her eyes flicker back and forth between mine. "No."

"I'll spell it out for you." My free hand threads in her velvet hair, and I yank her face to the side before whispering in her ear. "You can't kill Victoria, because there's so much more going on here than you realize." My voice is low but crisp enough for her one-track mind to understand. "Your actions could cause a domino effect that would destroy everything the Inferno Consortium has worked for."

"There is nothing you can say that will make me listen to you."

"Is that so?" I stare into her eyes then shove her backward until her back hits the floor-to-ceiling window. Air leaves her lips, and I use her dazed appearance to rip the curtains and bind her wrists, securing them to the railing above her head.

"Julian! What are you doing? Untie me right now!"

I ignore her.

Taking a step back, I admire her all tied up.

She sways left and right, putting force into untying her wrists. But the movement only serves to make my dick harden as her shirt rises, revealing more of her skin. She's standing on her toes. This position elongates her body, showing me more of her that I never considered branding as mine.

Her struggled noises echo throughout the room, a symphony of deprived need and hidden necessity.

She likes it.

Giving her my back, I rummage around the place. "See, this is what happens when you don't obey me," I tease as I pick up a bottle of body oil from her vanity and a scarlet feather bookmark lying on the floor next to the navy book she hurled at me.

"Really?" Her eyes narrow at the items in my hand. "You're going to threaten me with a feather and some coconut oil?" she scoffs.

I chuckle at how naïve she is. She has no idea what I have in store for her, and I can't wait to put that smart mouth of hers to better use.

With the items in hand, I ignore her comment and

move around the bed. Kneeling at her nightstand, I open the drawer and pick an old metal comb from inside.

"Julian, what are you doing?"

I'm ready to ensure that you will never defy me again.

But first we need an audience.

Walking over to the window, I open the other curtains, making sure what I'm about to do to her is visible from the outside.

"You know." I stand in front of her, making a scene of sliding my eyes down her body with tantalizing slowness. "As much as I enjoy seeing my shirt hugging those perky tits, I need it out of the way."

In a second my shirt is lying at her feet. In pieces. She squeaks in surprise, sprouting one question after another, while I intentionally focus on my next move, ignoring her countless questions.

The lid of the body oil joins my shirt on the floor as I let the liquid drip down her naked body, cascading between her breasts until it dips between her legs. Fingers twitching, I follow the trail, spreading the oil over both her nipples, swirling and pinching as she arches her body toward my touch.

Silently begging me for more.

"See, you should learn to do what I say." I slap her left breast, and a moan heaves out from between her parted lips. "Or I'll be forced to take something else from you each time you disobey."

I pull the old metal comb from my pocket, twirling it between my fingers before pulling out my lighter. Her eyes round as she watches the flame flicker to life, dancing before the comb as I hold it over it.

The silvery leaves adorning the antique comb turn a bronze shade before igniting into a ruby red. I keep the flame on it until the prongs are a scorching branding iron.

Color drains from her face.

"Don't worry, golden one," I whisper with a sinister smirk. "I'm not inconsiderate. I promise I'll make you come."

CHAPTER TWENTY-SEVEN

AURELIA

The material of the makeshift rope feels coarse against my skin.

I pull and twist my weight, struggling to untie my wrists above my head to no avail. The more I move, the more the material seems to tighten, obstructing the blood flow to my hands. Frustration rises within me, mingling with the bitter taste of desire. Somehow, having control taken away from me makes me desperate for the wrong reason.

Julian flicks the silver lighter he's holding close, and the dancing flame disappears with a satisfying click that echoes around us. He pockets it, and I press my lips together, calculating what his next move will be and what I can do to get him to free me.

Does he smell my fear—or lack of it?

The comb, a gift Adrian bought me when he saw me looking at it during our walk through the Ballard Avenue Historic District, is now a bronze color as it cools down slightly. He swings it in front of my eyes, making sure I catch his every move-ment, taunting me into wasting my time studying him, because he knows I won't find a way out of this.

He can read me like the pages of a diary. I hate him for that.

A wicked smirk plays on his lips the moment he sees I understand the game he's playing. A shiver covers my whole body. I know what that look means: it's the same look he gets before stepping into the ring. Only, this time, the dim light playing in his eyes doesn't show someone keen to finish, but someone who can't wait to savor every second.

"Don't even think about it." I narrow my eyes, glancing from the comb to him.

I know he wouldn't hurt me. Never physically at least. But the sight of that scalding comb so close to my face, my skin, makes me shudder.

"Don't what, golden one?" he muses, taking a step forward. "Don't *stop*? Don't *give me pleasure* . . . Don't *keep me tied up all night*?"

I instinctively step back, putting as much distance between us as I possibly can with my hands locked in place. But there's nowhere I can go. The rope yanks me back, and my bare ass bumps against the cold window behind me, making me gasp. Reminding me whose mercy I'm under and how there's no escaping it.

Eyes that look like a night sky gleam with mischief. "Enjoying yourself already?" he asks in a light, teasing tone, in contrast to the way his arm muscles bounce with the firm, unyielding grip he holds on the comb.

"Go to hell," I hiss, glaring at him for how much I detest his enjoyment in all this.

"I already am." He smirks. "Or I wouldn't be able to sin against your body."

For a moment I'm frozen, caught off-guard by the rawness in his words. I feel the heaviness of his revelation sliding down my spine. It's like he just peeled back a layer of himself and showed me how deeply he really feels for me.

Then why did you push me away? Why did you hurt me when we feel the same way?

Anger seeps into me, stirring all the conflicting emotions tugging at my insides. He's a hypocrite, or simply a sadist, because I can't find any better reason for the way he's treating me.

He grabs the body oil once more, dipping the still scorching comb into it. Then he stirs the liquid for a few seconds until the oil heats up and he can pour it onto my skin, tearing out another gasp from me.

A soft burning sensation spreads over my body as the searing droplets fall down my curves. And when the skin becomes too sensitive, his strong hands come down next, massaging the oil into my skin.

Sending shivers down my body.

Making me bite down on my tongue so I won't give him the satisfaction of hearing me.

"See how your body reacts to pain, golden one?" he whispers, hand brushing over my breast, covering it all before feeling its fullness. "To my touch?" He leans in close to my ear. "It *aches* for it."

"Y-you're wrong." I try to suppress the need from

revealing itself. "My body doesn't . . . it doesn't like what you're doing." *Am I trying to convince him or myself?* "You're delusional. It's shuddering away from . . . from your touch, not toward it."

Lies. Lies. Lies.

"Is it?" He moves his fingers lower, carrying on with their torturous dance across my oiled skin. "Your body can't lie, golden one. It's craving my touch."

My façade of defiance cracks and my body betrays me, yearning to get closer—for him to touch me everywhere. A spark ignites between my legs, and I sway forward involuntarily.

"Shut up," I say through clenched teeth.

He's right. I can't ignore the way his touch ignites every single cell in my body. Like a magnet, wherever he touches comes to life, luring him to never leave.

"Make me," he dares. Low and dangerous. His eyes are now the color of the abyss, the darkest shade they've ever been. "Tell me you won't kill Victoria."

"No." I spit at his face, and the corner of his mouth twitches before a low chuckle rumbles in his throat.

Julian takes a step away from me, his arms crossed over his chest. If the tattoos on his arms could come alive, they'd devour me whole. "This"—he waves his hand up and down my body—"was an entirely altruistic act. But maybe I should reconsider my tactics." His stare turns somber.

"I don't care what you do." I yank my hands one last time in an attempt to free them. "I just want you to untie me and leave!"

Lies. Lies. Lies.

He barely touched me, and I'm already squirming with need. Even the faintest brush of my skin and my body is ready to react. I've fantasized about Julian a lot of times in the dead of the night, but this is the first time I've experienced this raw need. My body is eager to succumb completely to his touch; to finally let someone else take care of me. To tie my hands and leave me just to *feel* for once.

"We'll see about that." His silent promises are loud enough for me to hear.

My body strains from holding its weight on my wrists and toes. The pain in my shoulders and my back calls for my attention, but I can't seem to think of anything else but him. I feel like a marionette as he deftly pulls on my strings.

I can't tear my eyes away from him.

He takes his shirt off, revealing his toned chest and the ink that adorns it, before disappearing into the bathroom. I follow each dip of his muscles, the ink giving depth to them, and for a second I forget I'm naked and tied up. I've seen him without a shirt so many times, yet it still irks me how affected I get.

I try to twist my hands, hoping to find a weakness in the knot, but all I achieve is grazed skin. Just as I hiss from the pain, Julian appears with a soaked shirt in his hands, beads of water following him on the floor.

He stops in front of me and in a slow act of torture regards me—every inch of my body—as he twists the shirt in his hands. Then I hear the snap of the material before I register the stinging sensation on my thigh, and a scream rips out of me.

The cold, wet fabric against my heated skin awakens all my senses. A surge of adrenaline rushes through me, leaving me gasping for air.

"Feels good, doesn't it?" He whips the side of my ass next, and I feel a hot streak of pain go through me. The sudden shock tears a scream out of me before it turns into a guttural moan.

My body trembles and my fingers claw at the ropes as I try to even my breathing.

"Fuck you," I grit out.

"Later." He smirks then whips the sensitive skin of my lower abdomen, making me hunch from the surprise.

And the pain.

My legs tremble with each colliding lash on my skin. Waves and waves of delirious pleasure flood my judgment.

"Tell me, golden one . . . what do you want?" he purrs, reading my mind, feeling my desire even as I fight it.

He moves closer.

"For you to untie me," I croak, hiding the desperation in my voice.

Lies. Lies. Lies.

"Your body says otherwise." Lost in thought, he traces a finger along my thigh. On the red patch he left on my skin from the whipping. "But I won't give you what you want . . . Not unless you tell me what I want to hear."

"Never." I gulp down the desire to let him do with me what he pleases. To lend him full control and see where he guides me. This is what falling into the abyss of pleasure truly feels like.

He just stares at me. Then, without warning, he whips my body again. This time harder. Faster.

Everywhere he sets his eyes on my body gets branded with the shirt as he flogs me.

Each hit leaves me gasping for air, craving for more as I slowly lose myself to the sensation, to insanity, as I keep my resolve from shattering. I clench my jaw, meeting his stare head-on even as my body trembles and my lower lip threatens to tear from the force I'm biting it with.

"God, you look so fucking good like this," he groans, watching my every reaction through his hooded eyes. "Your body is practically begging for my touch, isn't it?"

I don't answer. I can't.

If I open my mouth I might explode. The way he's making me feel would come out in the form of a moan. A plea for him to make me come.

Biting down on my lower lip harder, I restrain myself from moaning out loud as he flogs my nipple. Goose bumps erupt, and I feel my body shake with . . . *need*.

My orgasm builds.

If he continues, I might rip his clothes off and fuck him senseless. Or just collapse from the overwhelming sensation flowing over me.

I—

My lips part, and I rub my legs together, attempting to relieve the pressure as it mounts within me.

I'm so close.

I arch my back, the cold glass of the window heightening my perception, and my head falls back.

A wave of ecstasy floods through me, and just as I'm about to come, it quickly disappears.

Julian stops, leaving me hanging in complete desperation.

"You bastard!" I wheeze, boiling over in frustration. Tears threaten to fall down my cheeks from the electricity of the emotions coursing through me.

He wraps his hand around my throat, constricting my air supply, and presses his lips against mine. "Tell me, how much do you want to come?"

I wet my lips, battling with myself—losing myself in his tempting eyes.

Should I give in to him or not?

Something tickles the side of my hips. Up, under my breasts, then back down my stomach, getting a little stuck every time it runs over the oil. Heightening every agonizing feathery touch.

"Tell me," he whispers, tightening his grip around my neck. "How do you feel right now?" He tilts his head. "Are you drenched between your legs?" He moves the feather closer to my bundle of nerves. "Does the thought of all the dirty things I could do to you while you're tied up and helpless make you even wetter? Do you like the idea that people could be watching us through the window?"

I'm panting. Not from the lack of oxygen, but from his descriptive questions. From his words as they heighten my arousal, stealing the strength from my legs as the oil-slicked feather brushes over my clit, making my body twitch with need.

I can't take it anymore.

I need him. And I need him to make me come.

"Please," I whimper.

"Say it." His thumb caresses the pulse in my throat. "Tell me you won't kill Victoria tomorrow, and I'll give you what you want."

Gritting my teeth, I'm tempted to resist and disobey him, to spit in his face and tell him no, but the sensation between my legs is overwhelming. It's too sensitive for me to just ignore.

My body is burning up with each second he taunts me with the promise of release.

I want him.

I want him more than the thought of killing Victoria right now.

"Fine." A small part of me wheezes at the defeat, but the rest of me buzzes with anticipation. "I won't kill Victoria. Now make me fucking come."

He crashes his lips to mine, hungry for my taste as I fight for his. Our tongues meet, desperation evident in the way we cling to one another.

He plunges two fingers inside of me, and I gasp into the kiss. His lips devour any sound I make at the sudden intrusion. Thrusting his fingers fast, he adds another, and I moan in appreciation.

His other hand, wrapped around my throat, strains, squeezing my neck hard as he feels the pulsing sensation of my pleasure building between my legs. With each thrust, he hits the sweet spot inside of me and pleasure builds.

Until it becomes too much to bear.

A groan vibrates against my lips as I nip on his. With all the teasing from before, it won't take me long to come.

His fingers slide in and out, slick with my desire, and he can tell I'm close. He tightens his hand around my neck, completely choking me. I should be scared, but the lack of oxygen only intensifies the pleasure. I've never felt more alive than I do now.

My vision blurs, eyes drooping closed as I stare at him, his eyes glued to mine. The darkness that was there before is now gone, replaced by a warmth that envelops me as he breathes in all my pleasure.

I come undone, soaring along on the most intense orgasm of my life.

"Julian!" I choke out.

At the sound of his name, hunger shines in his eyes and he quickens his movement, meeting the tremble of my body with each thrust. My body convulses, and he thrusts deeper. Harder. Faster. Needier. *Desperate.*

His jaw clenches, and he watches as I submit to the pleasure he's driving into me.

Once the orgasm abates he removes his hand from my throat, allowing me to gulp in a lungful of air as I struggle to catch my breath, my body still quivering from the force of my climax. My vision fills with black spots as light slowly filters back in.

I stare at Julian. Both of our chests are heaving as a

mixture of satisfaction and hunger simmers right under the surface.

Licking my lips, a grin spreads across my face.

"More," I beg in a demanding whisper.

A predatory glint shines in his eyes, pupils darkening with lust. "Fuck, you're insatiable."

Lowering his pants, he doesn't waste any time.

In a second I'm being lifted by my ass. I wrap my legs around his waist, and then he's inside of me in one powerful thrust.

Pressing me hard against the cold window, he steals the satisfaction he gave me earlier, with his fingers.

I'm deprived now, stripped bare of any relief.

I need more. I want more.

"So wet for me," Julian growls, and I moan in response.

I'm more than just wet for him. I'm *his*.

I urge him deeper, moving my hips in sync with his thrusts. I wish he would untie me so I could make him mine too.

"Anyone could see how much you want this," he teases, reminding me of the window. Of the spectacle we're making of ourselves. "You're dripping for me, Aurelia."

Hearing my name leave his lips is almost overwhelming. The back and forth of his teeth and his tongue as he nibbles on my jaw fuels my desire. But it's the thought of someone possibly watching us from outside that really does it for me.

I clench my fingers around the restraints binding my wrists, wishing it were his skin instead, dreaming of my nails digging into his back, scratching him until they draw blood.

But I can't, so I bite his lower lip. Hard. Until the metallic taste of blood shakes my senses. I lick the crimson droplets away, savoring the taste before pulling him into a heated kiss.

The sound of his groans mixes with the thudding noise of my body as it gets pushed back and forth into the window. His hands part my ass with each thrust, slamming harshly into me.

Then I feel his thumb tracing over my puckered hole, and my breathing urges him forward. I want him to touch me there, to mark something never touched by anyone else as his. Adrian never did, and I was too self-conscious to ever ask him.

Julian puts pressure over it with his thumb and shivers rush down my spine, leaving me craving for more. Then he smears my wetness over the area, and I feel the heat flush over my face before he pushes his thumb inside.

I gasp. Every thought leaves my mind at the searing pleasure.

"God, you're so tight," he breathes out. His pupils dilate. He quickens his thrusts before groaning, "This is mine." Then he pushes his thumb inside, eliciting a whimper out of me. "My brother may have taken your virginity, but this . . . this is all mine."

He starts to move his thumb in and out, burning me in the process, until the pressure from his finger hits the pressure from his dick, making me see stars.

His words, along with the pressure growing between

my legs, send a shudder of pleasure through me, igniting a flame only he can stoke. This possessive side of him is strangely satisfying. Adrian was never possessive with me, only controlling, so seeing Julian this blinded by his need to own me is somewhat intoxicating.

Addictive, like I hold all the power.

The rawest form of pleasure builds between my legs, and I moan loudly as he continues to fuck my ass in sync with his thrusts. The combination is too much. In seconds I feel myself hurtling toward another climax.

I cry out, my voice breaking at the intensity of the orgasm. His reaction is immediate and as intense as mine. He doesn't take long to reach his peak. His breath hitches before a groan resonates deep within him. His body goes taut above mine, and with a final shudder of pleasure he releases himself inside of me.

I watch him from under my lashes, gasping for air as his grip on my waist tightens for one heart-stopping moment before it slackens. His eyes are still as dark as they were before, and I lose myself in their vastness. It's as if he's trying to commit this moment to memory.

He didn't use a condom, but I'm not concerned since I'm on the pill. Still, the tiny voice in the back of my mind nags about the risks we keep taking. Next time I won't give in to him if he doesn't use protection. Although I'm worried my resolve will be as frail as it was tonight.

We stand like that, panting and staring into each other's droopy eyes, until Julian carefully unties my wrists. I rub at the sore skin, flexing the muscles here and there. Then, when my legs threaten to give out, still weak and trembling, he lifts me up into his arms and lays me down on my bed, taking in the sight of my exposed body while his eyes flicker with something soft, something tender, that leaves warmth spreading through my chest.

But just as it appears, it's gone, leaving a trace of numbness in its wake.

He opens my legs, gathering his leaked-out cum with his finger before sliding it inside of me. I hiss at the touch, still sensitive and sore. It makes me shudder a little, but he covers me with the bedsheets. A soft moan leaves my lips at the warm feel of my bed as it lulls me to sleep.

"Don't wash yourself."

His low voice filters in, and I blink my eyes open, staring into a brewing tempest. I'm about to protest when his next words steal away any reasoning that remains within me.

"I want to know you'll be walking around tomorrow with my cum between your legs."

His crude words bring a flush to my cheeks. I can't walk around with his cum dripping down. Anyone could see it.

"Julian, I can't—"

He brushes the back of his hand over my reddening cheeks, and the tender gesture stuns me. He leans down, pressing a kiss to my lips, and I forget what I was about to say.

If doing what he tells me to do gets me this level of tenderness from him, I have no problem doing so.

He deepens the kiss, gripping my chin to close the distance between us. A flicker of desire forms in my lower abdomen, and I know if we were to go at it again, it wouldn't take me long to come undone.

I'm so consumed by the moment that when he straightens back up, the motion feels abrupt. He looks down at me, and the mixture of emotions in his eyes is long gone. In its place is his stoic, emotionless expression.

Without saying a word, he turns and leaves.

And I'm left alone again, with only my thoughts to pester my mind, clouding the remnants of what just happened between us.

The atmosphere turns cold again, creeping closer, as reality pushes through the cracks before sinking in.

All the warmth he enveloped me with is snatched away in seconds, leaving me with this itching sensation all over my skin. The wetness between my legs burns now with the doubt that this was all an act of manipulation. That maybe he didn't really mean each caress and kiss. He managed to play with my resolve, molding it with the promise of pleasure.

No. Impossible. That's not it.

But now he's gone . . . the fog of lust is lifted.

Tomorrow I'm killing Victoria.

Even if it kills us in the process.

CHAPTER TWENTY-EIGHT
AURELIA

"I'll be a little late. Make yourself at home. Xoxo."

I lift my head, Victoria's message fading as I switch my phone off.

The lobby of the Cascade Grand Hotel twinkles with the copious diamond chandeliers whose light reflects on the silver and red accents of the ceiling mural.

Plush velvet couches dot the outsides of the room, red cushions matching the heavy curtains, adding a bit of color to the monotonous cream.

It's like walking into a show of wealth from someone with a lack of style. They've just filled up the space with anything that had five zeroes on the price tag.

At the far end of the room, where the elevators are located, stand two tall pillars. The same mural pattern as the one on the ceiling adorns them. To my right is the reception desk. Behind it, a man dressed in a red suit types on the computer, unbothered by the breathtaking view of Elliot Bay through the windows at his back, the night sky reflecting over the black water.

"Welcome to the Cascade Grand Hotel." The receptionist's hair is slicked back with precision, and when he glances up at me, I notice how his eyes gleam under the light of the chandelier. "How may I help you?"

I meet his practiced, beaming stare. "Hello. I'm a guest of Victoria Marlowe."

"Ah, yes." He presses his lips together as he types on the keyboard. The pair of silver cufflinks he's wearing glint at his wrists. "Ms. Marlowe told me to let you know she'll be running a bit late. You're welcome to wait in her room." He turns around, grabbing a silver key card, and the leather *Tom Ford* shoes on his feet catch the rich light of the room.

His outfit is new—he must have just started working here. His shoes still need breaking in.

I slide the card between my fingers and read the engraved word "PENTHOUSE."

"Thank you." I send him a curt smile and turn to leave, heading to the elevators.

He'll be dead in the next hour. *And he just bought himself a pair of new shoes that cost more than some people's salary.* The thought tightens my stomach.

It's a bitter pill to swallow. Innocent lives shouldn't come between us in this war. It's sickening. But he's a free-running witness who could identify me. It's either him or me who dies, and the idea of those slimy bastards remaining untouched after what they did to my mother and others is too much to bear.

Valentine will kill him tonight so the guilty can pay for what they've done.

I step into the elevator. The metallic doors are on the

verge of closing when a hand springs out and abruptly stops them. A guy with a little kid slips in. My gaze skims over him briefly. He's dressed in black pants paired with a beige polo shirt. The small child is dressed similarly, in velvet brown pants and a slightly baggy white shirt.

Without exchanging pleasantries, the guy presses a number for his floor and turns forward, his back toward me. The kid, with his tiny hand wrapped around the guy's pinkie finger, can't be more than five years old. Those big chocolate-brown eyes keep peeking back at me, only to quickly look away whenever our gazes meet.

A smile threatens to curve my lips at how cute and innocent he looks. But as I watch the numbers on the panel rise, memories of the last time I used this elevator flood in. DeMarco splattered on the floor as the poison coursed through his veins, the Harrows' fundraiser just floors below.

It feels like a lifetime ago.

My very first kill.

I've killed more since then, and yet I'm not even close to the end. There are so many lives I still need to take. Lives that need to pay for the damage they've caused.

Acknowledging this reality leaves a heavy weight on me, making each step towards enacting this plan heavier than the last. This isn't my path of vengeance—I already knew that. But when the guilty have been punished, the consequences will fall on me. Not my mother.

A dull ache spreads through my chest at the thought. I feel guilt for the guilty. What a joke.

Or maybe you're the guilty *one*, the voice in the back of my mind hisses. *For lying to Julian. For throwing promises around like petals in a graveyard.*

How will Julian react? Will he be mad? I don't believe he cares about the Inferno Consortium enough to ask me not to do it. I thought he hated it. Hated Victoria and his father as much as me, if not more. He'll thank me when he sees his father's business tripping over itself. Seeing Lucian in disarray will be the highlight of the month, I'm sure.

I feel those cocoa eyes on me again. The little kid's curiosity is too strong to control as he peeks up at me, his little body pressed over the leg of the stranger.

When he notices me staring back, I stick out my tongue.

His eyes round in surprise, lips parting slightly before he says, "That's not very ladylike." His voice is a bundle of animated, high-pitched certainty. Those little eyebrows crumple as he scowls at me.

"Neither is staring." I arch a brow at him, causing a small smile to tug at the corner of his lips.

I pause at the sight, basking in the way he radiates simplicity. The life of a child, full of love, joy, and memories.

When does it stop? When does it disappear, stolen like dreams in the dead of night?

Maybe we all grow up to lose it. Or was I one of the lucky ones life decided to throw its worst challenges at?

"Well, I am a man." He sticks his button nose up in the air.

"Oh, sorry. I thought you were a gentleman." I rest a

hand on my chest. "My mistake. I was certain you were one."

He stomps his little foot on the floor, and I try my best not to smirk at his little scrunched-up face. "I am!"

Just then, the guy moves, and I remember we aren't alone. He turns his head slightly to the side, enough for me to catch the smirk appearing on his lips at our conversation. I trail my gaze at what little I can see of him.

Waves of dark golden hair combed backward and tanned skin. He's too young to be the father, but from the way he holds himself he appears older than me. But not in age. He appears mature, like someone who's been holding a heavy weight on their shoulders for most of their life.

Old in spirit.

"What's your name?" I ask the little *gentleman*.

"You can call me—"

The doors to the elevator open, and I gasp as I watch him get pulled out of it by the hand, leaving him scurrying behind the guy as he leads him away. They're about to turn the corner, the elevator doors closing, when he shouts back at me with the brightest of smiles, "Ciao, *ciumachella*!"

I watch, stunned. Then a sudden chuckle bursts out of me before I can suppress it, warmth spreading through me despite what I'm heading up to do. I wave at the little disappearing figure as the doors close and silence fills the space once again. His upbeat presence is still palpable as my lips twitch with the residue of a laugh.

That was the strangest encounter, yet it was exactly what I needed to lift the weight from my shoulders before going to murder someone.

What did he call me? *Chiumakel?* No. *Chiukella,* maybe?

All I got was the typical Italian word used for greetings and goodbyes. He must be here on vacation. Seattle is usually packed with tourists for the summer, but since we're a week away from September, this is the perfect time to visit. Less crowds, and the hotel prices are significantly lower.

At Victoria's floor the elevator doors slide open.

I'm greeted by a vast living room with an elegant stone design on the walls framing the French doors to a balcony. Cream-colored sofas and vases with blooming plants stand in the middle of the room.

The layout is somewhat similar to the room I was in with DeMarco, only this one has enough space for a cocktail party, and the other for a dead body only.

Walking around the space, I let my fingers brush the softness of the deep red curtains, the unexpected roughness of the rose jute material of the cushions, and the plushness of the couch situated in the middle of the room. The same vase that was in DeMarco's room is perched on a vanity, a bouquet of sunflowers arranged inside of it, and my lips curve at the memory. A melodic lullaby threatens to push past my lips in the form of a whistle, but that would be too creepy even for me.

Instead I strip bare.

With each step I take I undress, leaving each piece of clothing scattered on the floor.

Breadcrumbs for Victoria to follow.

I arrive at the primary bedroom completely naked. Pulling my hair up in a ponytail, I stand in front of the full-length mirror admiring the woman I've carved myself into. They may have chosen my life path for me, but everything else I am is thanks to me. My resolve, my strength, and my anger—I built it.

The tips of my fingers skim the pink scar on my neck. I angle my head, carefully roaming my eyes over it.

"You're next," I say under my breath. "I'm coming for you."

I slip into the adjoining bathroom, grabbing a white robe, which I drape over my shoulders. I leave the belt around my waist loose to reveal some skin as the robe hangs slightly open in the middle.

Walking back to the bedroom, I sit on a plush chair just as the sound of the elevator doors opening breaks the silence, followed by the click-clack of high heels.

"I hope you didn't wait too long." Her voice booms, echoing through the penthouse.

I don't answer.

"Aurelia? Where are—?"

She just found my light blue blouse.

And my white skirt.

Now we wait as the clothes lead her to me.

I watch the bedroom door, ajar, with bated breath. The spot I'm sitting in will give me the perfect view of her when she walks in, and it'll let her spot me immediately.

"Well, well," I hear her drawl right behind the door before she pushes it open. "You really took 'make yourself comfortable' to heart, didn't you?" My underwear gets wrapped around her fingers as she waves it like a trophy. "Not that I'm complaining."

"I hope you don't mind," I say before curling my lips, letting her bask for a few more seconds in the delusion she's created for tonight. Then, when I think enough time has passed, my smile falls. Arms spread on the armrests, I order, "Put my underwear in your mouth."

Victoria's expression falters. She wasn't expecting the sudden shift in my tone. "Excuse me?" Her eyes narrow as she tries to process my change in attitude.

"Put. It. In. Your. Mouth."

This is how it should start, with degradation. Just like how her mother treated mine.

One breath.

Another.

"Fine," she huffs, rolling her eyes as she stuffs her mouth with my *La Perla* lace.

Just having her wrapped around my fingertips, following my orders, sends an electric current of power through my body. I can't wait to do to her what her mother did to mine.

"Strip," I order next, "and crawl to me."

What little playfulness remained within her vanishes at my command. Her eyes narrow with rage, body tensing for a split second. A spark of worry ignites in my stomach, but I try to maintain my self-control and not let her notice it.

"Suit yourself." My voice is cold and unbothered.

Deciding to push my luck, I fix my gaze on hers and

slowly part my legs, enough to reveal just a hint of my nakedness. A tease. Bait.

Her tight expression loosens. She trails her gaze down to my parted legs. I can see her resolve vanishing as the seconds tick by. I know I have her wrapped around my little finger. She just needs a push.

"Strip."

She raises her eyes back to mine. I let a challenging smirk stretch my lips, and her eyes glow with the invitation to be dominated. She's loving this.

Unbuttoning her white shirt, she lets it fall. Then she takes the underwear out of her mouth, letting her next words reach my ears.

"Didn't expect you to be this slutty . . ." She wets her lips. "But then again, you are the golden one of the Inferno Consortium. Guess people-pleasing is what you do best."

She drops her beige pants, putting the underwear back in her mouth, eager for what's to come.

The muscles in my jaw twitch at what she said. Even now, as I treat her with inferiority, she still thinks less of me. A burning desire to shatter her illusion and prove her wrong gnaws at me.

Just as she's about to crawl up to me, I tsk loudly, letting the sound bounce off the walls.

"I said, strip naked and then crawl."

Her nostrils flare, probably hating being told what to do.

Without me having to tell her twice, she unclips her bra and steps around her underwear. Then, on all fours, she makes her way toward me.

Vulnerable. Laid bare before me.

She looks good. I won't lie. Her body is fit. Long, lean legs and a toned stomach, with boobs bigger than a handful. But as I look at her, I can't stop myself from wondering if Julian has ever seen her like this. On her knees for him. Black eyes looking up from under her long lashes. Mouth parted, waiting—

"Didn't expect you to be into this kind of kink." Her voice breaks the images forming in the back of my mind.

She's between my parted legs, long fingernails digging slightly into my thighs as the underwear that was in her mouth now dangles from her pinkie.

She's not good at following orders.

"Actually," I reply, grabbing it before binding her hands behind her back with the damp lace, "I'm into a different kind of kink." I whisper the words close to her ear before pushing her onto her back with my foot. Harshly—for fun.

Gasping, she struggles to sit back up.

I made sure to tighten the underwear around her hands well. It's going to leave a scar, but I don't think she'll mind in the afterlife.

"What the fuck? What's wrong with you? Help me up." She wiggles her body, really trying to get back on her knees.

Ignoring her, I just stare, head tilting to the side in appreciation.

"You won't get away with this, you little bitch," she huffs, focused on the task at hand.

I burst into laughter at her empty threat.

She won't be able to hurt me. There'll be nothing she can do once those makeshift cuffs come off.

I rise from my seat and wander over to the other side of the bedroom. Victoria's body twists at abnormal angles as she follows me with her eyes.

"I thought it would be more fulfilling to watch you slither at my feet." I pull a box of matches from the pocket of the robe. "I honestly don't understand why your mother found such fascination in it."

"My mother?"

Ignoring her question, I light up the candles in the room. One side first before moving to the next.

"You see,"—heat spreads over my fingers as the match comes to life—"I would've kept to the script, burned your skin with a cigarette over and over again, until your body contorted from the pain." I let the now spent match fall to the floor, turning to stare at her as I say, "But I'm not really a sadist, so I decided to go with an easier way."

I grab the flask I hid beside the matches in the pocket of the robe and take a long sip of its contents, hissing as the burning liquid slides down my throat.

"What are you talking about?" Her voice trembles at the end of her question.

I hurl the remaining liquid at her, drenching her in vodka. Then, with a finger, I let the first candle fall to the floor.

"Fuck! What are you doing?" she panics. "Are you insane?"

"Maybe." I walk to the next candles and make them fall one by one. "But now it's time for you to feel the heat." I lift a candle in my hand. "Your mother made the mistake of using mine as her personal ashtray. I'd like to repay the favor."

Her eyes round. A mixture of confusion and fear clouds her vision. But she doesn't plead for her life. Doesn't bat an eye as I hurl the candle at her soaked body.

Flames erupt on her skin, igniting a show of defiance that's almost admirable, if not stupid. And that's when she screams, finally finding the strength to get up.

But it's too late.

I lock the door to the bedroom behind me and quickly get to lighting the candles scattered around the rest of the penthouse before dropping them to the floor and letting them spread their deadly light.

She continues to scream, howling in pain. The notes are soothing, satisfying a part of me that longs to make her pay for her mother's sins. Yet the other part is simply satisfied at the prospect of being one step closer to finishing this massacre.

I don't have much time left before someone hears her or the fire alarm goes off.

Hurrying to the elevator, I press the button for the floor just below this one before adjusting the rope, tightening it around my body. I left my clothes on the floor of the penthouse, giving them the same fate as Victoria. The CCTV footage of me will be erased, but if anyone other than the hotel receptionist saw me, they won't be able to find the clothes and match them to me.

My heart gallops as the elevator descends. The moment I set foot out of it the alarm finally blares. It doesn't take long for the guests to spring out of their rooms, panicking, rushing toward the fire escape.

I join the crowd, concern etched on my features as I seamlessly blend in with them.

"Fire!" someone screams, causing more chaos to erupt. People start pushing past, desperate to escape and get to safety.

I'm running alongside them, but my mind is elsewhere.

Somehow the more I kill, the less satisfied I feel. The adrenaline I felt with my first kill was intoxicating, but I just feel empty right now. The image of Victoria being burned alive scratches behind my eyes.

The people surrounding me don't suspect me of anything. They think I'm one of them.

But I'm not. I just killed a woman. Set her on fire.

I know it was the right thing to do. *The only thing to do.*

So why do I feel like I'm losing a part of myself in the process?

CHAPTER TWENTY-NINE
JULIAN

A scream pierces my sleep.

A scream so guttural, so loud, it sharpens the further it cuts through, shredding the foggy tendrils of my dream.

I bolt upright at the third shriek, my ears pounding in sync with my racing heart. Sweat clings to my body, foreshadowing this very moment. Like it knew long before now I would get woken up by cries for help.

But this isn't one of those usual nights. My mom isn't screaming because of my father. My mother is screaming for something else.

I can hear it in the rawness of each howl, more animal than human.

She isn't screaming in pain, but for survival.

"Let him go!" Her words get swallowed by a scream —her scream—as desperation and anger meet.

I throw the covers off me, panic gripping my muscles as I stumble to my feet.

The house feels different. The air is denser. Night

shadows stretch out from the corners as the walls hold in their breath.

This isn't one of her usual screams. No—this is different.

This is the sound of someone dying.

The house passes me by in disorienting shapes as I run to her bedroom, legs pushing me forward with the urgency coursing through them.

"No!" Her voice cracks.

And something inside of me breaks.

A blind panic consumes me whole. Not even the cold marble floor manages to ground me. I just want to reach my mom.

Bursting through the double doors, I frantically scan for her and find her pinned against the wall. Someone taller than Lucian cages her in, blocking my view of her.

Where is Lucian? Did he give her to this man for the night?

No. At least not in his own bed. At four in the morning.

"Get the fuck away from her!" I roar. Everything inside of me gets drowned out by the rage that conquers my rationality. "Touch her and I'll skin you alive!" My fists clench.

I'll skin him alive either way.

At the sound of my voice, the man wearing the ski mask backs away from my mother before shoving past me to escape.

His abrupt action knocks me off-balance, and all I catch is a glimpse of his retreating figure.

"Guards! Stop that bastard!" I blare, voice echoing down the corridor, throughout the whole house.

A thump catches my attention, and I turn to see my mom crumpled on the floor, her right hand clutching the lower side of her stomach.

My throat squeezes shut at seeing her like this.

Kneeling beside her, I hold her chin up and look into her eyes. "Mom," I whisper.

Even in the situation we've found ourselves in, I'm searching for her reassurance. For her to tell me everything will be fine.

She hisses, and my eyes fall down her body to the stain on her white nightgown.

Blood seeps from the stab wound on her abdomen.

My hands tremble as I put pressure on it. But the blood keeps flowing out, drenching my hands. The metallic scent overpowers her flowery perfume, and I'm scared this is all I'll remember her by.

Nothing but her favorite white gown, ruined by her blood.

Nothing but her pink lips that always found the strength to stretch into a smile whenever she'd hold me, now the color of ash. Thin, crippled.

Or her blue eyes, the color of the morning sky, now the color of death. Of lost hope.

This can't be the last time I see my mom. I don't want this moment to taint all the memories I have of her.

I feel my spirit sink as I hold her life in my bloodied hands. I thought I was doing everything to protect her. I should have prevented this from happening. I should have done more. I didn't save her—I killed her. This is all my fault.

She looks at me with blinding terror. Tears fill her eyes as she gasps for air between jagged sobs.

Her lips drag at the corners as she struggles to form words through the soaring panic. The adrenaline must already be in full effect, or she'd be screaming out at the sheer force I'm putting on her stomach.

"Shh, it's okay."

But it's not. My hands are slick with her blood.

I can feel my own eyes pricking with unshed tears.

I can't lose her. Not like this. Not now.

Reaching to the left, I blindly grab the phone on the nightstand, leaving pressure on the wound with my other hand.

"Valentine!" I choke out the moment he picks up. "It's Julian. Someone broke into the house, tried to kill Mom. They're still here—find them!"

"Understood." His voice is calm. Receptive. Even if I just woke him up in the middle of the night with the worst news. "Is your mother all right?"

I'm about to answer when my mom manages to speak.

"Lucian . . . gone." Her voice is barely above a whisper, the words scratching the back of her throat as she uses all her strength to vocalize them.

Lucian is gone.

I was right then. He left her with that guy. But why? Something isn't adding up.

"Mom, what do you mean?"

"Julian?" Adrian's voice echoes around the room as he bursts through the door. His eyes round when he catches us on the floor, but the color completely drains from his face when he looks at the bed.

I follow his gaze.

My heart lurches, turning rigid with realization.

"Valentine," I say through the phone. "Lucian is dead."

Adrian takes a step forward, a haunted look in his eyes as he stares into the blank eyes of our father.

"I'll be there shortly," Valentine finally says, his tone shifting from calm to one I've never heard coming from him. From the right hand of the Harrows.

The phone call ends. A beeping sound wraps itself around us as everything slows down, fading away, except for my mother's heavy breathing. Her blood warms my hands while freezing my heart.

I see Adrian crawl on top of Lucian's body to push and push with his hands on his chest, hysterically trying to bring him back to life.

I see my brother deliver orders, his face contorting with pure rage. I see his hair sticking out in every direction, blood smearing his cheeks, his neck, his hands, his clothes.

Everywhere.

There's blood everywhere.

I see guards filtering in to later rush out in search of the killer.

I see everything.

But I don't hear.

I hear nothing but the labored breathing of my mom as her life slips through my fingers.

"Who did this?"

Adrian's question stirs something within me. His eyes dart around the room, searching for any clue.

"Who was it?" He turns to us, his gaze locked on the barely open eyes of our mother. "Mom, did you see who it was? Their face—anything?"

I know.

I know who did this.

She went behind my back.

She killed Victoria.

All the pieces fall into place. I now have a clear picture of what happened tonight. The reason why my mom is bleeding on the floor and Lucian is dead.

Something soft falls on my cheek. My mother's hand calls for my attention. Her touch is weak, but the light behind her eyes is so fierce. So full of determination.

That's why it stuns me to hear her say the next words.

"Julian," she stutters, "I love you so much. You and Adrian need to take care of the business and the Inferno Consortium now that we won't be here with you."

I get a hold of myself, keeping my tears from spilling.

"Mom, don't talk like that!" I shake my head, pinching my eyebrows. "You're not going anywhere! *Where's the fucking ambulance?*" I scream the question out, all my frustration bubbling to the surface.

A lump forms in my throat.

Her eyes flutter closed, and I shake her.

"Hold on," I whisper, my words choking out. "Hold

on, Mom. You have to hold on." I brush a hair away from her forehead. "Lucian is gone. You can finally live your life, but you have to hold on."

God, *please*.

"Julian . . ." she whispers. A small smile stretches her dry lips. "Having you brought me to life, and I've loved every second."

A tear escapes and streams down my face.

Mimicking hers.

But her eyes close next, and mine remain wide-open as I watch her get picked up from my arms and carried away by paramedics.

I continue to watch.

Is this the last time I'll get to see her? Will this become a haunting memory or a distant one?

My tears fall silently, mixing with her blood on my skin.

And in a beat she's gone.

For how long?

"Julian." Adrian turns me toward him. "Listen to me. I'm going with them to check on Mom. Can you stay here and take care of Dad?"

I feel utterly helpless.

He doesn't wait for an answer. He takes off behind them, and I'm left standing in my parents' room with the one person who hates me the most, while the only one who ever loved me fights for her life.

Adrian's figure disappears, and in its place appears Valentine.

As composed as always, he looks over my shoulder at the resting body of his boss.

Ex-boss.

I am his boss now.

"We'll take care of him," he says.

"Where is she?"

"Who?"

I push past him without another word.

"Julian!" he shouts after me.

Shouts.

The only time you shout at a member of the leading family of the Inferno Consortium is when you're getting tortured by them.

I ignore the blatant disrespect and rush down the stairs, my mother's blood drying on my skin, and in an instant I'm in front of her apartment. Barging in.

She's sitting on the couch chewing on her lower lip, but she stands immediately at my appearance. The light speckles in her eyes are visible from this far away as her eyes widen in shock, taking in every brush of crimson on my clothes. On my skin.

"Julian—"

"You promised."

She flinches, regret in her eyes.

"You promised me." This time I growl. "And you still went and did it." My mouth pulls down in disgust.

She moves around the coffee table, and I hold up a hand.

"Don't come near me," I spit.

The sight of her twists my stomach. My hand shivers slightly, and I clench it back down, not wanting her to notice.

Her eyebrows crease, mouth twisting, as she tries to

hide the hurt my words caused her. But whatever pain she's feeling right now can't compare to the turmoil brewing inside of me at having watched my mother nearly die in my arms.

Because of her.

"Julian, I didn't expect this to happen." Her voice is small, tentative.

"Didn't expect it?" I glare. "You knew exactly what you were doing! I don't give a fuck that Lucian is dead, but your actions caused harm to my mother, and she could be dying because of you!"

She flinches from the anger slithering out of my pores. From the rise and fall of my chest as I fight for a breath.

Regret overtakes her face. Remorse burns in her eyes.

"You asked for the impossible. You know about my mom. I couldn't let her live, Julian. You asked for too much."

I know.

"You needed to wait . . ." My lower lip quivers with the intensity of my emotions. "I told you I wouldn't stand in the way of you killing Victoria—just not the same fucking day she had a meeting with my father!"

"What?" she whispers, color draining from her pink cheeks as she shakes her head. "I had no idea." Then, unexpectedly, she yells, "You could have told me!"

"Maybe you should've trusted me!" I shout back.

We stand there with silence hovering between us, our chests heaving as we stare into each other's eyes.

There's a tangible weight between us, suffocating us. A glint of sadness evident in her eyes.

But does she regret it? Would she have waited if I'd told her to?

"Julian," she tries, taking a small step toward me.

I'd forgive you in a heartbeat, is what I want to tell her. *If I had the strength to, I would.*

"Let me at least help." Tears brim in her eyes. "What can I do?" she asks softly.

But I don't have the strength to forgive her. To let her back in.

Not when my mom's life is hanging by a thread.

"Stay away from us." The words are acidic in my mouth. "That's all you can do."

I don't believe a single word.

"You don't mean it," she whispers, her head shaking with her typical stubbornness.

I don't mean it.

"Right now my only family is fighting for her life at the hospital." My voice pinches, straining, as my throat clogs. "She's all I have."

Tears shine in her eyes as she fights them back. Taking another step closer, she murmurs, "I know." Her voice is heavy with emotion.

She repeats the word as she wraps her arms around me, her warmth erasing the anger boiling within.

My body trembles, and I break down, sobbing into her shoulder.

"I'm sorry." Her voice breaks as she holds me close to her, my tears soaking her shirt.

She runs her fingers through my hair, caressing the pain away, but it only heightens it. A hole forms in the center of my chest, and the more I let my emotions lead me, the more I get swallowed by it. Losing myself in it.

The world outside ceases to exist as she holds my weight up.

Our heartbeats sync as I cling to her.

Then I feel her muscles loosen. Her sigh of relief breezes through my hair, and I pull back enough to whisper in her ear. Enough to let the venom set in.

"Pray she survives."

Her body tenses.

I grip her arm harder, not caring if it bruises. "For your own sake."

I turn around and leave her apartment.

The sun is slowly beginning to rise, devouring the night sky as I head to the hospital, swaying between cars with my bike.

Light may be stretching its way through the buildings, but it's not enough to reach the darkness raging within me.

———————————————

The muscles of my legs strain as I pace back and forth, my footsteps silent against the bland linoleum floor.

The sterile scent of the hospital burns my nose, the white furniture blinding me.

If I have to stay one more hour in this waiting room, I'll go insane.

"Julian."

Adrian's voice cuts through the tension coiling tightly within me.

"She's out of surgery. She's resting now. The doctor said we can bring her back home tomorrow, but she'll need bed rest for the next two weeks."

His eyes are underlined with shadows, heavy from the past five hours. The concern and fear are gone, but their mark remains.

"None of this should have happened in the first place." I clench my fists at the image of her bleeding on the floor, her gasps echoing through my mind. "If only I hadn't let my guard down . . ."

"Hey," he snaps. The weight of his hands on my shoulders follows next. "This isn't your fault. You couldn't have known what would happen."

His words force me to look at him.

"Couldn't I?" I whisper. I was angry before, but now I only feel guilt. It's heavy as it presses down on me like concrete. "I should have seen it coming. Aurelia . . . she warned me. And I didn't listen."

The waiting room isn't the issue—I could pace the length of it for days to come. It's what's inside of me that will crush me to death if I don't share the weight with someone else.

"Wait . . . Aurelia knew about this?" Adrian's fingers dig into me. "How? What did she say?"

I shake my head, unable to meet his interrogating gaze.

I can't tell him.

"Julian, talk to me." He shakes me. The action

inspires flashbacks of me shaking Mom's fragile body as I tried to keep her awake.

I feel the weight in my chest pressing down again. Like clay, it takes the shape of my insides as it resides there.

"What did Aurelia know?"

The memory of her standing before me, eyes laced with tears as she asked for my forgiveness, haunts me.

The weight amasses, becoming unbearable.

"Enough," I hear myself murmur. "She knew enough."

Taking several steps back, I try to put some distance between us. The burning sensation spreading over my skin is enough—I can't have his presence suffocating me too.

"She killed Victoria."

"Damn it, Julian," Adrian hisses, running his hand through his already disheveled hair. "You knew she was going to kill her?" His eyes are bulging out. "I— What the fuck! Why didn't you tell us? We're family. We could have helped you stop her!"

Maybe I should have. That would have prevented Victoria's family from sending someone to kill Lucian and attempt to kill Mom in retaliation.

Aurelia isn't the only one who follows the "an eye for an eye" motto. Every member of the Inferno Consortium does. We've been bathing in it for decades, generations.

"Family." The word tastes like ash in my mouth. "And look where that got us."

Adrian sighs, eating up the space between us with one long step. "We'll figure this out, Julian. But we need to stick together. We can't let whatever reason she had for doing this tear us apart."

I scoff, a headache forming from the force I put into clenching my jaw. "I know exactly why she did this."

Vincent DeMarco humiliated her mother. Made her feel like less of a person and more of an object.

Marcus Whitman played his filthy psychological games with her mother before using her worn-out body all night.

Lady Marlowe scarred her mother's body, bruising it or burning it depending on what she was feeling that night.

And my father? Lucian imprisoned her, exploiting her sexually and mentally. Lavishing her in fake love. He stole her life in the name of greed.

"Is there something else you're not telling me?"

So much more.

I glance at the closed doors separating me from our mother. "Does it matter?" I look back at him, reading every micro-expression. "What matters is that our mother almost died because Aurelia was too selfish, too blinded by the desire for revenge."

The slight twitch in his eyes tells me he knows there is so much more I'm not telling him. And the smoothness in his forehead tells me he will seek to find out, with or without my help.

"We will get through this. We always do."

I shake his hand off my shoulder. "You don't under-stand, Adrian. This isn't like before. This . . ." I swallow to wet my dry throat. "This could break us."

Break us. Tear apart what fragile strings remain between me and Aurelia.

"We won't let it." He places his hand back on my shoulder. *He thinks I'm talking about our family.* His grip is like steel on my skin. "We'll find a way to make things right. I promise you that."

Promise?

A numbness settles deep within me.

What good are promises when everything we thought we knew has been ripped away?

CHAPTER THIRTY
AURELIA

I bite down on the cookie.

Chocolate crumbs fall on my pants as I swing my legs. My phone is beside me on the kitchen counter, and I peek at it every three seconds, waiting for the screen to light up and for Julian's name to appear.

I haven't heard from him since last week when . . . everything changed.

Why hasn't he called? At least to let me know how his mother is doing. Although I already know—Valentine told me. They brought her back home this morning. She still has a long way to go, but she's alive.

He could have at least sent me a quick text.

Maybe he's still mad. But it's not like I personally stabbed his mother.

He warned me what would happen if she died, but what happens now that she didn't?

I grab another cookie from the jar and bite down aggressively, my feet bouncing impatiently as I eat all my frustration away.

I'm on my last bite when I hear the metallic sound of keys and then the thud of the front door closing. Valentine's looming figure appears next, and he stops to stare at me, clearly not expecting to find me here.

Raising my brow, I watch him as my fingers search for the next cookie to taste.

Without voicing a word, he opens a kitchen cabinet and pours himself a glass of rum. A golden droplet slides down the side of the short glass.

"Needed something stronger than coffee today?" I tease, though concern laces my voice.

Exhaling a long breath, he hangs his head. Warm light from the living room paints the deep lines on his face. His tiredness is evident in the dullness of his skin.

"Long day," he says faintly before straightening his posture and taking a sip. "I don't think even coffee would take the edge off today." He tilts the glass in his hand, twirling the liquid inside of it.

Taking another cookie, I bite into it.

Valentine looks more than just exhausted—he looks beaten down. His usual strong posture now sags with whatever weight he's holding alone.

"How many of those have you eaten already?"

"Excuse me?" I say between a mouthful of cookie.

He eyes the half-eaten chocolate chip cookie in my hand and looks back at me, arching his brow.

"Hasn't anyone ever taught you not to ask those kinds of questions to a woman?"

Mumbling something under his breath, he takes a sip of his drink before making a show of rolling his eyes.

My mouth twitches, the ghost of a smile curving my lips.

But just like that, it disappears. My chest tightens, twisting as I remember Julian.

"Is Julian okay?"

"Considering his mother nearly died,"—he takes another sip, tasting the liquid without even a hiss—"he's holding up as well as anyone could."

"And a dead father." The words flow out of me.

"Right, and a dead father." Valentine sighs, rubbing his temples.

"Maybe I should go see him."

Or maybe he should have called, the intrusive voice says.

Valentine nods. "Couldn't hurt," he says before downing the rest of his rum. "He wasn't even at the funeral today."

My heart drops.

"What? There was a funeral today?" Hurt washes over me. *No one told me.*

Why?

Cursing under his breath, he sets the glass down. "Sorry." He rubs the back of his neck. "I've been so busy with everything, keeping the press and the police at bay. I thought someone else would have told you."

"Great," I mumble, picking at the crumbs on my sweatpants.

Not even Valentine thought about sparing the time to let me know.

Someone died. *Don't be so full of yourself*, the voice in my head says.

What is Julian thinking right now? He doesn't know I wasn't told. He probably thinks I didn't care to attend. And I don't care—they could have done whatever they liked with Lucian's body. I just wanted to be there for Julian.

Just then my phone lights up.

Impatiently, I pick it up, fingers dirty with cookie crumbs and chocolate stains. I expect to see Julian's name, but another Harrow name appears instead.

Adrian.

Why is Adrian texting me?

"Meet me now on the floor below ours. Need to talk."

I reread his message. There's no mention of the subject or why the unexpected urgency.

My curiosity piqued, I hop off the counter. I could meet up with him and then head to their apartment to finally see how Julian is doing.

"I'm going to meet Adrian real quick," I say over my shoulder as I walk toward the door.

My hand is on the doorknob when Valentine unexpectedly calls out, "Aurelia, wait!"

Something in his voice stops me.

"There—" In his haste he knocks his glass off the counter, sending it crashing to the floor, where it shatters into a million pieces. "Fuck." He hisses, looking down at the mess he made.

I feel my fingers twitching with impatience and swing the door open before rushing out. "You can tell me later," I yell as I run down the corridor to the elevator, leaving the front door open.

I press the button for the twenty-ninth floor over and

over again, until the elevator doors close. Turning around, I catch my reflection in the mirror. I'm wearing light green sweatpants with an oversize white shirt, and my red hair is pinned in a messy bun.

I may have missed the funeral, but I play the part of the sad family friend perfectly.

Friend? No. "The culprit of the attack" sounds better.

The elevator doors open and I find myself in a corridor bare of doors. Walking farther in, I brush my fingers over the freshly painted walls. They probably joined the apartments together, creating one.

The Harrows own the building, so they can mix and match the place however they like.

I've been walking for what feels like forever when a black door catches my attention.

Finally.

The door is unlocked, and when I walk in, I expect to find Adrian waiting for me.

Instead all I see is a room covered in plastic sheets, buckets of maroon paint waiting to be dipped with a paintbrush.

Why does Adrian want to talk to me here?

The sound of my weight crushing the plastic sheet under my feet fills the silent room as I venture farther in.

"Adrian?" I call out. "For someone who urgently needs to talk to me, you're making this quite the mystery."

My foot knocks against a paint roller on the floor, nearly making me stumble.

"Shit," I whisper under my breath.

Thud.

A noise drifts past the double doors on the far side of the room.

"Adrian?"

Sighing at the lack of a response, I make my way toward the door.

"Did anyone ever tell you how exasperating you are?" I push the doors open and cross my arms when I see him just standing there in the middle of the room, his back to me.

A bed stands on the left side of the empty room. There's no furniture—if you don't count the metallic nightstand holding a lamp and a plastic cup of water.

"You said you needed to talk to me, so . . . here I am." I close the door behind me as I lean my weight against it. "Adrian?"

He moves his finger almost imperceptibly.

"Is everything okay?"

Did something else happen? My spine tingles with dread.

I move away from the door. "Adrian, seriously, what's going on?"

He doesn't answer me. He doesn't move.

"Can you at least look at me?" Frustration grows deep within me.

His shoulders fall, and with heavy steps he turns toward me.

Bile rises in my throat.

His blue eyes are as vast as the ocean, lips parted as he gasps for air.

But it's the hand clutching his stomach and the blood

gliding from his lower abdomen that rips a scream out of me.

"Adrian!" I rush to his side. "What happened?"

My breath hitches as his body falls on me. I wrap my arms around him and struggle to keep him on his feet as his blood seeps through his clothes onto mine.

He looks at me, eyes pleading for help. Fear clutches my heart as I try to think of what I can do. But I can't seem to think. For the first time ever, someone is dying in front of me and I don't know what to do.

I immediately thrust my hand into my sweatpants pocket but find it empty. My phone isn't there. I search the other pocket, patting around, hoping to find it, but I know it's not there. How did I leave it behind? How stupid can I possibly be? I always bring it everywhere with me. Yet I had to mindlessly rush out of the house this time.

Despair starts to gnaw at my insides.

"Tell me what to do," I whisper, my voice cracking. "Please, Adrian. Tell me how I can help you."

His hand grips my shoulder and pain shoots right through me. His legs give out, and we both fall to the floor.

It only takes me a second to forget about the pain pulsing in my ankle. Instead I'm too focused on him. I kneel in front of him, pressing my hands on the seeping wound, but the blood keeps flowing out. With all the force I apply, I can't undo this.

"Adrian, stay with me!" I yell as I watch his eyes flutter closed. "Stay with me," I whisper before shouting with all my strength, "Help! Someone help us!"

I feel lightheaded, my vision blurring as I push my hands over the hole on his lower abdomen.

Adrian grunts, his mouth opening and closing on empty words. His eyes burn with something else that mixes with the fear and the pain that should be there.

"Talk to me," I beg, tears streaming down my cheeks. "Please, just talk to me. Don't close your eyes."

I can see him trying to refrain from falling asleep. From giving up. From dying.

Cradling his head in my lap, a touch of hope rises within me as I remember about his phone. I pat around his trousers in search of it, but I only find empty pockets and a heavy sense of despair.

His body quivers, and I know I'm running out of time.

He's too heavy—I can't carry him out of here. But I also can't leave him here alone while I call for help. What if he dies while I'm away? I can't let him die alone in this cold room.

"Adrian." I caress his cheek. I need to distract him. "Do you remember the time you made fun of me because I didn't know how to ride a bike?"

I swallow down the lump in my throat, brushing away my tears with the back of my hand before they fall on him and force a reassuring smile.

He coughs. "You . . . you were sixteen."

Warmth spreads in my chest at hearing his voice. "And you were such an ass."

His mouth curves into a lopsided grin, and I lie to myself that we aren't on the floor of an unknown apartment as his last breaths heave out of him. Instead I pretend we're at our favorite Italian restaurant, making fun of the tourists as they share plates of spaghetti and meatballs.

I lie to myself and think of those years when I didn't hate spending time with him. When he gave me the love I sought, even though I knew in the back of my mind he didn't truly love me.

I lie to myself and think of the first night we slept together, and how gentle he was with me. How gentle he always was with me before the final two years, when I couldn't live with the thought he was trapped with me anymore.

Blood bubbles out of his mouth, and I'm brought back to the present.

"Tell me what happened. Can you tell me who did this to you?" I murmur.

If I can't save him, maybe I can exact my revenge the only way I know how.

My vision blurs with tears as I watch him fight to speak through the blood seeping from his mouth. I desperately wipe it away.

"It's all right. I'll figure it out. Don't worry. Don't force yourself."

But he doesn't listen to me.

His gaze falls to my right and remains there until I see the gun lying there. Then he turns to me and chokes out, "T-take it a-and l-leave."

The hairs on my arms prickle at his warning. "I can't leave you."

"You'll d-die." He chokes on his blood, spitting more of it out. "You a-are nex—"

A whisper of breath leaves his mouth, and he closes his eyes.

"Adrian . . ." I whisper.

"Adrian?" I scream.

"Adrian!" I shake his body, a sob rising in my throat, but he remains still, his body slack.

No.

An ache pushes against my heart as sobs rock my chest. I stroke his cheeks, soaking up the warmth still radiating from his dead body.

"I'm sorry."

I couldn't save him. I should have saved him.

"I'm sorry." My voice wobbles as I lean down and kiss his cheek.

My lips tingle, and I brush my fingertips over them.

He didn't shave this morning.

And he won't tomorrow.

Tears blur my vision, my heart turning cold at the realization.

"*I'm sorry.*"

Glancing one last time at him, I close my eyes.

Before the sound of something jolts me toward the other door connected to the room. I didn't notice it when I walked in—I was too preoccupied with Adrian's strange attitude.

His earlier warning echoes in my mind, and I scramble toward the gun.

Picking it up with trembling hands, I stand back on my feet, pointing the gun at whoever is waiting behind the door.

At whoever killed Adrian.

I wait.

My chest rises and falls while fresh tears run down my cheeks, and I dry them with the sleeve of my shirt.

The door creaks open, the sound sending shivers down my spine as I steady my grip on the gun. My breath is heaving, but I hold it in, waiting for whoever is behind it to reveal themselves so I can exhale, aim, and shoot.

But a voice reaches me first, setting my nerves on fire. Stealing my breath altogether.

"Oh, look what you've done."

I know this voice. I've heard it many times before.

The person steps forward, tsking at the body lying between us on the floor.

Not just a body. Her son.

Lady Harrow stares back at me. The playful smile curving her lips vanishes as her distant gaze drills into mine. "If only you'd never been born, none of this would have happened."

CHAPTER THIRTY-ONE
AURELIA

The woman in front of me isn't the same woman I grew up with. Gone is the obedient wife who took her husband's beatings without protest. This woman here, staring at me with the most wicked of smiles, is a fighter. Someone finally ready for battle.

I wish I'd met this version of her under different circumstances. Maybe then I would feel proud of her.

Her stare is glacial, the complete opposite to how she presents herself with the gauze wrapped around her stomach and the slight wiggle of her knees.

I glance around the room and realize this is where she's supposed to rest. Her sons took a whole floor and made her a new home far from the haunting memories of her husband, so she could recover in peace.

And yet she killed Adrian.

I know she did. The fact she isn't running to him in complete agony or shedding tears tells me she pulled the trigger.

She killed her son.

"Why?" I ask her, still having a hard time believing a mother could ever do this. "Why would you do this to your own son?"

A chuckle parts her lips. Her hand falls to her chest as she looks at me like I've just asked her the most trivial of questions. "Oh, dear, everything happens for a reason. People believe God plans their destiny—I guess I've been playing God for quite a while now."

My knuckles whiten as I jerk the gun at her. "Why. Did. You. Kill. Adrian?" I grit out, each word punctuated with poison.

She may feel like the most invincible person ever, having accomplished the impossible from the shadows. But right now light is shining on her. And I see her for who she is.

"For Julian, of course."

"Julian?" I whisper, my thoughts fogging as I try to make sense of what she just said. "How does killing his brother help him?"

Ignoring my question, she limps toward the bed. "You'll have to excuse me." Her voice is so calm, like we're catching up over tea instead of in a room with her dead son. "I was stabbed recently, so I can't stand for too long."

She sits down on the edge of the bed, blue eyes challenging me to put an end to this.

I follow her every movement with the gun, making sure my aim remains glued between her eyes. I'll kill her in an instant if the need occurs.

"Go on." I flick the gun, motioning for her to continue. "Tell me why you did what you did."

She grunts, sighing as she says, "I thought you were smarter than this, Aurelia. Must I really spell everything out for you?"

"Same goes for you," I snap back. "You shouldn't be testing the person holding the gun."

I could kill her in an instant if I wanted to.

"Very well." She clears her throat, threading her fingers through her black strands as she ruffles her combed hair. "You see, sometimes, in order for one person to rise, another must fall. I killed Adrian to put Julian next in line to lead."

"But Julian doesn't want to be the leader." Confusion etches itself onto my face. It feels like there's a missing piece to the puzzle. "He never wanted to be involved in the family business," I argue back, trying to make sense of what she's saying.

Lady Harrow lifts a shoulder. "Life isn't about what we want." Her voice drips with certainty. Experience. "He'll change his mind once he tastes how intoxicating it is to be in charge. I'll make sure of it."

I stand still, gun trained on her as I struggle to swallow the bitter truth.

How can this woman who always seemed so weak and submissive be so cunning? How did she orchestrate all this without anyone ever noticing? How long did it take for this plan to take shape?

"This was your plan all along?"

Or did this happen because I killed Victoria, killing Lucian in the process?

"Since the day I saw my husband's eyes glued to you. Since the day both of my sons did nothing but spend time with *you*." She spits the last word before her features morph into a look of content. "Oh, and of course, since the day I planned for you to help me with it."

"What?" I breathe.

She doesn't answer me. Instead she goes on to say, "I would have killed my abusive shit of a husband sooner or later, but you killing Victoria was really a gift from above." She smiles.

Smiles.

"I needed to find someone to blame for his death, and your recklessness was just fantastic." She looks me dead in the eye. "Oh, don't make that face. It was time for him to die. Julian gave me the strength to do it, but you gave me the chance."

"I don't understand." My voice is fading, but my grip on the gun persists. "Tell me everything. From the beginning, or I swear to God,"—my voice trembles with impatience as I clench my jaw—"I'll shoot you just once . . . you'll die a slow death."

Anger for what she did to Adrian swirls inside of me as she just . . . sits there, the calmest I've ever seen her. Her hair and her clothes are in disarray, but she's anything but.

"Your time is running out." And so is my patience. I just want to kill her and give Adrian the funeral he deserves. "Start fucking talking. If you killed Lucian, did he stab you?"

"With that foul mouth . . ." Her face twists in disgust. "You really are your mother's daughter."

At the mention of my mom, my chest constricts.

"Speak," I grit.

I'm struggling to control my emotions. The last thing I want is to bring my mom into this.

Sighing, her cold gaze locks onto mine. "Of course I didn't let the pig stab me. I had someone else do it, making sure not to injure vital organs. I didn't want to die."

"That would have been such a shame."

"Watch your mouth."

"Or what?" I take a step forward, making sure she sees the barrel of the gun pointed right between her brows. "Now speak."

I need to get as much information out of her as possible before I kill her.

"What do you want to know?"

"You said I helped you. How?" My finger twitches next to the trigger, ankle pulsing in pain with all the weight I'm putting on it. It's not broken, but I'm pretty sure I sprained it when Adrian's body fell on mine.

"I knew since the day you were born that you were going to be a pain in my ass. So I made you useful. I planted your mother's diary so that Valentine would find it and give it to you. All at the right time."

My mother's diary?

I feel my legs shake.

"Was the diary fake?" I demand, desperation clawing at me.

She scoffs. "I don't have that much free time to write a whole diary filled with such disturbing details."

"Then why did you give it to me?"

I already know the answer. But I need to hear it from her.

"Because I knew you were going to kill them." She stands. "I needed those powerful people out of the way so they wouldn't challenge Julian for the position."

Disgust filters in, flipping my stomach.

You were going to kill each one of them either way. They deserved it, I tell myself.

The blood on my hands suddenly feels thicker than ever before. I was a key player in her scheme.

She made me her queen.

"You manipulated me into killing people for your own selfish reasons?" I spit at her, anger vibrating my whole body. "Is that all you have to say?"

"Selfish?" Her voice is shrill, piercing my ears. "Everything I've done has been to ensure my son's future as the leader of this family."

"What about Adrian!" My voice breaks as I scream. "Did he mean nothing to you?"

"Adrian was a necessary sacrifice." She talks about him like he's nothing but a recent acquaintance. "Julian is the one I chose to lead our family. I made sure of that."

"How could you kill your own son?" I seethe.

She doesn't lower her gaze. Doesn't even feel the need to look at her son's body lying there.

She tilts her head, considering my question, as my stomach turns over. "I simply love Julian enough to keep him alive."

Her words petrify my insides.

How can she say something like that? What kind of mother is she?

"Julian will never forgive you for this." My voice trembles with rage—with sadness for the neglected boy lying on the floor.

When Julian finds out about this, he won't be able to look at his mother the same way again. It'll ruin the memory he has of her, but fuck if I care. She deserves far worse than this.

"Perhaps not." She stands and takes a step toward me, and I steady my grip. "But sometimes sacrifices must be made for the greater good." Her gaze is unwavering, blue eyes staring deep into my soul.

Julian's same eyes.

"You're a monster," I seethe, eyes filling with unshed tears.

"Maybe so." She casually lifts a shoulder, her short hair bouncing with the movement. "But I'm a monster who gets what she wants." She takes another step closer to me and sticks her nose in the air. "It's your turn now. You are the last part of my plan. I need you gone. I can't have you threatening his position." At my confusion, she adds, "Ah, you still don't know who your father is."

I lose it.

She thinks I give a shit about my father? I know he must be a member of the Inferno Consortium, but she must have lost it if she thinks I'd ever want to take the position of leader. I don't want to know who my father is. I don't want to know who the asshole who raped my mother is.

A hysterical laugh bubbles out of my mouth as tears finally roll down my cheeks. "My turn?" I shout. "I'm the one holding the gun, or have you forgotten?" My voice grows louder with each word.

She finally eyes the weapon in my hands. "Yes. The gun. So powerful, so deadly." She takes a step forward.

"Stay back!"

She takes another step, ignoring my warning. "And yet sometimes the person not holding the gun is the one with all the power."

I aim the gun an inch away from her face and fire.

The noise rings in my ears as the bullet slams into the wall behind her.

Lady Harrow smiles. "I told you."

She glances over my shoulder before her face suddenly changes. "Julian!" she cries out. The purest form of fear stretches her features.

In an instant she's staggering into his strong arms as he appears in the doorway.

"Julian," I breathe, and I turn to see him standing there, his chest rising and falling as he breathes heavily, as if he just ran here.

He looks at me with confusion, eyes narrowing as he takes in the gun I'm pointing at them—at Lady Harrow. Then his body tenses, wrapping around his mother in comfort and a hint of protection.

"Stay back!" I try to warn him. "She's dangerous." My voice cracks under the weight of the situation. The heaviness from before is lifted from my shoulders at knowing he's here to help.

"Is that so?" he says.

His mother sobs into his chest, her body trembling like a leaf as she clings to him like a lifeline.

"It's all an act!"

His eyes fall to the spot behind me. Adrian.

The cold steel of the gun bites at my skin. Its presence is heavy as he glances back at it.

Before I can find the words to explain the absurdity of the situation, Lady Harrow's voice fills the dense atmosphere of the room, panting as she paints a story of tragedy. Of lies.

"I was resting in bed, with Adrian keeping me company, when Aurelia just . . . walked in and . . . shot him!" She breaks into sobs again, tears streaming down her face as she clings to his shirt.

"Julian, that's not true!" I feel panic rising in my chest. "Please, Julian, listen to me!" I stammer, struggling to find my footing in the lies she just spilled. "She killed Adrian. And Lucian. She planned all of this!" I yell, feeling myself going mad.

He needs to believe me. He needs to believe the truth.

"Put the gun down, Aurelia." His voice is low, almost threatening. "You're only making things worse for yourself." He moves his hand behind his jeans. To the gun he probably has hooked there.

No.

"Adrian sent me a message to meet here, but when I arrived he was already dying. She's lying! She killed your brother!" I'm panting, tears burning my eyes, my skin, as they slide down. "I can show you the texts! I left my phone at home, but I—"

"How convenient," Lady Harrow drawls.

He doesn't say a word. His eyes are the blankest they've ever been as they take me in.

"Julian, I swear," I whisper, eyebrows pulling in at the middle as I slowly realize. As I see his resolve. "I didn't kill Adrian." Desperation fills my voice. "You have to believe me."

"Believe you?" His jaw clenches. "You're standing here covered in my brother's blood, pointing a gun at my mother. How can I believe you?"

"Because it's the truth!" I cry out, my voice breaking under the weight of my emotions as the gun I'm still pointing at them shakes.

My whole body shakes.

"Julian, please, just listen to me!" I scream. "She killed Adrian because she wants you to take your father's position. She's behind everything! *Everything!* She-she made sure I'd find my mother's diary and kill all those people. She used Victoria's death to pin your father's death on it! God, she got someone to stab her!"

I'm panting, my vision blurring as I frantically blink the tears away.

"She killed Adrian," I whisper, my voice breaking.

But he doesn't seem to hear me. He stares at his brother's lifeless body as he holds the only family he has left in his arms.

"I heard the gunshot, Aurelia," he whispers back. Like he doesn't want to believe a word he's saying. "What were you doing?"

My lips wobble, my head tilting to the side in a plea, begging him to believe me.

"She tried to shoot me, but she missed!" Lady Harrow says. "Look, Julian," she urges, calling his attention away from me. "See for yourself." She points to the hole in the plaster where the bullet went through.

My heart sinks.

"It's not . . . it's not what it looks like."

"So you didn't shoot at my mom?"

I feel my feet threatening to give way. The look on his face carves a hole in my heart, numbness filling it.

"I told Adrian about Victoria," he says. "I know he must have texted you to talk about that . . . and now he's dead."

No, no, no.

"No, Julian, it's just a coincidence," I insist. "I didn't kill him." I shake my head madly. "I never would! You have to believe me—please. *I promise!*"

Something flickers in his eyes. The moment those two words reach his ears, his face turns to stone, mouth setting in a hard line.

"Please," I beg.

Believe me. Believe me. Belie—

He raises his gun.

ACKNOWLEDGMENTS

Did we just write a book? Oh gosh, we did, didn't we?

This section of the book is dedicated to every single beautiful soul who helped bring Julian and Aurelia's story to life. YOU are the reason this story exists.

To my loving boyfriend, thank you for encouraging the little girl who used to write stories in her small bedroom at night to follow her dreams and become an author. Thank you for loving me, holding me when times got tough, and always believing in me. You are the reason I wrote a childhood friends-to-lovers story.

To my bestie and PA, Kylie (@buriedwithinpages), thank you for showing enthusiasm for this story from the very beginning! I still remember the day I messaged you and how my life has changed since then. You nurtured this story as if it were your own, and for that, I will be forever grateful. P.S. Adrian loves you too.

To my editor, Bryony Leah (@bryonyleahsmith), thank you for staying up all night and working your magic on the manuscript. You always know how to add that perfect touch. You didn't just help with this book; you supported me through the query trenches and book-related drama. I want you to be my editor until I'm 80 and still writing stories.

To my development editor, Zee (@thebluecouched-its), thank you for listening to my countless voice notes during the editing rounds. You saw the potential in this story and went through every challenge with me to transform it into a book.

To my Beta and Alpha readers—Kylie, Brittany, Ellie, Leslie, Tammy, Kenzie, and Ariana—thank you, thank you, thank you! Your enthusiasm and suggestions were the final push this book needed to become what it is today.

To my bestie and twin, Sophie Grace, you are so special to me. Thank you for always having my back, especially during my tantrums, and for being my number one cheerleader. I feel so lucky to have met such a wonderful soul through this book. I still can't believe we've been talking non-stop for the past six months, and I wouldn't want it any other way. Are you ready for the next six months? Ooh, those are going to be spectacular with everything we have planned!

To everyone I've met through this incredible journey, thank you for your love and support.

Thank you, my flames. Now go set the world on fire.

ABOUT THE AUTHOR

Aveline Knight can't help herself from writing about morally grey idiots that struggle endlessly to repair their broken hearts. She especially loves matching them to badass ladies and creating the perfect world where love stories flourish in the depths of darkness.

You can find her on Instagram @avelineknight_author

Made in United States
Orlando, FL
13 September 2024

51476635R00243